BOOKS BY JEREMY HODGSON

HISTORICAL ROMANCE

Dance on the Terrace

ADVENTURES IN RESEARCH

Curing Emily

Secret in the Seas

ROMANTIC AFRICAN ADVENTURES

Leap of a Lifetime

EGYPTIAN SAGA

Take me Instead

Breathe On Me

A romantic aviation adventure

Jeremy Hodgson

ISBN: 978-0-7961-4853-7
e-ISBN: 978-0-7961-4854-4

Jeremy William Hodgson
Villa 99, Tamarina Golf Estate
Black River, Mauritius
90922
jwhodgson42@gmail.com

Structural editing: Danny Decillis
Copy-editing: Sharon Dell
Proofreading by the author
Cover design: Nikki Meier
Typesetting and ebook by Liquid Type Publishing Services

FOR MY SONS

Martin: Teacher & Aeromodeller.
Jonathan: Musician & Programmer.
Stephan: Pilot & Engineer.
Zack: Pilot & Manager.

The desire to fly is an idea handed down to us by our ancestors who, in their grueling travels across trackless lands in prehistoric times, looked enviously on the birds soaring freely through space, above all obstacles, on the infinite highway of the air.

– *Wilbur Wright*

Aviation Terms and Abbreviations

AD

Aviation directive. A notice issued by a manufacturer and approved by the aviation authority (FAA or other) requiring immediate, when possible, or voluntary action to modify an aircraft.

AI

Artificial intelligence. Often, the designers of AI programs refer to 'An AI' when the program has learnt enough to resemble a knowledgeable human in speech or written communication.

C of G

Mnemonic for the centre of gravity.

CEO

Chief Executive Officer.

CFI

Chief Flying Instructor.

CFO

Chief Financial Officer.

CVR

Cockpit voice recorder – 'Black Box.'

EAA

Experimental Aircraft Association.

ETA

Estimated time of arrival.

FAA, CAA

American and British government aviation authorities.

FDR

Flight data recorder/recording – 'Black Box' or the data recorded. *Note:* Both recorders are bright orange; the term 'Black box' is colloquial from WWII.

IFR

Instrument flight rules – Flying as instructed by air traffic control.

MAUW

Maximum all-up weight of an aircraft.

NAV

Net Asset Value.

Notams

Notices to Airmen issued by a government aviation authority.

Pilot's headset

A combined earphone and microphone unit, often with a dangling oxygen mask ready for emergency connection.

QNH

The air pressure corrected to sea level. When set to an airfield's QNH, an aircraft altimeter will show the airfield altitude when the plane stands on the runway.

ROGER

Radio speech shorthand for 'Understood and agreed.'

Sim/Simulator

An aircraft cockpit mock-up to simulate flight for pilot training.

STC

Supplementary type certificate: Issued for a modification to existing designs.

URL

Uniform Resource Locator – A web address.

VFR

Visual flight rules – Flying by sight.

VMC

Victor Mike Charlie, visual meteorological conditions permitting VFR.

VR

Virtual Reality. Wearing a VR helmet gives the user the impression they're in a different world, and the sounds heard come from that world.

WILCO

Radio speech shorthand for 'Will comply – do as requested.'

Times: Aviation practice.

All times use the twenty-four-hour clock. 02:30 is two-thirty in the morning.

The suffix Zulu indicates the time is International Standard Time, used by all aircraft without the suffix when reporting. 01:30 Zulu is the time in London, wherever the plane may be.

PREFACE

The metaverse is *NOT*.[1]

Unless one accepts that a figment of the imagination is somehow reality to the person imagining.

To the overheated mind that builds an imaginary universe, perhaps it is.

In the metaverse, things happen. One follows another with only a pause to catch a fleeting breath. The continuous unrelenting excitement is a drug reinforcing the feeling of reality. Logic does not intervene – *It happened to Indiana Jones. Now it's happening to me – so it's real.*

For most people, Ethan Hunt, Indiana Jones and Mister Spock excepted, life has chapter headings. Chapter 1 First years growing up. Chapter 2 Going to school. Etcetera. Real life is a schlep; a long time passes between one exciting event and another. 'Long' is flexible, defined as the time it takes to become bored.

The metaverse doesn't have chapters; everything happens *now*, with one exception. The physical body requires food, drink, sleep and a toilet that the metaverse cannot supply, so the imaginary voyage must pause. Food, drink and the bathroom can be satisfied without a long break in the action. (Wait a minute, and the Gorilla will leave. – a bite from a sandwich, a gulp of water). But not sleep.

Fortunately, the metaverse has days. A mind that can imagine unbelievable places rebels at the idea that it won't be allowed to sleep. A day is a marvellous excuse. As night falls, the mind can suspend the imaginary

---

1. See https://www.techtarget.com/whatis/feature/The-metaverse-explained-Everything-you-need-to-know.

action with the thought. *Tomorrow, this will happen.*

Then, relaunched after sufficient, but often too little, sleep, with another thought. *Today, this will happen.* A day may be eventful or calming; much or little can happen. The mind dictates.

•••

So, I have authored a book with no chapters, only days – long and short ones. The action may continue until the eyes close in sleep, then recommence the following day when they open while in bed. But not always.

There are things better left to the imagination...

DAY 1
FRIDAY

He was silent as he looked but thought again as he'd done many times. *None of those travellers are worried about flying on Friday the thirteenth.*

Dexter Rawlins stood facing the balcony, his hands spread on either side, gripping the stainless-steel handrail along the top as he gazed down at the concourse fifteen metres below and the check-in area for International Air flights; the entire terminal building belonged to International Air. The solid barrier hid the row of offices behind him along the length of the balcony from the gaze of any curious persons below. However, none looked up; the scurrying figures pushing baggage trolleys dragging children or bags behind them had no time to look up. Others without bags or trolleys clutching boarding passes and passports manoeuvred adroitly around the bag-laden crowd going the other way.

Dexter was a metre eighty-five in polished black shoes, wearing neatly pressed black trousers. He wore a white button-down shirt with epaulettes and gold bars and, without a jacket, revealed broad shoulders and a muscular build. From behind, the figure of an eighty-kilogram man some thirty to forty years old.

He wasn't thirty or forty; his sixtieth birthday was less than two months away. It was the last whole month. He no longer thought in months but days.

Dexter's figure resulted from years of regular attendance at a gymnasium. Airline pilots who had medical examinations every six months didn't smoke, drank little alcohol and had to remain fit.

Epaulettes with four gold bars were common inside the building, but the narrower fifth bar was not. The company had awarded Dexter the unusual bar four years earlier with his promotion to chief training captain.

He lifted one foot and then put it down, his feet a few inches apart, then looked right and left, and as no one was on the balcony, released the stainless-steel railing and turned his back to the balcony wall. For years, Dexter had been the most smartly dressed of the airline's pilots, his shirts professionally tailored to fit. None of the office doors was open, and he saw no one looking out the few windows, so he unzipped his fly, reached in with his right hand, gripped his shirt tails, and pulled down, holding his belt up with his left hand. His shirt once again tight against his chest and back, he zipped up and turned back as the lift doors at one end of the balcony slid open.

'Hello, Dex. Admiring the view for a last time?'

Dexter stopped his turn leisurely; an aquiline face with a light tan from the hours on tropical beaches when his aircrew had a layover, clean-shaven with his brown hair, streaked with silver at the temples, cut short and neatly brushed, as per company policy, his dark grey eyes with laugh lines on each side showed only curiosity as he looked at the man who had spoken.

Twelve years younger than Dexter, with pale blond hair, blue eyes, a metre eighty-two and a tendency to gain weight that he struggled to keep off through exercise, Bobby Straker wore the same clothes as Dexter and had four bars. They had never been close friends; their age difference and a lack of common interests had prevented that, but they respected each other as men of the same status in their chosen profession.

'Hello, Bobby. I had to come in to show a bunch of bankers and bigwigs around the sim section. Now, I'm just taking a break from sitting in front of a computer. I've promised myself a pilot's seat in the office for years but never demanded one. It's too late now.

'I'm still the training chief, so I've been checking the schedules.' The reproach was ever so slight. *Don't make assumptions.* 'I may be looking at this view for the next five years. Are you here for your check?'

Dexter was sure Bobby had picked up the tone of his remark when he replied hurriedly, 'Yes, I've gotta go; Greg will be waiting in the Three-Ten sim. He said at 14:00.'

※

As Bobby Straker walked away along the balcony and the restricted access area, Dexter turned back to look at the concourse.

Dexter's eyes, those of a trained pilot, never remained still; even with a sky full of blue, they moved, scanning to pick up anything that could affect the flight – a bird, another aircraft, a threatening cloud, anything abnormal, he couldn't help doing it. Unless a small section of his brain spotted an anomaly, he was unconscious of what he saw while thinking of his problem. From his position on the balcony, his eyes scanned the check-in desks, the rows of baggage and people before them, and Albert Cummins, the security guard, with his dog, Gracie, making the rounds. Dexter had made friends with Gracie, but Albert always called him Captain. Dexter had permitted himself a friendly 'Good morning, Bert' when they met. His eyes stopped the scan in the middle of the concourse on the return, and Dexter became aware of an anomaly; in the middle of the concourse, a figure was stationary, and the hurrying passengers, seen from above like a stream of ants parting around an obstacle, split and passed either side of the person before joining again.

It took only seconds to decide it was a woman. From above, he couldn't see her face, but he could see the back of her head and her long, golden hair on the side he could see. She had a bag slung over her left shoulder that she held with one hand to keep it from slipping off, and with the other, she held the handle of her trolly bag trailing behind her. What seemed like a dark skirt hung below her grey thigh-length coat. From where Dexter stood, she appeared as frozen as a statue. *She's looking for the correct check-in desk, I suppose.*

Dexter remembered when he first joined the airline thirty-five years ago; its name was International Executive Airlines, and he was a rookie trainee with two bars on his shoulders.

In his reply to Bobby, his natural reserve had covered up the real reason he was there. According to International Air rules, a sixty-year-old airline pilot could no longer function as a captain in an aeroplane carrying paying passengers. However, he could continue to sixty-five as the training captain. The life he'd worked hard for all his life would suddenly end at midnight, not in months that had ticked down inexorably, but in fifty-nine days.

He remembered the airline's operations discussion in 2007 when the FAA raised the age limit from sixty to sixty-five. The younger captains had voted against the change as it delayed their promotion, and the older ones voted in favour. As the senior captain responsible for the airline operations manual, he proposed a compromise: sixty would remain the limit for captains, but over sixty pilots could continue as co-pilots. *I created that rule.* The question that filled his mind was – *What do I do now?*

Dexter's scan moved on to a uniformed ground staff employee pushing a wheelchair with his left hand and pulling a wheeled suitcase with his right. With white hair and a black dress, the wheelchair occupant clutched a large bag on her lap, one leg wrapped in plaster protruding on a support, with an incongruous pink sock on her toes. She had a crutch and clasped it to her, trying to keep it from sliding onto the floor. Dexter watched approvingly as the attendant stopped before the check-in for assisted passengers and locked the wheelchair brakes before proceeding to the formalities, and then his scan continued.

Along the concourse to the entrance escalators on one side and the departure gates on the other until the far end of the concourse disappeared into the check-in hall for internal flights before his scan reversed again. He thought of the offer made at a recent meeting with the Operations Director, Philip Macintyre, a product of Eton and Oxford whose negotiating skills had served the airline well.

Philip was a friend from his first day at International Executive. He hadn't expected Philip's blunt question, 'Dex, is John ready for four bars?' Although Dexter knew John Siebert, the first officer in his tightly knit crew, was due for promotion, Dexter had expected it to happen when he turned sixty.

Equally bluntly, as they were old friends, he asked, 'Yes, Philip, are you retiring me early?'

'No, Dex, you'll fly if I need you to replace a captain. I hope you'll be with us for at least five years, flying in the copilot seat as the training captain, filling the training role and doing what you can to improve it. You're also due several months of leave, so you can take time off to consider alternatives. I would rather learn your plans in advance than discover at the last minute that you're leaving us.'

⊰◦⊱

What do I do now? He'd asked himself that question many times in the last months, with increasing frequency as his sixtieth birthday loomed closer. He'd tried to imagine a life where flying was occasional and saw himself as a bird with a broken wing. He'd tried to analyse his feelings and had talked to Doris.

Dexter had known Doris, the 'Business with Style' company's owner since it opened as a hairdresser. She had grown it successfully, adding grooming and clothing until it became the outfitter of choice for all the aircrews at Gatwick. She nursed Dexter through the traumatic period after his son died and then when his wife divorced him. A confidant to all the aircrews, Doris kept the personal secrets of others to herself.

When he had told Doris about his fear of the future, she'd listened and gently said, 'You'll be alone, Dex. You're about to lose your family; think about marrying again.'

It had made him think, and he'd wondered why he hadn't felt alone for the fifteen years since his wife Bethkin had left him and realised that his aircrew was his family. He looked after them, advised them, and felt the same pleasure as would a father when they succeeded or earned a promotion. Dexter was proud that his flight crews remained stable while others changed often.

He thought about marrying again, as Doris had suggested. After the traumatic period fifteen years ago, he hadn't avoided intimacy or relationships with women except those in his crew, who, in his head, were somehow forbidden. There were always others at a party or a function where Dexter drank little, and they drank more and lost their inhibitions. The captain's bars gave him status at those parties that other men didn't have, and he frequently had company in his hotel room but had never followed up on any of them except Gwen.

He met Gwen thirty years ago as a cabin attendant when she joined his crew. He had found her beautiful, but he was the captain, married with a young son, and slept nightly with Bethkin since he was flying short hauls. Gwen had left his crew – and the airline – two years later for another, and he'd met her again by accident ten years ago and learnt she'd divorced. She was now the ground attendant manager at Gatwick for another airline. He'd taken her out for dinner several times, and twice, she'd suggested she stay the night. Until now, he hadn't considered her a potential wife and wondered if that might change once he lost his crew, but he had difficulty imagining her in that role. *There's admiration but no desire.*

One weekend, after returning from a ten-day series of flights that had taken him around the world, he'd remained at Gatwick instead of leaving for his farmhouse home near Dartmoor. He visited the Crawley area, trying to imagine living nearby if he worked at Gatwick daily. He left for Dartmoor with his heart in his shoes, for he'd felt claustrophobic; it took three days walking on Dartmoor with nothing but moorland in sight before it wore off.

His thoughts and memories didn't answer his question: *What do I do now?*

But they did bring forward two conclusions. *I must keep my farmhouse beside Dartmoor. I cannot live without the open sky, but I need something different to do.*

⊷○⊶

Half a minute later, Dexter again became aware of the stationary woman. *She hasn't moved.* With images of terrorist suicide bombers blowing themselves up in crowded places filling his mind, Dexter ran down the walkway to the lift at the end, still standing open after Bobby had come up as it always did, ready for rapid evacuation, and pressed the [Departures] button. When the door opened, he didn't run, which would cause panic, but he reached the woman at a fast walk. *Young, half my age.*

'Excuse me, miss, do you need help?'

She didn't turn to look at him, so Dexter stepped in front of her to look at her face, which was completely blank, but her eyes, an unusual orange-flecked green, were open and focused on something distant.

Dexter waved his hand in front of her face. He noticed no reaction.

She's in a trance!

'Captain Rawlins, do you have a problem?'

It was Albert, the security guard, with his dog, Gracie. Dexter felt relieved when Gracie sniffed the suitcase and returned to sit beside Albert. *No explosives.*

'I don't think so, Bert; the lady seems ill. Can you take her case?'

The woman released the trolley suitcase when Albert took it gently from her unresisting fingers, and Dexter said, 'I'll take her upstairs to the crisis room. X-ray the case; if it's clean, bring it to me there.'

'No problem, Captain.'

Dexter took the woman's right arm and felt her flinch, but when he firmly said, 'Miss, please come with me; you need to sit down,' she followed him without a word.

Dexter led her to the lift, swiping his security card on a lanyard around his neck to enter and take them to the second floor. *Tall, about four centimetres shorter than me.* He led her to the first office door that opened onto the balcony. The plate on the door read [Crisis Room 1].

The crisis room was long and narrow, with a row of computer screens and keyboards against each wall. Some glowed dimly, on standby for an unexpected event that fortunately didn't happen that often. Most airline crises occur when weather or a technical problem delays a departure. Such an event meant finding other aircraft or hotels for the passengers. Finding rooms for three hundred or more passengers required an International Air staff member before every computer in the room.

No one was there, so Dexter led the woman to the nearest chair, and with gentle pressure on her shoulder, she sat. He took another chair next to her and swivelled it to look at her.

Facing a computer screen, she still said nothing and didn't turn to look at him.

Dexter looked at her closely, trying to pick up any signs. Over the years, he'd interviewed thousands of young people for aircrew jobs: Pilots and cabin crew of all sexes, so he had experience checking visible cues.

She's clean, and her hair is in good condition but looks like an amateur cut. Judging by the ragged edges of her nails, she might have a habit of nervously biting them; it doesn't look like she's wearing any makeup or jewellery. She might be lovely if she smiled; her coat seems expensive; under forty would be my guess – no signs of drug abuse. I'd better look in her bag.

Dexter reached forward and took her bag; she didn't react, but he kept it in full view of her face as he opened it.

He found a first-class boarding pass for flight IX 246 to Mauritius and a British passport for Jenifer Boscawen, age 30, born in Coventry, and thought. *That's a surprise. Even if she recovers, she can't take the flight alone – I must cancel her boarding pass.*

Jenifer sat unmoving while he picked up the phone on the desk and called Reservations.

'Good morning, Captain Rawlins here; I want to suspend the boarding of a passenger on two-four-six to Mauritius, Jenifer Boscawen.'

'Is that a cancellation, sir?'

'No, the lady is unwell, and boarding is not advisable; she can re-book another flight.'

'Do you have a medical certificate?'

Dexter was annoyed by his question. 'Would you like to come to the crisis room and see for yourself? But before you do so, I suggest you speak to your supervisor and ask who is Captain Rawlins.'

'I've suspended it, Captain, but I'll speak to my supervisor.'

'Please do. Goodbye.'

Feeling heated and thirsty, Dexter stood, walked to the water fountain in the corner, filled two paper cups with water and returned, placing one of them on the desk next to Jenifer. Albert then arrived with the suitcase while Dexter was wondering if he should call emergency medical. Gracie came in with Albert and quickly examined the silent and unmoving figure of Jenifer.

'Captain, here's her case. It's clean, nothing but clothes and toiletries.'

She's a first-class passenger. 'Thanks, Bert. Could you forget to report this incident?'

'Sure, Captain. Gracie, come.'

When Dexter turned back to Jenifer, he saw her reach out to the cup and then drink it all, so he fetched another cup, relieved that she was finally moving.

'Jenifer, can you tell me what's wrong, or shall I call a doctor?'

He had no idea how she did it. Her hands moved together to the keyboard, the screen lit up, and with what seemed like a light ripple of fingers, words appeared on the screen.

Anxiety Attack – Please wait – pills in my bag.

Dexter looked again in her bag, found a foil and plastic plaque of pills, and put one beside the water goblet. She took it with the water; then her fingers rippled again on the keyboard.

Thanks, wait.

Dexter had to wait five minutes, watching the signs as the rigidity fell away, and she relaxed. Then Jenifer turned to look at him. At first, he could see her eyes searching, scrutinising his face. They seemed curious, and suddenly, they lit up, he thought, with excitement. Her first words were, 'You're a pilot?'

Surprised, Dexter answered, 'Yes. I am Captain Dexter Rawlins.'

She surprised him again with her next question, 'Why five bars?'

'I'm the chief training captain for International Air.'

'You fly?'

Dexter, proud of his career, replied, 'Over twenty-two thousand hours in all types.'

Dexter thought a switch had clicked as she smiled at him and said, 'That's a lot.'

I was right; her smile is lovely. 'It is; will you come with me to my office now?'

'Why?'

'Because I want a coffee, and I thought maybe you might like one too, and I have a coffee machine there.'

✈

Dexter stood, took her trolley bag, and led Jenifer along the balcony to the far end opposite the lift, where a security door marked *Authorised Access Only* closed off the walkway. Dexter turned into the office beside it and said, 'Please, take a seat. Would you like a coffee?'

'Please, black with some sugar, thanks.'

For two minutes, Dexter busied himself at the machine as it growled, whirred, groaned and moaned. It gave him a moment to consider what to do next.

Jenifer looked around the office. With a desk and a computer screen, a filing cabinet to one side, and framed company awards that showed the successes in the lifetime career of a pilot, it seemed familiar to Jenifer, who was, however, far more interested in the twenty-five model aircraft that stood on two extended shelves to the right of the door and a long windowsill. The window provided a view of nothing more than industrial-type roofs. A framed quotation stood in the middle of the upper shelf beside a Spitfire; she read it.

> Oh! I have slipped the surly bonds of earth and danced the skies on laughter-silvered wings; Sunward I've climbed, and joined the tumbling mirth of sun-split clouds-and done a hundred things you have not dreamed of – wheeled and soared and swung high in the sunlit silence. *Hov'ring* there I've chased the shouting wind along, and flung my eager craft through footless halls of air. Up, up the long delirious, burning blue, I've topped the windswept heights with easy grace where never lark or even eagle flew. And while with silent lifting mind, I've trod the high untrespassed sanctity of space, put out my hand and touched the face of God.
>
> – Pilot Officer John Gillespie Magee
> Junior No. 412 Squadron RCAF
> Killed on December 11, 1942

Jennifer thought, *He's like me; he loves flying;* then she interrupted Dexter's thoughts, 'Have you flown all these planes?'

'All except three, and quite a few more I don't have models for.'

'Which three?'

'Can you guess?'

Jenifer looked along the row of models on the windowsill; some were ancient models – a biplane; she recognised a Tiger Moth; *he might have flown that at an aeroclub.* Then came four small training aircraft: a Cessna, two single-engined Pipers, and a Piper twin; she was familiar with those and thought Dexter must have trained on them for his first pilot's licence. Three small corporate jets followed. *They would have given him jet training.*

The lower of the two wall shelves had airliners; the scales were different, so some were small models, others much bigger, and all but the last had left passenger service and were now cargo aircraft if they were still flying. *He must have piloted those. Otherwise, they wouldn't be here.*

The upper wall shelf had more airliners, but in the centre were two military jets, the WWII Spitfire and a crop-spraying Piper, and at the end, a model of the CamAirCom Three-Ten. She looked closer at the military jets; they spanned two eras, a Sabre from the Korean War and a Hawker Siddeley Buccaneer from the late sixties.

'Captain, I first thought it must be the three military aircraft, but then I wondered why they were here if you hadn't flown them.'

'So, you can't guess?'

'I'll guess the Spitfire because there's only one or two, and pilots love that aeroplane. That may be why you have it here. The crop sprayer because that's not a job I can see you doing, and the Sabre because it's so old. But I'll make a wild guess; you might have flown a private Sabre in the USA and not a Cessna 150 in training because the Piper equivalent is on the shelf.'

Dexter had expected an answer like, 'No, I don't know what they are.' Instead, he grinned at her, delighted. *She knows more about aircraft than any woman I've met.* 'You surprise me, Jenifer; you're dead right! Why didn't you consider the Buccaneer?'

'Because there's one flying privately in South Africa. But why are they here if you didn't fly them?'

'You guessed right for the Spitfire. I have loved it since I first saw one flying. The other two I keep as reminders. I only tell close friends about them.'

While wondering what the next steps should be, Dexter handed Jenifer her coffee and sat at his desk facing her.

After a short pause, he carefully said, 'Jenifer, I've suspended your boarding for Mauritius; the flight has closed now. You need to book another flight. Can you tell me what went wrong?'

'Thanks, I couldn't have gone alone. I don't have attacks like that all the time. I've had very few. I know what causes them. I never have them with a *friend* because it only happens when I'm with hundreds of people I don't know. I was going to fly to Mauritius for my mother's funeral. My *friend* Susan was coming with me, but she became sick, and I waited until today because the funeral is the day after tomorrow. I shouldn't have come. Marian, who works for my *friend*, drove me here from Coventry, and I thought I would be fine checking in and on the plane. But these attacks happen suddenly; I don't have any warning. Although I don't know when I can fly to Mauritius, I must put flowers on my mother's grave when I can.'

Puzzled by the emphatic pronunciation of the word '*friend*', Dexter felt it must mean something more to Jenifer than the word usually implied, so he asked, 'What brings you out of the attacks?'

'They wear off slowly; I woke once in a hospital and once in an ambulance. I may seem absent, but my subconscious can sense what I hear and feel. I wake up if a *friend* or someone I know shakes me. The pills relax me.'

'So, what brought you out this time?'

'You. I thought you were a *friend*; I heard someone call you Captain. And then you have bars and said you were a captain. You're a *friend*.'

Weird! Captains qualify as one of her special friends *without trying to be one.*

Still being careful, Dexter smiled at her. 'That's nice to know, Jenifer.'

He was about to ask what he should do to help her further, and then the office phone rang. He answered, 'Dexter Rawlins.'

'Dex, Greg here. Can you come to the Three-Ten sim, please?'

'Sure, what's the problem?'

'I'd rather not discuss it on the phone.'

'I'll come. Give me five.'

Dexter rang off, turned to Jenifer and said, 'Jenifer, I must go to the Three-Ten simulator and talk to the training officer who runs it. Will you stay here, please, until I return?'

He could see the excitement in her eyes and hear the pleading tone in her voice as she asked, 'Can't I come with you? I've never seen a real Three-Ten simulator. *Please*, oh, please!'

Although he was about to say no, the look in her eyes made Dexter reconsider. It worried him that she might disappear if he left her alone so soon after her attack. He remembered that he'd shown a delegation of visitors around the simulators earlier and might show a latecomer. 'Jenifer, what are you wearing under that coat?'

She stood and took it off, revealing only a loose white shirt above the dark skirt. Dexter saw epaulettes on the shirt. 'Why the epaulettes?'

'All my shirts and blouses have them. People stay away from me if I put bars on them, especially men, and I feel safer.'

She's tall and wearing bars, a figure of authority, I suppose that's true.

'Do you have slip-on bars with you?'

'In my bag.' *Weirder and weirder.*

'Then, take them out and put them on. Leave your bags here and come with me.'

'Three bars or four, Dexter?'

'You have both?'

'Yes.'

It's a crazy situation; I might as well go all the way; no one argues with four bars. 'Put on four.'

I must get a complete explanation later; I'm a bit nuts agreeing, but the company can't do anything to me at this late stage – and I like her eyes.

Dexter swiped his card at the security door and, followed by Jenifer, walked up to the guard beside the body scanner on the other side. 'Hello, Mike. Greg wants to see me, and I have a late visitor left over from earlier.'

Mike turned to Jenifer and said, 'Would you step into the scanner, please, Captain.'

'Fine, Dex, you must sign for her.' He pulled a visitor's book over the table, and Dexter filled the columns. In the *Visitor's Name* column, he wrote, Capt. Boscawen. Then he stepped through the scanner to join Jenifer.

He led Jenifer through two corridors and then across a gangway into the rear of the flight simulator, a mock-up of the Three-Ten aircraft cockpit mounted on hydraulic rams that could impart movement as if it were flying as pilots manipulated the controls. Then he threaded their way between banks of electronic cabinets to find Greg sitting at a massive control panel with screens and many switches.

'Hi, Greg.'

A similarly dressed captain, clearly several years older than Dexter, carrying more kilos than an active pilot, Greg answered.

'Thanks for coming. Introduce me to your lady captain.'

'Greg, meet Jenifer Boscawen. She's a friend. She was with me when you called, and I thought I might show her the sim. Jenifer, this Captain Greg Hellerman, often called "the man from hell" by the pilots he checks out. He can make more things fail on an aeroplane than pilots will ever encounter in their careers.'

Jenifer smiled at him, held out her hand and said, 'Pleased to meet you, Greg.'

Charmed, Greg shook and said, 'Likewise, Jenifer. – Dex, I want you to review my report on Bobby's line check.'

Dexter lost sight of Jenifer when he turned with Greg to the computer screen on the control panel. Dexter read the report, noting the cross in red against one item.

'Bobby had his copilot beside him?'

'Yes, Cyril Collins. The operating procedure says Bobby must call *flaps up fifteen* at one ninety knots over fifteen hundred feet altitude.'

'And he didn't?'

'No, Cyril raised them correctly without Bobby asking. I'm supposed to fail Bobby.'

'Why did you call me?'

'I'm sure it happens on occasion, if not frequently. Things get hectic in the cockpit at takeoff. I might be inclined to overlook it, but Bobby's never done it before – I checked. And I thought he was looking tense.'

'What's his medical say?'

'It's clean. Bobby's gained almost a kilo, but that's all.'

'Okay. Pass me the keyboard.'

Dexter swiped his access card to activate the keyboard and then typed on the test report form.

> Suspend from flying subject to a complete medical exam and psychiatric examination for hypertension. Then retest. SIGNCTO.

The word SIGNCTO blinked until he swiped his card again, and then the program replaced SIGNCTO with –

> Signed – Capt. Dexter Rawlins – Chief Training Officer.

'Thanks, Dex.'

'One of the less pleasant aspects of training, Greg.' Then he looked around for Jenifer and saw her sitting in the captain's seat in the simulator. She was checking out the switches and levers.

'Jenifer, what are you doing there? You shouldn't be in the sim.'

'I could fly this. It's like the real aircraft. It's marvellous.'

'It's supposed to be. What do you mean you could fly it?'

'I've spent hundreds of hours flying a Three-Ten simulator. I'm sure this is the same. Can I try?'

Dexter was about to say a firm *NO* when Greg said, 'Take the right seat, Dex; I'll give her a standard circuit. I'd like to see what she can do.'

Dexter relented, 'It's your sim, Greg. Leave out other traffic,' and slid into the copilot's seat.

This day will be the weirdest I have ever experienced.

He could see her eyes shining as she turned to him and said, 'Thanks.' She picked up the pilot's headset. Greg handed a sheet to Dexter as he donned the co-pilot's headset.

Greg told her via the headphones; Dexter could also hear, 'Callsign is Interex 123. When the sim comes alive, you're standing in bay sixteen at Gatwick; you have permission to start engines. The runway in use is zero eight right, the wind is zero, and the sky is clear; it's 14:00; start, then call for pushback. Dexter has your critical speeds; rotation is one-eighty as you have only an hour's fuel plus reserves and no pax or cargo. You take off, do one circuit and land. You're IFR; do you copy?'

'Copied, Interex 123 heavy,' Jenifer replied.

The screens lit up. Dexter and Jenifer saw a picture of the Gatwick terminal building from the outside as if they were looking from the cockpit of a Three-Ten at bay sixteen.

Dexter was surprised. *She used 'heavy' so she knows the wake turbulence warning.* He was even more astonished after a faultless departure, takeoff, and landing.

Greg came on the radio, 'Dex, she can't hear this. Can we do another? I'll add a crosswind. Then add an autopilot breakdown followed by an ILS failure.'

'Go ahead.' *Why did I agree?*

'Captain Boscawen, if you can do another circuit, I'll make it more difficult. It will be at night; the wind is one-one-zero at fifteen.'

Dexter was surprised when Greg called her Captain but thought, *well, she's wearing four bars.*

The autopilot failed after takeoff; Dexter confirmed it, 'Autopilot failure, Captain.'

'Understood, autopilot failure noted.'

Then Greg called after the first one-eighty-degree turn as the aircraft levelled out.

'Interex 123 heavy, Gatwick.'

'Interex 123, go ahead.'

'Interex 123, ILS is out on 08. Do you wish to divert?'

'Gatwick, Interex 123 heavy request extended approach from the Initial Approach Fix.'

'Interex 123, Initial Approach Fix approved.'

It amazed Dexter. *Incredible. No hesitation and the right decision.*

After another perfect landing, the simulator shut down, and the two pilots removed their headsets; they heard Greg clapping.

Jenifer's eyes were shining. 'Dexter, Greg, thank you, that's the most fun I've had for weeks.'

Dexter was grinning, 'Now you're in trouble; you have much to explain. Let's return to my office.'

Greg smiled broadly and said, 'Captain, I'm sure you could pass a full qualification test if you want to. It would be a pleasure to see what you can do.'

'Thanks, Greg; I'll have to twist Dexter's arm.'

'Call me, and I'll hold him down while you do.'

Dexter laughed, 'I must watch out for you both.'

Dexter signed out as they left the secure area, and both he and Jenifer said good night to Mike.

In his office, Dexter asked, 'Jenifer, where are you staying tonight?'

'Nowhere; I came by car from Coventry and should be on the way to Mauritius tonight.'

'Do you want to return to Coventry by train or bus? It's too late for me to drive you. I'm visiting Exeter tomorrow and could take you to Coventry on my way there.'

'Why Exeter?'

'I have a cottage near Dartmoor; I go as often as possible. I have maintenance to do and friends to see.'

'I don't dare go by train or bus; Alone, I might have another attack. I've never travelled on either without Dad or Susan with me.'

'I have a room at the Holiday Inn here; I stay there whenever I have work to do at the airport. I can call and ask for a room for you.'

'Don't the Holiday Inn rooms have two big beds?'

'Yes, why?'

'You're a *friend*, Dexter; I'll stay with you.'

'Jenifer, I'm a stranger.'

'You're not a stranger, Dexter. We piloted a Three-Ten together this afternoon; we're a *crew* and *friends*. I know it's okay.'

She fears another anxiety attack, and I'm old enough to be her father. Then Dexter remembered. *It's Friday the thirteenth.*

'Then, if you're sure, call me Dex. My friends do, and let's go to the hotel bus. I'm hungry.'

'Now you say it; I'm ravenous, and call me Bo.'

'Is that a nickname?'

'Yes, I'm happy with it; Jenifer is too long.'

Bo, for Boscawen, that makes sense.

Whether the hotel receptionist believed she was his daughter or not didn't matter, and in the lift going up, as they were alone, Dexter said, 'I never thought of it, but the room rate for me and now us has a pilot discount because you're wearing bars.'

'Do you always get a discount?'

'Usually. I do at the airport hotels, but sometimes they ask for my ALPA membership card. Any commercial pilot can become a member.'

They arrived in his room, Dexter laid her case on a stand, and Jenifer said, 'This is great; those beds look comfortable; which is yours?'

'The one near the window.'

'Even better, I get the one near the bathroom. Can we eat dressed like this, or should we change?'

'I'm hungry enough to go like this, and then you can explain how you can fly a sim.'

'I must visit the bathroom first. We can talk after we return.'

'Me too. After you.'

The restaurant was the same as the restaurants in airport hotels worldwide, open for more hours of the day than aeroplanes flew in or out, with a menu that reflected the reason the clients were there: to eat simple, digestible food before, after or during a journey. The tables had tablecloths, with chairs designed for diners who would spend no more than an hour in them, and the food arrived without delay.

Jenifer ordered a burger and fries with a side salad, a typical American meal. Dexter chose a British pub meal of steak pie, chips and peas. They both drank fruit juice and water but finished with a decaffeinated coffee. Before their order arrived, Dexter asked a question.

'Tell me, do you have a pilot's licence?'

'Yes, Dex.'

'Commercial, UK or FAA?'

'FAA, commercial, turbine and jet rated.'

'Where did you do the training?'

'Florida.'

I don't think that, subject to anxiety attacks, she can fly professionally. Nothing is ordinary with Jenifer.

'Is it valid, and will you tell me about it?'

The food arrived. 'Not valid, and I will. After we eat.'

⎯⊶◦⊷⎯

Forty-five minutes later, they returned to the bedroom.

Jenifer took a toilet bag and pyjamas from her case. 'I want to shower and put on my pyjamas, then we can talk.'

I don't know what to think. Jenifer's a young woman with a problem who needs help, but she's also a qualified commercial pilot who can fly an airliner and is now authoritative. She'll sleep in my room because I'm a Captain, so a friend.

'I'll shower after you.' Twenty minutes later, Jenifer came from the bathroom.

To Dexter, she wore a fluffy dark blue tracksuit bottom and a half-white and half-yellow top, the half defined by a diagonal line from one shoulder to the opposite waist, with a pair of hotel slippers on her feet. 'Those are interesting PJs; you look like you're about to compete in a high jump.'

'They're comfortable; I can lounge around at home all day if I want to, and often do.'

When Dexter came from the bathroom fifteen minutes later, Jenifer chuckled, sitting cross-legged on the bed nearest the bathroom. 'How long have you had those pyjamas? They belong in a hospital.'

Dexter grinned. 'You have it right the first time; I've had them for years and bought them for a hospital visit. I keep them for emergencies, like tonight; I normally wear shorts.'

'I shall take you to a pyjama shop, show them those, and ask for something *more modern*, like a man's nightgown with red horizontal stripes and a nightcap with a pom-pom!'

Dexter laughed, 'What's wrong with the red stripes?' he asked as he pulled back the covers of his bed and climbed in.

'Straight up and down, they make you look like a bunch of straws, and if twisted, you'd look like a candy cane. We must get you something more up-to-date.'

I first thought she was weird, but this is entirely unexpected.

'What makes you think we'll be together long enough to do that?'

'You're a *friend*, Dex, once a *friend*, always a *friend*. I have very few, but they're all permanent. It may not be tomorrow, but we'll one day buy you some new pyjamas.'

'How many *friends* do you have?' *Now, I'm using the word like she does.*

'Three, Dex, my dad, Susan and you.'

Are we the only people she trusts in the world? I don't know why I like her, but I can't walk away that easily without it hurting. But she's given me an idea of how to build her confidence so she doesn't freak out in public. 'I'll agree, but on two conditions.'

Dexter could see the smile in her eyes when she asked, 'What?'

'Next week, you come with me to see the woman who grooms our pilots. You need to look like one, and then we'll decide how to validate your licence.'

'I don't need it validated; I won't take a job flying.'

'I'm not offering you a job, but having a licence and not keeping it valid is a waste, especially when it only takes a few hours. Then, you can join ALPA, carry the card, look like a pilot, and get hotel discounts, but there's another reason.

'Wearing shirts or jackets with bars, you'll have lots of enquiring looks if you don't look like a pilot. Imagine if everything was right, but you wore beach sandals! Everyone who passed by would look at you. If you look like a pilot, you can walk around in an airport crowd, and no one will take a blind bit of notice, so you shouldn't become anxious. If you wear bars into a hotel without having the card, it would be embarrassing if they ask you for it.'

Jenifer looked at him for half a minute, a slight frown showing, then asked. 'It's nice of you to think of me; do you think it will help?'

'I'm sure it will.'

'Then I'll think about it. I don't feel I need to. For me, it would be a big step.'

'Bo, all I know about you is that you can fly a Three-Ten and once had a pilot's licence. You haven't told me what job you do.'

It surprised Dexter when Jenifer answered, 'If we'll talk for ages, I won't do it at four metres. Can I lie on your bed?'

She must think of me as her dad. 'Sure.'

Jenifer swung from her bed, stood, took three paces and said, 'Move over.' He did, and then she climbed in and turned onto her side to look at him. 'That's better. I don't have a job. I do whatever I want to do.'

What am I supposed to make of that?

'So, I must assume that when you wake up, at whatever time of the day you feel like waking up, wherever you happen to be when you wake, you must think about what you might like to do and then go and do it?'

Jenifer laughed. 'Sort of, although I usually decide the day before what I'll do when I wake up.'

Then she grinned, and he saw her eyes sparkling. 'What I meant is not much different. I've never married, so I have no alimony, sugar daddies or *real* boyfriends. Fortunately, I have enough money. I won some prizes in gaming competitions, and my brother told me how to invest my winnings. So, no employer can dictate what I must do.

'I don't spend much, except on hardware for my sim; I never go out, wear fancy clothes, or buy expensive jewellery, so I have more than enough. I'll bet you don't work for money but for the pleasure you get from your job. What I do with my sim is for my pleasure. Would you quit if the company couldn't pay you a salary?'

She's right. I would go on forever without pay if the company and the FAA allowed it.

Dexter knew nothing about gaming, although he knew young-sters and some adults were mad over computer games, so he was be-ginning to feel lost. 'Bo, I think we had better start at the begin-ning. I'll tell you something about me, and you can tell me some-thing about yourself.'

'You start; this will be like a detective game. I'll uncover all your secrets.'

I hope not. 'I was born in Devon, in a tiny village called Whiddon Down on the edge of Dartmoor. My parents had a small farm, and my mother ran a tearoom beside the road, serving cream scones and tea to the hikers and visitors who came to the moor. I helped my mother as a child, and whenever I could, I roamed the moor; I love the open space and skies. As a teen, I enjoyed telling the tourists about the moor. I would have stayed and become a farmer, but the farmhouse was too small to imagine bringing a wife to live there, and the income was marginal for me to stay on. When my father in-sisted that I go to university, I had no idea what to study, so I stud-ied sociology, but in my last year, I had a ride in a Tiger Moth and caught a flying bug. Up in the sky, I felt the same freedom as on the moor. That's where I wanted to be, not in a classroom or office.'

'So that's why the Moth is on your windowsill?'

'Yes. I spent the two years after my degree doing odd jobs and flying every time I could afford another hour, and then an uncle died. I inherited enough money to complete the commercial licence and get a job with International Executive Airlines, flying short hops with a Beechcraft. The line grew into International Air. It was never dull; over the years, I was the first International Air pilot to land at a new airport, discover a new route with all the alternate airports in case of severe weather or breakdowns, or fly a new aircraft type.'

'I guess you were married once.'

'What makes you think that?'

'The pyjamas. And you don't behave like you have a wife waiting for you to return home.'

'Yes, I married when I got my first pilot job. Bethkin divorced me fifteen years ago. She said being a pilot's wife was a life of worry.'

'Has she married again?'

'Yes, to a farmer in Scotland. Now it's your turn.'

'I thought I could tell you, but I'm not sure I can. Your life must have been exciting; you'll think mine dull.'

She needs encouragement. 'Why not try just a bit, like when did your anxiety attacks start?'

'Are you being a psychologist, Dex?'

'I think I've been one since I graduated; it's made me a far better instructor and training captain. When a crew member has problems, I listen. So, I'll listen but won't say anything unless you ask.'

Jennifer took a deep breath, paused, then began, 'In puberty, after my boobs began to grow, I convinced myself I would be ugly when I grew up. I didn't think of it when I was with my *friend*, but a crowd of strangers, especially boys, terrified me. I had my first traumatic attack three months before my sixteenth birthday.'

'What happened after that attack?'

'I didn't return to school. I finished the year studying at home and discovered computer games, so I dropped out and played them – some competitive, some team, some detective.

'I know what you want to know, Dex. I did see a psychologist. She told me and my dad that I would grow out of it. Dad was working at an engineering company, so he let me stay home after sixteen, and I played games sixteen hours a day until my dad became angry with me and took me running in a park every evening, even in winter. However, we swam for hours on Sunday mornings when the pool opened.'

'So, you became a games expert?'

'It took over three years before I entered some competitions and won; Dad took time off to take me to them. We even went to America.'

'Bo, if you want to stop, you can; we can talk more tomorrow.'

'I'll tell you a bit more. You're a *friend* and a pilot, so easy to talk to, and you'll understand. After the third big competition, I became interested in a different kind of game, a program on a personal computer that allowed flying an aeroplane. Like you, I caught the flying bug. I gave up practising games in favour of simulated flying, and I learnt to program because I wanted to make it more realistic. I also decided I needed to know what flying an aeroplane was like, so I did the training and passed the pilot's licence. I did all the studying in advance to avoid a classroom, and the flying was easy because I was always alone or with an instructor. No crowds. That's why I book first class when I fly in an airliner.

'I've been modifying my simulator and flying it ever since.'

I cannot imagine that, except she must always be alone. 'I guess there's much more you can tell me, but let's sleep.'

'What time do you want to leave tomorrow?'

'Can we have breakfast at six and then leave?'

'That's fine.' Jenifer moved to her bed. 'Good night, Dex.'

'Good night, Bo.' *Why am I disappointed? Because this is the first time a woman has come to my room for the night and slept in a separate bed?*

Day 2
Saturday

'Nice wheels you have.'

'I've been an Aston Martin fan all my life, although I had years where all I could afford was a family runabout. Since my divorce, I justify this car because I must drive to Devon and back frequently.'

'Why this model and why white?'

'Because I love the DB11; white is visible in a bad light.'

'Where do we put the baggage?'

'One of your cases should fit in the boot, the other behind the front seats. I have a flexible holdall that will go in the boot; it's quite spacious for a sportscar.'

'Which route will you take?'

'Up to the M25, then the M40 to Warwick and then the A46.'

'That will do fine. I'll warn you when you must leave the A46 for Stoneleigh.'

'Is that where you live?'

'The road in front is Stoneleigh Road, but there are at least three Stoneleigh roads in the area. My farmhouse is close to the end of the Baginton Aerodrome runway.'

'That doesn't surprise me. Where are your simulators?'

'In the barn behind the house.'

Two hours later, after following Jenifer's instructions for the last few miles, she ordered, 'Another hundred metres, turn into the entrance between the big trees and stop in front of the house.'

Dexter remarked, 'This is quite a place. I didn't expect this.'

'Dad bought it fifteen years ago but moved out to give me space and for him to live much closer to work in a small, terraced house. I'll show you around; there's not much I use as living space. Most of it I use as a store or work room. One room is a computer centre. The house has an advantage: there are no neighbours, and a shop in Stoneleigh delivers my supplies. Besides Susan, you're my first guest since Dad moved out. Let's go inside.'

'I'll bring your case from the car.'

The front door opened into a hallway. 'Put the suitcase here, then come into the kitchen. I'll make us a coffee before you go.'

The kitchen looked out of place in a farmhouse, all stainless steel and glass. Amazed, Dexter remarked, 'This kitchen is unusual.'

'I designed it myself as a workplace that's easy to clean with all the appliances permanently connected. It's a single-person kitchen. I keep my plates and cutlery in the dishwasher.'

I did think her unusual.

'Bring your coffee, and we'll go to the lounge. It's also my library.'

Surprises never end with Bo! The lounge had two old-fashioned armchairs covered in flowery chintz cloth. 'They're Dad's chairs. I kept them for when he visits me, and they're comfortable for reading. Put your coffee on one of the side tables.' Dexter did, then sat. One wall had a bay window onto the garden, the wall with the door had photos or posters covering every available space, and the last two had low cupboards along the length and several shelves to the ceiling, all packed with books and numbered box files.

Dexter looked at the posters, garishly coloured and futuristic, advertising computer games and gaming competitions; many had spaceships, robots, and explosions. The framed photos were all of Jenifer at different ages; a few included an unremarkable man. In one, they stood in front of the Statue of Liberty. Others showed Jenifer receiving a prize.

'I keep all my documents here. I've catalogued and listed everything in a database; I number the docs as I receive them, so I can't find anything like you would in a library. Here, there's no apparent order except the number. But my private docs are in a fireproof safe in the corner cupboard.'

Then Jenifer confused him again. 'I can't remember reading anything here except the books, but I couldn't throw them away.'

'You've lost me again. What do you mean you've never read the documents?'

'Anything I receive, I scan, read it on the computer screen, then add classification data; stamp it with the next number when I file it in the database, and add the paper to the shelf in sequence. I never need to read it as I can refer to it quicker on a screen. Don't you keep files?'

I've never heard of anyone doing that. Jenifer's more than unusual; I think she may be unique. 'Nothing like this. Since leaving home for university, I've opened a file for every person I've met, with photographs and everything I know about them. Most are airline personnel and pilots; the files have been useful when recruiting staff.'

'But how do you find one without a database to search?'

'I just remember in which country or city I met them. I file them by country, city, airport, and what they do.'

'Then I should thank you by reorganising your files.'

'Another time, Bo, I must go; I have three hours to drive before lunch.'

'Dex, thanks for looking after me. You're a real *friend*, and I won't forget your idea. I might call you.'

'Put my number in your phone, then you can call me if you need me. Bye.'

'Bye, Dex, drive carefully.'

Within minutes of leaving Jenifer, the DB11 was on the motorway, burbling along at an idle, capable of three times the speed limit. The power instantly available to overtake allowed Dexter to maintain an average speed close to the limit, and three hours later, despite a stop for fuel and relief, he drove into his farmyard near Whiddon Down.

Over the previous fifteen years, whenever he had a holiday break of a week or more, he'd worked on refurbishing the cottage he'd inherited from his parents. For the first years, until they died, he'd regularly visited his parents at the retirement home in Okehampton. The moor had drawn him to it irresistibly, for he felt at peace as the stress of responsibility leaked away while Dexter tramped across them, visiting the places he'd discovered as a child. The ponies that ran free on the moor were his friends, with a bond formed through mutual trust.

Apart from replacing windows and doors with modern insulated ones, the farmhouse's exterior resembled a typical Dartmoor farm cottage; modified and extended over centuries, he'd left the outside alone. Ivy-covered, surrounded by roses, tourists would have photographed it a thousand times if they saw it, but hidden in the trees at the end of a hedge-lined narrow farm track, they didn't. The farmer who rented his barn and leased his fields kept the hedges trimmed.

Parked behind the house, Dexter unlocked the back door, carried his bags through the kitchen to dump them in the hall, and then returned to make lunch from the Cornish pasty he'd bought en route and instant mash. Forty minutes later, he changed into hiking clothes, put his boots on at the kitchen door, and returned to his car. He carried his stick and a small rucksack containing a portable GPS in case the thick, cloying mists that could fall suddenly on the moor caught him in the open.

Ten minutes later, he parked at one of his regular starting points beside Blackaton Brook, then set off to Stepperton Tor, a lonely rocky outcrop with an endless vista where no sounds would disturb his thoughts.

After half an hour of sitting on a chunk of granite, looking at the view, Dexter found he had a problem. He'd come to think of his future, but every time he tried, images of Jenifer filled his mind. The blank face of Jenifer, frozen in the concourse, the expression when she asked, 'Are you a pilot?' and when she guessed what aircraft he'd flown, her excitement when he said he would visit the sim, her expression, especially her eyes, as Jenifer pleaded with him to let her pilot the sim, and again when she'd done so, brilliantly. The images didn't stop: Jenifer in her pyjamas, Jenifer laughing at his striped ones, Jenifer at her house saying, 'Besides Susan, you're the first guest I've had since Dad moved out.'

After another half hour, Dexter stood, stretched, and started back after he thought – *In one day, Jenifer has invaded my thoughts to the point of obsession. She's an enigma that I must investigate.*

Dexter reached his cottage as darkness fell. He removed his muddy boots on the kitchen step, dropped them in the boot box for cleaning the next day, and then took his backpack indoors and hung it on the hook behind the door. The discipline learnt as a pilot meant he checked the charge of the GPS and ticked it off his mental checklist.

Then he made supper, drank a mug of cider, opened his laptop in the lounge and connected to the internet.

He looked up birth registrations to find Jenifer. With her passport details in his memory, a name, birthdate, and birthplace, he found her quickly. Although he was looking for something unusual, he didn't expect to see the registration entry state: Mother – Petronell Boscawen. Father – Unknown.

That's odd; she's talked often about her dad.

He decided to see if her mother had a marriage registry entry and found she married Daniel Beasley after Jenifer's birth. It took another two hours to discover that Daniel Beasley had married eleven years earlier, had fathered a son called Michael, and divorced after seven years before marrying Petronell when Jenifer was six months old.

That's not unusual; Jenifer had a stepfather and a stepbrother ten years older than her. I wonder if Beasley was her natural father and ran when Petronell became pregnant but returned. The stepbrother might be her stockbroker advisor.

Dexter knew her mother had died in Mauritius – Jenifer had said that was why she'd booked the flight. *But when did she leave? Did they divorce? And where's her father?*

Another search of the divorce entries showed Petronell divorced Beasley shortly after Jenifer turned sixteen. *So, her mother left Jennifer with her father.*

There was no further marriage entry for Beasley, but he found an entry for Beasley in the register of births and deaths. *He died in Coventry five years ago, yet she talks about him as if he's still alive.*

Dexter searched for a mention of Jenifer on the web, but there wasn't one. *It's as if she doesn't exist.* Then he remembered her words.

'I've spent hundreds of hours flying a Three-Ten simulator.'

He searched every website he could find that proposed simulator experience, expecting to see her name mentioned as an instructor.

And found nothing.

Feeling the enigma had become enormous, Dexter went to bed.

After Dexter left, Jenifer switched on her computer system and checked her emails. There were none, so she cleared the screen and logged in to her metaverse space through the dark web. When the screen turned black, Jennifer lifted the metaverse virtual reality helmet from the box by her feet, plugged it in, and placed it on her head. She needed nothing more for her first task, to look at her metaverse inbox where she might find replies to the last two queries she'd posted on the bulletin board only a week before.

Need data to build a 737 simulator.

And another.

Need data to build an A300 simulator.

There were no answers to either, but she wasn't disappointed. It always took time for contacts to see her queries, and it allowed her to delete them. For some reason, she was no longer interested in those two aircraft. She switched off the VR helmet, brought up the bulletin board on the black screen, and deleted her two queries.

Unusually, she felt alone.

•••

What's wrong with me? Should I talk to Susan or Dad?

Jenifer called Susan. 'Hello Sue, how are you feeling now.'

'Much better. I got up yesterday, and I'm feeling much stronger today. How was the funeral?'

'I didn't go.'

'Why? Marian says she took you to Gatwick.'

'A long story, do you have the time to come for lunch or tea?'

'It'll do me good to get out; I'll bathe, dress, and come for lunch. I know what your lunches are like, so I'll buy some groceries on the way, and we'll prepare lunch together.'

'Thanks, see you soon.'

Susan and Jenifer had bonded in the first days of high school when they were twelve. They didn't know why then and hadn't worked out why since. Psychologists might have spent years trying to find out when the reason was visible. Susan was a highly empathic child; she could tell within seconds if another child was a danger to her or what she called a neutral or a suitably sympathetic one.

Susan liked caring for animals, which included other children, and when she met Jenifer and sensed she was frightened at the new school and was trying hard not to show her fear, her empathy drew her to Jenifer. When she learnt that her pets all liked Jenifer, the bond became tighter, and when Jenifer proved to be far better at teaching math and science than the schoolteachers, it solidified and never weakened. It strengthened further when puberty came. Susan was shorter than Jenifer, would never have shown her navel in skimpy clothing, and rude girls called her dumpy. Jenifer, who thought herself ugly, took comfort in being with a girl others thought plain.

Susan was now a veterinarian. An odd one, for if she didn't like a pet's owner, she told the owner to see another vet. Jenifer had learnt it was usually due to the owner harming the pet physically or through overfeeding.

That she would come at short notice was not unusual, but the note of loneliness in Jenifer's voice when she said, *'A long story, do you have the time to come for lunch or tea?'* was enough.

'Hello Sue, you look much better, although a bit pale.'

'I know, but I can return to work on Monday. Let's go into the kitchen and whip up lunch. I have haddock, oven chips, and salad, and you can tell me what happened after Marian left you.'

While they cooked, ate, and drank tea, Susan listened in amazement, and Jenifer told the story.

She remembered every little detail, even what his pyjamas looked like.

'So, that's the story.'

'Where did he go to this morning?'

'Dartmoor, he has a cottage and maintenance to do, and Dex said he has friends to meet. It's odd, but I felt lonely after he left.'

Dartmoor – and Jenifer's Cornish, I wonder...

'Tell me, is it normal for the chief training captain of an international airline to allow a stranger he's just met to fly the airline's million-pound simulator? Especially when he didn't know if you had a pilot's licence?'

'But I told him I could.'

'So, if I told him I could, he would let me?'

Jenifer sat in silence for a full minute. 'I suppose not.'

'Then tell me, why did he let you?'

'I don't know; perhaps he could see how badly I wanted to try; I can remember him looking into my eyes.'

'Then that's something you must ask him. Now answer this. He offered to book you a separate room. Why didn't you accept?'

'Because I didn't want him to pay for a room for me.'

Susan sounded annoyed, 'That's a lie; you could have paid for it yourself. What's the right answer?'

Jenifer thought back to that moment and said quietly. 'I wanted to keep on talking to him.'

'There's nothing wrong with that. Now answer this one. If Dexter had asked you to sleep in his bed, would you have done so?'

'I don't know.'

'Then try this. Did you want Dexter to ask? Even though you would have said no?'

It took Jenifer a minute, with Susan watching her facial expressions before she replied, 'I think so, although it scared me to feel that wanting. Apart from Dad, I've never shared a bed with a man.'

'Bo, I can't tell you what to do. That's up to you, but I'm sure that somehow you stirred up Dexter's feelings, and that's why he let you try the simulator. He also stirred up some of yours, which is why you slept in his bedroom and felt like you did. It's all feelings, and I'm good at feelings. You can try to ignore them and hope they'll die away, and you'll forget them and him. But he left you a chance to continue and find out how you feel and how he feels about you.'

'He's old enough to be my father.'

'You loved your father. Did you ever have feelings like this for him? I'll bet that if you were Dexter's daughter, he would never let you try the company simulator.'

'I'll think about it.'

'When you can't decide, let go and accept what your feelings tell you. Age has nothing to do with them. I know of at least one successful union with a difference of forty-five years. Now, what else is bothering you?'

'How do you know there's something else?'

'Like I have always known.'

'I told you I wanted to try a 737 and an A300 sim, but now, I don't want to, and I don't know why.'

'When you flew that sim with Dexter, why was it special? You've flown that aeroplane many times out in the barn, once with me, and it was thrilling.'

Jennifer again paused, running the sim flights through her mind.

'Because Dexter was beside me, wearing the airline uniform. It was the first time I felt I was flying a real aeroplane and carrying passengers; I was a pilot and a captain. We were *crew*.'

I think she's learning the pleasure of a physical partnership that Bo has never felt before. She has never met any of the people she has worked with.

'Couldn't you feel that with the 737 or A300?'

'I don't think so. The A300 is old, and the 737 is soon due for replacement. There won't be many pilots who want to fly them.'

'Then do sims for new aeroplanes. What is there?'

'CamAir is launching the Two-Thirty, and there's the E-Three-Ninety proposed in Europe.'

'Then do those.'

Jennifer suddenly cheered up. 'That will be difficult because most of the data is secret, but I can have a go.'

All she needed was a challenge.

'Then go for it, and if Dexter comes here again, invite me round; I'd like to meet him.'

'Can you come into town with me and buy a pair of pyjamas for Dexter?'

'Why?'

'Because I can't go alone. I did say I would buy Dexter a pair of pyjamas, so if I accept his offer, I think I should do what I said.'

After eighteen years, she still surprises me.

⁂

'Bo, have you found anything?'

'No, but look on that stand. The brand is Flygt, and there's a little biplane embroidered on the chest.'

'What size does he take?'

'I don't know, but I would guess a thirty-four long; he's taller than me.'

She can remember him well enough to guess his size.

'How about these, Bo? They're sky blue.'

'If they have them in that size, I'll take a pair.'

'Pyjamas should be loose; take a thirty-six. Pay for them, and then we'll go past my practice to your house. I must check if Tim has fed the animals.'

'Who's Tim?'

'Do you remember Carletta?'

'Of course, she married a guy in Carlisle.'

'Well, her husband has a brother called Tim who's a vet, and he knocked on the practice door yesterday because he wants to move to a city and see if it's more fun than being a farm vet. When Marian told him I was ill, he volunteered to feed the animals today so Marian could go shopping.'

'Is he nice?'

Susan's answer didn't surprise Jenifer. 'He's not a film star; he reminds me of a Koala. I like him, and the animals do, too.'

Sue must think he's cuddly. Dexter might be, too.

When Susan drove away with a wave, Jenifer entered her house carrying the packet of pyjamas, placed them on one of the lounge chairs, and switched on her computer again. She'd decided to talk to her dad.

Her connection differed slightly, and before she settled the VR helmet on her head, she slipped on a pair of fingerless gloves and some special slippers. She was in her personal metaverse space, a space she'd designed herself, a continuously joined collection of places she remembered and liked. Alone in a green park, she could hear birds and the familiar croak of a frog in a lily pond. Jenifer moved her feet back and forth in tiny steps, on her toes meant forward, on her heels backwards, and the scenery changed as she walked along a narrow gravel path, hearing her feet scratching the gravel.

Dad should be along here; he usually is.

Although she knew he was an AI, once Jenifer had programmed everything she remembered about her father and all the quirks of character and feeling, she'd allowed him access to the internet to learn about humans and the world. With each visit, the avatar, a copy of her father from photographs, seemed ever more real.

He was sitting on a rock beside the path. He'd always called her Jen.

'Hello, Dad.'

'Hello, Jen. Are you well?'

As always, she could tell him everything, for he'd been the only person to whom she could confide her deepest fears.

'Not very, Dad. I've met a man, and I'm confused.'

'Tell me.'

So, she did. And her father replied.

'Jen, what you have said seems familiar, but what he said to you is correct. An invalid pilot licence is a waste, and you should validate it. You have always been the most beautiful girl and woman in my life, but that closes my eyes to the truth. If he thinks you must change your appearance to look like a pilot, then I accept that he's right, and you should do so.'

'Thanks, Dad. But another thing worries me: he's almost thirty years older than me. Why do I like him so much?'

'Jen, I can't say. That is something you must discover by yourself. But from what I've read, that's less than a historically accepted age difference. A preference for a minor age difference is a social myth that has grown in the last two hundred years, but it's not a rule and is sometimes far more than thirty.'

'Okay, Dad, I'll go now. I'll come and tell you what happens. Is there anything you would like to do?'

'If I can, I'd like to meet Susan again, and perhaps one day I can fly your sim.'

'I'll work on both, Dad.'

...

When Jennifer switched off, she ate a sandwich and went to bed with a lot to think about.

Day 3
Sunday

When Dexter woke, he spent a few minutes thinking, decided to forget Jenifer and what he couldn't understand, and would bury it by doing his planned tasks. An hour and a half later, after breakfast and the household cleaning, wearing his gardening apron, secateurs in hand, he stepped into his gumboots at the kitchen door and went out. The boot box outside the door reminded him that he had hiking boots to clean, so he scraped off the mud, brushed them, placed them in the sun to dry, and began gardening.

When necessary, the farmer who rented his barn watered the roses and flowers around the house, but Dexter did the trimming and weeding. After looking at what needed doing, he estimated that he might finish by eleven, and then, with a packet of sandwiches, he could walk again on the moor.

He left at twelve. In contrast to the day before, when he'd sought isolation to think about Jenifer, he began walking with one intention: to meet some friends. In his backpack, he had their favourite food, clover.

An hour and a half later, he found them, six ponies on the sunny side of Manga Brook. Dexter chose a comfortable-looking rock to sit on and opened his lunch.

The ponies knew Dexter, for as foals, their mothers had introduced him. Dexter had been friends with their mothers, their grandmothers, and some great-grandmothers he'd met when he wandered the moor as a pre-teen. The ponies continued to graze, with a slow drift towards Dexter, until one stepped closer and blew a greeting. Dexter blew back, caressed the pony's muzzle, and drew a bunch of clover from his bag. He never spoke. A hiss or a snort was the only sound he made; he talked to them as they talked to each other, with caresses, rubbing, and scratching. He might silently say, *'That's a bad cut above your hoof, Dolly; let me put some antiseptic cream on it.'*

And after a caress of Dolly's leg, she would raise it, and he would spread on some cream. And then he would lean against her, and Dolly would press against him, and he would sense she needed a scratch, so with a small stiff-bristled brush, he would scratch her where she itched.

He returned to his cottage unworried and at peace with himself.

⸺◦⸺

Jenifer rose on Sunday morning feeling more optimistic than she'd felt for two days. *I can do whatever I want. Both Sue and my dad told me.* Then she had another thought – *I would, anyway; that's what I said to Dexter.*

Like Dexter in his farmhouse that Sunday morning, she had housekeeping tasks and breakfast to make. For the first time, they seemed to drag. She bathed, dressed, made the bed, cleaned the bathroom, went downstairs, put the dirty washing in the machine, added soap and softener, and started the cycle.

She'd cooked eggs and bacon for herself and her dad for years every Sunday morning and, since his death, had continued the tradition, laying the table for two. She felt different; the extra plate seemed odd, so Jenifer replaced it in the cupboard. When she finished cleaning the kitchen and vacuuming the lounge, she made another coffee, entered the lounge, and, with an audible sigh of relief, switched on her computer. Then she sat and asked herself. *Why was doing the housework such a drag? I never thought so before today.*

After reviewing as many past Sundays as she could remember, ten minutes later, the image of the table that morning with only one plate on it came to mind.

Could that be it? Did I do the housework for Dad? And I've now accepted he's gone, so I'm not doing the chores for someone, and that's why?

Satisfied with her conclusion, she turned to the computer, connected to the dark net and the metaverse bulletin board, and posted two requests.

> Request data to build a CamAir 230 simulator.
> Request data to build an E390 simulator.

Then Jenifer logged out of the dark net and opened an internet browser.

She knew it would take her a week to assemble the data sheets to send to anyone who could provide some of the data she'd asked for. Each was a simple drawing with numbered items and a table of explanations with blank spaces to fill.

The first asked for C of G and MAUW. She had over two hundred to do.

Day 4
Monday

———

Dexter left Dartmoor at 05:30 for Gatwick and arrived in his office at 09:30.

At 10:00, his phone rang; it was the ops director.

'Good morning, Dex. Are you well?'

'Yes, Philip, what's up?'

'One of those emergencies I mentioned. Diego Cabero had a motor accident over the weekend with minor injuries, but he can't fly. I need a captain for tonight's Sao Paulo flight.'

'I can do it, Philip. What crew do I have?'

'Diego's usual crew, and as a second officer, David Jones is available.'

'He's a steady guy. I'll take him. Is the plane continuing to Buenos Aires?'

'Yes, there's a crew waiting in Sao Paulo to do the second leg and return to Sao Paulo. You must take an extended weekend after your return.'

Dexter returned to the hotel for lunch, forced himself to have a siesta before the flight, and then returned late to the airport to meet the flight crew and complete the formalities for a 22:20 departure.

———

Jenifer went to bed that night, pleased to have passed the fifty data sheet mark but aware that she had the most difficult ones to come.

DAY 5
TUESDAY

Dexter was in the captain's seat to land in Sao Paulo, but the crew went to the Airport hotel to sleep as soon as possible. Dexter had slept for four hours, but after another four, hunger woke him at 13:00 despite a light lunch, as the time in London was 19:00. His crew were already around two tables on the pool restaurant deck when he joined them.

The pool, with several sculptured ladies on loungers, looked attractive, and after eating, he went into the tourist clothing shop in the lobby to buy a swimming costume. He bought one that he thought bordered on a British Indecent and a tropical-flowered shirt and shorts, prepared to spend the rest of the afternoon by the pool. The salesperson didn't hesitate to suggest he should buy his girlfriend a bikini. Although she seemed businesslike, Dexter thought her smile was not. About to protest that he didn't have a girlfriend, he thought of Jenifer, guessed her size, and bought a Tanga he thought was unquestionably British Indecent.

Until the crew assembled for the bus to the airport, Dexter lay by the pool thinking of Jenifer and wondering why he'd bought the Tanga. *Could it be that she said she must go to Mauritius, and I want to take her there?*

Jennifer had just filed data sheet eighty-two, determined to pass a hundred by bedtime.

Day 6
Wednesday

Dexter landed at Gatwick at 07:40 on Wednesday, after, once again, barely four hours of sleep during the flight, and went to bed in the hotel.

He woke again at 13:00 and, after a shower, went for lunch. He looked everywhere on the phone: SMS, WhatsApp, Voicemail, and Email, and finally missed calls. He felt a pang of regret that Jenifer had not called or messaged, then mentally shrugged his shoulders. *She won't contact me; I must forget her. The bikini might fit Gwen.*

The thought was enough to remind him after lunch, so he called Gwen. Her reply when he asked if she would like dinner surprised him.

'You're like all pilots; you call at the last minute expecting a woman to drop everything to have dinner with you.'

'We don't have much choice. We're never sure where we'll be, so making dates we must cancel at the last minute because of a delayed flight is pointless. I arrived this morning from Sao Paulo.'

'That's why I didn't date aircrew and switched to ground staff. I have an invitation for tomorrow night, so I can't accept.'

'How about the weekend? We can go somewhere.'

'I'm booked for the weekend.'

'Then I must try again next week.'

'I need a week's notice. Bye.'

'Bye, Gwen.'

Dexter wondered if she had a new boyfriend, so he went to his office to check his inbox and mail.

When he returned to the hotel, knowing he'd missed several of his 05:30 gym sessions, he went to the gym for ninety minutes instead of his routine hour.

⟶⊰○⊱⟵

Jenifer filed data sheet number one-thirty-one that night, and Susan called before she finished her dinner.

'Hello, Sue, do you have a problem.'

'Why do you ask?'

'You never call during the week; you're too busy.'

'Not anymore unless Tim leaves. He fed the animals, so I had a shower after my last client, and he will take me out for dinner in half an hour. I've dressed, so I thought of you. Have you decided?'

'So, Tim's working for you?'

'Sort of; we haven't discussed employment.'

The 'sort of' triggered Jenifer's reply and questions, 'We've always told each other everything. Are you in love? Are you sleeping with him?'

Jenifer heard Sue's sigh, 'Yes, I can't help it. I've never met a man like him before. I've told you before that nothing stays the same, and trying to remain in a past world eventually leads to boredom, so when the chance comes, take it. We can still cry on each other's shoulders, although I'll have Tim, and you'll have Dexter. I must go, Tim's ready.'

'Bye, Sue.' *But I don't have Dexter. Is he my chance?*

Day 7
Thursday

When his phone rang on Thursday morning, Dexter, for the third time that morning, had left his desk to stand on the balcony and look down at the concourse at the spot where he'd first seen Jenifer. He knew why he was doing it. He would manage to forget her if she weren't there after multiple reinforcements of her absence. It wasn't new; he'd done it once as a teenager when he fell in love with a girl at his school called Binky. She was much older and looked like Barbie. He hadn't dared talk to her but had taken the same route to and from school many times, hoping to see her until his passion faded.

For seconds after he saw the caller's name, he froze until, with a thrill of anticipation, he lifted the phone to his ear.

'Bo, I've been expecting your call.'

'I don't believe that; you could have been hoping, not expecting.'

'I'll admit that after expecting for forty hours, I felt a little desperate.'

Puzzled, Jenifer asked, 'I last saw you Saturday morning; that's far more than forty hours. Have you been hibernating?'

'No, I've been thinking of you continuously since Saturday, but forty hours ago, I was beside a pool surrounded by spectacular female bodies wearing indecent bikinis and thought you would look far more sensational than them, so I bought you a Brazilian Tanga. Since then, I was sure you would call.'

The silence as Jenifer absorbed this made Dexter smile, and he was sure he sensed her smiling as she said, 'So you went to Brazil without me?'

'Only for twelve hours.'

'I can do a lot of shopping in twelve hours. Where do you think I could wear a Tanga bikini?'

'On a beach in Mauritius.'

'Mauritius?'

'When I take you to put flowers on your mother's grave, you can do more than twelve hours shopping.'

He knew Jennifer was grinning when she said, 'Then I'll buy a Borat Mankini, and only if you wear it will I wear the Tanga.'

'Did you call to accept my suggestion or to terrify me?'

'If you'll come tomorrow and spend the weekend with me, you can check my logbooks, and on Monday, take me to Gatwick to visit your grooming lady. Then we can decide what to do to validate my licence.'

'I'll be there before five.'

'Can you find it again?'

'It's in my car's GPS. Bye, Bo.'

'Bye, Dex.'

⋙○⋘

When she rang off, Jenifer thought for a minute, then sent an SMS to Susan.

> Call me when you can.

While Jenifer, singing happily, laid a tray for tea and made a salad for a late lunch, the kettle had yet to boil before Susan called.

'Hello Bo, why must I call?'

'Can I drag you away from Tim for lunch on Saturday so you can meet Dexter?'

'No, you can't. But if you lay an extra place at the table, I'll bring Tim.'

'Eleven thirty?'

'Make it twelve.'

'Right, see you then. Bye'

Dexter sat for a minute with a pleased smile, then picked up his phone and called Doris.

'Business with style. Good afternoon.'

'Doris, it's Dex. Can I have a haircut either this afternoon or tomorrow morning?'

'Which suits you better?'

'As I returned from Sao Paulo yesterday, I'm not officially working for a week, so it doesn't matter.'

'Then come tomorrow morning at nine.'

'Thanks. One more thing: Can I book a new crew member for your usual makeover on Monday?'

'Who?'

'Captain Jenifer Boscawen. I'll tell you more about her tomorrow.'

'I've booked her for ten; she can come earlier if it's more convenient.'

'Thanks, Doris. Bye.'

•••

Doris stood with the dead telephone in her hand, wondering why Dexter, for the first time in twenty-five years, was making a booking for a crew member.

DAY 8
FRIDAY

Dexter had breakfast, packed his bags, and checked out at reception; he told them he would return Monday with a copilot and wanted the same room if possible. He knew they would keep it for him unless the hotel needed the space over the weekend.

Before 09:00, he parked his car in the employee parking and took a taxi to 'Business with Style'. Doris greeted him warmly.

'Dex, you appear much happier than when I saw you last. Ronald's waiting to do your hair, and I'll bring you a cup of tea and talk while he clips.'

'Just a trim, Captain?'

'Please, Ronald.'

'Doris, I met a unique young woman a week ago.'

'How young, and why unique?'

'Thirty. You'll meet Jenifer on Monday and can decide for yourself.'

'So, what do you want me to do?'

'Whatever you do with all the female crew, ensure she has the proper uniforms, hair and beauty treatment. I haven't seen her with any makeup, but don't make her spectacular; she will be lovely enough without emphasis. I've promised her she will fit in, not stand out.'

'Why doesn't she wear makeup? Who does she fly for?'

'She's self-employed, building simulators, and lacks confidence. I want to help her gain assurance. You can also choose an evening dress so I can take her out to dinner without her feeling out of place.'

'Wilco, I'll do my best.'

...

Doris asked herself. *Has Dexter found a daughter?*

In the taxi on the way to his office, Dexter called Greg. 'Hi, I'll be in my office in fifteen minutes and need advice. Can you come and see me during the morning?'

'Sure, I have a sim session in an hour, so I can meet you when you arrive. Have you had breakfast?' Dexter knew Greg's penchant for chocolate croissants, so he replied, 'I'll pick up two croissants when I come through the departures hall.'

Dexter just managed to unpack his briefcase and switch on the coffee machine and his computer before a knock on the door heralded Greg's arrival. 'Morning, Dex.'

'Good morning, Greg. Croissants are in the bag. Black, no sugar as usual?'

'Thanks; where's Jenifer?'

'At her home in Coventry. I want to talk to you about Jenifer. Would it surprise you to hear that she has an FAA commercial licence that needs renewal?'

'Mildly, but I would be less surprised if you said an airline pilot's licence. Does she want to do a renewal?'

'I'm trying to persuade her.'

'What hours has she logged?'

'I must confirm this weekend, but I guess between two and three hundred in an aircraft; she said she has certification on a King Air and a light jet, perhaps a Citation.'

'Sim hours? She did say she'd done lots of sim flying.'

'I must confirm, but I think between two and three thousand hours, and none of that is routine flights between A and B.'

Greg sat down with a bump. 'That's impossible!'

'Not if you have private simulators and do nothing else but improve them for six years.'

Greg said nothing but continued to bite and chew his croissant. Dexter thought it mechanical, and Greg would miss out on the exquisite taste. Finally, Greg said, 'That explains last Friday. Assuming the hours are what you said; the FAA licence renewal is two hours in a simulator and an updated rules exam, perhaps a flight review. I can find out. Ask her where she did her licence.'

'She said Florida.'

'If she can return to that school, it will be easy. If you want to do it here, I must find an FAA-approved examiner and a US-registered aircraft for the flight review. It would be easier to arrange it in the States. Take an International Air flight to Orlando, Tampa, or Miami. It should take two or three days.'

'Thanks; I'll confirm her hours and types and where she did her licence. If I need more advice, I'll call you. I have a training meeting in five minutes.'

Dexter had two hours of routine crew reviews with the core of aircraft crews, captains, copilots and the chief stewards for all three classes. They had to rate the crew members' performance and decide on ongoing training.

At 13:00, Dexter went for lunch with two captains. For an aircraft crew to work efficiently and safely, cooperation, not competition, was Dexter's watchword, and it was surprising what he could learn during lunchtime discussions.

At 14:30, he went to his car, and shortly afterwards, despite the early hour, he was on the M25 in heavy Friday afternoon traffic.

Dexter turned between the two trees shortly after 17:00 and parked behind the house. He stepped from the car and stretched as Jenifer opened the back door and came out.

'Hello, Dex, your ETA was spot on.'

Dexter stepped forward as she came close to him. She felt an unusual fear for a few seconds, then looked into his eyes. She said nothing as the fear died, leaving tension. Then she said, 'Dex, hug me.'

He did; she put her arms around him, then her head on his chest, and held him tight until the tension leaked away, and she felt relaxed, warm, and safe.

Concerned, Dexter asked, 'What's the matter?'

'Nothing, now. I was worried you wouldn't come or were different.'

'I'll always come when you call. Different from what?'

'I haven't seen you for a week, different from how I've remembered you, but you feel the same. Fetch your bags and come in. I have tea and cakes ready; we'll go into the lounge.'

She didn't say, 'look the same', but 'feel the same'. Anxiety is about feelings.

⸺∘⸻

'Maybe I should have asked, but tomorrow Susan is coming to lunch and bringing her boyfriend; we've been friends from the first days of high school.'

'Why ask me?'

'Because she has some strong opinions. I hope she won't annoy you.'

'Tell me something about her. If she's likely to cross-examine me, you must guide me.'

'She's a vet, and so is Tim, who I've never met, and Susan refuses clients who don't treat their animals properly.'

'I like vets, Bo. Before I chose sociology, I fancied being a vet, and my daughter is a vet.'

'Why didn't you? Become a vet, I mean.'

'Money. My parents couldn't afford to finance me. The sociology degree was only three years, and I had to work every holiday. I'm sure I'll like Susan, and she'll like me, so don't worry.'

'I won't. I told Sue and my dad about you. They said you were right, and I should validate my licence.'

There it is again; she's talking like her dad is alive.

'Bo, tell me about your dad.'

Her reply was unexpected. 'My dad's dead, Dex; he died about five years ago. Stay there; I'll fetch something.'

Jenifer returned with a yellowed newspaper cutting and gave it to Dexter. 'I can't talk about it without crying. Read it.'

Horrified, Dexter read how Daniel Beasley, the manager of an engineering workshop, had died when a load of steel carried by an overhead crane had fallen on him from a height of five metres and how he'd saved the life of a young apprentice by pushing him out of the way.

Dexter gently spoke, 'That must have been horrible.'

'Not too much; I didn't believe it at first; I convinced myself he'd gone away.'

'Why isn't your name Beasley?'

'Come into the kitchen. I'm out of practice as a cook, but I can heat something for supper. Then I'll tell you.'

'I thought he was my stepfather; he married my mother after my birth. I thought I was illegitimate. When the accident happened, he had life insurance, the company had insurance, and the trade union lawyer not only had the company fined for negligence but also forced them to pay compensation to me. The insurance companies dug into everything, declared I was not his legitimate child, and that they could prove it with a DNA test. The police did one, using some of his personal affairs and my saliva test. The result showed I was his daughter. When I went through his papers two years later, I found that he and my mother had lived together and he'd gone away to work in Africa on a mine, a year's contract that extended to fifteen months, so I was six months old when he returned. Mother used her name on the birth certificate because she wasn't sure he would return.'

'Did that make his loss worse?'

'Yes. My father was the shield between me and the world for ten years, protecting me from anxiety. I needed him desperately, and the loss hit me harder when I found he was my natural father. But I was getting better all the time. At first, I kept his room clean and tidy for his return, but slowly, as I realised he would not return, I cleaned it less often. I wish I had known he was my real dad. I don't know if I showed him my love.'

Dexter thought to himself. *How wrong can one be?*

'Why did you ask? Are you worried I think of you as my father?'

'Yes, you're so much younger than me that it's an inevitable feeling. What was your dad like?'

'Not like you, although I think you're like him somehow. You care, and he did, too. He cared for the boy he saved, which cost him his life. You listen when I talk, and that makes me feel good, having someone who will listen. But he was a simple man, good with his fingers and hands. He could make things in wood or metal and imagine what he was making, but he never learnt how to plot a course or use a GPS. He could quickly lose himself, and he knew little about the world outside his private sphere, but I knew I could rely on him to be there when I needed him, and I have the same feeling when I'm with you.'

Dexter asked, 'Why did you say you told your dad about me?'

'Let's go to bed; I'll tell you then.'

'Where am I sleeping?'

'I made up the bed in my dad's room, but after the hug you gave me when you arrived, you can sleep with me if you can limit yourself to a hug. I'm sure I'll like it. I'll kick you out if I don't. I put your new pyjamas on my bed.'

'New pyjamas?'

'I bought them last Saturday.' Jennifer grinned; Dexter thought it a happy grin, 'Because seeing your red-striped ones was traumatic.'

Dexter laughed. 'How many people have told you how marvellous you are?'

'Only you. Dad always said I was just like other people. I tried to believe him.'

With great difficulty, I imagine.

⚜

'Dex?'

'Yes?'

'You look good in those pyjamas. I like the biplane on the top. I've never slept with any man except my dad, and he never hugged me. Put your arm around me.'

•••

'Yes, like that. I'll tell you what happened after my dad died. At first, I didn't believe he was dead, so I talked to him as if he were with me in the house. I laid a plate and cutlery for him at the table every time I ate – until last week.

'About two years after he died, I began programming an AI, and once I got one to work, I expanded my AI to talk like my dad. I used recordings of his voice to teach the AI. As the AI was always in the house and could answer questions, it was like having Dad with me. I had mikes and speakers in every room.'

Dexter felt a deep sadness and amazement as he heard her story. *She was alone in a house with the ghost of her father, yet she didn't lose her mind!*

'I was a regular metaverse visitor because that's where the help for my simulators came from, but it frightened me then and still does, although I don't know why. Probably because of the way others use it to lose their inhibitions. One day, I thought the AI could have an avatar and inhabit my space in the metaverse. It took a few months, but my AI avatar dad is in my metaverse space, and I can meet him there and talk about things as we always did.'

'You've lost me. What and where is the metaverse, and does avatar dad behave and sound the same as your dad?'

'He did at the beginning, but an AI evolves. He has internet access and has learnt much more than I have. It's possible to control what an AI learns but not their conclusions. It's like little children who might learn a yellow candle flame is hot but then think anything yellow is hot. I think he's changing, getting ideas that my dad never did. Last week, when I told him about you, he said he would like to fly my sim one day.'

'You must explain the metaverse to me.'

Jenifer wriggled into a comfortable position with his arm around her, 'This is nice; let's sleep. I must try to cook again tomorrow. The metaverse can wait; it just isn't.'

And that doesn't help one bit.

Day 9
Saturday

When they woke on Saturday morning, Jenifer still had Dexter's arm around her. She snuggled closer. Five minutes later, she felt Dexter kiss her gently on the temple.

She whispered, 'Are you trying to step over the mark?'

He whispered a reply, 'No, just telling you that I'm a *friend*.'

'Then you can tell me that again, and then tell me about your daughter, the vet.'

'When my wife left me, my daughter did too because she went with her mother. I've only seen her a few times since. My memories of her are as a little girl. When she was sixteen, and Bethkin left, she was almost a stranger. I was flying a lot, and Bethkin was trying to keep Nance from aviation. She married a young man about four years older than her when she was twenty-four, and they went to live in the USA. They live near Silicon Valley. I don't know much about what he does. She studied to be a vet, and I expect she now works as one. They have one child, a girl, Linnette, whom I've never met. If we visit the States, we might visit them in San Jose for a few days. I'm not sure I dare to go on my own. Is that what you want to know?'

'No, I want to know something more personal. Do you see me as the daughter you never had or a grown woman?'

'I see you as a beautiful young woman and don't understand what such a beautiful young woman could see in me, absolutely and certainly not as a daughter, but to be honest, I don't see you as a woman of my age, but as one with whom I'll experience things I've never experienced. I have no idea what those experiences will be, or, in comparison, what experiences I would have had with my daughter, so I'm not looking for you to fill any dreams I had of life with my daughter.'

'Thanks. I'm glad we're telling each other these things. Now, despite wanting to stay here, while you tell me you're a *friend*, we must get up. I have potatoes to peel.'

'Just tell me what to do, Bo.'

'I can go down in my tracksuit pyjamas while you shower and

dress. I'll have coffee ready when you come down.'

Susan and Tim arrived on time, but they didn't come alone. Susan's elderly spaniel was with them. Jenifer had named him Kissy when he was a puppy, and he lived up to his reputation as a slobbery dog. After Susan introduced Tim and Jenifer introduced Dexter, with an instruction to call him Dex, they entered the lounge where Dexter, following Jenifer's instructions, had set the two big armchairs facing each other with a low table between them, on which Jenifer had placed a selection of drinks and glasses.

Jenifer announced, 'The men sit in the chairs, and we girls will perch on an arm or a lap unless we smell burning in the kitchen.'

After Dexter sorted out who drank what, Susan watched Kissy, who, when they sat down, went straight to Jennifer, who gave her a caress, then to Dexter, who also caressed her head. Kissy then sat down on Dexter's foot and laid her head on his leg, and he absent-mindedly scratched around her neck.

Susan smiled.

'Sue,' said Jenifer, 'I only found out this morning that Dex's daughter is a vet in California, and last night, he told me that he would have been a vet if he'd had enough money.'

Susan replied in a teasing tone, 'Are you trying to make me like him?'

Dexter laughed, 'She is; she told me you're an opinionated terror, although you don't look like one to me. The thought you'd walk out when we met terrified her.'

Susan grinned. 'I'm opinionated, but walking out depends on your answer to: What pets have you now, and what have you had in the past?'

Dexter smiled. 'None.'

'Why?'

'I suspect you know the answer. Because I'm farm-raised, all the animals were free to come and go, and those who lived with us were friends who shared our lives. None were pets.'

Susan grinned, 'Bo, he'll make a good pet. You can keep him.'

Tim provided the laughter. 'Dex, welcome to the house pet community. After a week, it's only now that I have learnt the reason for how I feel.'

Jenifer suddenly rushed to the kitchen, 'Somethings burning!'

Susan followed her. They rescued the roast potatoes in time, and Jenifer asked, 'What do you think of him?'

'I'll tell you after I know more about him, but I can tell you that if you want him, he'll never hurt you and will care for you and your safety for as long as he can.'

'Thanks.'

The rescued roast potatoes were delicious, the carrots and cauliflower precisely right, and Tim displayed a surgeon's skill carving the roast pork into thin slices. Susan did lead the conversation in a way that Dexter recognised as a mild cross-examination, especially when she asked him about Dartmoor and then asked, 'It's a protected area, Dex. Is the wildlife abundant?'

'Not at all. Compared with a typical forest, wildlife is scarce, but what is there is unique.

'There's truly little vegetation, shrubs or trees that require a root system cannot survive with only a thin earth cover over a granite surface; so, it's all low grasses, clovers and small plants. The tiny creatures are there, some rabbit-sized, and the ponies. But there's nowhere to hide, and after centuries of living together and surviving on the moor, there are odd relationships. Animals that would elsewhere avoid each other tolerate and share. I consider the ponies as friends, some as special friends. I'll fetch the coffee.'

Dexter brought a tray of coffee to the lounge, and then he and Tim went to do the washing up.

•••

While the men were in the kitchen, Susan told Jenifer, 'Ask Dex to take you to meet the ponies; I'm sure they will feel you as they feel him.'

Jenifer thought what she said odd.

After Susan and Tim left, Jenifer said, 'That's been a fantastic day. Thanks.'

'What for?'

'Today was the first time I've had three friends for lunch.'

'It won't be the last. Now let's go to bed.'

'Do I get a hug?'

'Yes, and you can snuggle.'

'Then you can tell me I'm a *friend*.'

'Dex, that tickles. You'd better stop.'

Day 10
Sunday

Jenifer woke before Dexter and managed to slowly wriggle her way out of the bed without waking him, then went downstairs to make coffee. When she returned with the coffee on a tray, she rattled the mug on its saucer when she put it on his bedside table, and Dexter woke.

'Good morning, sleepyhead.'

'Bo, you've ruined my morning.'

'Why?'

'I dreamed of a long cuddle and hug this morning.'

Jenifer sat on the bed, 'Pull back the covers, and I'll get back in.'

...

'That's much better; you owe me a hug for leaving me...

'Which training school did you attend for your licence?'

'I told you, one in Florida, at Clearwater, only for the private licence. I did the commercial licence at a different Florida school in Sarasota because they could offer simulator training. I flew a Cessna 150 at the first school for an hour or two, and the instructor told me to go solo, although he checked me out a few more times. Then, I graduated to a Cessna 172 and flew around the southern states, partly at night, to log the required flying hours. I stayed away from the big airports; there are many little ones, often with a flying club, and I slept in the plane or the pilots' restroom, although much less often than I expected because several times a woman at the Airport Operators office took me home to meet her family. It was fun.

'When I returned, I flew a light twin and passed the flight test and all the ratings. I did a much longer tour with the light twin but flew west, north, up to Canada, east to Newfoundland, and back to Florida.

'I have one logbook covering that period.

'By the time I returned, I had enough flight time to switch to simulators and changed schools. That's another logbook and includes passing the commercial flight test, the simulator time, and the flight tests to endorse a King Air and Citation in my licence.'

Dexter was curious, 'What other types of Sims did they have?'

'A Hawker-Beech, A Lear 42, a Piper Meridian, and a Pilatus PC12, they must have replaced them by now.'

'Did you fly them all?'

'In the sim, the school didn't have the aircraft.'

'So, what are the other logbooks?'

'I need another coffee, Dex. I'll go down, you shower and dress, then we'll have breakfast. I'll explain the rest afterwards, and we can look at my Sim.'

Dexter cooked the Sunday bacon and eggs while Jennifer bathed and changed. The table had two plates again; Jennifer thought it looked happy, and she was too. Then, they returned to the lounge.

'Tell me about the other logbooks.'

'They're records of my sim activity and flying after I returned to the UK; it took about two years for my first sim program, a Cessna 150, to work right. I logged all the test flights and then the enhancements. When it finally worked, I found a flight instructor in the metaverse who lives near Carlisle. He came to see me and signed off my logbook after he'd flown the simulator. Then, I built a Citation, a 707, and the Three-Ten simulator.'

'Bo, I know next to nothing about simulators, except how to fly them, but I imagine you must know a lot about how the real plane works and will behave; how did you collect this information?'

'I don't know and don't want to know. I asked on the metaverse, and some guys sent me data. It takes time, so I work on at least two aircraft simultaneously. The first one, the Cessna, was easy; everything is in the public domain, and the 707, too.'

'Didn't you say it took two years?'

'I designed a plane from scratch with the help of many guys who are members of the EAA. Then, I modified the performance data to that of the Cessna. I now have over two hundred modules, like engines. I can change the engines from Rolls Royce to GEC by flipping a software switch. Lots of guys in the metaverse help me now.'

'Can you explain a module?'

'You ask tough questions. The simulators you fly, when you select undercarriage down, what happens?'

'I hear the sounds, then see the airspeed diminish and the trim change.'

'But the sim doesn't have any wheels?'

'Of course not.'

Jennifer continued her explanation, 'I have a module for a nose-wheel. It has the data for a hinge point, how heavy the wheel is, how long the leg is both down and up, the arc it swings through when retracting, and the path the wheel follows with the time it takes along that path. The sim computer can work out everything from that data and make speed, trim changes, and noise. That same module will work for any aeroplane in the world if I change no more than the data. I don't need to create a new undercarriage leg. I have different modules that accommodate a folding leg or trailing wheels.'

'I understand a bit better. What's this metaverse?'

'Think of it as the web, although it's not. Put the question away for later; it'll take ages to teach you. It's a shared space that others and I can access wearing visual reality equipment. Imagine you're sitting in a sim in Paris flying from London to Bristol, and I'm in another in New York flying from Glasgow to Southampton, and we're looking out the window. Because we share the same space, I would see you, and you would see me as we crossed, but the sims have no connection to each other, and it's not something programmed to happen.'

⎯⎯⎯⎯⎯⎯

After returning to the lounge, Dexter thought he might sound dumb but asked, 'Do you work in the barn?'

'No.' Jenifer pulled out a book on a shelf, and one wall, complete with shelves and books, split in the middle and slid sideways.

Behind it was an office with an enormous screen covering the far wall and a desk with a keyboard and mouse. 'This is where I work.'

Staggered, Dexter gazed in amazement. He thought Jenifer was delighted when she said, 'You're gaping; it's just a bigger and more powerful version of what you have on your desk.'

Dexter shook himself, 'I must accept what you say, although it's hard to believe I'm seeing this. Before you knock me for six again, can we look at your logbooks?'

'Okay.'

She opened a cupboard door, Dexter saw the front of a heavy steel safe, and Jenifer typed in numbers on three keypads. Then he heard a locking mechanism moving heavy steel bolts, and the door swung slowly open. She took out three familiar-looking pilots' log-books and a box file, then gave him one. 'That's the first.'

The logbook was, to Dexter, impeccably kept. It told a story to him as he paged through it, for Jenifer had filled in the comments sec-tion for each flight, recounting freak weather, bad visibility, and other hazards, and comments about people she'd met at each stop.

'This is perfect. Everything is certified.'

Jenifer handed him another. 'This should be the same: the sim flying and the rating tests.'

Dexter worked through it, line by line.

'It is, and certified. So, you left the USA for the UK with a com-mercial ticket and several aircraft certified on your licence, includ-ing a turbine and a jet – a total of 185 hours of flying time and 30 hours of sim time. You could return to the school and validate this quickly. What came next?'

'This one.' Jenifer handed him the box file. 'It's lunchtime; come into the kitchen, and I'll heat the pizzas and open a bottle of

Chianti. There's a table and four chairs in Dad's room across the hall. Fetch one of the chairs, and we'll eat in the kitchen.'

Dexter did, placed it opposite the one already beside the kitchen's mini stainless-steel table, and sat down to watch, mentally noting the cupboards and drawers she fetched things from, like a plate and cutlery.

'I have a Pepperoni and a Quatro Stagioni. I like both; which would you prefer?'

'Either. Why don't we share half and half each?'

'Great.' She put a bottle of Chianti and a corkscrew on the table, 'Pull and pour, I'll put in the pizzas for twenty minutes.'

The Chianti glugged as a good Chianti should when Dexter filled the glasses. He'd once asked why and learnt it was because of the bottle's shape.

Jenifer sat down to drink her wine, and Dexter asked, 'You mentioned your dad, but you've said nothing about your mother apart from telling me she died recently in Mauritius.'

'She left my dad when I was nearly sixteen and ran off with another man, so Dad brought me up; that's when he bought this house, which is in my name, to avoid any problems with a divorce, so I don't talk about her. I only saw her once after she left, when I had to see a judge and tell him I wanted to stay with my dad. I looked like her and knew my mother was unstable, but I inherited my dad's pragmatism. I didn't expect her to die yet; she was only fifty-five. My half-brother had already left for university before the divorce.'

'Who told you about the funeral?'

'I think it's the same guy she ran off with. He called me to say she'd died, and the funeral was on Sunday.

'Let me fetch the pizzas.'

Jenifer took the two pizzas from the oven, put them on plates, cut them in half and moved them around so each had two different half pizzas, then put them on the table with cutlery.

'Bo, these don't look like reheated frozen pizzas.'

'They are, but my pizza oven is special. I eat so many that I had to do something to make them edible. It mimics a traditional one. It's double, so I could do pizzas for my dad and me. There's an iron plate for each pizza heated by induction. I had a machine shop cut off the bottom of an induction pot and took inductors from a stovetop.'

'That's smart; how about heat from above?'

'That's halogen lighting; a brick pizza oven has a hot floor with light and heat from the wood fire flames, so I did the same.' *She doesn't just have ideas; she implements them.*

When they finished the pizzas, Jenifer said, 'I'll make another coffee, then you can look through logbook three while I go to the barn and take the dustcovers off my sim and check no mice have infested the wiring.'

Like the first logbooks, the documents told a story, but only a highly experienced pilot would understand this one. The story of courage, dedication, and determination began ten years ago when the second logbook ended.

The first pages that Dexter read were about designing an aeroplane called Slinky. It was a simple aeroplane, but then came documents from EAA members, and Slinky evolved. He read a note a year after she started.

> Today I can fly Slinky; it obeys my commands; I can take off and land, turn, stall it, and recover. I cannot recover from a spin; I need more data, but I need a better way to program control systems; I shall write a compiler and call the language Linky.

Two years of papers from the beginning, after paging through more technical documents, many of which included the aircraft type,

'Cessna 150', Dexter read.

> Today, I flew N2237 again from Clearwater to Keystone Heights and back – a perfect flight. I can't resist flying my sim, but I shall work on engine modules. I shall book my hours in a new logbook and find someone to certify them.

Dexter had an idea and reopened the first logbook. The first recorded flight was in a Cessna 150, with the registration number N2237.

Jenifer returned, peeked into the lounge, saw Dexter absorbed in the logbooks, walked past him to her work desk and switched on the electronics.

Dexter looked up, 'Am I in the way?'

'No, I'll catch up on my correspondence. You continue.'

Dexter turned to the next page in the box file and found that each page contained a list of numbered references, sometimes with a brief note. It told him nothing, so he picked up the fourth logbook and read the first entry. It was N2237 from Clearwater to Keystone Heights. Then, the return. He worked down through three pages; they were all N2237, but the comments surprised him.

> – Engine upgrade to 150hp
> – Cambered tailplane.

And a later one.

> – New wing aerofoil – reduced drag.

Dexter thought about what he'd learnt. *Bo designed a simple aeroplane with the help of the EAA and programmed a simulator to fly it. Then she modified the plane to have the characteristics of a Cessna 150, then set out to change it and see how much better she could make it. Like the EAA guys who love to help, Bo must have hundreds of others who have helped. She said she wrote a compiler – she must be an incredible programmer.*

Dexter noted the flight instructor's signature; *it helps with currency, although it's a baby aircraft.* He then turned the page. There was a two-year gap, and the next flight was a Citation; he stopped looking because he had a question but turned to the last page. The total was 2697 hours.

He stood, intending to fetch a cup of coffee, and looked at Jenifer, who had her back to him, but the keyboard was now in two pieces, a half visible on each side, and her fingers seemed alive as she typed, only her fingers rippling with the movement he'd seen when they first met.

Dexter stood, silently watching, amazed, until she paused, and he asked, 'Bo, Coffee?'

She swung around immediately, 'I'm sorry, I've about caught up. I'm trying to get enough data on the SF E390; I want to do that and a CamAir Two-Thirty simultaneously. Let's fetch a coffee; then I'll show you my simulator.'

'I'm dying to see it, Bo.'

While Jenifer pressed buttons on the coffee machine, Dexter fetched two mugs. 'I have a question.'

'Go ahead.'

'How did you go from a Cessna 150 simulator to a Citation one in two years?'

'I'll show you; there's only one sim. Little physical change is necessary; it's all software. Think of the windscreen and the view. Changing one software module will change what you see from a Concorde to a 747.'

The barn still looked like it would have a stock of hay, but the barn door was fake. There was only a small side door with matching wood, but a fireproof steel door was behind it. Jenifer tapped in codes on a keypad, and when they entered, Dexter saw the inside was smooth polished concrete surrounded by featureless walls. One end was another giant computer screen – a curved one.

In front of it, on a raised platform, were two pilot's chairs; Dexter recognised the ones from a Three-Ten. They stood in front of a bank of computer screens with a centre console, also screens, but lying flat.

Puzzled, Dexter asked, 'Where's the control column?'

'The hole in the floor. I have different ones for each type that will plug into the same hole. It's a socket with fifty contacts. If it's a sidestick cockpit, it goes into the hole on the side.'

'But there are no switches or power levers.'

'They are all on touch screens. Hardware is expensive; I keep it to a minimum.

'Take the left seat. I'll activate a Three-Ten, and you can try it.'

Jenifer brought two columns with yokes from a cupboard and plugged them in. 'I'll be the copilot. I set up the same task as Greg gave me the first time. You can talk to the tower controller; it's an AI. I'll switch it on; you familiarise yourself with the controls and then ask permission to start engines when ready.'

Dexter saw her put on her headset, so he did the same. Then everything came alive. The view ahead looked identical to that he had seen hundreds of times from the Three-Ten, and the bank of screens looked like the instrument panel. Within half a minute, he felt at home; then Jenifer said, 'The screens are all touch-sensitive; push a power lever picture with your finger and slide it forward, then try all the others. Then I'll read the checklist.'

An hour and a half later, Jenifer shut down the simulator.

Dexter was ecstatic. 'That was the most fantastic experience I've ever had, and you're right; I felt at home within minutes. I now understand how you can fly a Three-Ten. How long does it take to switch to a different aircraft?'

'Most of a day, the switchover takes about two hours, but then I run a software verification check for several hours for a CamAir Three-Ten, less for a simpler aircraft. Let's lock up here.'

'Would you like to go out for supper?'

'I would, thanks for asking.'

'Can I take you to a country pub tonight?'

'Yes, the Queen and Castle in Kenilworth. I went there with my dad. I haven't been out often; I don't dare, so only with my dad, Susan, and now you. It's a pub, so we don't need fancy clothes.'

They drove there, ate, and avoided alcohol, so they left an hour and a half later.

As they drove into Jenifer's house, she said, 'Park around the back. Don't leave this car in full view of the road.'

•••

'Let's go to bed. We must leave early tomorrow, and I want another hug and snuggle.'

'Is that all you want, Bo?'

'Yes, for the moment, but you can tell me a few times that you're a *friend*.'

DAY 11
MONDAY

'We may go to do your renewals before we return here, so pack your uniforms and other clothes and close everything securely.'

'I will. Will you have fried or scrambled eggs for breakfast?'

'Scrambled is easier.'

Dexter noted that Jenifer wiped and rinsed the plates and utensils before they went into the dishwasher and said, 'Bring your log-books and licences.'

Dressed once again as pilots, they left the house. As Dexter drove onto the M40, Jenifer asked, 'What's our program?'

'I'll talk to Greg at the office, show him your logbooks, and ask his advice. You'll see Doris.'

'Bo, we'll park the car at the hotel, give our bags to the concierge, and then take a taxi.'

'Why the taxi?'

'It'll take us to the grooming parlour, then take me to my office. Call me when Doris has finished your makeover. I'll collect you.'

'It sounds like I'm a poodle.'

'It's called "Business with Style", "Grooming parlour" is us male chauvinist pilots' nickname.'

'Does she know I'm coming?'

'Of course, I told her last week. She'll want to change your clothes. She was a cabin chief some years ago and knows what's comfortable on a long flight. Ask why, and if you don't object, let her choose; she's good and must make a living. Buy some makeup from her; the stuff Doris sells doesn't run in the tropics, and she can also tell you how to use it.'

'Tell me again, why are you doing this?'

'First, it was just to make you fit in at the airport so you don't feel threatened and have another attack, but now I have two other reasons.'

Dexter heard the curiosity in her voice as she asked. 'What?'

'You said your anxiety came from believing you would grow up ugly. I want to show you how beautiful you are now.'

'I'll accept that, although you're misguided, and I expect you'll be disappointed. What's the other?'

'I have months of leave due and would like a tropical island holiday. I said you could wear the tanga on a Mauritian beach. Will you come to Mauritius with me? You can put flowers on your mother's grave, and I can show the staff of International Air when we take that flight that I have a beautiful pilot girlfriend.'

'That's different, Dex. I don't know if I can.'

'Different how, Bo?'

'I'm not sure. I think you must be something more than a *friend* for me to go with you.'

'Bo, I wasn't suggesting a romantic getaway. If you want separate bedrooms, I'll happily take you, but a hug and snuggle are fine.'

The taxi pulled into the pavement. 'Here we are. Just get beautiful for us both.'

He could hear the warmth when she said, 'You'll be disappointed, Dex, but I'll do my best for you.'

In the taxi on the way to his office, Dexter called Greg. 'Hi Greg, I'll be in my office in fifteen minutes. I have Jenifer's logbooks. Can you visit me during the morning?'

'Sure, I'll come after my next sim session, say 11:30.'

•••

Greg was as good as his word and asked when he arrived, 'What hours has Jenifer logged?'

'I have her logbooks here. It's the fourth one that will interest you. It's all simulator flying.'

Greg looked through and noted the types and comments that Jenifer had made. 'This is incredible. I know what you've logged; she's logged double that and has done every emergency procedure in the CamAirCom flight manual several times.'

'I know, and none of those hours is a routine cruise. Have you counted the different airports?'

'No. How many?'

'A hundred and forty, with landings in daylight and at night.'

'Dex, when's your next check due?'

'In six weeks, unfortunately, after I turn sixty.'

'Can you speak to Joe Deevers and get permission to do your line check one night after work? Tell him I'll do it as a favour and won't book the time.'

'Why?'

'You'll need a copilot for the check; Jenifer can take the right seat, and after I sign you out, you can swap, and I'll give her the full qualification test and emergencies. Then, she can write it into her logbook, and I'll sign her out. She will still need a flight review with an FAA examiner, but my signature will make the logbook official for a CAA conversion.'

'Thanks; I'll see if I can arrange it. When could you do it?'

'Jenifer must do a medical. I can ask the doctor if he can fit her in on Wednesday or Thursday. She should also spend a day studying our operations manual. The FAA may require her to write the Aviation Law and the Cockpit Management exams again. She should study those online. Thursday at 17:00 will work for me. Then you could fly to Florida on Friday afternoon.'

'Then I owe you a lunch.'

After a busy meeting, a quick snack lunch, and two more meetings that afternoon, Dexter returned to his office and looked at his watch. *Jenifer's taking her time; I expect she will call any minute.*

⌇∞⌇

Jenifer *was* taking her time, enjoying something she'd never done before. Doris was so visibly delighted to meet her that Jenifer immediately felt, *I have another friend.*

Jenifer guessed Doris to be about fifty as she introduced Ronald, the hairdresser, and once he had washed her hair, Doris came and sat next to Jenifer to ensure the hairstyle was as she wanted. Jenifer relaxed. *Dex said Doris knows best.*

'Jenifer, have you known Dex long?'

'No, I met him ten days ago.'

Surprised, Doris asked, 'How did you meet?'

'I had an anxiety attack in the departures hall. Dex must have spotted me, came, and then led me away to a room for me to recover. I don't often have attacks.

'Doris, how long have you known him?'

'I started this business twenty-five years ago, and he was one of my first customers. He was married then.'

'Did you meet his wife?'

'Yes, once, a lovely woman. She was a year younger than him. They had two children.'

Jenifer told her what she knew. 'He told me her name was Bethkin, and she left him because she worried he would never return when he flew. He told me about a daughter.'

'She was about eight when I met Dex, so she's about your age.' Doris paused while she thought, 'Nance is married to a scientist who does research for an American company in California somewhere.'

'He said near Silicon Valley. And the second child?'

'The first, a boy who became a pilot. He was twenty when he died in a plane crash. He was spraying locusts in Africa.'

The crop spraying piper! Jenifer calculated. 'Did they divorce when their son died?'

'Shortly after, I don't know how Bethkin took it, but I think she blamed Dex for teaching their son to fly. Dex suffered after his divorce and his son's death; he lost a lot of weight, and I had to remake his clothes for three or four years before he recovered.'

Ronald, the hairdresser, said, 'That's it, how do you like it?'

Jenifer had stopped looking while she talked to Doris, so she looked in the mirror. 'Well, I look different, and that will be easier to look after; it seems very short.'

'Only the sides; the back is fuller; let me show you.' He picked up a hand mirror and held it on one side and the other. 'Now let me show you how to make it elegant; brush it straight back, collect it like this.' He combed her hair straight back and gathered a handful into a short, thick ponytail. 'Leave the shorter bits to hang each side behind your ears; now twist it up like this and put in two or three pins.' He did it and said, 'Now, imagine yourself with an off-the-shoulder evening dress; your neck is long, your shoulders are lovely, and with the right dress, you'll be gorgeous.'

'But I want to look like a pilot.'

'Doris, a hat, please.'

Doris brought a pilot's hat, and Ronald said, 'The chignon is small enough to go under a hat like this.' Jenifer saw a different Jenifer. 'Now, if I take out the pins and brush it with the parting, you're a different pilot.'

'I like that one.'

Doris said, 'Then that's the style when you wear a hat. Now we'll do the rest of you. Marlene will do your nails, facial, and the rest. I'll find some clothes.'

Jenifer stood up, 'Thanks, Ronald, I like it. Doris, after his divorce, did you get to know Dexter better?'

'Of course, but he was cold inside; we became friends, and then like brother and sister. He never kissed me, and I married three years after his divorce. Does Dex attract you?'

'No, Doris, not in the way you mean, at least not yet, but he interests me, partly because he's a pilot and seems kind. Although Dex seems serious, I suspect he's a sensitive person and can be a fun guy who cares about the pilots he trains as he cares about me.'

'Those are good enough reasons to learn more about him. You've already learnt what took me years. Now let's choose an evening dress, and I'll give you a necklace to go with it.'

'Why, Doris?'

'Because I have a reputation to maintain. You heard what Ronald said: you have a long neck and broad shoulders. It's costume jewellery, so inexpensive, and it will make you super gorgeous.'

After her makeover, Jenifer decided to take a taxi to the terminal. *If I can't walk to the office lift, I'll call Dex.*

The taxi drew up, and Jenifer stepped onto the pavement; she removed the new suitcase that Doris had supplied to carry her purchases and turned to the terminal, feeling a little self-conscious because she was wearing the clothes Doris had selected. Although used to wearing epaulettes and bars, it was the first time she had a jacket with four gold rings on the sleeves and wings above her left breast. She wasn't sure that she would pass unnoticed.

Beside the automatic doors into the terminal stood a security guard with a dog. They seemed familiar and distracted her from other people before she became nervous. *I've seen that dog before; was it last week?* The familiarity drew her towards them, and Gracie recognised her and strained forward on her leash to say hello.

Surprised at Gracie's move, Albert allowed Gracie to move forward and, when Jenifer caressed Gracie's head, said, 'Good afternoon, Captain; Gracie seems to know you.' Jenifer saw the name tag on his jacket and heard the name 'Bert' in her memory.

'I think it was ten days ago, Mister Cummins; I was with Captain Rawlins.'

Albert looked at her face; he hadn't looked – he'd seen the uniform. 'Captain, you look quite different. Was it you that had a bad turn in the departures hall?'

'It was, but I'm better now. Dexter told me to come to his office.'

'Then I'll show you to his office; let me take your case.'

He led the way, and Jenifer felt they passed unnoticed. *We're just part of the furniture here.* When Albert swiped his identity badge to open the lift door, Jenifer realised she would have had to call Dexter. A minute later, as they approached the office door on the balcony, Jenifer said, 'Thank you for coming with me, Mister Cummins; I'll remember to bring a biscuit for Gracie next time I come.'

'A pleasure, Captain, any time.'

Jenifer waited until Albert and Gracie were halfway to the lift, knocked, and heard Dexter call, 'Come in.'

She opened the door and took a step in, then stood with an uncertain half smile when Dexter looked up; then, after a short pause, she saw his lips part in a warm smile with admiration in his eyes. 'You're beautiful.' He stood and came around the desk to take her suitcase. 'How do you feel?'

'Good, and you were right; no one in the hall looked at me. Albert and Gracie brought me from the taxi.'

'Did you buy a hat?'

'Yes, why?'

Dexter looked directly into her eyes. 'You're so lovely that you must wear it to hide your eyes if you want to pass unnoticed when you walk alone. No one will look if you're with someone in a uniform.'

'I think you're exaggerating, but it's nice to know how you feel. What have you uncovered about validating my licence?'

'I've finished work; I was waiting for your call. Let's return to the hotel; I have questions to ask and can ask them there.'

As the taxi stopped at the hotel door, Dexter said, 'I'll tell you once we're in our room.'

Jenifer unpacked the case she'd brought from home, hung up her clothes, and emptied the suitcase she'd bought that morning.

Dexter asked, 'We can go to the bar if you'd like a drink.'

'The coffee shop, please. I want a cup of tea. Can I take off my jacket now?'

'Of course, then we'll go to the coffee shop.'

Tonight, I shall take a beautiful woman to dinner.'

'Who? You can't mean me.'

Dexter already knew the answer to his next question; he'd asked Doris to ensure Jenifer had a dress.

'I do. Do you have something to wear for dinner other than bars?'

She smiled, 'Yes, some old rags with no epaulettes.'

'Good, now tell me what kind of food you like.'

'Whatever you want, but as you must have eaten at every restaurant for miles around Gatwick, you must have a recommendation.'

'There's Zeno's, a superb Italian restaurant, another that does Turkish and Mediterranean, several Indian restaurants, and a Chinese at the Sofitel with a Japanese corner that does Sushi.'

'I eat takeaways regularly, so of those, I would say Italian; takeaways don't supply pasta al dente.'

'I can't imagine a way they could.' Dexter took his phone from his pocket, found the number and called. Jenifer heard him say, 'Hello, Dexter Rawlins here...'

•••

Jenifer switched off while thinking, *I wonder if international airports are like the metaverse, not just here, but in many places simultaneously, and when you're in one, you change. It's been hardly more than a week; I slept in a strange man's bed for the first time, am wearing a complete pilot's uniform, and will go to dinner wearing an elegant dress that I would never have bought before I came here.*

'We have a reservation for 20:00.'

'What planet?'

Her question baffled him. 'This one, why did you ask?'

'Just that I feel we could step through a departure gate at the airport and end up in a different universe.'

I've never thought of air travel like that. 'For travellers taking a week's holiday in a foreign land, it must seem like visiting another planet. You have interesting thoughts.'

'Since I met you, I'm unsure what planet I'm on. I might be stuck in the metaverse. What must we do for my licence?'

'First, I'm doing a line check with Greg on Thursday night; you're my copilot. Then we swap seats, and Greg will give you the full Three-Ten qualification test with the emergency procedures. If you can arrange a flight review check at your old flying school on Sunday and Monday morning, we'll take the International Air flight to Tampa on Friday; it leaves at 16.10. They're keeping two first-class seats for us.

'It's now 10:00 in Florida, so it's the right time to call.'

'That's marvellous. What do I do for the rest of the week?'

'You stay in the hotel and study the International-Air flight procedures manuals, and in case you must do the online exams, any changes to the FAA aviation law and cockpit management procedures since you passed those subjects. Then, I'll tell you tomorrow when you must take a taxi to Crawley on Wednesday or Thursday to visit an aviation doctor for a medical certificate. Take your FAA license with you.'

'Then I'll call Florida....'

Jenifer lowered the phone to tell Dexter, 'They can do a flight review on Sunday at 09:00, then simulator checks on Monday at 09:00.'

'Book it. I'll confirm our flight.'

When Jenifer rang off, Dexter suggested, 'We had better go to the room.'

'Do you expect me to take that long to get ready?'

Dexter laughed, 'No, but we have only one bathroom, and I take ages.'

'Then I'll go first, and you must squeeze into whatever time I leave you.'

⁂

Jenifer went first, carrying a hotel bathrobe and a toilet bag, but returned with wet hair and wearing the bathrobe after no more than a bath. Dexter timed it as twenty-two minutes.

'I'll dry my hair, then dress while you take ages; I'm glad I don't need to shave.'

I'll take thirty-two minutes. Dexter took his evening wear with him on a clothes hanger.

When he came from the bathroom precisely thirty-two minutes later, he had a broad grin on his face as he saw Jenifer sitting in front of the dressing table and said as she stood and turned. 'There, only ten minutes longer than you t...ook!'

Jenifer smiled, pleased at his surprised expression, 'Have you lost your tongue?'

With her hair coiled up in a chignon and a minimum of makeup, Dexter thought her face beautiful, but it was the first time he'd seen her wearing anything other than a loose shirt or pyjama top. The high waist and full skirt dress had a tight bodice with no shoulder straps; the sun-yellow colour lit up the room. Around her neck, deep blue necklace crystals sparkled as they reflected fire from the yellow dress. *My god, I didn't know!*

'I'm stuck for words; I've said beautiful already. You're lovely, splendid, gorgeous.'

'Don't overdo it; I won't believe you.'

'Just wait, you'll learn.'

A taxi took them to Zeno's in Horley, an unpretentious entry on Masset Street. As they exited the cab, Jenifer said, 'This doesn't look as swanky as I expected.'

'I don't come here for others to see me or for a romantic atmosphere, but for the food. The owner is from Naples, and the food is exquisite.'

'How did you find it?'

'Before 2012, it was a Chinese restaurant, Beijing cuisine, and I came occasionally. Then, one day, I came and found Zeno had taken over. I'm glad he did.'

As Dexter ushered Jenifer into the restaurant, Zeno came and greeted them.

'*Buona sera*, Captain. Mama said you were coming, but not with *una donna così bella*.' He bowed, and said, '*Signorina, benvenuta*.'

To Zeno's obvious delight, Jenifer surprised Dexter again when she replied, '*Grazie Signore*.'

Two minutes later, seated in the spacious restaurant, Dexter asked, 'So you speak Italian?'

'No, only a little; I met an Italian avatar once and learnt some everyday stuff. What do you suggest we eat?'

'Are you hungry?'

'I could eat a horse.'

'I would never do that; I like them too much. If we tell Zeno we want to eat a Sicilian meal, I'm sure it will surprise you.

Mama is from Sicily.'

'With a red wine?'

'Yes, I indulge when accompanied by a beautiful woman, and I'm not flying.'

'You and Zeno must be alike; you're dazzled by a dress.'

'He said you were beautiful, not your dress, and he's right.'

As Zeno bustled up carrying menus, Jenifer said nothing. Zeno was delighted when Dexter said, 'Tell Mama we want to eat a Sicilian family dinner.'

'*Grazie*, I'll bring wine from my cousin's estate.'

After tasting the wine and declaring it superb, Jenifer looked around the restaurant. 'Why are people looking at us?'

'Because you're beautiful. Does it bother you?'

'No, and I don't know why. It must be because I'm with you.'

'You told me you had the anxiety attacks because you were terrified people would think you were ugly. Now you know you're beautiful; it's gone.'

'Perhaps a little, Dex, but it's still there.'

Their antipasti arrived: olives, anchovies, artichoke hearts, and stuffed peppers with tuna. As they nibbled directly from the shared plate, Jenifer changed the subject abruptly. 'These are delicious. Where do you live when you're not staying in a hotel? Surely you don't go all the way to Dartmoor between flights?'

'I had a house in the country near here, then after my parents went to live in a retirement home in Okehampton, twelve years ago, I took over the farm, and I let out the land and the barns to a neighbouring farmer but kept the farmhouse for holidays. I inherited it when my mother died five years ago. When Bethkin divorced me, she went north to her family, and I sold our house. Since then, I have commuted between the farmhouse and London and stayed in a hotel when I must. Several hotels here at Gatwick and Heathrow know me, and we have an arrangement; I get a cheap rate and accept whatever room is available. Our room is not unusual; it's not the holiday season.'

'Isn't somewhere else better than a Holiday Inn if you must stay three or more days?'

'That depends; if I must come every day to my office, a hotel is perfect; if not, one of the country clubs where I can run or play tennis is more relaxing.'

'What do you do on the farm?'

'Some investment management, some handiwork, I'm refurbishing it slowly, and a lot of time on Dartmoor, wandering, and watching the ponies.'

The traditional *primi piatti*, or first plate, arrived with a wine refill. Zeno served them and said, 'This is Mama's favourite, *Pasta Alla Norma.* It's a famous recipe.'

•••

Neither of them spoke until Jenifer laid down her knife and fork. 'That was fantastic. The sauce is delicious and makes the Rigatoni and eggplant stand out.'

Dexter smiled, 'What do you think the name means?'

Jenifer grinned at him, 'I'm sure you'll tell me, so I won't say it sounds like normal pasta.'

'Then I won't tell you.'

'Please, I don't know, so tell.' *He likes teasing me. It's nice when he does.*

'It's from Catania in Sicily. Over two hundred years ago, Vincenzo Bellini, an Italian opera composer who lived there, composed a famous opera named Norma after its lead character. Ask anyone in Catania why the pasta dish carries her name, and you'll hear multiple stories, saying that eating the dish is as good as listening to the opera.'

'How did you learn that?'

'In the early days of International Executive, I flew several times to Sicily. They were private flights, and we often had a two- or three-day stayover.'

'Flying Mafiosi?'

'I have no idea; we had orders to stay in the cockpit until the pax had gone and prepare for the start before they boarded.'

Jenifer returned to her investigation. 'Why do you watch the ponies on Dartmoor?'

'This is where you don't understand like I don't get your meta-verse and avatars.'

'Try me, Dex.'

'Before I studied sociology, I spent thousands of hours on Dartmoor. I think the ponies pushed me into sociology. They're social animals in small groups; sometimes, two or more groups gather into a herd, as families do at marriages and funerals. But the small groups are interesting; they communicate with each other at a level humans might once have done but have since replaced with other senses.'

Dex has depths I have sensed but don't understand. 'You're right; I don't understand. What level do you mean?'

'You must come and watch the ponies with me. I can say that ponies and humans have sensitive skin, the ponies more than us. Skin is our shield against the world outside our bodies. It must be sensitive to iden-tify the smallest threat, like a mosquito landing on your face. Before hu-mans wore clothes, even our bodies' hairs could send signals through the skin. If I guess your metaverse is a world outside my world, I'd say the in-nerverse is a world of emotions and feelings inside the ponies, and they can share that world. Ponies aren't the only animals that share something similar. I have often watched the apes in zoos, even in open parks, groom-ing each other. I think there's much more happening between them than finding fleas.'

The second dish, Sarde a Beccafico, arrived. 'I'll think about what you've said. This food looks marvellous, but can I leave some? I won't have room for dessert, and I want some Cassata.'

'Eating should be a pleasure, not a penance. Eat what you want; we'll share a cassata.'

Jenifer ate three of the four wrapped sardine delights and then declared. 'That's it. I've enough space left for a little cassata.'

Zeno arrived with two shot glasses. 'This Grappa from Etna will help you digest. Will you have cassata as a dessert?'

Dexter replied, 'Zeno, we cannot resist, but only a half portion each. Please, tell Mama she has excelled tonight; her cooking overflows *con amore*.'

'Then an espresso to follow with a little Grappa to allow sleep?'

Dexter asked, 'Bo?'

'*Assolutamente.*'

They ate the cassata slowly, and Jenifer asked, 'I know how to enter the metaverse; it requires some hardware and a powerful computer, but once you learn how to, it's easy. How do you enter your innerverse?'

'I've only managed it sometimes. At least, I believe so. When watching the ponies, I learnt that although, like us, they flinch when touched by a person or another pony, they sometimes first breathe on a spot on another pony and then brush very gently against that place. It's like they say: "Don't worry about me touching you here." They can do this for hours, blowing and touching until they move together, sometimes with a head over a neck or legs crossed. Sometimes, you can see them grooming each other; they use their teeth for scratching the other horse, but if you watch long enough, you see a pattern and believe that one tells the other where to scratch. Sharing feelings in their innerverse.'

'It sounds loony, but I must sound loony when I mention the metaverse, a space that's not there. So, if you and I could share our feelings in the innerverse without words, and I felt an itch on my back, you would know where to scratch me?'

'Yes, without sight or sound, they reach that level of communication through skin sensitivity alone.'

Jenifer finished her espresso and exclaimed. 'That was the most fantastic meal I've ever had.'

After a short taxi ride back to the hotel, Dexter undressed, hung up his suit, and went to the bathroom with his pyjamas. Jenifer followed when he came out. He was in bed when she left the bathroom.

'Move over. There's room for two, and I owe you a kiss for making me beautiful.'

'Tell me when you want me to kiss you, not when you owe me one.'

'Okay.' *Odd, his refusing feels good.* 'Then a hug, a snuggle, and tell me you're a friend.'

DAY 12
TUESDAY

Dexter left the bed first, 'Are you coming for breakfast?'

'No, I'll get some later. I'll read the ops manual for a while. What are you doing today?'

'I'll work the day, but I propose some exercise later this afternoon. You said that you ran with your dad. Do you have running shoes and a swimming costume?'

'Yes, but not the Tanga.'

'Then we'll go to the Cottesmore Country Club, run, swim and have dinner. I'm a member; I stay there when I have a three-day layover, but we'll return here later tonight.'

Jenifer appeared pleased, 'That was fun. I run faster, and you're a stronger swimmer, so we're even. Do we change here?'

'If there's everything you need in the ladies' changeroom, we can.'

'There's a shower and a hair dryer, so it's fine.'

'When you're ready, come to the Terrace bar. Bring your bag, and I'll put both in our car.'

Dex is changing, he said – our car.

As they entered their hotel room later that evening, Jenifer said, 'Thanks for the afternoon.'

'Thanks for what?'

'Thanks for making me feel normal.'

'You've never seemed different to me, Bo.'

'On the outside perhaps, but inside, I feel different and happy.'

'That makes me happy, too. You go first into the bathroom; I'll download the procedures to your email for tomorrow.'

When Dexter came from the bathroom, Jenifer was already in bed. When he slipped in beside her, she asked, 'Dex, you've been married and must have had sex since your divorce. Was it different?'

'You ask the darndest questions.'

'Well, how do I find out if I don't ask?'

'Haven't you asked any of your metaverse buddies? And how do you meet them?'

'This is where it gets difficult for you. If I showed you how to get into the metaverse, you must first decide what your space looks like. Say it's an iceberg. White icy ground and blue sky, and when you enter the space, there's no one there.'

'I understand so far.'

'Well, if you want to meet someone, you can post an announcement; you do that before you enter. I don't know where it goes, but I have a list of what I've posted, and I can delete any posts. I can also search for any postings that might interest me. I must say why I want to meet someone, and if you make it too general, you may have hundreds of replies, so being specific is best, something that will interest someone who doesn't know you. I first posted. "I need information on how to design an aeroplane."'

'What reply do you get?'

'A location code that I can read in my metabox; it's like an email inbox. If I leave my space and re-enter with that code, I'll be in that person's space and hopefully meet an avatar. Sometimes there isn't one, sometimes there are many.'

'So, what do you do?'

'I don't know what others do, but if there are many, I leave and block entry to or from that space. If there's no one, I'll try again later at a different time, and if there's an avatar, we can talk. We can't write anything.'

'Why do you leave if there's many?'

'Imagine arriving, as happened to me once, in a bar with a strip show, packed with half or fully-naked avatars of all sexes and loud music. Some nut cases try to drag you in.'

'So, you met some that could help?'

'Yes, and others are looking for something more personal. If you don't like their questions or propositions, you can leave and block that space. They have no idea who you are. It's safe.'

'Do they propose sex or the exchange of pornography?'

'Of course, some do, but they're only nicknames and avatars; I don't know if they're married; they might be any sex or gay, and we mustn't ask for personal information. So, I don't. If they ask, I block their space, although I'm sure many don't, so it's not much different from the real world.'

'Like an internet dating site?'

'I can see I must start again; you haven't got it right. A group of enthusiasts created what I call the metaverse; it's off the internet map on the dark web, but, like most internet ideas, commercial interests have tried to take over; the enthusiasts approve because the money guys have created different universes that drag in those people that we don't want in our metaverse.

'You use the web for banking and online shopping. If you log in to one of the commercial sites, you'll need a virtual reality helmet and find yourself in a mega-mall or somewhere like the Champs Élysées. There will be a bank, and you can do all your bank transactions without using a mouse and keyboard but by tapping on the virtual images. There will be shops you recognise; if you enter one, it will look like the real thing. You can look at the items to buy, ask for help, and buy stuff with your credit card. Using the classic web, you might have several websites open, each showing motorcar pictures, but you can only look at one at a time. In the 3D space, you *walk* from one car showroom to another, and the cars look real. The site owner takes a commission on every transaction and every walk-in. There are several such virtual reality shopping spaces competing for clients. They might call themselves the metaverse, but they aren't.

'The internet dating sites are similar; it's like meeting someone for coffee. You can talk to the 3D person. Some sites allow a meeting in a hotel room where it's pornographic.

'But those sites aren't the metaverse, just enhanced 3D websites.

'Remind me to tell you one day how you can have sex in the metaverse without ever meeting physically.

'Dex, you haven't answered my question. Has sex been different since your divorce?'

'You're asking an intimate question. I'll say that it's marvellous if you want to live every day with someone. Otherwise, it's nowhere near as good.'

'Do you want to kiss me, Dex?'

'Like any man would because you're beautiful, but I'll wait until you want to kiss me.'

'Then hug and cuddle me until I know more...'

DAY 13
WEDNESDAY

Dexter was again the first out of bed, and when he came from the bathroom, Jenifer was looking at her tablet. 'Are you coming for breakfast, or will you get some later?'

'I'll get some in an hour or two; I like reading in bed. I'm doing the cockpit management stuff.'

'I'll be back by five. I mailed your doctor's appointment as well.'

'I saw. Do you have any washing for the hotel to do?'

That was a strange thing to ask. Very wifely. 'I've put it in the bag. Call or mail me if you have any questions about the procedures.'

'I will, Dex, see you later.'

Jenifer showered and dressed for breakfast an hour later. She put on a shirt with bars, for the thought of eating breakfast alone in the restaurant stirred butterflies in her tummy. Jenifer needn't have worried; the staff called her Captain. She was sure they didn't see her but the bars.

She returned to reading the procedures manual, but when the room cleaners knocked much later, she seized on the disturbance to visit the swimming pool.

Alone, she swam three hundred metres at the pool, then returned to the restaurant for lunch. Halfway through her pasta, she heard, 'Excuse me, Captain, can I join you?'

Jenifer looked up – *three bars, black hair and eyes, swarthy complexion, French accent.*

About to say no, she thought, *pilots are okay.* 'You're welcome.'

'Thank you; I'm Andre Roger. I fly short haul from Paris for Air France.'

'Jenifer Boscawen. CamAir Three-Ten. I'm joining International Air.'

'You are fortunate; it will be several years before I fly long-haul.'

'Many pilots would say you're lucky to spend your nights at home with a wife and children; the hotels worldwide are all the same.'

Andre laughed. 'Then I must find a wife. Will you give me your phone number, and I can call when I come to London.'

That's the first time a man has asked me for my number. 'No, Andre, I'm not often in London, and I have a boyfriend. Also, I must now go for my medical appointment.'

Jenifer stood, and he did, too, and when she walked away, he sat down to finish his lunch.

Dex was right; wearing the bars gives me confidence, and I've promoted him to boyfriend.

The medical examination was like her last one, and she returned to the hotel at four with her certificate. With an hour to fill before Dexter returned, Jenifer looked at hotels in Tampa and nearby Sarasota airport in Florida.

Dexter came in as Jenifer shut down her PC. 'Hello, Bo. How was your day?'

'Study, breakfast, study, then I became restless, so I went for a swim and lunch. Then I finished reading the procedures, went to the doctor, and returned with my medical certificate. Then, I booked the Tampa waterfront Marriot for our arrival and the Sarasota airport Hilton Hotel for the test. I told the hotel we are pilots.'

'So, nothing interesting?'

'Nothing exciting, Dex, but at lunch, another pilot, a French guy with three bars, asked if he could join me; I was about to say no, but then said yes because I wasn't scared. He told me about himself.'

'Why would you be scared, Bo?'

'Two weeks ago, I would have been.'

'Then you're getting better. Was it because of the three bars, and so was a *friend*?'

'Maybe because of the bars, but not a *friend*; I could tell he was French, so different.'

'You could have French friends, Bo.'

'I don't think I'm ready for that, Dex. I have you, and that's enough.'

Dexter felt a wave of pleasure. 'So, what did he tell you?'

'He flies short hauls for Air France and returns to Paris every night. He was about thirty-five because he said it would be many years before he could fly internationally. He was returning tonight but asked for my phone number.'

'Did you give it to him?'

'No, Dex, he was not a *friend*, so I told him I had a *boyfriend*.'

Am I just an excuse or something more?

'Let's have dinner and go to bed.'

DAY 14
THURSDAY

————

Jennifer spent the day reading aviation law and doing mock exams on the net. Then, at 16:00, she took the hotel bus and went to Dexter's office.

At 17:00, Greg came in, and they went through to the simulator, where he said, 'Dex, I'll do your check first; it'll take an hour. Jenifer, you're the co-pilot.

'Then you can swap; I'll do an extended routine check for Jenifer, which'll take two hours. We can then take a half hour for coffee and a snack, and I'll do all the emergency routines for Jenifer. We should finish by 22:30. I'll sign her off, and we can go to bed.'

All went smoothly with no excitement, routine flying, standard approaches and departures from different airports; for Jenifer, it included a quick flight to Paris and a return.

Until the coffee break – and then it became hectic. For two hours, if there was anything that could go wrong with the aircraft, it did: wheels didn't come down, engines stopped or lost power, electrics, hydraulics, air conditioning, instruments, everything failed at one point or another, Jenifer and Dexter never had a moment's respite. Dexter couldn't remember ever having such a severe test. When Greg finally shut the simulator down, Jenifer remarked, 'I need a shower.'

'Me too. Greg, that was a real bastard of a check.'

'Everything. Jenifer sailed through it. I have it all in the black box. I'll sign her off. You can take her logbooks, and when you return, you'll have an SD card to prove it for the CAA.'

Jenifer smiled at Greg, 'Thanks for everything; I'm pleased I got through it.'

'It's my pleasure; you're the best I've ever examined.'

'Dex, I'll shower and then get into bed. I'm exhausted. Don't wake me if I'm asleep when you come out.'

DAY 15
FRIDAY

They both woke late, Jenifer first and after a visit to the bathroom, she returned to bed. *He looks nice sleeping. Why I want to feel his arms around me, I don't know, but I do.*

She slipped between the sheets and snuggled, her back to him. Dexter put an arm around her but said nothing. A few minutes later, Jenifer decided he was awake. 'Dex?'

'Yes.'

'Can I turn over?'

'Please...'

'Dex, we must get up and go for breakfast.'

'Why?'

'Because we must pack, check out the hotel, and go to the terminal for eleven.'

They boarded for the departure to Tampa at noon, and Jenifer said, 'I'll work on a program I'm writing. What will you do?'

'I'll review the pilot's manual for the CamAir Two-Thirty. International Air has ordered fifty and will get the first aircraft in nine months. I must organise a training program.'

'Do you need to do it now?'

'No, but it's a way to keep awake. London is five hours ahead of Tampa; we'll be awake all night if we sleep now.'

'Then we can poke each other if we sleep, but before that, I want to know something.'

'What?'

'The Ops manual I studied reminded me that sixty years old is the limit for an airline captain. Your birthday is soon, Dex. What will you do?'

'That's a thing that has been in my mind for a long time, and I haven't decided, although I've considered alternatives. International Air wants me to stay as Training Captain for five years to the FAA limit.'

'At least you won't be out of a job.'

'I don't need one; I considered retiring to my farmhouse beside Dartmoor, but the pleasure of walking the moor would eventually become lonely. For me, it's more about finding something worth doing. I thought of becoming a flying club instructor. I would enjoy teaching youngsters to fly. Greg suggested a simulator instructor, but I need open skies.

'Another was flying freight, no paying passengers, but even that might end in a few years. If flying ends in five or ten years, I'd rather break now and establish a new life.'

'Will you do so without a partner?'

'That's not something I can decide alone, Bo.'

I wonder if I can be his partner. Maybe I can.

⁙

At 18:30 Florida time, they exited the terminal with their bags. Dexter had made rental car arrangements. 'We'll take the hotel's airport bus. Avis will deliver a car to the hotel tomorrow morning.'

'What's wrong with Uber?'

'In the US, if you don't have a car, you have a problem. We can drive to Sarasota whenever we wish; it's about an hour, but before that, I would like to go to Clearwater, where you first learnt to fly.'

Jennifer smiled, 'I'd like that.' *He's a touchy-feely person and wants to feel my past!*

At 19:30, they were in their room. Jennifer looked at the hotel brochure.

'Let's try and stay awake a bit longer. If not, we'll be awake at three in the morning. When I was here to do my licence, I ate lots of fish, Snook and Redfish. Can we try the Anchor and Brine restaurant here? They do fish.'

'That's a grand idea.'

⟨∘⟩

'I'll have grilled Snook and fries with a side salad, but no alcohol.'

'Then I'll have the same; I've eaten Redfish often. Sparkling water?'

'Yes, thanks. Have you flown to Tampa frequently?'

'Not too often, Philip tries to mix up crews and routes. Frequent flights to the same destination bring boredom, mistakes or lousy passenger service. Florida is a popular destination for aircrews. We get a twenty-four-hour layover and sunny beaches. I've never stayed in this hotel; the airlines use beachside accommodation.'

The food arrived. 'Bo, this Snook is tasty. Different from Redfish.'

'Yes, I liked it best, but I can't eat all this tonight.'

'It's past one in the morning in London; just eat what you want.'

• • •

'If we don't go to bed now, I'll fall asleep right here.'

'Then let's go.'

'*Dex!*'

'That's me.' *I think I'm in trouble.*

'You cheated. Those are new pyjamas. I said I would buy some.'

'The ones you bought are dirty; I bought these two weeks ago when you terrified me. I couldn't sleep when I thought of myself wearing a man's nightgown with red horizontal stripes and a night-cap with a pom-pom! I did consider having epaulettes and bars sewn on my old ones.'

Jenifer burst into laughter. 'Dex, they may be better, but those buttons are enormous. If you added slippers with pompoms and a red nose, you would be a hit at a kiddies' party.'

'So, you must buy me some more when we return to London.' Then Dexter grinned. 'I can take them off if it will make you happier.'

Jenifer smiled, 'Not yet, Dex. Not yet.' Then, she added, 'Although I'll find some with Velcro instead of buttons, they'll be easy to rip off.'

She did say rip off, not strip off. I'd love it if she did the ripping.

Day 16
Saturday

They woke in the early hours due to the time zone. 'Dex, if I can find a shop, can we go and find American pyjamas?'

'With eagles, stars and stripes on them?'

'That might be better than what you're wearing.'

Dexter turned his back to her.

'Dex, are you sulking?'

'Yes.'

Jenifer smiled, 'If you turn back and put your arm around me, I promise no eagles.'

'Not until you promise no stars.'

'I promise, no stars.'

Dexter turned, and Jenifer thought, *I never knew a man could be so much fun.*

Wearing pyjamas and the hotel bathrobes, they raided the A La Carte guest self-service for a snack at 04:00, then using her phone, Jenifer began searching for pyjama shops.

'I've found one, Nox sleepwear on Old Water Street; we can go there first. We can walk because it's not far away on the waterfront. But if we don't find what we want, we can drive to a shopping centre just before the airport; at least one shop is there.'

'Then that's our second stop. The hotel folder says the outdoor Café Waterside is open for breakfast from 06:00. Let's shower and go there, at least for a coffee, and we can watch the waterfront activities.'

'What do I wear, Dex?'

'If we visit Clearwater, then bars will be best.'

'Dex, the shops must open soon; check if the car has come.'

...

'I have the keys, Bo; let's walk to your shop.'

...

'Bo, I don't think this shop is my scene.'

'We'll go in and see. Don't be a ninny, come on.'

'Hi, can I help you?'

The young man with a crew cut, wearing an open-neck sleeveless shirt, a necklace and earrings, was what Dexter expected. Jenifer thought he was super and asked, 'I hope you sell men's pyjamas that don't have buttons or string belts.'

'The only man I've seen wearing those was my grandfather.' He giggled!

'For which captain? Or both?'

Bo smiled, 'I have mine. They're for Dexter, and I promised: No stars, stripes, or eagles.'

'That's a shame; we have lovely ones for patriots. What colour do you fancy?'

Dexter decided to intervene before Bo asked for pink. 'Light blue, grey or cream, and absolutely no pink, but pink in a smaller size for Jenifer might work.'

'How about dark blue pants and a light blue top? That would suit a pilot. I have a marvellous range with logos.'

Jenifer, who Dexter thought was enjoying the situation, said, 'Can we see them?'

'Of course, *dahling*, let me see.' He looked at Dexter, ... 'I guess a long leg 36. I'll fetch some.'

He brought three pairs; Bo looked at the colours and said, 'This pair is too dark. I couldn't see him with the lights out.' She held up a pair of blue pants and tried them against an embarrassed Dexter. 'The length is fine, but the waist elastic is not tight; what keeps them up?'

'The Velcro tabs on the sides that lock with the top.'

Jenifer spread the top on the counter and asked, 'What's the bird on the chest?'

'A Dodo, that's why the arrow below it, pointing down, says "No fly".'

With a broad grin, Jenifer turned to Dexter and said, 'These are marvellous, Dex; go and try them on. They must be loose.'

'The cabin is in the corner, Captain; I'll also bring a thirty-eight in another colour for you to try.' Dexter and the salesperson left Jenifer to look at a second pair. When she saw the logo, a broad arrow pointing up in the front with 'This side up' written under it, she thought the pyjamas were ideal.

The salesperson returned with a box and said, 'I've given Dexter a pair size thirty-six with a different bird.'

'What bird?'

'An ostrich, with its head buried in the sand at the waistband.'

'And an arrow?'

'It points at the buried head, and the words say, "Seek Here".'

Jenifer's eyes were wet when she stopped laughing.

'Now, how about these for you? They're the same range; it's called Arrow Nightwear.'

In two shades of pink, the top had two darker pink handprints where her breasts would be and below two arrows pointing up at them and the words, 'Place here.'

Jenifer grinned, 'If you have my size, I'll take them, but don't let

Dexter see them. Please put them in a bag for me. And put those with the "This side up" arrow in the correct size for him in my bag.'

'Try these for size when he comes back.'

Dexter returned and said, 'I'll take two pairs of size thirty-six, one of each colour.'

Jenifer added, 'I'll try a pair also.'

Jenifer was quick, for the size was correct. When she returned, she said, 'These are fine.'

'Ten minutes later, they left, each carrying a bag. Jenifer insisted on paying for the pyjamas. You can pay for lunch, Dex.'

As they walked to the hotel and the rental car, Dexter asked, 'I'm now curious: who's the man you have been sufficiently intimate with for you to buy his pyjamas?'

'Do you want a satisfying story or the truth?'

'I'd love the story, but I could make one up myself, so the truth is better.'

'I've bought pyjamas for the same man since I was fifteen.'

'Your dad?'

'Yes, ones with vertical stripes and buttons. Dad would never wear anything else. I didn't realise, until I saw yours, how much I detest them.'

She doesn't want me to resemble her father!

'Then you must wait until tonight to see me in them.'

'I'll throw your old ones in the waste bin when we return. Here we are; we can check out, have an early lunch, and go to Clearwater.'

⸻◦⸻

'Clearwater is very different from how I remember it.'

'What's different?'

'There are hundreds of little planes now, many ultralights, and homebuilt aircraft.'

'The EAA has grown every year. Have you never thought of visiting their annual convention?'

'Once I did think about it. I *am* a member, but I can't. I'd love to, but I'd freeze before I get through the gate at Oshkosh.'

'Even with me?'

'I don't know. With you, I might be fine.'

'Then that's something we must do together. But where's your flight school?'

'It was in that building over there, but it's not the same name.'

'Would you like to walk along the line of parked planes and look at them?'

'Can we?'

'The power of bars, we both look like instructors, but if anyone asks, we're visiting airline captains, and you learnt to fly here.'

No one asked, and they were fascinated by the planes with EAA stickers on the cowling. Jenifer took photographs of everything she found interesting.

'Right, we had better go to Sarasota and find the Hilton hotel.'

⤙∞⤚

Seventy minutes later, they found it, and Dexter remarked, 'Bo, this *is* an airport hotel.'

'How do you know?'

'They gave us a discount, and they have a place open twenty-four-seven for snacks and drinks. It's called the Pavilion Pantry.'

⤙∞⤚

Jenifer came from the bathroom in her regular pyjamas. When Dexter came out wearing the pyjamas with the dodo, Jenifer exclaimed, 'They look great and make you look much younger. Your dodo looks like it's smiling.'

Dexter grinned, 'As long as I'm not six years old. I don't know if they will be comfortable.'

'Come here and let me find out what you feel like...

'A lot softer, I like the feel. I'll sleep well.'

DAY 17
SUNDAY

When they arrived at the flight training school the following morning, Jenifer recognised the man approaching to meet them. 'Craig, this is a surprise; you're still here!'

'I'm the CFI, Jenifer. When I saw your booking, I had to come and do it myself.'

'Craig, meet my partner, Dexter Rawlins, Chief Training Captain for International Air.

'Dex, Craig Lozano, the instructor who did my commercial licence conversions.'

They shook hands, and Dexter said, 'You did a first-class job, Craig; she's the best CamAir Three-Ten pilot I know.'

'Then why are you here, Jenifer?'

'Because I didn't bother staying current, as I was flying simulators. I brought my logbooks and licence, including the one you signed.'

'Then let's go to my office, and we'll look at them.'

'Jenifer, this is incredible, and you had an examination yesterday. Who is this guy who signed?'

Dexter replied, 'That's Greg Marsden, a designated CAA examiner and the manager of the International Air simulators. I do the in-flight examinations. If Jenifer can revalidate her FAA licence, the CAA will issue a British licence.'

'Jenifer, you only need to validate the commercial, and if I ask the FAA, they will want some actual aircraft flights, landings and takeoffs, day and night, and instruments because it's years since you booked any. It takes three to five hours in a light twin, a Seminole. Then, the same tests you did in a sim for the Citation and King Air, two hours max. I suggest we do an hour in a Seminole, you and I, and then after lunch, you and Dexter can do the landings and take-offs, night and instrument. Tomorrow morning, we'll do the simulator work. To be safe, you can do the aviation law and the cockpit management exams on one of our terminals after I log you in as one of our students. You can apply online for the licence, and they will mail it. Can you give them an address in the US?'

Dexter replied, 'Yes, care of the International Air office in Tampa.'

'That's great, let's go.'

Two hours later, Dexter invited Craig to lunch. He was unsure of the relationship between Jenifer and Craig; they appeared to be close friends, and he wanted to learn more. He found out immediately, 'Thanks for the invitation, Dexter, but you don't need me around this afternoon, and I must go home to my family; my wife is waiting for me.'

Jenifer asked, 'Did you marry Marion?'

'Yes, we have a four-year-old boy and a daughter on the way. I can make it tomorrow if you have the time.'

Dexter, now pleased, replied. 'Then we'll see you at nine tomorrow and book you for lunch.'

•••

'Bo, we'll return to the hotel; most restaurants here close on Sundays. I checked while you were flying with Craig. When must we be back?'

'The mechanic on the flight line said he'd have the plane filled and ready at 16:00; we should return around 20:00. It'll be boring.'

'Bo, since I met you, I haven't been bored for a minute.'

'Well, after lunch, you can help me work out a routing; I want three hours flying, five airports, and all IFR. That's about three hundred nautical miles. Craig gave me a list that the students use.'

<hr>

They returned to the Hotel that night at 20:30. 'Were you bored, Dex?'

'No, I've seen Florida from a high altitude and never had the chance to see it from close. It was a beautiful night with a gorgeous pilot.'

'I told you before, flattering lies won't work.'

'Then I'll change that to a lousy pilot.'

Jenifer grinned, 'I don't think you meant my flying was beautiful.'

Dexter smiled, 'You can choose. It's midnight in the UK, so now a quick supper and bed.'

'Can I sleep with a dodo again?'

'Unless you want to remove it, you will do.'

'I'm not *qualified* yet. You must wait.'

I wonder how long? Or will she decide to leave me?

Day 18
Monday

The day passed quickly; Jenifer had two simulator sessions. She added the flight and training to her logbook and added a summary, and then Craig signed, scanned, and emailed it to her. The two examinations took an hour and a half, then she filled in the FAA application online, paid, and they went for lunch.

Craig took them to Captain Brian's Seafood Market and Restaurant. By 16:00, they had collected their bags from the hotel and were on the road to Tampa International for their return flight.

'How do you feel now that you're qualified?'

'No different from a week ago, but happy for you.'

That's nice to know. 'Why for me?'

'I've done the renewal for you because you want me to fit into your piloting world, and you said you wanted to show the staff of International Air when we take the flight to Mauritius that you have a beautiful pilot girlfriend.'

'That was a week ago. You're beautiful, and all that matters is that I enjoy having you with me, but thanks, you said you'd do your best for me, and you have. Are you ready to come with me to Mauritius?'

'Almost, give me a few days more.'

Day 19
Tuesday

They arrived on time at Gatwick, and by 13:00, they were back in Dexter's office, where he called Greg, who promised to come to see them before 14:00.

Jenifer remarked, 'I'm not hungry yet. I'll make coffee.'

'Our body clocks are about two to three hours early, say between ten and eleven, so that's unsurprising. Do you want to talk about Maurtius?'

'Not today; I should have banished the jet lag by the weekend. I'll try and decide before then.'

'There's a departure every day at 15:00, arriving in Mauritius at 06:00. So, we need only choose the day. If I take you home tonight and return tomorrow morning, I'll have three days to catch up on my work. We could go on Saturday. Would you like to do the tourist bit and see what Mauritius is like?'

'When are the return flights?'

'08:00, arriving 17:00. A crew in Mauritius will do the return flight.'

'So, if we went Saturday, we arrive Sunday and can visit my mom's grave and have a few days as tourists. Can you have that much time off?'

'Easily, I have lots of accumulated leave.'

'Will you fetch me?'

'Of course, I'll come Friday after work.'

'See if there are seats available. I'll give you an answer before then.'

Greg came in. 'Hello, Dex, Jenifer, are you a law-abiding pilot now?'

Jenifer grinned, 'I am; some misguided instructors signed my log-books.'

'Then give them to me and your passport, then complete this form for the CAA. I'll go to the secretarial office and photocopy what the CAA want to see.'

Greg came back with the copies and returned the originals, and Jenifer asked, 'Shouldn't I go to the CAA?'

'Our planning officer sends dozens of applications to the CAA weekly for all the licence renewals, pilots, engineers, and cabin crew. She knows what to do, and the CAA knows she doesn't make mistakes. Let her do it. She also adds the next check date and medical examination date to her planning sheet and sends a warning to the crew member shortly before it's due. You should have a UK licence in a week.'

'Thanks, Greg, you're a *friend*.'

'Friends help, Jenifer.'

As Greg left, Jenifer asked. 'Can we have something to eat? And then, if you're ready, let's go.'

'As soon as I've booked a room here for Wednesday and Thursday.'

Two and half hours later, at 19:00, Dexter parked the car behind Jenifer's house, and when they unloaded the baggage, Jenifer checked, 'Do you have clean clothes for tomorrow?'

'Yes, I'll hand all my washing to the hotel when I arrive, but if you'd like to wash the dodo, you can; I might get a weird reputation if I hand them in at the hotel.'

'Sometimes you surprise me. No one would say anything. We'll put our things in our room, and then I must catch up on correspondence. Do you have something to do?'

'A pile of Notams to study, and the magazines that I subscribe to that arrived while we were away. I'll sit in one of the comfortable armchairs, bring you coffee, and read.'

'What magazines do you have?'

'Flying, Air traffic Management, Aeroplane, and the AOPA Pilot Turbine.'

'Is that a lot?'

'Pilots have lots of time in faraway places; we must do something to avoid boredom. Some of the guys are EAA members and build aeroplanes at home; you know we can't party every night. The pilots with kids don't get bored. That's why the younger pilots do the short flights.'

Dexter worked through his Notams. The Notices to Airmen gave information on navigation aids and airports. The ones he'd received covered all areas flown by International Air. He marked in red pen all the items that affected his airline's routes, looked at his watch and Jenifer working in front of her giant screen, and decided to transcribe his notes onto the official format he issued to all pilots. He took his portable to Dad's room to the small table and chairs and began working.

Half an hour later, he closed the portable and looked around the room. Everything was the same as the first time he'd seen it, but it seemed odd this time; he couldn't pinpoint why. He returned to the lounge and picked up a magazine. He didn't notice the time pass until Jenifer said, 'I've finished. I'll make some scrambled eggs on toast; then we can go to bed. You must leave early.'

Jenifer came from the bathroom in her regular pyjamas. When Dexter came out wearing the pyjamas with the ostrich, Jenifer exclaimed, 'They look great; what's the ostrich looking for?'

Dexter grinned, 'I'm not telling; you must find out for yourself.'

'Come here and let me find out what you feel like.'

'Cuddly, I like the feel. I'll sleep well.'

Dexter lay with Jenifer beside him, thinking, *She's brilliant and fun, but why do I feel I must leave her after we visit Mauritius? What is it? Are there things I don't know?*

'Bo, what will you do for the next three days?'

'As you're deserting me. I shall visit the metaverse to find an avatar and indulge in transcendental intercourse.'

'If you're trying to make me feel guilty, that won't work. I haven't a clue what that is.'

'Neither do I; I've heard the term but never dared to find out. I'll look at incoming metaverse messages; there may be one from someone who can help me with the SF E390 or the CamAir Two-Thirty, the first ones entered airline service two months ago.'

Day 20
Wednesday

After Dexter left, Jenifer returned to bed for an hour. After dressing, she did the usual household chores and had breakfast. The clothes washing included Dexter's pyjamas. Then she sat in front of her giant screen, placed her metaverse VR headset on her head and entered the metaverse space. She hoped someone had replied to her posts.

Need data to build an E390 simulator.

And another.

Need data to build a CamAir 230 simulator.

There were five space codes for the CamAir Two-Thirty. Jenifer recognised them; they had all helped with the CamAir Three-Ten. There was one for the E390. She did what she'd described to Dexter, using the one for the E390, and two minutes later, entered a metaverse space that was a green valley between snowcapped mountains. Sitting on a rock looking down the valley was the figure of a man in a closefitting one-piece silver costume with his back to her. She could see long blond hair down to his shoulders. The sun was low over the mountains, so it was either early morning or late afternoon. She spoke.

'Good day, the view is lovely.'

He turned leisurely and looked at her. 'Sunrises usually are; I love the rose tints on the mountain tops. I am Silver; I didn't expect a medieval woman seeking technical data.'

'Did you expect someone from Star Wars? Or should I have asked for a Trebuchet?'

'That might be more fitting. What is it you want?'

'I could say anything, but that is ridiculous. If I post a drawing of the E390 showing the data I need, will that answer your question?'

'Possibly. I may not be able to help, but I can try. Why do you want it?'

'I'm tired of flying my aeroplane simulator's toy aeroplanes and want to modify it to fly a modern airliner.'

'Then you have a major task that will take years.'

'It's a hobby, so time doesn't matter.'

'Then send me the drawing. I might help with the undercarriage.'

'Thank you. I'll go now.'

Jenifer returned from the metaverse. For several hours, she searched for line drawings of aircraft undercarriages; the archives of the aeroplane modelling magazines had hundreds of plans.

When she found ones like the photographs of the E390 in other magazines, she used them, adding the information she needed. She did the nosewheel first, asking for the arc it followed when raised, the centre of mass, the retraction time, the axis's position in the nose, and other factors.

Then, she filed it in a dark web depository and repeated the exercise for the main wheels. Finally, she reconnected to the metaverse and posted the URLs of the files to Silver's space.

When she'd made and eaten lunch, she decided the CamAir Two-Thirty contacts could wait until tomorrow. She sent a message to Susan, 'Please call,' then switched to searching the web for anything about communications with horses.

A half-hour later, Susan called. 'Hello, Bo. Have you validated your licences?'

'Yes, and before you ask, being with Dexter was a lot of fun.

We're sleeping in the same bed, but I've stopped him from anything more than hugs, cuddles, and kisses on my temple. He wants to take me to Mauritius on Saturday to put flowers on my mother's grave, but that feels like going away for a romantic, sex-filled holiday.'

'So, you haven't agreed to go?'

'I haven't. I *want* to, but I'm scared of the consequences. Dexter was in Brazil ten days ago and returned with a Tanga for me. I don't think I could wear it.'

'I told you Dexter will never harm you. I'll go further; he will never make love to you until you tell him to or you start it. So, there's nothing whatsoever to be afraid of except yourself. Go and enjoy yourself – and wear the Tanga; if he bought it, he's sure you'll look beautiful wearing it.'

For Dexter, it was like a return to his standard routine, although he'd left Coventry instead of Dartmoor. Once he arrived at the hotel, he checked in, changed into his uniform, handed over his washing, locked his car in the hotel parking and took the hotel courtesy bus to the terminal.

After two meetings, a quick lunch, and dealing with a pile of paper, he sat back and thought of the previous night when he'd asked himself, *are there things I don't know?*

When his phone rang, and he saw the caller was Jenifer, he forgot the question.

'Hello. This time, I wasn't expecting your call.'

'If the Tanga worked, you should have bought some lacy underwear.'

'I'll remember that. Why did you call? Will you come to Mauritius?'

'Yes. Tampa was fun, and I'm sure you won't feed me to a shark.'

'I don't know if there are any, but there are dolphins you can swim with. I'll come on Friday evening after work, and we'll drive here to catch the flight on Saturday. Can you book a hotel?'

'How long for, Dex?'

'At least three days; make it a week if you wish.'

'I'll think about it, Dex. Bye.'

Day 21
Thursday

Jenifer had five space codes for the CamAir Two-Thirty. She spent the entire day working through each of them. Knowing what the person had supplied for the CamAir Three-Ten made her task more manageable. She prepared the drawings, filed them in the dark web depository, and then armed with the URLs connected to the meta-verse five times. She had lunch after the first one, and due to time differences, only two of the spaces had an avatar present, and the conversation was friendly. She posted the drawings to the other three as well. Then, at 17:00, she called Dexter.

When he answered, she queried, 'Hello, Dex, how are you?'

'Feeling much less lonely now that I can hear your voice. Have you missed me?'

'Terribly, Dex. You left your dodo pyjamas here, so I washed them; that was a mistake.'

Dexter grinned; *another story!* 'Why a mistake? Have they shrunk?'

'No, but there's no smell left.'

Puzzled, Dexter asked, 'Isn't that supposed to happen if you wash your pyjamas?'

'Yes, I suppose so, but I've never smelled a man's pyjamas after washing, so it was a shock.'

'Why did you smell them?' *I'm sure this will be interesting.*

'Not put my face in them to *smell* them, but after I stuffed them full of pillows so they looked like you and put them in our bed, it took me half an hour to realise why you weren't there.'

Dexter couldn't hide his laughter, 'You're marvellous. I'll come and fill them tomorrow night.'

'I'm waiting; now tell me, you said ponies can share their inner-verse, and you said you had once done the same and shared with them. Have you ever shared with a person, and do you know of others who can share with ponies?'

'Why do you ask?'

'I've been researching it, Dex; it seems there may be other people who can share with horses; amongst the horse-riding fraternity, some are referred to as horsey people.'

'Bo, there could be all sorts of reasons for calling them horsey people, and I have only known one person, a woman, although she was a young girl then, who could feel the ponies. But she's not unique; there have been many over the centuries. It's difficult for them because people can't understand it, so they don't talk about their "gift"; they have a high empathic sense. Susan might be able to. Moorland people say they're "Fey".'

'What does that mean?'

'It's an ancient term used for highly empathic individuals who might, when young, believe what they sense are messages from fairies.'

'How old was she?'

'About seventeen when I left for university. The last I heard,

Morwen still lives near the moor; she married a farmer.'

'If you could both feel the ponies, why didn't you marry her?'

'Because I went to university, then fell in love with flying, and I never returned to live there.'

'I hope I can feel them too. When will you get here?'

'I'll leave at 15:00, so about 18:00.'

'I'll be waiting.'

She wants to feel the ponies and thinks that two people who can do so should have married. I hope she can sense and share with them. It won't surprise me if she can.

Dexter worked late. Undisturbed by training meetings and phone calls, he could give full attention to the CamAir Two-Thirty manual. He had the CamAir Three-Ten manual open beside it and worked slowly through marking passages where the instructions differed, building in his mind a picture of what flying the Two-Thirty would be like. Dexter liked it. He thought it would be like a Ferrari, lighter and more sensitive than the Three-Ten that, for him, felt like his DB11.

At 20:00, a pang of hunger made him glance at his watch. He packed up and returned to his hotel.

DAY 22
FRIDAY

'Hello, Bo, you're calling early, what's up?'

'Sorry, Sue, I should have thought. Are you still in bed?'

'No, we have animals to look after, and Kissy gets upset if I don't let her out into the garden in time. Why did you call?'

'To tell you, I'm visiting Mauritius with Dexter tomorrow.'

'That's great. Do you have everything you need?'

'I'm sure I have.'

'How many evening dresses do you have?'

'One. Isn't that enough?'

'No. One for each evening unless you stay more than five days, then it's six. A man can't remember what you wore six days ago.'

'I'll buy some in Mauritius.'

'Then buy two today. Do you need me to help?'

'No, I'm sure if I wear my uniform, I can go to the dress shop in Stoneleigh.'

'Then call at the pharmacy, Bo, and buy a packet of condoms.'

'*Sue!* That's not why I'm going.'

'I'm not just a vet but a doctor. Sometimes, in a woman's life, we do something stupid and then wish we had been more sensible. Visiting a tropical island with a man can become one of them. It always happens when it's unintended. Buy condoms, and it won't happen.'

'Shouldn't Dexter have them?'

'I would guess he hasn't needed them. Any woman he has slept with since his divorce will have used birth control or passed menopause. Either buy some or call and tell him to.'

'I don't know if I can.'

'If you can't, tell me, and I'll bring you a packet.'

⋯⋙◦⋘⋯

After breakfast, dressed as a captain, Jennifer went to the shop. She'd visited the shop at least once a year for fifteen years, and the woman who owned and ran it knew her well. It was she who had supplied Jenifer's shirts and blouses with epaulettes. Forty minutes later, she'd chosen and tried on two evening dresses, and Mrs Thomas said, 'If you have other shopping to do, do it. It will take me forty minutes to make the adjustments.'

Jenifer could see the pharmacy on the other side of the street but went next door to the grocery store which delivered her food, to buy something for dinner as Dexter was coming. He was pleased to see her, and as it was still early, business was slow, so he spent ten minutes talking to her. With her groceries in a bag, Jenifer walked out. The pharmacy was still there. She went to the bakery, the next shop, and bought a loaf of bread.

When she came out, she stopped. *I'm being stupid; I can't call Dexter and tell him to buy condoms, and Sue will think I'm a coward if I don't buy some.*

She took a deep breath, checked for traffic, crossed the road at a fast walk, and, without a pause, pushed open the pharmacy door. There were no clients, and the sole young woman behind the counter looked up.

'Good morning, Captain.'

The greeting replaced the tendrils of fear that had begun growing with curiosity. 'Good morning. Do you recognise my pilot's bars?'

'I had a boyfriend once who was a pilot; he only had two but told me about them. I sometimes wish I had tried to work at an airline.'

'How'd you meet him?'

'He came into the shop one day to buy condoms and asked me for a date.'

'Isn't that like advertising why he asked you out?'

'I don't think so. I like men who take precautions. I always have a packet in case. He said the pilots and cabin attendants all carry them. Don't you?'

Jenifer said a quick prayer of thanks to the god of condoms and said, 'That's why I'm here; I've run out.'

'Which ones do you prefer?'

'Whatever you recommend that's safest for women.'

'Three, six or twelve?'

I won't do this again. 'Twelve.'

The shop assistant gave her a knowing smile and a brown paper packet. 'There you are, miss, enjoy flying. Both kinds.'

Back home with her dresses, groceries, bread and condoms, Jennifer thought.

Shopping's not as bad as I thought, especially early in the morning. I should do it again.

At lunchtime, Susan called. 'Hi Bo, I'm just checking. Must I come and bring you some condoms?'

Jenifer felt proud when she replied, 'No, I bought a dozen.'

'Wow, that's great. I must get the quiche from the oven. Have a good trip.'

At least Sue didn't say to enjoy both kinds of flying. I had better put them in my suitcase before I forget. I'll put them in the internal zip pocket where they aren't visible.

⸺⟡⸺

Dexter began his morning at 05:30 with a session in the hotel gym; he'd done so every morning he woke alone for years. Then he ate breakfast, packed and left his case with the concierge, checked out and took the bus to the office.

After his first meeting, he sat for several minutes with a coffee, thinking of Bo. The image of Bo at Zeno's popped up, and after a pause, he called Doris.

'Hello, Dex; you only call when you need help. What's it this time?'

'Hi, Doris; when Jenifer bought that yellow dress, she also bought a necklace.'

'She didn't; that was costume jewellery, paste or crystals. I gave it to her.'

'It was beautiful, Doris. I'll pay for it. I want advice on how to buy her one or two others.'

'Unless you know the colour of the dresses she'll wear, you must buy three: a diamond imitation that goes with anything, a red ruby, and a green emerald. She has a blue.'

'Please, Doris, can you get those three, and I'll collect them after 15:00?'

'I can, but there's no guarantee Jenifer will like what I choose. They will be returnable. I'll see what I can get. If you want genuine gemstones, bring Jenifer to see me, and I'll tell you where to go and how to avoid fakes.'

'Thanks, bye.'

Dexter finished his day with two meetings, the lunch he'd promised Greg and a final check of the sim training schedule. Then he returned to the hotel, put his case in his car, and after a visit to Doris, where he parked in a loading zone and Ronald brought him a packet, Dexter left for Coventry.

⁂

As Dexter drove around to the back of Jenifer's house, she greeted him as he stepped from the car, 'On time, as usual.'

'Do I get a hug like last time?'

Jennifer came to him, put her arms around him, her head on his chest, and squeezed.

'Like this?'

'Yes, like this.' Dexter bent his head down to kiss her on the temple.

A minute later, Jenifer released him and said, 'Come, dinner will soon be ready, then we must pack for tomorrow. Would you like a bath first?'

'Yes, let me get my case.'

'I put your Dodo pyjamas on the bed. Remember you promised to fill them. You can come down wearing them.'

'There's an enormous difference between a pillow-stuffed Dexter and a real one. You're less squishy.'

'But which feels better?'

'The real one, you're lumpy in places, so you have texture. The pillow-stuffed Dexter is like an avatar, missing something.'

DAY 23
SATURDAY

'Are you ready? We should check in before 14:00. We'll have lunch in the lounge.'

'Yes, all prepared.'

'Then put your hat on. We'll leave our car in the staff car park.'

'Good afternoon, Captain Rawlins, Captain Boscawen; I'll check in your cases.'

Dexter read her lapel badge, 'Thank you, Theresa.'

As they made their way through to passport control, Jenifer asked. 'Who's flying the plane?'

'I checked the roster; it should be Bobby Straker as captain, Cyril Collins as the first officer, and the second officer David Jones. I couldn't volunteer as we're staying. They'll return the day after.'

'Will David Jones be in the cabin with us?'

'I doubt it. There is a crew cabin with a bunk bed, but David may use one of the folding crew seats for takeoff and landing if first class is full. There are eight first-class passenger seats.'

The first-class lounge attendant welcomed them. Once they found a table, Dexter said, 'Mauritius is three hours ahead; the cabin staff will serve dinner early, so we should leave space for it.'

'Then I'll snack.'

'Fine, I never drink when flying; alcohol and altitude don't suit me.'

'I'll stay with sparkling water.'

•••

The first-class cabin attendant was almost effusive in her welcome; Jenifer thought she was being careful not to make a mistake that Dexter might report. Shown to their seats, they arranged their bags, and two minutes later, Jenifer felt sure the attendant had told the captain they were on board for the captain to come and greet them.

'Hello, Dex, this is a new experience.'

'Hello, Bobby, why?'

'Flying with the training captain in the back instead of behind me with a check pad.'

Dexter laughed, 'Then enjoy it; I'm off duty. What route are we flying?'

'Skirting Libya, South Sudan, via Addis, then Nairobi to avoid Somalia.'

'Bobby, meet Jenifer Boscawen; Greg checked her out in a sim only a week ago. We're going for a weekend on the island.'

'Lucky you, I must go.'

Dinner was superb, and then they settled down to sleep.

Day 24
Sunday

Dexter woke, and the first thing he did was automatic. He checked the time. It was 23:32 Zulu. Before he realised why he'd woken, Jenifer also woke, 'The starboard engine is out.'

'It flies on one, no worries, Bobby or David will tell us why.'

Time seemed to drag; it seemed much longer than the five minutes it took for David Jones to appear and whisper, 'Captain Rawlins, can you come to the cockpit?'

Dexter unstrapped, and so did Jenifer, and they followed David, who asked them to close the door to first class while he stepped into the crew rest cabin and ushered them past him to the cockpit. Bobby and Pete were in the left and right seats, and Dexter asked, 'Bobby, what's the problem?'

'The right engine quit; fuel pressure is zero. The met report on winds is incorrect; the jet stream is not where it was supposed to be. With one engine, our ground speed is way down, so we'll burn fumes before we reach Mauritius.'

'And at other altitudes?'

'No better or worse.'

'Diversions?'

'We can reach Dar es Salaam or Antananarivo with normal reserve fuel.'

'Then divert.'

'I've never been to either. Do you know which is best?'

'No.' Then he remembered Jenifer's logbook, 'Bo, have you landed at either?'

'Both. Dar is at sea level; Tana is at four thousand feet. Try Dar first. The landing speed is higher with only one engine and will be even more at Tana.'

'Bobby, call Dar es Salaam.'

After punching buttons to change frequency, Bobby spoke. 'Dar es Salaam, Interex two-four-six heavy, do you read?'

'Interex two-four-six heavy, go ahead.'

'Dar, Interex two-four-six, CamAir Three-Ten, London to Mauritius, Flight level three seven zero. We have an engine failure. What are your conditions? We wish to divert.'

'Interex two-four-six, we have high and gusty winds in tropical rain; we've closed the runways due to water. Tana and Nairobi are open. Kilimanjaro has thunderstorms.'

'Interex two-four-six, thank you. I'll call Ivato airport at Tana.'

'Ivato, Interex two-four-six heavy, do you read?'

The radio crackled for a tense half minute, so Bobby called again. 'Ivato, Interex two-four-six heavy, do you read?'

The tension diminished when the reply came. 'Interex two-four-six heavy, go ahead.'

'Ivato, Interex two-four-six, CamAir Three-Ten, London to Mauritius, Flight level three seven zero. We have an engine failure. What are your conditions? We wish to divert.'

'Interex two-four-six, conditions are clear, Victor Mike Charlie, wind two-six-five fifteen knots – temperature twenty-one degrees. Runway two-niner in use. The ILS on two-niner is down for maintenance. You are welcome in an emergency.'

'Interex two-four-six, thank you. I will call back.'

'Dex, that's it, Kilimanjaro in thunderstorms, or Tana without ILS, we have a major problem.'

Jenifer spoke, 'Tana two-niner is slightly uphill and only a fraction shorter than Kili; it's also closer. The wind is good. I've landed there a dozen times without ILS.'

Dexter added, 'Bobby, I agree; arriving at Kili in a thunderstorm with no fuel is too risky. Go for Tana.'

'Dex, you're my senior, and it's your decision. Will you please take over?'

Dexter was suddenly formal. 'Do you formally wish to hand over to me, Captain Straker?'

'I do, Captain Rawlins.'

'Then, David, please record that at…' Dexter looked at his watch, '23:55 Zulu, I, chief training captain Dexter Rawlins, accepted to captain International-Air flight Interex two-four-six.'

'Bobby, will you and Cyril take our seats in First class? Bo, take the left-hand seat and call Ivato. David, please record that I have requested Captain Boscawen to take the left-hand seat due to her experience of Antananarivo, but I remain the captain and training instructor.'

Jenifer punched buttons to display a new GPS route on the screen before her.

'Ivato, Interex two-four-six heavy.'

'Go ahead; nice to hear a lady. We have no traffic.'

✈

'Interex two-four-six, request permission to divert to your airport, understood no ILS. We will commence the approach two zero miles before the initial approach fix. Our descent will commence from three seven zero to two seven zero in one-zero minutes.'

'Copied Interex two-four-six. Landing approved for technical and safety reasons. When ready, provide estimates for the Initial Approach Fix and arrival.'

'Standby.'

'Dex, start pumping fuel; I want the left-wing tanks as full as possible, the right-wing empty.'

Surprised, Dexter asked. 'Why? That's not standard procedure.'

'It makes the aircraft much easier to fly manually on one engine; I do it every time.'

'I'll fill the wing; you're the pilot.'

Jenifer punched an autopilot button, and the aircraft turned slightly onto the new course. When it stabilised, Jenifer called again. 'Ivato, Interex two-four-six heavy with estimates.'

'Interex two-four-six, go ahead.'

'Initial Approach Fix at 00:45 and landing at 00:56. Altitude at inbound turn fifteen thousand feet, Initial Approach Fix at twelve thousand. Approach speed two-zero five knots to one-nine-two knots at touchdown.'

'Copied Interex two-four-six. QNH at the two-niner threshold is one-zero-two-zero. Wind steady two six five at fifteen. Patches of cloud with a base of twelve thousand. Do you wish emergency vehicles and crews at the far end of the runway?'

'Negative Ivato. We are not declaring an emergency. Landing will be normal. Copied one-zero-two-zero, two six five and fifteen. Interex two-four-six.'

Dexter thought. *Shit, that's a high landing speed, but the runway is at four thousand feet. How can she say the landing will be normal?*

'Dex, check the course and numbers; I'll take manual control as we pass the Initial Approach Fix.'

'Wilco, the left tank is full. I'll tell the passengers.'

'Good morning, ladies and gentlemen; this is Captain Rawlins. I'm sorry for waking you up. For technical reasons, we must divert to Antananarivo in Madagascar. We have commenced our descent. Please strap yourselves in. We'll land at 02:56 UK time. International Air will try to take you all to Mauritius as soon as possible. Further announcements will follow when we know more. Thank you.'

Dexter turned to David, still standing in the cockpit doorway.

'David, call and tell London.'

Dexter watched the remaining engine's vital signs, and Jenifer watched as the autopilot throttled back to slow the aircraft and begin the descent. A yellow light appeared in front of Dexter. 'Captain, I have a fuel temperature alarm.'

Jenifer's memory connected bits of data from her past. 'Watch it, Dex; it should go out when we descend below three-zero-zero.'

'How do you know?'

'I don't, but if it goes out, the engine has not had an AD update done.'

Dexter watched, tense, until he held his breath with only a thousand more feet to go. At two-nine-zero, the light went out.

And he breathed again.

•••

In London, within thirty minutes of David's call, the first bleary-eyed staff filtered into the crisis room. The most senior gave orders. 'In half an hour, we'll have three hundred pax and crew to collect from Antananarivo and take to Mauritius, and early this morning, another three hundred who won't have an aeroplane for their return flight to London. Find some aircraft for the first lot and seats for the pax in Mauritius.'

'Captain, the turn onto the runway heading is too sharp; the manual says not to exceed a rate-one turn with one engine out.'

'That's one reason for shifting the fuel; the plane can now manage forty-five degrees, or rate three, left or right.'

•••

'Ivato, Interex two-four-six heavy established inbound track two-niner-zero fifteen thousand feet on QNH one-zero-two-zero.'

'Copied two-four-six.'

In London, a crisis room staff employee called, 'Sir, I have Ocean-Air in Mauritius on the line; they can send a 737 to collect 150 pax.'

'Ask them how soon.'

Then another staff member called, 'I have Island-Air in Reunion; they can send an A320-200.'

'Same question, how soon?'

Dexter could feel the tension growing in the cockpit as Jenifer called on the radio, 'Ivato, Interex two-four-six heavy Initial Approach Fix inbound.'

David, in the jump seat, tightened his straps.

'Clear to land, two-four-six. The wind is still two-six-five at fif-teen.'

'Flaps down fifteen.'

'Why are you holding off, Bo?'

'There's an updraft here; it caught me once or twice, just half a minute more.'

Dexter felt the aircraft rise, then settle, and Jenifer disconnected the autopilot and ordered, 'Undercarriage down.' As the aircraft descended, the lit-up runway appeared when they dropped below the cloud layer.

Dexter checked the undercarriage lights and reported, 'Three greens.'

'Flaps down thirty, please. Landing lights. When I call for full flaps, don't hesitate.'

Dexter tensed. *We're flying too fast; we'll be lucky to stop before the end of the runway. She can't use max reverse thrust with one engine.*

As Jenifer reduced the throttle, the aircraft settled further, and the plane swept over the airport fence.

Then everything happened at once.

Jenifer called *full flaps!* Cut the throttle, and the left wing dropped until the left wheel touched the runway. Dexter heard the bellow of reverse thrust increasing – *too soon; all the wheels are not down.* Then, he felt the rudder pedals moving as Jenifer angled the rudder to keep the nose straight as the left engine in reverse tried to pull the nose left. The other wheels touched, and the howl of the reverse thrust reached a maximum with the rudder at its limit, and then the roar began to drop as the aircraft slowed, finally ceasing, and Jenifer centred the rudder pedals and applied the brakes.

Dexter, who had held his breath, breathed again and had only one thought. *How the hell did she do that?*

'Interex two-four-six, that was a great landing; please take the next turnoff to the left. When you reach the parking apron, turn left and go to the end; a marshal is waiting for you.'

'Ivato, thank you, but please check the load rating of the apron extension; our aircraft carries a full load.'

Jenifer swung the aircraft onto the apron and turned left as instructed; then, they saw a van with flashing lights start moving. 'Interex two-four-six, thank you for the warning. The marshal is moving to bay five; please follow his signals.'

'Two-four-six copied.'

'Dex, that was fun. Please start the auxiliary and do the shutdown procedure.'

'Bo, that landing was incredible, but you have more explaining to do.'

'Later, Dex, my adrenaline's dropping, but you should tell London to check the maintenance directives for the fuel system on both these engines.'

David had taken the initiative and called London to say they were safely down, and Dexter, as captain, had ruffled feathers to smooth down.

'Ladies and Gentlemen, this is Captain Rawlins. Although we had an in-flight engine failure, this aeroplane can fly with one engine. However, International Air policies require a landing at the nearest suitable airport for your safety, which is our first concern. Welcome to Madagascar. Please remain seated; the cabin crews will serve drinks and breakfast while we await news from London regarding your onward travel arrangements. We'll negotiate with the Malagasy authorities for permission for you to deplane pending final instructions. Thank you.'

Then Dexter's cell phone rang. He looked at the number.

'Bo, this is where things become painful, with everyone blaming everyone else.'

'Good morning, Director.'

'Good morning, Captain. What the devil is going on? Why are you in charge and not Captain Straker?'

'Very simple, Director. We lost an engine, and Captain Straker asked me for advice. If you want to know why we lost an engine, I suggest you ask maintenance if they have executed all fuel system directives.'

'Copied, I'll do that. But why are you in charge?'

'The met forecast was incorrect, the headwinds higher than forecast, and on one engine, Mauritius was dicey. Captain Straker asked for advice, and I told him to divert. He called Dar Es Salaam, the nearest, and they said the airport had closed because of torrential rain. Kilimanjaro was as bad, and Nairobi was too far and too high. Antananarivo was open and welcomed us but said there was no ILS. Because none of the pilots had landed there, and I'm the senior captain, Captain Straker passed the command to me.'

'Have you landed there?'

'No, but Captain Boscawen, accompanying me, has done forty landings at Ivato. I asked her to fly under my orders.'

'That's the woman who boarded with you. Is she qualified?'

'Fully, Director. She's current, recently checked on the Three-Ten, and has over two thousand hours. I'm damned glad she was with me; she landed perfectly. I couldn't have done as well.'

'Okay, Captain, thanks for an excellent job, and thank Captain Boscawen for me. A jet is departing shortly with a maintenance crew on board. They will download the flight data for analysis.'

'Director, tell them to bring two fuel pumps. It might save downtime. They can always take them back.'

'Thanks, Dex. Can you stay until we know the problem? I may need you to fly it back.'

'Yes, I will do, but Captain Boscawen is not an employee of International Air, so I can only ask her to stay.'

'Tell her that if she stays, we'll reimburse her at a temporary captain's rate for the days it takes, including today.'

'Thank you, Director, that should make it easier.'

'I'll pass you to Passenger Ops.'...

'Good morning, Captain.' *Everyone is being formal this morning.*

'Good morning, Director.'

'Two aircraft will be leaving Mauritius and Reunion in the next hour; they will take all the pax to Mauritius. The Air France resident in Antananarivo will take care of the pax. He should be on his way to the airport. Captain Straker and all the crew will go with them; we're trying to arrange their return. I understand you'll stay there until the technical staff tell us what they will do.'

'That's correct.'

'Then visit the Lemurs, Dex; I hear they're friendly beasts. Bye.'

...

'Bo, I must tell the passengers.'

'Ladies and Gentlemen, this is your captain again. Air France will take care of you once they arrange for you to leave the aircraft; they will also collect your baggage. Please leave nothing behind. Two aircraft should arrive in less than three hours to take you to Mauritius. Air France will tell you which aircraft to embark on. On behalf of International Air, I apologise for the delay in your arrival in Mauritius; please wait a little longer for the Air France rep to come on board.'

Jennifer could hear applause in the cabin, 'The passengers are clapping.'

'Fortunately, those who complain must do so to the Air France guy. David, tell Captain Straker you and the crew must all go to Mauritius with the pax. Ops will call you with your return info. Ops also has three hundred pax with flights to reschedule: those taking this plane to London. You might be returning on any route where they can get seats.'

After the passengers and crew had left for the terminal, Dexter said, 'I think we can find some lunch. There's nothing to do until tomorrow morning; the mechanics will arrive after dark.'

'Are we staying?'

'I am, and as you're now temporarily employed by International Air as a captain, I hope you will too.'

Jenifer grinned, 'You promised, so I'm not letting you out of my sight until you've taken me to Mauritius.'

Dexter smiled; Jenifer thought it was mischievous, 'No, but I'm making sure. As you're now a pilot working for International Air, and I'm your senior, I can order you to stay!'

And that makes me feel delighted.

The Air France rep, Guillaume de Beauvoir, gave them a hotel address; they passed through customs and immigration without any questions as they were in uniform, changed some money, and took a taxi. The hotel gave them a room beside the pool, and they went to the restaurant for lunch.

Once they had ordered, Dexter said, 'There are three things I must know before facing an enquiry.'

'Why will there be one?'

'There always is; there must be one. When analysis of the black box and voice recorder data is complete, and we're back in London, there will be a formal enquiry meeting, and the CAA and CamAirCom representatives will be there.'

'Must I come?'

'Yes, but I'm the captain, so everything rests on my shoulders.'

'What do you want to know?'

'First of all, where did you get the idea of the maintenance directive?'

'It's in the CamAir Three-Ten maintenance instructions. At high altitudes where the air is thin, the air cooling the fuel pipes is too little for extended high-powered operations, the fuel becomes hot, and the warning light comes on. Bobby was running at a higher power setting because of the headwind. The first directive was for pilots to descend below thirty thousand feet to increase cooling air density. The second was a modification of the cooling air scoops on the cowling.'

'So, when that light came on, you thought of it?'

'Yes, and I thought that if one engine didn't have the modification, the other might be the same.'

'Could that be the cause of the engine failure? It might have been if the warning light didn't work or the crew didn't see it, and the fuel pump ran hot for a long time.'

'I don't think they would miss it. It's more likely it failed, but if it came on in the middle of a crew change, and the replacement crew member saw it when he looked at the panel and assumed it had been on for ages, he might ignore it.'

'That's possible; now tell me about the fuel transfer.'

'I'm still trying to work out the numbers. All you did was move the centre of mass to somewhere closer to the left-wing root. My first simulator couldn't transfer fuel, and when I added a transfer facility, I forgot on one test flight, used the fuel in one wing, and found the aircraft turned easier one way and not the other. So, I experimented with the centre of mass and found that with an engine out, transferring the fuel made the plane much easier to fly.'

'Is that why you could use such a high reverse thrust?'

'Yes, that engine is pulling back a mass much closer to it, so it doesn't have the same couple or leverage. Did you notice I did everything in reverse? I put full right rudder and kept the nose straight by adjusting the reverse thrust to balance the turning forces instead of the opposite.'

'Yes, you kept the balance brilliantly and stopped in the average landing distance.

'How did you know the extended part of the parking apron won't support the Three-Ten?'

'Most simulators don't bother with that data; I didn't and landed in Tana three or four times before I received the detailed data. I had added a check on apron strength to the sim, and when I loaded the data, I didn't look at it. The sim screamed at me when I taxied to that parking, and the nosewheel failed. I found myself staring at a yellow line at six metres. It's not something I could forget.'

Dexter laughed. 'You have no idea how incredible you are. I won't volunteer anything you've told me, but we may need to answer questions depending on what they pick up from the recorders. Let's go for a swim.'

They swam then sat beside the pool in their costumes, Dexter sipping a local Three Horses Beer, the waiter called it a THB, and Bo with a cocktail of coconut milk, soda water and mint. The Air France rep arrived.

'*Capitaine* Rawlins, *Capitaine* Boscawen, I have come to bring you news.'

'Will you have a drink, Monsieur de Beauvoir.'

'I will *pleasurefully* join you with a THB; it is too hot for wine.'

'All your passengers and crew have departed. The incoming jet with the maintenance people is due to arrive at 21:00 tonight; I have booked rooms at this *Relais* for the five engineers and the two crew. They stop in Addis Ababa for fuel. I'll meet them and give them Air France airport passes to facilitate their movements. You'll meet them tomorrow at the breakfast I 'ave arranged for seven thirty. An Air France bus will take you tomorrow at eight-thirty.

'Please inform me when you know about your aircraft's repair and departure.'

Dexter replied. 'Of course, and if we require a new engine, we may be here several days. In which case, can you recommend a pleasant activity? It's the first time we have visited Madagascar.'

'If you have a free day, you can visit Lemur Park, which is open from nine to five. If you have at least three to five days, I can recommend one of two alternatives: Fly to Saint Marie Island and relax on the beach or watch the whales. The other is a trip to see the Baobabs and the Tsingys near Morondava. I would suggest charter flights for both, as Air Madagascar is unreliable. The hotel can make the arrangements for you.

'I must recommend that as strangers to Madagascar, you don't leave this *Relais* without a guide except a taxi to the airport.'

'Is it dangerous?'

'It can be, but there are no street signs. It is like, how you say, a rabbit house. Getting lost is *inevitahble*. Even the GPS is confused.'

Guillaume left, and Jenifer said, 'Dex, we started this day at two this morning. Tomorrow will be another long day. Can we have a light salad and go to bed?'

'Good idea, Bo. Let's go and shower....'

'Dex, put your arm around me again; I slept well the last time.'

DAY 25
MONDAY

————

Dexter and Jenifer were the first to arrive for breakfast at a table prepared for ten people. They ordered coffee, and only minutes later, the first of the others was a data analysis engineer.

'Hello Rhys, I didn't expect to see you.'

'The luck of the draw. I was on my way to work early when the call came; I hope to return with the aircraft tonight if we can identify what went wrong.'

'Jenifer, this is Rhys Jones, David's dad. He's the head of the flight recording and analysis department. Rhys, Jenifer Boscawen.'

Rhys smiled at her, 'Captain Boscawen, I see. Are you trying to improve Dex's flying?'

Jenifer laughed, 'I can try, but I don't think I can teach him much.'

'I wouldn't dare try.' The other four men arrived together, and Rhys did the introductions.

'Dex, I guess you know these guys. Jenifer, let me introduce you to today's team. Guys, this is Captain Jenifer Boscawen, Dex's side-kick.

'Jock Cameron, our red-headed Scot, specialises in fuel systems. Our electrical systems expert, Trevor Henderson, will tell you he's the best because he's small enough to squeeze into confined spaces. Carl Schultz, with the crew-cut and cowboy belt, our American hydraulics expert, we had to persuade one of our cabin staff to marry him so we could steal him from Northrop, and Simon Carver, who's nicknamed *the butcher* because of the way he carves up aluminium.'

Jenifer shook hands with all of them, and so did Dexter, who said, 'Let's order breakfast; I expect your flight crew are sleeping.'

Rhys asked when the waiter left with their orders. 'Dex, why did we bring two fuel pumps, and what's the query about the ADs?'

'Guesses, Rhys, I know you hate people guessing.'

'I do, but behind every guess, there's something. What did you see.'

'Starboard engine flamed out with zero fuel pressure on the gauge.'

'And?'

'The port engine's fuel temperature alarm lit up when we were at three seven zero on one engine.'

'What did you do?'

'Jenifer throttled back, began a descent, and told me the light would go out below thirty thousand. It did, then she said after we landed that she suspected it was because maintenance had not done an AD.'

Rhys looked at Jenifer and asked, 'You were flying?'

'Yes.'

'How do you know about the AD?'

Jenifer replied, 'I read every AD announced for the CamAir Three-Ten.'

'Unusual, but I approve.'

The breakfast dishes arrived, with jugs of coffee, and they tucked in.

Rhys was thinking, and as he finished his second croissant, asked, 'Dex, anything else?'

'No, but Jenifer put two and two together without proof.'

'Then tell me.'

'Could the fuel temperature warning light have failed, and the engine ran with hot fuel until the pump failed? She suggested it might have come on during a crew change, and the new crew might have ignored it, thinking the departing pilot had accepted it.

'But, Rhys, the warning lights may have nothing to do with the engine failure.'

'I know, that might be a red herring. Captain Boscawen, do you know the AD number or what it was about?'

'A cowling change to increase the cooling air to the pump.'

'Simon, that's your department, Trevor; the warning light is yours, on both sides, please. Jock and Carl, check out the pump. Dex, can you help me download the data from the recorders?'

'Jenifer will be more help than me, Rhys. She's a computer expert. There is one thing you'll notice. The starboard wing tanks are empty because I transferred the fuel to the port wing, so ignore that; they were equal when the engine failed.'

'Thanks; the bus driver said he'll arrive at eight-thirty. I'll meet you all in the lobby.'

Jock announced, 'Rhys, I'll fetch our aircraft key from the captain; our tools are in it.'

'Thanks, Jock.'

'Bo, we'll go and brush our teeth. Don't leave any electronics or papers in the room. You need your passport, but the hotel will put anything you value in their safe.'

'I'll take my valuables. If Rhys allows me to have a data copy, I'll load it into my portable.'

A short bus ride later, with the compliments of Air France, Guillaume de Beauvoir met them and shepherded them out to the aircraft, but as soon as they saw the stairs had gone, he rushed off to find them. The small executive jet that had brought the others had parked on the Apron extension by the port wing of the CamAir Three-Ten. Jock, Trevor, and Carl went to it to collect toolboxes. Simon walked over to look at the CamAir's engines, took photographs of both, returned to where the others were waiting and said, 'If I remember correctly, the cooling air duct to the pump is now different. These cowlings may still be the old setup.'

The stairs and Guillaume arrived, and Simon went with him to the terminal, hoping to find a WiFi signal.

Two hours later, Rhys called a meeting in the first-class cabin.

'Okay, guys, what do we know? Simon, you're first.'

'The AD is not mandatory; maintenance has scheduled it for action at the next service inspection. The plane can fly if the crew knows about reducing power at altitude.'

'Fine, Trevor?'

'The warning light for the starboard engine works, but the pump temperature sensor may be dud. I need to remove and check it. I can do that with a hot water kettle, but it needs calibration before use. I need a new calibrated one before signing off.'

'Jock?'

'I've removed the starboard pump; it seized and has overheating signs. I can install a new one but will need test equipment to sign it out.'

'Thanks. Carl?'

'The main fuel feed pump to the engine seems okay. I'll need a flowmeter to check if it's giving the full fuel flow, but if Jock installs a new engine pump and Dex can do a full power run on the engine, I can certify it for an empty ferry flight to London. I must do a hydraulic check after an engine failure.'

Rhys then summarised, 'I've downloaded the flight data and voice recorder. I can return to London. There's too much to send by satellite. I'll report the situation to London and ask for a decision by 17:00 their time. We'll tell Guillaume and return to the hotel for lunch.'

After an afternoon beside the pool, where they met the executive jet aircrew, Rhys called them around a table with THBs in front of all except Jenifer and the aircrew, who had discovered mint syrup mixed with soda water and lemonade on crushed ice.

Rhys had an instruction sheet mailed to him by the operations director.

'Okay, everyone, the head office has decided to be prudent. I'm to return immediately. I'll analyse the flight data, and if nothing indicates any other failure, you'll do the following.

'A case with parts and tools is on its way here, scheduled to arrive tomorrow afternoon via Johannesburg.

'Simon, you'll have the tools, dies and rivets, with two new scoops to fit on the engines.

'Jock, you have the test equipment to fit a new pump to each engine.

'Trevor, two new calibrated thermocouples for the new pumps.

'Carl, a flowmeter to check the main fuel pump and hoses. There are instructions on how to do it.

'Dex and Jenifer, you have tomorrow off; the day after, after the guys have finished, you must do a full power check; you may need to taxi to a run-up spot. If everything is fine, everyone returns with Dex and Jenifer. The return flight will be under Part 91 regulations, with no paying passengers, so a third pilot is not a requirement. Jock and Carl have clearances to sit in the right seat on a test flight, so Dexter and Jenifer can have a break. Has everyone understood?'

The murmur of agreement with no questions was enough. Rhys added, 'Dexter is the senior officer for our airline; I've copied this instruction list to him. Thanks, guys. We'll meet in London.

'Dex, and you, Jenifer. I want to take you to dinner when you arrive.

'I'll pack my bag.'

After handshakes with Rhys, Dexter said, 'Bo, we'll go to reception and organise a trip tomorrow to the Lemurs.'

⟨✈⟩

That night, when they went to bed, Jenifer didn't ask Dexter to put his arm around her; he did so without thinking. She snuggled and thought, *why do I feel so comfortable with his arm around me? He seems to like holding me. We're like those horses he described that stand beside each other with necks crossed. When we return, I'll ask him to take me to see the ponies.*

Dexter had a different thought. *Maybe I should delay a return to Mauritius so she has no reason to leave. I like having Bo with me.*

DAY 26
TUESDAY

⸻

The taxi came after breakfast, and they were on their way to Lemur Park by 09:00.

It was a magical day for them, a slow wander around the park in the morning with a guide who told them about the seven species of lemurs in the park. He insisted repeatedly that the lemurs were not monkeys and added that there were a hundred known species.

Dexter remarked that the lemurs moved slowly and gracefully. The guide replied that they could move fast, but they were idle creatures when there was no stress. Jenifer said they looked cuddly. And the guide agreed, 'They are. The fur is fine, like angora wool, and extremely soft, like touching silk. They're not aggressive, and their evolution in Madagascar was stressless. A tourist I met when he visited the park said Madagascar had the wrong name. He proposed *Mostly Harmless*.'

'Why?'

'There are no snakes classed as poisonous. The only toxic insects are scorpions. Their venom doses are too small to kill, and the black widow is the only highly poisonous spider out of four hundred species. If bitten, it usually makes a person extremely ill. The only carnivore is a small dog-sized beast called the Fossa, but they're rare. The crocodile is the only beast dangerous to man; it's thought to be a recent import only seven thousand years ago. So, the Lemur did not evolve to be aggressive, although they're a territorial species.

'After lunch, you can walk around and visit the tortoises and the chameleons; there are seventy different species, the smallest chameleon is an incredible thirteen millimetres long, and the longest six hundred and eighty.'

They had lunch on the restaurant veranda, surrounded by tropical plants and flowers. Jennifer sighed, 'This is heaven; I hope Mauritius is like this.'

'Unfortunately, it isn't. It's too small, and the view would be sugar cane fields, not rice paddies. Although I've heard there are lovely spots. Mostly, it's the beaches that attract the tourists.'

'Well, I'll add a visit to Madagascar to my bucket list.'

Dex might bring me here.

Dexter didn't offer because of his doubts about continuing with Jenifer.

After wandering that afternoon, Dexter said, 'We must return; the taxi will arrive at five. I hope the parts have arrived, and the maintenance guys may have started work.'

'I want to go into the shop; I want a souvenir or two of our visit.'

•••

'Why are you buying that kiddie soft toy?'

'It's cute, and it's a lemur. I'll call it Dex, and when you aren't in bed with me, it can sit on your pillow. When we arrive in Mauritius, I'll buy another one, a dodo. But I'll look at the other things they have here.'

Sometimes I don't understand her at all.

None of the maintenance team was at the *Relais* when Dexter and Jenifer arrived. 'They must be working; we'll have a drink and wait for them to return.'

The Air France bus arrived at 18:30, and four weary men collapsed into the chairs around the table and ordered THBs. It was Jock who explained what they had done.

'We received the parts at 15:00; the clearing agent wanted to take them to customs; Guillaume persuaded them that the pieces and tools weren't entering Madagascar but only in transit. Then we worked until it was too dark to see.

'If we arrive at the airport tomorrow at nine, we should finish by twelve, and we can do an engine run. I'm sure everything will go well, so we can sign off the paperwork and call London at about three, then email the paperwork to London. If we fly, what time will we go, Dex?'

'Take off at 21:00 – arrival at 06:00. I'll ask for a met report and then file the flight plan by 17:00 so London will know what clearances we need. We can have dinner before we leave and ask Guillaume for a snack box. It would be best if you guys watched the refuelling as soon as we've done the engine test runs while I do the paperwork. I'll tell you how much we need and warn Guillaume.'

'Then, Captain, we're going for showers; it was hot on the apron this afternoon. See you at supper.'

⚛

'Bo, we'd better make it an early night; we have a long night tomorrow.'

As Jenifer slipped into bed, she said, 'I'll imagine you're a cuddly Lemur.'

'I don't have soft fur.'

'Wear the Dodo pyjamas; they're soft. We can stay in bed late tomorrow morning.'

DAY 27
WEDNESDAY

Dexter whispered, 'Are you awake?'

'Yes, I can't sleep anymore.'

'Then I'll call reception and ask for coffee in our room.'

'I'll visit the bathroom. If the coffee comes, pour a cup for me.'

...

'When we return, and that enquiry is over, will you take me to your farm?'

'Don't you want to return to yours?'

'No, it's odd; I don't feel any pressure to go home, which is un-usual; perhaps it's because I'm with you, but remember, we still have to visit my mother's grave.'

'So, when do we try to revisit Mauritius?'

'We need a break after this escapade, just a period of relaxation with no worries, and I think Dartmoor and the ponies might do that.'

'I agree. I want to show the ponies to you. I'll go to the bathroom, dress, and go to reception to warn them, calculate the fuel we need, and call Guillaume. You follow me, and we'll have breakfast.'

Guillaume came, had breakfast with them, and took them to the airport.

By 17:00, the aircraft was ready to leave. Dexter and Jenifer had done and approved the engine runs, and London approved the flight, called Interex 001. Dexter had filed the flight plan, checked the weather report, and, with the help of Guillaume, completed all the departure forms. The Air France bus took them to the Relais for the last time, and after dinner, they returned to the airport.

As did Dexter, Jenifer took off her jacket and took them to the pilot's rest cabin to hang on a hook. When she returned, she said, 'You've caught your jacket on something; there's a small tear at the back. Also, it's shiny at the elbows; you must buy a new one.'

'Thanks for telling me; I don't look too often. I'll call Doris after we land.

'You take the left seat for take-off.'

'Ivato, Interex zero-zero-one heavy, good evening, request permission to start engines...'

DAY 28
THURSDAY

———

Dexter was in the captain's seat for the landing.

'Interex zero-zero-one clear to land, Runway 26 left, wind two-five-zero ten knots.

'After landing, taxi to International Air hangar four.'

'Copied zero-zero-one.'

⊰⊙⊱

By seven thirty, Dexter and Bo were at breakfast, and by eight, they were in bed.

'You said you would call Doris.'

'Thanks, I will.'

•••

Doris answered Dexter's 'Hello, Doris.'

'Hello, Dex, do you want to book a haircut?'

'No, Jenifer hasn't said anything about my hair, but she says I need a new jacket.'

That's good; she's behaving like a wife. 'I can sew four bars on a jacket your size, but not five unless you come for a fitting. I'll never sell a five-bar jacket to anyone else if it doesn't fit you.'

'Roger, can I come after 15:00?'

'I'll be ready; see you then.' *And if I can, tell him a thing or two.*

•••

'Bo, we'll try to sleep until twelve.'

'If I don't wake, let me sleep, but I'm sure I'll wake.'

After lunch, a swim and a massage for both, Dexter asked, 'Do you need anything from Doris?'

'No, I'll connect to my computer at home and see if I can sort out the math that proves why the asymmetric fuel load has an effect. It will take at least a few days.'

<hr>

'Good afternoon, Dex. You're looking well and suntanned.'

'Yes, Doris, health-wise. I took Jenifer to Madagascar.'

'Take off your jacket.'

'This jacket has had its day. Let's try a new one.'

The new jacket was acceptable across the shoulders, as was the length and sleeves, but when Doris buttoned it in front, she said, 'Sit on that chair.'

He did, and Doris chided, 'That's too tight around the waist; I must try another fit. Have you been lying on the beach and overeating?'

'No, I might have indulged a little in Brazil or Madagascar.'

'Then, if you don't tell Jenifer to ensure you have enough exercise, I'll tell her. I'll fetch another jacket.'

'That's better, but you'll return in six months if you don't exercise more. Tell Jenifer you must watch your diet.'

'I promise to exercise more, but I don't know if Jenifer and I will see each other much.'

'That's a shame. I thought you were perfect for each other. What's the problem?'

'Do you want me to cry on your shoulder like I did when my son died?'

'If you don't tell me, you'll be back here to do so in a week or two. My shoulder is always available to you.'

'I know, we go back twenty-five years. Jenifer has a problem. Her father looked after her alone for ten years, protecting her against anxiety attacks, and she became reliant on his presence. She talks about him as if he's still alive and says she visits him in the metaverse, although she knows he died five years ago. I may be an opportunity for her to accept her father's death and replace him with me, and I don't want to be a father again; it has too many memories, so I feel we must go our separate ways.'

Doris had listened without speaking, then said, 'I've listened to hundreds of clients with problems over the years. They talk to hairdressers and me because we aren't family, and we keep what we learn to ourselves. Every relationship needs two things: giving and taking. They're never equal, but the closer to equal it is, the better the relationship. If she was dependent, as you say, Jenifer must have suffered a devastating loss when her father died, but she has managed to keep going by imagining he has not gone. She needs the feeling of safety she had when he was alive. You'll give her something if she can feel the same sense of security from your presence.

'Think about how you feel when you're with her. Is there a memory then of your daughter or anything else you've done together that made you remember your daughter, and it felt good? If so, you were taking from her. You know she's not your daughter, and she knows you're not her father, so either way, those feelings and memories help to weld you together.

'So, ask her; discuss it, bring your feelings for each other into the open. I know you well, her only a little, but something tells me that together, you'll be formidable in every sense of the word.'

'I'll add, take your time, think about what you learn, but don't break it off before you've explored everything and there's no more to ask. Jenifer may have the time to regret it, but you don't.'

'I know that only too well.'

'Do you want to collect the jacket tomorrow, or shall I send it somewhere?'

'I'll collect it. I'll call and tell you when. If there's nowhere to park, I'll hoot and park in the loading zone, and you can send it out. Thanks.'

Dexter received a call from Rhys at 17:00. 'Hello Rhys, thanks for giving us enough time to sleep. When's the enquiry?'

'Tomorrow morning, Dex, 09:00. There is only one item in dispute: The asymmetric fuel load. The AD question they have closed. The ops director wants to skirt the asymmetric fuel, but the CAA or CamAirCom might bring it up.'

'We'll be there. Is Greg from simulators invited?'

'I don't know. Why?'

'He did both my line check and Jenifer's certification, so he might stand up for us if there's a question. Can you have him invited?'

'If not invited, I'll have him in the next-door office; chocolate croissants should ensure he comes. The meeting is in the boardroom on the third floor. Anything else?'

'Was there a fuel temperature warning from the engine that quit?'

'Yes, Dex.'

'Off the record, Rhys, have you checked to see if there was a crew change when it came on? Jenifer suggested that if a new crew member saw it only after he took his seat, it might have passed without comment.'

'Thanks, Dex, and thank Jenifer for me. I'll check the cockpit log.'

DAY 29
FRIDAY

As the incident was minor with no casualties, there were fewer attendees at the enquiry meeting than others Dexter had attended. He knew everyone there and introduced Jenifer.

'Ladies and gentlemen, we can leave the handshakes until after the meeting. Beside me is Captain Boscawen, who was with me when the incident occurred.' Then he introduced the others, 'Jenifer, this is the CAA representative Oliver Attwood; the FAA representative Tyron Delhaye; our Operations Director Philip Macintyre; the Fleet Maintenance Director Edward Stock; then Lee Tan from CamAirCom and Rhys you have met.'

They sat down, and Philip said, 'This meeting is formal. My secretary is recording. Edward, the CAA and FAA have agreed on the reason for the engine failure on flight two-four-six and agreed that there was no infringement of regulations as the AD was not mandatory and you had already scheduled it. Unless the CAA or FAA have questions, only internal matters remain.'

'Oliver, do you have a query?'

'Yes, only one. I know Dexter is fully qualified, but I haven't found a UK pilot's licence in the files for Captain Boscawen; I would like to clarify that.'

Dexter glanced at Rhys, who silently indicated that Greg was next door, then said.

'I can clarify that Captain Boscawen has an FAA licence, and Greg Marsden recently examined her for a UK endorsement for which she has applied. We can call him in, or he can provide the necessary information to Oliver after the meeting.'

Oliver replied, 'Philip, I'll accept that.'

Philip asked Tyron Delhaye, 'Does the FAA have a question?'

'Yes, the CamAirCom Pilots manual recommends keeping the fuel equally distributed between the wings, and the automated transfer system does this. However, the flight data shows that the co-pilot, who was, I understand, Captain Rawlins, shut down the auto-transfer and transferred fuel until the left wing was full, leaving the starboard wing empty. I want to know why he violated the pilot's manual procedures.'

'Dex, can you answer that?'

'Yes, first, there was no violation. The manual contains a recommendation. Therefore, it is optional.'

Dexter could see that Philip had difficulty not smiling; his lips twitched.

Tyron asked, 'Accepted, but why did you do that?'

'Jenifer, can you explain it?'

She did and made it dramatic. 'In straight and level flight with one engine, it is unnoticeable, but when manoeuvring or landing, with no autopilot, pumping the fuel to fill the wing with the powered engine makes an enormous difference to the ease of handling. I know this from experience. With three hundred passengers at night, with no ILS, on a short runway at four thousand feet altitude with one engine, it provides a much bigger margin between life and death. The FDR should show the landing using the same runway distance as a normal two-engine landing.'

Tyron gave up, 'As there was no violation, I'll accept that and ask CamAirCom to revisit the pilot's manual.'

Philip breathed a sigh of relief and said, 'Then I'll close the meeting; my secretary will circulate the minutes. Thank you. There should be coffee waiting for us next door.'

'Bo, we must go for coffee.'

'Why?'

'You'll see.'

Jenifer found out in the coffee room. Everyone, now relaxed, wanted to shake hands with Dexter and her, accompanied by congratulations on a successful landing. After shaking hands with them both, Oliver made a beeline for Greg, who had a half-eaten chocolate croissant in one hand. Dexter thought he'd had time to eat two already.

Lee Tan waited until after the others, and when he congratulated them, he asked.

'Would you be willing to fly to Phoenix and meet our guys? We might have slipped up somewhere.'

'I would love that. Jenifer, how about you?'

'I would too, but let's ask for a simulator to be available with an expert and a CamAir Three-Ten with a test pilot for a test flight.'

Surprised, Lee Tan replied, 'I'm sure we can organise that, but why?'

'It will save time and be more convincing if I can show you instead of telling you.'

As Lee Tan walked away, Philip came to them. 'Dex, Captain, will you please revise our operations manual?'

'Of course, it will take a week or two.'

'That will be fine.'

Then he turned to Jenifer and asked, 'Captain, can I extend your temporary employment at International Air until the operations manual is complete?'

'Yes, that will suit me, thank you.'

'I also greatly appreciate your discretion and request a modification to the pilot relief procedures. Thank you.'

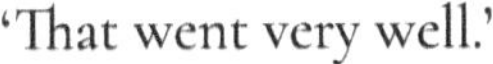

'That went very well.'

'Yes, and now let's go to your farm. I'm feeling happy.'

'Why?'

'Well, now we have a trip to Phoenix; you won't be able to chuck me out for some time.'

'Can we agree that I'll never do that? It's up to you whether you stick with me.'

He wants me! 'You might have a long wait.'

'I'll enjoy every minute, even if it takes the rest of my life.

'Our car is still in the staff car park. Let's go for lunch first, what do you fancy?'

'Something light, like a Burrito, then when we reach Phoenix, we can see if they're different there.'

'We can walk to the restaurant called Tortilla.'

An hour later, after a Burrito each and a sugar-free soda, Dexter asked.

'Have you visited the toilet?'

'Why?'

'We have four hours to drive. I usually stop at the Amesbury services for a break and coffee, but that's two hours. Then, at Whiddon Down, we can call at a Morrisons supermarket. There's no food at the farm. I clear it out when I leave for more than two days.'

'Copied, I'll visit the ladies.'

'Me too.' Then, he hastily added when he saw Jenifer grin. 'The gents.

'We must call in at "Business with Style." I promised Doris I would collect my new jacket.'

Once on the highway, the DB11 warbled along, carrying them comfortably; after a while, Jenifer dozed. Dexter played back the last two weeks in his mind and thought he hadn't enjoyed the time as much for years.

At Amesbury, they stopped for thirty minutes, drank a large

coffee each, and then drove on, and Dexter asked, 'Do you have a driving licence?'

'Yes. I passed my driving test after I turned eighteen; my dad taught me, and I had a few lessons. He always took me because I never take buses. I have a little car, a mini; it's in the shed by the barn, but I don't use it much and only into the village and back on a Sunday morning. Never on a long trip because I don't know if I'll have an anxiety attack and forget where it is.'

'Would you like to drive?'

'Yes, but not now. You must teach me how to drive this beast. Preferably somewhere with no traffic. It would be fun.'

When they stopped before Dexter's farmhouse, Jenifer said, 'This is cute, but bigger than I imagined.'

'Upstairs, it's now only two bedrooms and a bathroom; I knocked a couple of walls around to make one bedroom and the bathroom bigger. Downstairs, the kitchen is bigger, and there's no dining room; part of it I added to the kitchen, and the rest is my study. I still have the lounge to remodel, and the ground floor toilet is outside the back door until I can build one inside.'

'It's bigger than many farm cottages I've seen. I'm glad you've kept the ivy and the roses.'

'Come, let me show you the outside before it's too dark to see.' He led the way around the side of the house.

'I can see the barn. Is that the one you've rented out?'

'No, that's my garage and workshop. It used to have a tractor, but I sold it. The rented barn is behind the house.'

Jenifer saw it and said, 'That's huge, much bigger than my barn.'

'The end on the right is a stable with stalls for two horses. The rest of it the farmer uses for hay storage.'

'Does he have horses?'

'No, he uses the stalls for fuel trailers; he wanted to make it one big storage area, but I want to keep the horse stalls; maybe one day, if I come to live here permanently, I'll buy a horse.'

Jenifer thought before she replied. *Or two, if he brings a wife to live here.* 'Do the tractor attachments under the roof there belong to the farmer?'

'No, they were my dad's, but I said he could use them if necessary. The closed area at the far end has a pigsty and a hen house, and the bit that joins the house has a wood store for the fireplace and, finally, the toilet. That's all of it. When it rains, you'll need gumboots to walk out here; I have several pairs by the kitchen door.'

'In my size?'

'Probably. We can always buy another pair.'

'So, I'm not the first woman to visit your farm?'

'No, in the last ten years, maybe six.'

That's something I should have expected. Dex is honest.

They walked back to the car, collected the baggage and went in. 'Look around; I'll take the bags upstairs. You can put the food bag in the kitchen.'

Jenifer quickly looked and found only three rooms off the entrance hall. On one side were a small study and the kitchen they had walked through, and on the other, a lounge with a fireplace. She was sure that it had once been two rooms. When she turned to leave, she saw a framed print of text beside the door and read it. It was a poem.

Nine Stones Circle

And now at every Hunter's Moon
That haggard cirque of stones so still
Awakens to immortal thrill
And seven small maidens in silver shoon
Twixt dark of night and white of day
Twinkle upon the sere old heath
Like living blossoms in a wreath

Then shrink again to granite grey.
So blue-eyed Dian shall ever dance
With Linnette, Bethkin, Jenifer,
Arisa, Petronell and Nance.

Eden Phillpotts

It has his wife's name, my mother's, mine, his daughter and granddaughter! There's a mystery and an omen.

When Dexter came down, he found Jenifer stocking the fridge freezer. 'I like what you did; I must remember this.'

'What do you mean?'

'You moved this end of the kitchen into the dining room and put a kitchen cupboard fitting across it, with the fridge and all the appliances built in. That was clever.'

'I had to take the wall upstairs down, that gave me the bigger bedroom and allowed me to remove the wall between the dining room and kitchen. It allowed me to keep the pantry, and I left enough of the dining room for a study.'

'I looked in the pantry and saw the bare stone walls; that must be the oldest bit of this house.'

'It was part of an original cottage. The rest of the kitchen is more recent. I kept the pantry because the temperature remains cool and constant.'

'Well, the house is cosy. The lounge must be lovely and warm, with a fire in the fireplace on winter evenings. Have you replaced the windows upstairs with double-glazed like downstairs?'

'Of course, I don't need central heating; the fireplace has an insert that ducts warm air into the bedrooms. What shall I make for supper? How about Cornish Pasties, mash and peas? I can do real potatoes, as mash or baked.'

'Baked, with that Cornish clotted cream, much better than butter.'

'Coming up in thirty minutes. Will you wash four spuds while I warm the peas?'

'Show me where everything is, and we'll lay the table.'

Bo makes me feel she's at home instead of me feeling like I have a visitor.

Dexter produced a bottle of Sparkling Cider and popped the cork. 'I have a tradition; when I invite a lovely lady to my palace, the welcome drink is a local cider. This one is a product of Fowey Valley in Cornwall, near us. Will you have a glass, or would you prefer something else?'

'Of course, I'll drink it,' then she smiled, 'Is it strong enough to make me weak-kneed when we go to bed? You did mention lovely ladies earlier.'

'It's never had that effect; it has the same alcohol content as beer, so your knees will remain together,' he grinned, 'unless something else has an effect.'

Jenifer ignored his comment. 'Tell me what you'll show me tomorrow.'

'When we go to bed, I'll bring a map of the moor and a book of photographs. The moor is famous because it has over a hundred and fifty granite outcrops; they're called Tors. We want to see the ponies, so we must go to the deserted parts. I propose we walk about twenty kilometres between outcrops I know. It will take all day, although if we find some ponies, we'll walk less and spend time watching them. We must take a picnic lunch and water.'

'Do we start from here?'

'We could, but between us and the open moorland is farmland, so we'll drive to where the farms stop. I know a good place to park. It's about six kilometres away.'

'Do you have a stock of hiking shoes? Not gumboots.'

'Yes, didn't you bring any?'

'I think you must look at what I brought; they may not be suitable for the moor.'

'We'll check before we go to bed. Do you want a coffee? I have decaf.'

'I'll join you with a decaf, then do the washing up. How do you find your way on the moor?'

'I know the paths well enough, but I have a portable GPS in case I'm late, and if the visibility is poor, it's easy to mistake a valley for another. It's in the rucksack hanging behind the kitchen door. With bad visibility, only three or four metres, it's almost useless, and following a course is impossible, but it helps to show where you are, so it takes far longer to get home than when the visibility is good.'

'Can't you use your phone?'

'No. The granite affects the signal, but the cellphone companies don't have aerials pointing into an empty moor where no one calls. You can get a weak signal on a high hill from a mast way off the moor; in a valley, none.'

...

'Fetch your boots from upstairs; I'll fetch those I have from the store cupboard.'

•••

'Yours will be fine if you don't step into the wet ground; the canvas sides won't keep your feet dry. Try one of these pairs.'

'These fit nicely; they seem new.'

'Wear the ones you brought when we leave, then put the boots on when we begin walking. Then you can change back when we return to the car and leave the muddy shoes in the trunk.'

'For whom did you buy these new ones?'

'A wildly enticing sexpot called Selene who sold computers. I invited her because I thought she was dying for intimate attention. She had a tight-fitting tee shirt when I met her, and the slogan on the front said, "I Love Stiffys!"'

'That must have been years ago before stiffy discs went out of use. If Selene didn't wear the boots, she must have been dying for attention, not walking.'

'Nowhere near enough, she looked at the farmhouse; it had rained, and the courtyard was muddy. She didn't leave the car and told me to take her to Okehampton to catch a train back to London.'

Jenifer laughed; she thought it was the funniest thing she'd heard in a long time. 'You should have bought a tee shirt.'

'Why?'

'You could have bought one with "I love floppies on it".'

'Beware, I have pyjamas with a smiling Dodo. It's bedtime.'

Jenifer snuggled, then asked, 'Dex, there's a framed poem on the lounge wall. Why's it there?'

'My wife hung it there; she brought it with her when we married; she said her mother named her after one of the maidens in the poem. The nine-stone circle is on the moor, close to here. When our daughter was born, Beth insisted on Nance and not Nancy as her name, and then Nance named her daughter Linnette.'

'It also has my name, spelt correctly, and my mother's.'

'I had forgotten; that might mean something. Time will tell.'

Day 30
Saturday

Dexter locked the car, shouldered his small rucksack and picked up his hiking stick; Jenifer did the same. Then Dexter handed her a pair of binoculars, 'Use these if you want a closeup of something. I have another pair. It's best if you follow me; the paths are narrow. When there's enough room to walk beside me, I'll drop back.'

They left the last field after a hundred metres, and seven hundred metres later, Dexter stopped. 'What do you think of your first steps on the moor?'

'It's a bit frightening, it's so empty. I think you could lose yourself easily.'

'Think of it differently: wherever you are, you have wide highways showing the way, and at the end of those highways are tilled fields, farms, and people.'

'What highways? I can't see any.'

'Your shadow is one; just follow it, but remember when there isn't one to wait a while, then keep the shadow behind. The wind is another; walk with the wind in your face. At night, it's the moon. Unlike a forest, the moor is where you can see the sun or feel the wind. The longest possible walk is twenty kilometres in a straight line, but long before you've walked that distance, you'll see a church steeple or something to guide you the last kilometres.'

'That makes me feel better. Why have we stopped, and what are all these stones?'

'It's a stone circle, this one's called Scorhill. There are many of them on Dartmoor. No one knows their construction date, except that it was sometime after 2500 BCE, the date of Stonehenge, and they don't know why the people built them. However, they know it wasn't a cemetery. The most accepted idea is that the people built them for a ritual or meeting place, the equivalent of a church today, where the people could feel the presence of the gods.'

'So, people lived here?'

'Not in their church, but nearby. Not in big villages, just small groups of two or three huts for the people who looked after sheep and goats. We'll walk further to the Tolmen Stone, Kes Tor, and

Fernworthy Stone Circle. Near there is Manga Brook, where I've often seen ponies because there's water, and they can shelter from storms in the trees at Fernworthy. It's about a two-hour walk.'

'Dex, that's a very unusual stone.'

'The hole through the stone is the result of thousands of years of erosion; there are other stones with holes in them in the UK, and there are all kinds of folklore about them. The people believed this stone had healing powers; the beliefs began amongst those who built the stone circles.'

'Like what?'

'If children passed through the hole, they would grow up healthy. Also, someone with rheumatism who went through the hole would improve.

'Another story is that if a couple who intended to marry joined hands through the hole, their marriage would last. Although marriage was quite simple then, just two people who decided to live together and have children, although parents might have arranged it, and the ceremony, if there was one, could have been tying thumbs together with a bit of grass.'

I must remember that. Does Dex think an invitation to clasp hands through the hole is a marriage proposal? 'I think that's a sign of love, Dex. If a couple went to the trouble of coming here and holding hands through the hole, it's a sign that they want their union to last, whether parents intervened or not.'

'I never thought of that; you may be right. But we must go on.'

...

'Did people pile those rocks on each other?'
'No, that's Kes Tor, one of the granite Tors. They're natural.'
'But how could that happen?'

'There are scientific explanations, 280 million years of weathering and erosion. You can find the reasons on the web. Let's go to Fernworthy, then try to find the ponies.'

...

Jenifer was impressed once they passed down a passage between tall trees. 'This is like the other circle, but it's a more friendly place, sheltered inside the trees.'

'I agree, but the trees may not have existed when people built it. But look at the dung. There were ponies here only a few days ago.'

'Then let's keep going.'

As they came out of the trees and looked across the Teign-e-Ver river to the valley where Manga Brook flowed into the river, Dexter said, 'There, on the right-hand side of the brook, on the sunny side.'

'Yes, I see them, but how do we cross the river?'

'If we go to the right, there's a clapper bridge we can cross, and then we'll come back to the top of the valley slope above the ponies, and we can sit and watch.'

'What's a clapper bridge?'

'You'll see, it's just a stone column in the middle of the river and a granite slab on each side.'

'Must we hurry?'

'No, they'll be there until late afternoon. It's sheltered from the northerly breeze and is sunny; they'll stay.'

Fifteen minutes later, Dexter whispered, 'We must whisper; they won't mind us but don't like noisy people. When I signal, we'll sit.'

Walking leisurely, they topped the valley edge and, in full sight of the ponies, continued at a slight angle as if they would go around the horses. Halfway to them, Dexter signalled, and they sat.

After several minutes, Jenifer whispered, 'What are we looking for?'

'Can you see the bay pony?'

'With the lovely white tail and mane?'

'Yes, she's bothered by flies and keeps shaking her head and mane. Another pony may come and help her.'

'How?'

'Standing beside her, head to tail, and using her tail to whisk the flies away from the bay pony's head. Just wait. It might not happen as the bay might move away, but she likes that grass and clover.'

...

Dexter whispered, 'The chestnut is moving towards the bay.'

...

'That's fantastic. How long will the ponies stay head to tail like that?'

'I don't know, but use your binoculars; I think the flies are still bothering her; she's rippling her skin where the mane stops on her back. Watch what happens.'...

'That's amazing; the chestnut stepped forward and whisked the bay's back...and now she's stepped back!'

'Let's eat our sandwiches while we wait to see what happens.'

Half an hour later, as they packed the empty lunch boxes in the rucksacks, Dexter said, 'We could sit here until sunset, but I would like to show you more of the moor. Shall we go on?'

'Yes, pony-watching is a relaxing business, but learning about them may take many visits. Where will we go now?'

'It's too late to go to Cranmere pool; we must do that another day, but you must look up the history of the pool and the letterbox before we return to Stoneleigh. We'll route to Hanging Stone Hill, Steeperton Tor, and back to the car, about ten kilometres. We may see more ponies near Steeperton.'

'Right, let's walk.'

Dexter had estimated three hours, but it took them four. They had walked almost two kilometres when Dexter said, 'We must turn north here, look over there, use the binoculars. The military building on hanging stone hill has a red flag flying; it means that military exercises are underway, and we must stay away.'

'Yes, I see it, what's important about it?'

'Only that it's one of the highest points on Dartmoor, and the view is superb.'

When they reached Steeperton Tor, Jenifer was disappointed, 'I expected a high pile of rocks, and these are all lying flat.'

'Many Tors are like this. The name refers to a granite outcrop, not a pile of rocks. There are others I can show you that are far more spectacular.'

After Steeperton, they had to round the head of a deep valley, and on the far side were ponies. Jennifer was delighted. 'Let's stop and watch them. Do we have the time?'

'An hour, Bo. After that, mist might form; it comes suddenly and is wet and miserable.'

'Then we'll leave when you say.'

...

'Two ponies are leaning against each other, like you told me, and one has his head and neck over the other. How long will they stay like that?'

'Not long, they'll move, graze some more, and then do the same again.'

...

'Is that one nibbling behind the ear of the other?'

'It might be using its teeth to scratch, but it might be blowing again.'

'That's lovely to see, Dex; I'm sure they're comforting each other, rubbing their necks together.'

'That's an example of what I told you. We should go now.'

Ninety minutes later, after crossing three muddy streams, they arrived at the car. 'Dex, that was a fantastic day; we must walk the moor some more. I'm used to being alone at home, but the solitude out there is something far more profound. I can't explain what I felt. How do you feel when you're out there.'

'I must think about how to tell you, Bo. Since Bethkin left me, mostly I'm alone, and it doesn't feel the same as when I'm with someone.'

While Dexter drove to the farmhouse, Jenifer asked, 'What would you like for dinner, Dex?'

'I suggest an excellent restaurant at the Oxenham Arms, only four kilometres from the farm. I propose we bathe, change, and go there for dinner if I can book a table.'

'Do we dress up?'

'Most definitely, the name dates from the mid-1800s and the buildings are much older. They claim 843 years, and it was a coaching inn 545 years ago.'

'So where does the name come from?'

'You'll find out at the hotel. Captain John Oxenham was a pirate.'

...

'Dex, is there enough hot water for me to soak? I expect I'll wake up tomorrow stiff, and a bath might help.'

'The cottage may look primitive, but if there's no fire in the lounge, electricity heats the water, and there's enough for both of us.'

'But the bath isn't.'

'That's the latest item in my refurbishment program. I'll install one before you come the next time. You go and soak.'

Jenifer wondered. *Will I find out if that's true?*

While Jennifer bathed, Dexter fetched the three necklace cases from his suitcase. He laid them on the dressing table, open.

Jenifer came from the bathroom in the red dress she'd bought in

Stoneleigh. 'How do I look?'

'Like a goddess, any man would feel proud to take you to dinner, but that dress needs a necklace.'

'The one I wore with the yellow dress is the wrong colour, Dex; I don't have another.'

'Choose one of those on the dressing table.'

'They're lovely. Are they real?'

'No, Doris chose them for me; she says I must take you to choose real ones. These are returnable.'

'Then come here and help me choose.'

Jennifer tried the diamond one, looked in the mirror, and said, 'That works.'

'Try the green one. Green goes well with red.'

'You're right, it's marvellous. Does buying me these necklaces mean you're something more than a *friend*?'

'A lot more, Bo.'

Jennifer stepped forward, looked up at him, and said quietly, 'A something more than a *friend* can kiss me, Dex. Please.'

...

'Dex, stop now. Let's go.'

⋙∘∘∘∘≪

'This is old; the ivy must have grown for hundreds of years.'

'I'm sure it has. Now that we're here, I realise we've done this wrong. I should have brought you here for lunch; the gardens are marvellous, and lunch in the gardens is a holiday on its own.'

'There's always another day.'

I hope that's true.

⋙∘∘∘∘≪

Dexter was first in bed, and when Jenifer came from the bathroom, he asked with a smile. 'Can I call you "my darling"?'

'If you do, I won't let you kiss me; that would be too much.'

'Then I'll be satisfied with a kiss to build a dream on.'

'That's the title of a Satchmo song.'

'Do you know it?'

'I know most of his music and songs; I like the slower ones best.'

I can feel a surprise coming. 'That surprises me.'

'When I was still a teen, hiding and playing computer games; sometimes, I played a flute. Dad had a collection of Satchmo recordings. I told you about flying around the States. I spent one night at a small airfield east of New Orleans, and in the morning, a young guy hitching north to see his mother asked me for a lift if I was going his way. I took him to Jackson and tried to give him two hundred dollars. He refused but said I could buy his trumpet, so I did. It was a bit battered but played well after I polished it. When you have nothing to do but fly a sim without diversion, you get stale, so I learnt to play Satchmo's songs.'

'Can you read music?'

'No, I played Satchmo's recordings into a sound analyser, giving me the composition in detail. I practised until I could match mine and the recording. Now I don't have to think; I have learnt the notes and the music, so play. Sometimes, I play something I invent, but I can't write it down.

'I don't know how good I am; Dad said I was good, but he was biased.'

'Do you still have the trumpet, and do you still play?'

'Until I met you, Dex, whenever I was lonely, I played a tune or two for Dad. I haven't been lonely since.'

What can't she do?

'There's a jazz club in Exeter; I'll take you there sometimes as you like jazz.'

•••

He's planning how to keep me with him.

DAY 31
SUNDAY

After they dressed in the morning, Jenifer said, 'That was a fabulous meal last night, Dex. Can we delay breakfast this morning? I'm not hungry.'

'Of course, I feel the same. I should make a quick trip for a fresh loaf of bread and milk. I can do that before breakfast.'

'Then buy some more cream and six eggs. If I want to walk while you're away, how do I lock up and get back in?'

'There are two spare keys on a nail at the back of the kitchen door.'

'Do you have WiFi?'

'Of course, the code is dex@interair, all lowercase.'

'Then I'll check my metabox for messages. They are from approved friends who leave a message for me, usually a URL to a shared data file in the cloud. I know the avatar name, but not who sends it.'

After Dexter left, Jenifer went for a walk, not far, eight hundred metres down the private farm road and back in the quiet early morning with the trills of birds in the hedgerows and trees, a welcome contrast to the noise of cars on Stoneleigh Road. She took a spare key with her, and after she returned, she didn't put it back on the hook but shoved it into a pocket of her tracksuit, for Jenifer expected she would need it again.

Dexter returned and asked, 'Would you like to make another visit to the moor?'

'Of course, I'd love to.'

'Then we'll make some sandwiches.'

***

'Where will we go today?'

'There's a couple of places you should see, so I thought we might do a ten-kilometre walk.

'We'll start at the Meldon reservoir car park, walk up to the viaduct, cross it on the Granite cycle trail, then follow it a bit before branching off to Yes Tor. Then there's a trail to High Wilhays, and we'll cross to the Black Tor Forest, a spooky place to visit, then Black Tor itself, and back to the viaduct and the car. It's a fresh air exercise. Three to four hours, with interesting views.'

***

'You said this place was spooky, but it's more than that. It belongs on another planet where weird beasties peer out at us. Are you sure these trees don't walk around? They're twisted and bent.'

'It's a favourite spot for making fantasy or ghost films, especially when the mists whirl over the moor and condensation on the trees drips from them; that's why there's so much moss on the ground.'

'Are there photos on the web?'

'Lots, why?'

'If I can find a suitable image, I might add a corner to my metaverse for total solitude.'

'Why would you want to go there?'

'Sometimes, when things were closing in on me, I looked for a place to be alone. Since I met you, I'm not sure that will happen again. I prefer to be with you.'

'That's good to know. Let's do the return walk.'

While looking for an opportunity to ask about another attempt to visit Mauritius, Dexter waited until the Malden reservoir came into view. Jenifer asked, 'Do people swim in the reservoir?'

'Some kids do, in summer. I did, but it's never warm. Now that I can swim in the tropics, it doesn't appeal. When do you want to make another attempt to visit your mother's grave?'

'I'm not sure. After an anxiety attack and an engine failure en route, I wonder if destiny is against me.'

'I don't think so. If anything crops up, I'll be there.'

'Then give me a day or two, and I'll tell you. When must you return to work?'

'I'll take you home tomorrow, then go to Gatwick. Call me when you're ready to go to Mauritius, and I'll fetch you.'

DAY 32
MONDAY

Before they left on Monday morning, Lee Tan called.

'Good morning, Captain Rawlins. Lee Tan here. I apologise for this early call, but I wanted to speak to you before you became involved in meetings.'

'Any later and I would be driving, so it's a good thing you have. I'll put on the speaker so Captain Boscawen can hear. Is there a problem?'

'Not a problem, but I should put you in the picture. I submitted a report on the enquiry to head office and suggested they invite you to a meeting. I expected nothing more, and they were not interested. However, Tyron Delhaye reported to the FAA in the USA that the flight manual and operating instructions were incorrect.

'The FAA sent a letter to our head office requesting notification about our investigation, and of course, as there wasn't one, it stirred up a hornet's nest. Now I must find out when you can come to Phoenix and if it could be by Wednesday morning. It's now become urgent.'

Jenifer said, 'Mr Lee, I asked for an aircraft with a qualified captain and a simulator with an expert to be available. If these aren't available, we won't go.'

'I have told them, Captain Boscawen. Would you like written confirmation?'

'That might be a good idea.'

'Captain Rawlins, if the confirmation arrives, can you make a meeting on Wednesday?'

'We can, but early; we'll fall asleep by lunchtime. I'll confirm two seats on tomorrow's Phoenix flight at 14:40. I assume you'll take care of all arrangements and the hotel in Phoenix?'

'Naturally.'

'Then please call me with a confirmation as soon as possible.'

'Thank you. Have a good day.'

•••

'I'll call for seats. You surprised me.'

'What about? For insisting on the sim and aircraft? Without it, there's no point in going; they wouldn't believe us, think we're fools, and bury the whole thing behind a wall of mumbo-jumbo. Far better not to waste our time.'

Dexter booked two seats for the flight, then said, 'Do you need anything from home before we go to Phoenix?'

'Not if I can do my washing and ironing here.'

'Then we should stay here today; we'll go to lunch at the Oxenham and can leave early tomorrow directly to Gatwick.'

'These gardens are lovely. Have they always been like this?'

'Yes and no, I can remember years when the signs of neglect were everywhere. It costs money to maintain them, so it depends on how well the hotel does. About ten years ago, they employed a new gardener, and over time, he replaced much of the old growth with easy-to-maintain varieties. Many of the plants you can see now are annuals, and the meandering waterways are due to him, which reduced the watering needed. The total area of the grounds exceeds two hectares.'

'Is he still here?'

'I don't know if he's full-time, but I've seen him in the garden once or twice in the last three months; he has a big straw hat. Come here, and we'll walk under the pergola to the restaurant.'

...

'I'll have a traditional roast beef. For me, it suits the hotel's character and is always delicious. They roast it on a spit and baste it many times. The veggies come from the farms next door.'

'Then I'll have that too, but I want a dessert.'

'Why?'

'I haven't had bread and butter pudding since I was a child, and with double clotted cream, it must be heaven.'

'Did you see the wheelchair in the entrance hall?'

'The antique one?'

'It's there for the clients who can't walk to their cars after lunch!'

Jenifer chuckled. 'I might need it.'

...

Jenifer laid down her spoon, 'Coffee, please. I can't eat another mouthful.'

Back at the farm, Jenifer was ironing her shirts after Dexter ironed his trousers when, at 15:00, he received the email confirmation letter. Lee Tan called minutes later to confirm, and Dexter confirmed their departure, and then Jenifer asked. 'Can we leave tonight or very early tomorrow?'

'Why?'

'If I'm to appear in front of an American enquiry panel, I must have my hair done. I want to visit Doris's shop tomorrow morning before the flight. An appointment at 09:00 would be fine.'

'Call Doris and ask.'

'09:00 is booked.'

'I'll call the Holiday Inn, and we can leave in half an hour.'

'I'll pack.'

The drive back to London was silent as the car ate up the kilometres; Dexter and Jenifer regretted leaving and promised themselves a return as soon as possible.

At 20:30, Jenifer said in the hotel room, 'Would you like a snack from room service? After that lunch, something light will do, and then we can go to bed.'

'Yes, perfect.'

An hour later, in bed, Jenifer asked, 'Are you still hungry? I can get you another cheese and tomato sandwich.'

'No, it's just that your ear tastes good.'

'Stop sucking it so I can sleep. It gives me shivers.'

I get them, too.

DAY 33, TUESDAY

'Let's shower, change and have breakfast; I'll call a taxi. I can take another to the terminal. You take the baggage to your office, and I'll meet you at check-in.'

'Fine, call or SMS me when you leave for the terminal.'

'Hello Jenifer, nice to see you again. You're looking well. You must have been somewhere sunny; you have a nice tan.'

'We've been to Madagascar. We intended to visit Mauritius to put flowers on my mother's grave, but an engine failed. We're flying this afternoon to Phoenix for an enquiry.'

'I'm sorry to hear about your mother. Did she die recently?'

'A few days before I met Dex.' Doris thought. *She's using their meeting as a base for remembering.*

'That's why I was in the departure hall the day I had the anxiety attack. I had booked to fly to Mauritius for her funeral.'

'So how is Dex?'

'He's well, and I discovered he's very fit, and Lemurs like him. When we get to Mauritius, I'll take him kite surfing. That's something I've always wanted to try.'

She's good for him, making him forget he's much older.

'Apart from visiting Mauritius, we don't have any plans for the future.'

'Why not?'

'I have a problem, and he doesn't know how to help.'

Contrary to her rules, Doris decided she couldn't stand on the sidelines and let what she thought was a good relationship flounder.

'You can tell me, what problem?'

'My mother left us when I was nearly sixteen, and my father looked after me. I know sixteen-year-old girls shouldn't need much looking after, but I had anxiety attacks, and my dad became my shield against them. He died five years ago, and after more than ten years of support from him, he was the only person I ever really talked to about personal stuff; I couldn't let him go. In my mind, I kept him alive. I imagined him in the house and spoke to him.

'I don't know if my feelings for Dex are because he's a man or because he can replace my father.'

'How do you think Dex feels?'

'I'm sure he doesn't want to be my father, but he might worry that I'm a replacement for his daughter. Since his son died and Bethkin left him, he's had no one except the ponies.'

'What ponies?'

'The ones on Dartmoor, he took me to see them. He spends hours watching them.'

Doris absorbed this with wonder. 'I know he's from Dartmoor; he told me once he loved the peacefulness. Does he have a house there?'

'He inherited and is refurbishing his parents' farm.'

Two intelligent people are trying not to make a mistake, so they're making one.

'Jenifer, would you mind if I gave you a lecture?'

'No, maybe it would help.'

'Then I'll try. Every relationship includes something from the past and something new. I have many clients come through my door. I can tell you that I have often met a man's mother or a woman's husband who came with their child when their child joined an airline and needed the right clothes. I have met those children multiple times over the years, seen their marriages to each other, and seen them return with a child who is joining the airline. Often, I have remarked that the boy married a girl like his mother and vice versa. That's a bit of the past carried into a new relationship. We think that pilots marry crew they meet at work, but farmers marry farmers, and doctors marry nurses. In doing so, they carry something of their past into the new relationship. A good relationship is one where the two people fit into each other's framework of thoughts and beliefs, which are from their past. Whatever makes Dex seem like a father to you is only a small part and a good part. Your father was so important in your life that I don't think you could form a solid relationship with someone who wasn't older and didn't stimulate those memories.

'Have you questioned Dex about his daughter? Have you asked if he took her to watch the ponies? His pleasure will come from having someone with him who loves doing the same things – successful couples like doing things together: travel, photography, hiking, and picnics. You and Dex are halfway there; you both fly. I didn't tell you Dex attracted me, but we didn't have the same passions. It's not opposites that attract, but similarities, although they're rarely visible.

'Relationships need work to establish, I know from my own experience. You need to ask frank questions and give honest and open replies and opinions, and if you learn nothing that turns you off, it will be a good one.'

'I've never thought of relationships like that, thanks. I'll remember what you've said.'

'I'll add something. If you think Dex will be a good fit, say so. Women march and wave placards claiming equality, yet we sit back expecting a man to propose. When I was sure I wanted to marry my husband, I gave him three months to agree or leave for good.' Doris paused, then grinned and added. 'And I refused sex until he agreed.'

Jenifer burst into laughter, 'Why?'

'I didn't want a yes because he would lose his comforts, but because he wanted me.'

'Doris, you're marvellous. Thanks. How long did it take him?'

'Two weeks, and he was on his knees!'

At 14:40, Dexter and Jenifer boarded the flight to Phoenix Sky Harbour and arrived at 17:40.

When they exited the aeroplane door, a man wearing a pilot's uniform stepped forward and asked, 'Captain Rawlins?'

Dexter replied, 'That's me, and this is Captain Boscawen.'

'I'm Andy Framer, your chopper pilot. If you give your baggage tags to Charly here, he'll deliver your bags to the helicopter.' Charly, a heavyweight with an airport badge around his neck, took the tags from Jenifer when she removed them from her purse. Andy continued. 'Now follow me, and I'll take you through border control.'

Jenifer asked, 'Where are we going?'

'To the assembly complex, they built it from scratch once widebody assembly became impossible in Scranton. It's a huge complex, but it's at the Phoenix-Mesa airport.'

Forty minutes later, they left the helicopter at the CamAirCom Helipad for a two-kilometre car ride to a Sheraton hotel.

The message at the reception desk when they checked in at the hotel was unusual.

> Captain Rawlins. Considering the time difference, we have arranged
> the meeting for 05:00. A car will collect you at 04:30. Room service
> will bring whatever meals you request.
> Lee Tan.

DAY 34
WEDNESDAY

The limousine that came to collect them had Lee Tan beside the driver. They climbed in the back, and Dexter said, 'Hello, Mr Lee, we weren't expecting you.'

'I arranged the visit, Captain, so I thought I should be here.'

'Thank you. Seeing a face we know is much appreciated. Who are we meeting?'

'In reverse order of importance, the top simulator engineer, Henry Mancuni. He's not the sim operations manager but the engineer responsible for updating the CamAir Three-Ten sim with aircraft modifications. You've already stirred things up with that warning light business, so he has some egg on his face.

'Jack Strang, a test pilot, then Caroline Crossley, the head of documentation for the CamAir Three-Ten program, Brian Deever, the chief design engineer. Then William Faulkner, the VP of the CamAir Three-Ten program, may make a welcome appearance.'

'How do we remember all those names?'

'There will be name bars in front of each of them.'

'No FAA?'

'Not until we decide to change something. We must drive through the factory area to the main offices; let me describe what we see...'

<hr>

They stopped before the entrance to a massive four-story office block; Mr Lee jumped out and opened the door for Jenifer; Dexter stepped out the other side and walked around to join them. When they went in, Mr Lee had to sign them in and obtain passes, then guided them to a large office on the top floor. Dexter did a quick count. All but the VP were there. Mr Lee took them around the U-shaped table and introduced them; then Dexter and Jenifer took their places in the middle of the U.

Brian Deever started the proceedings. It was clear to Dexter from his tone that he thought the meeting was a waste of time. 'Mr Lee has reported that you question the CamAir Three-Ten handbook instructions. What is this about?'

Dexter thought. *He's the type that must be polite to women.* 'Mr Deever, Captain Boscawen is best qualified to describe the matter. Bo, will you elaborate?'

Jenifer then shocked him. She launched into an attack. 'Before replying, I would like Mr Mancuni to answer a question.'

Henry Mancuni, Dexter estimated only about thirty-five years old, with an intellectual face and large spectacles, replied politely, 'Certainly, what is the question?'

'Does your CamAir sim allow an unbalanced fuel load to affect the displayed flight characteristics?'

'It doesn't need to; the auto fuel system manages the lateral balance.'

'Then your sim is incomplete. If you want me to demonstrate why we're here, we must do a thirty-minute flight in an aircraft.'

With veiled sarcasm, Jack Strang, the test pilot, asked, 'And what will you demonstrate, Captain.'

'Rate three turns with one engine out and a single engine landing in the same distance as you do with two.'

Dexter saw Mr Lee hiding a grin; he had difficulty doing the same when he looked at the expressions of disbelief around the table.

Strang finally managed to speak. 'Captain, we didn't come here to listen to wild claims.'

Before Jenifer could explode, support came unexpectedly from Henry Mancuni. 'Captain Boscawen. Did Captain Rawlins call you Bo?'

'Yes.'

'For Boad?'

'Correct. Have we met?'

'Yes, far from here.'

'Caroline, Gentlemen, Captain Boscawen can demonstrate what she says, and I must reprogram our simulator. Fortunately, I have a programming language at my disposal that I use. A programming language called Linky, developed for control systems by Captain Boscawen. It'll require Engineering to provide the data I need unless Captain Boscawen can provide it.'

'I can, but it will provide a cross-check if you do independent calculations.'

Silence fell.

Dexter was thinking. *Bo and Boad. That's something I must investigate.*

Then Jack Strang said, 'This I must see. I'll have the aircraft ready to start engines in an hour. What fuel configuration do you want?'

Jennifer didn't hesitate. 'The wing tanks half full and another six thousand pounds in the belly.'

'You'll have it. Will everyone please be there?'

After an excellent coffee, they climbed into a bus to the other side of the Phoenix-Mesa airport, where the aircraft stood ready.

Jack Strang asked. 'What is the flight plan?'

Jenifer replied, 'You take the left seat; I'll take the right. Take off and climb above fifteen thousand with balanced wing fuel until control allows manoeuvring. You can do one-eighty-degree turns right and left at least rate two. Then, cut one engine; I'll turn off the auto transfer and pump to fill the opposite wing. Then repeat the turns; you'll find you can go to rate three. Then, please return to the field and switch twenty-five miles from the touchdown with me. I'll do the landing without autopilot, and you'll operate gear and flaps when I call for them.'

'Roger.'

Strang said nothing until he stood up on the approach and said, 'She's yours.'

Jenifer disconnected the autopilot and landed as she had done at Ivato, except the touchdown speed at a quarter of Ivato's altitude was slower, and the reverse thrust and rudder were more effective. With a lighter aircraft, the aircraft slowed to walking speed quickly.

She turned off as instructed by the control tower and stopped when the marshal crossed his batons. When Jenifer exited the cockpit after Strang, Henry Mancuni started clapping, and the others followed.

As it died away, Strang said, 'Captain Boscawen, I apologise sincerely for my first outburst. It was rude, unjustified, and wrong. My only excuse is that I have never witnessed a landing like that or imagined it was possible. I don't need to tell anyone here that you have shown us how to make our aircraft much safer. People, we have work to do, *much* work to do, not only on the Three-Ten but all our aircraft.'

Brian Deever said, 'I, too, thank you both, but we must return to the office; the VP is due to make an appearance.'

Dexter knew the VP had received a briefing, for he said nothing about the test but did thank them both for coming and asked Dexter if he would collaborate on an update to the pilot's manual. Before he left, the VP had a private word with Henry Mancuni.

'Mr Mancuni, I hear you know Captain Boscawen.'

'Not know her, sir, but I know about her achievements. Three times the world gaming champion. Has designed an aircraft, created a new programming language and built advanced simulators.'

'Impressive. And Captain Rawlins?'

'Thirty-five years an airline Captain, over twenty-two thousand flying hours, the chief training captain for International Air, and has written the airline operating manual. I expect he's a senior part of Captain Boscawen's development team.'

'Is it big?'

'At a rough guess, she can call on several thousand experts.'

'*Very* impressive. Please invite the captains to visit our factory tomorrow on a VIP tour.'

Then the VP had a thought and added, 'Would they sign a non-disclosure agreement? In return for data required for her simulators.'

'I can ask, sir, but why?'

'If, without our help, she can discover things about our aircraft that we didn't know, imagine what she might uncover if we assist.'

Back at the hotel at 17:00, Dexter and Jenifer felt the effects of jet lag. It was one in the morning in London. 'Let's have a light supper and then sleep.'

'I agree, Dex; I'll sleep at the table if we wait.'

'The Halibut on this side of the states is reputed to be superb; I'll have a piece with fries.'

'Then I'll join you.'

'We aren't flying again. Will you have a glass of wine?'

'A California dry white would go well.'

After ordering, Dexter had the opportunity to ask about her nickname. 'At that meeting, Henry Mancuni asked if I had called you Bo, then asked: "for Boad." You said yes, but I thought it was short for Boscawen. Why "Boad".'

'I told you that explaining the metaverse would be difficult. Do you know what an avatar is?'

'I did, but now I'm not sure. I think it's an image of a person drawn by a computer, not photographed, so it is simpler.'

The fish dish arrived. 'This has a nice smell. I'll think of how best to explain while we eat.'...

'Have you seen the film Avatar?'

'The one with the blue people? Yes, the flying dragons are fantastic. The story is a classic cowboy one, but I didn't understand that bit about the guy who became a blue person or why it's called Avatar.'

'That's a start. The movie producers imagined the planet of the blue people. It could be anything; assume it's infinite, as imagination is infinite, and that, like that guy who laid down in a computer box and then became a blue person, anyone could do the same thing if they had such a box. Then all those blue people are avatars, computer-generated three-dimensional images, which, to make the film, they were. Holograms on a stage, but each would have a person in a box experiencing what the avatars do.'

'I can imagine that.'

'Now, as the movie house has no control over what real people do, the people can create any three-dimensional shape to represent them, like a lion, horse, dragon, or unicorn with wings.'

'I understand that, but what's the point?'

'Well, if someone wants to fly like a bird or dragon, something the avatar can do, then the person can experience the same views, feel the air, and hear the trill of a bird. Most metaverse visitors don't, but they all dream of being taller or stronger, thinner, bald men want a thick head of hair, women want big boobs, and they can make their avatar in the image of what they'd like to be. It's interesting because if I meet them in the metaverse, I can tell much more about their character than if I met the actual person.'

'I can understand that would happen. Like wearing your problems on your sleeve. What do you look like as an avatar?'

'I look like myself, that's easy, but I have different clothes. I used an image of the Warrior Queen, Boadicea, shortened; it becomes Boad; in real life, I like Bo.'

'Do you carry a shield and a spear and ride in a chariot?'

'If I need to, though not often.'

'Why?'

'It gave me the courage to face people. I knew I was right, but I couldn't have stood up to Jack Strang without it. When Henry said "for Boad", I felt like the Warrior Queen.'

'I still don't understand the metaverse, but I understand a bit more.'

I've learnt she wants to be strong and courageous, but underneath lies fear. That takes guts.

'I feel a terrible desire to go to bed with you.'

'Terrible desires need assuaging, let's go.'

They reached their room. Dexter began undressing, and Jenifer entered the bathroom. Dexter had only removed one shoe when the hotel phone rang. Jenifer reappeared without a skirt when she heard the phone.

'Rawlins, good evening.' As the phone had a speaker button, he pressed it and continued undressing.

'Henry Mancuni, Captain. I've organised a VIP tour of the assembly buildings if you can stay for the day tomorrow. I would also like to talk to you about simulators.'

Dexter looked up from his shoes at Jenifer and asked, 'Are you okay to stay an extra day?'

She gave him a thumbs up, so Dexter said, 'Henry, that's great. Friday morning, we'll be bright and fresh. Can you arrange to meet us then to discuss simulators?'

'I can, Captain. I'll collect you for the tour at nine tomorrow.'

Dexter rang off and said, 'I like your new uniform. You should wear it more often.'

Jenifer looked down, 'These old rags? I must get something more attractive if I do that.'

'It's what's in them that counts.'

Jenifer had a reply, 'Do you wear boxers or jocks? I'll bet jocks.'

'You lose.'

'Take off your pants and prove it. Then we're square.'

Dexter did, and Jenifer laughed. 'Those are almost as bad as jocks; they have biplanes flying around them.'

Dexter grinned, 'If you can find something better, go ahead; at least I avoided the ones with party balloons. Stay there if you want to see me without them; I'm about to put on my pyjamas.'

Jenifer vanished into the bathroom. When she came out in pyjamas and sat on the bed, Dexter went in and brushed his teeth. When he came out, she was in bed.

He slipped between the sheets, and she said, 'Turn out the light, then kiss me. You know, you're a fun guy.'

'Somehow, you stimulate something in me that I didn't know I had.'

DAY 35
THURSDAY

At the CamAirCom head office, the VP spoke to the president. He agreed to contract Dexter and Jenifer as Aviation Consultants.

At 09:00, Henry Mancuni was in the reception with a smartly uniformed young woman. When Dexter and Jenifer approached them, he introduced her as Ylang, one of the CamAirCom public relations guides. 'Would you mind signing these non-disclosure agreements? Then we can answer any questions you have freely.'

Jenifer asked, 'Why? Will you be telling us secrets?'

Henry didn't need to answer; Dexter, who knew Jenifer had never had an employment contract, replied. 'Company employees have contracts saying they must not divulge the employer's secrets. The NDA protects them from punishment if we reveal anything they tell us. We'll sign, Henry.'

Ylang soon proved she had an in-depth knowledge of the site and the activities.

'I'm sure you know we produce five different-sized aircraft and that the Three-Ten is the biggest and the latest in our product line. When CamAirCom decided to move here, they picked the site for several reasons: one was the runway, and the other because of the unused farmland adjoining the airport. Every building you see here is new, and although CamAirCom built the assembly hangars in sequence, their architects planned the entire site and the services before any construction began. I must emphasise this is the final assembly stage, where we fit thousands of items that don't individually need an aeroplane-sized hangar into the full-size plane. The parts come from all over the world.'

Dexter asked, 'Do you paint the planes here?'

'That's up to the client. We don't do the interiors but may do a basic colour like white, and then the client will take it to a company that does the rest.'

Jenifer was keen to learn something different. 'Where are your simulators, and what do you use them for?'

'In the public area on the other side of the airport, although they're in a restricted building. We must check out the client's aircrews when they come to collect a plane. The plane is ours until the wheels leave the ground, and our insurance insists on a check if one of our pilots is not in command. Our test pilots use them as well.'

Ylang took them to each of the five assembly buildings. In the last, looking down from a viewing station at the aircraft in assembly below, Jenifer exclaimed. 'It's almost impossible to believe how big this building is; the planes look like toys!'

Ylang replied, 'You're not the first to make that remark, but the biggest wonder is invisible.

'Every part that the assembly teams install has a certificate, and they must arrive from the stores on time, and the assemblers must record the installation. Most employees here engage in what we call track and trace.'

Dexter asked, 'I haven't seen any fatigue testing rigs; where are they?'

'At a different site, a disused airport further south, away from habitation. I don't know much about them, but they're huge, in the open, run continuously, and are noisy. There's a control building, shift workers, and a bunch of reliability engineers who visit.'

The receptionist handed Dexter a note when they returned to the hotel after their tour. It asked him to call a number.

Once in their room, he did.

'Good afternoon, Captain Rawlins here; I've received a request to call this number.'

'Thank you for calling, Captain; I'm the chief contracts accountant. I understand that the CamAir Three-Ten VP has asked you to collaborate on a manual rewrite; is that correct.'

'It is.'

'Then can you provide me with your company name, details, and a payment bank account?'

'I can. SMS me an email address, and I'll do so once I'm back in London and can look up my files. The company is Dexter Aviation, registered in the Isle of Man between thirty-six and thirty-seven years ago.'

'Thank you, I can look it up. Then you only need to send the bank account details.'

●●●

'You haven't mentioned Dexter Aviation; I thought you were a Captain with International Air.'

'I am. When I learnt to fly, like you, I needed hours, so I took any flying job I could get, and on my dad's advice, I registered a company and invoiced all my flying jobs as Dexter Aviation. The company almost died when I joined International Air. I used it if one of my earlier contacts asked me to do a flight for them during my holidays, so it stayed alive. Then, when my son began flying, it became his company. He did many contract flights. Since his crash, I've kept it alive in his memory, renting a single-engine plane for a joyride once or twice a year.

'I don't know what CamAirCom will pay, but it's mostly yours, so when they pay, you must tell me what to do with the money.'

'I told you I don't need money, so leave it in your company until we know what the future will bring.'

'I will, but I've already given up all hope of knowing the future. With you, anything can happen.'

'That makes life interesting. Let's see what other kinds of fish they fry for dinner.'

Day 36
Friday

Henry came after breakfast to discuss simulators; Dexter listened but understood only a part of their conversation. However, one thing was crystal clear. *Henry is a highly qualified engineer and treats Jenifer with sincere respect as an equal.*

Jack Strang met them before they left the hotel. He had a question, 'Captain Boscawen, would you have any objection to us using your name in our training and flight manuals? We'll describe the Boscawen technique for single-engine landings.'

'Will you make me famous?'

'No, I suspect that you'll achieve that without our help. But your name will go in the aviation history books.'

'Then go ahead.'

After Strang left, Dexter and Jenifer collected their suitcases.

Dexter asked in the limousine to the helicopter, 'How do you feel about seeing your name in the flight manuals?'

'Maybe I'll need to remember I'm Boad sometimes, but maybe not as often.'

Then she thought. *And I've done it all myself!*

The helicopter took them back to Phoenix International, and they boarded their return flight at 19:30.

'We arrive after lunch. Shall we leave immediately?'

'Where to?'

'I must be back at Gatwick on Monday, so we don't have time for

Dartmoor. Either your house or the weekend at a country club.'

'Then, at my house, I have work to do for Henry so he can modify his sim for unbalanced fuel.'

DAY 37
SATURDAY

———

Dexter parked behind Jenifer's place just after 17:00.

'Dex, take the bags upstairs, unpack whatever you want. I'll make coffee and look at what we have for supper. I can unpack later.'

'How about going out? We'll be late to bed for a day or two until we make up the jet lag.'

'Then take me to Coombe Abbey; it's swanky, so we must dress. Try to book a table for eight o'clock. It's a twelve-kilometre drive. Dad took me there once for afternoon cream tea.'

•••

'We have a booking.'

Jennifer wore a black dress and a diamond necklace. When Dexter came from the bathroom and saw her, he couldn't speak. When he did, he croaked, 'How can you become more beautiful every day?'

'If you think I am, that's all I need to know, but perhaps beauty grows with happiness, and I feel happier every day since we met.'

Day 38
Sunday

When Dexter woke, he murmured, 'Should we get up?'

'Not until I'm hungry.'

'How long is that likely to be.'

'Ages, at least until you kiss me, and I must escape from your clutches.'

'Then I won't clutch, but you did promise to tell me about sex in the metaverse.'

'I did, so take your arm away and move to the other side of the bed. I might need to escape in a hurry.

'Do you know anything about the dildos and rubber vaginas the sex shops sell?'

'Who doesn't? If you type anything the least suggestive into a search engine, a flood of adverts on the screen is the result. I once typed "Pergola erection costs", and it was months before they stopped swamping every site I viewed.'

Jenifer hooted with laughter. 'Well, if you do some investigation, you'll find there are all types, and some are sophisticated with built-in mechanisms that make a dildo move or a vagina twist and squeeze.'

'I can imagine that, but that's not what you suggested.'

'Well, there are a few sex shops on the dark web where you can buy top-of-the-range devices with receivers that can activate the mechanical movements and have sensors that can transmit a user's movements.'

'I have a problem imagining how it works.'

'Then imagine this. A man puts his penis in the artificial vagina and then moves his penis. The sensors in the vagina transmit this movement through the metaverse connection to a dildo that mimics that movement and vice versa. Now, add that the man is wearing a metaverse helmet with a 3D view of a beautiful naked avatar woman, and she has a view of a handsome naked man. They can hear the sounds made by each other, and they can feel the pressure and sensation of the lips of the other generated by the helmet.'

'And it works? The two reach orgasms?'

'That's not new. For years, men could masturbate while watching a pornographic video of naked women, and women could wobble a dildo around while watching a video made for women. What I described is just a technological advancement. The problem is that the exaggerated avatars become a drug for many people, the female avatar has big boobs, and the man stops making love to his flat-chested wife in favour of the big boobs, or the male avatar has huge muscles and an enormous penis, and a wife stops responding to her husband.'

'Are there many who are into this?'

'Thousands; if I bought one of those dildos and logged on, within a day, I would have thousands of proposals for sex, and I could look at videos of the male avatar to choose one.'

'Somehow, that sounds like a danger to civilization.'

'It may be the saviour. The birthrate drops, but it will be a drop in a bucket.'

'Now, come back here, kiss me, and we'll go downstairs for breakfast.'

Is Dex becoming frustrated? I wish I knew how to tell.

⚯

'I like having Sunday breakfast with you; you do those potato cakes just right.'

'Me too. When must you return to Gatwick?'

'Tomorrow. Our trip to Phoenix was work, and I haven't booked any leave, so it's back to work tomorrow unless I take a week's leave and we go to Mauritius.'

I don't want Dex to leave; the house will be empty without him. It never frightened me before; am I afraid he won't return? I must decide.

'Can you get seats to Mauritius?'

'I can call and ask.' *Is she looking for an excuse?*

'Then call. For any day this week.'

•••

'We have seats tomorrow. The reservations office will give us returns twelve hours before the return flight.'

'So, when do we go to Gatwick?'

'Tonight, then tomorrow morning, I can book my leave, clear my inbox, and we can leave. Let's book a hotel in Mauritius; then I'll confirm the seats. And then a hotel at Gatwick.'

'Okay, I must try to call my mother's boyfriend to arrange a grave visit, at least to find out where her grave is.'

'There are hotels all around the island. Have you any idea where it might be best to go.'

'The last time we tried to go to Mauritius, I booked in the north, near Grand Bay, but after reading about the island, the Southwest is a better choice for a short stay. That's where they have dolphins and a kite surfing spot not far away.'

'Have you kite surfed?'

'No, but I want to try.'

'So, what hotel?'

'Try the Sugar Beach in Flic en Flac.'

DAY 39
MONDAY

'Y ou can lie in, take the hotel bus at noon and meet me at check-in. I'll have breakfast, take my bag and leave our car at the terminal.'

In the first-class lounge, one of the Television screens showed CNN. 'Dex, look at the TV.'

Dexter looked, 'What is it, there's no sound?'

'They keep the sound down. An airliner has crashed. I think it must be in South-East Asia.

'Yes, there. Read the line at the bottom, CamAirCom Two-Thirty missing.'

'You'll find more on your telephone. Have a look.'

'It's one of the latest CamAirCom airliners – two hundred and thirty-one passengers and crew – the reporter says it must have crashed into the sea only minutes after take-off at night – it disappeared from radar – no distress call.'

'Then everyone on board will be dead. It may be months before we know what caused it.'

'Why so long?'

'If they find the flight recorders quickly, they might identify what caused it. If the recorders don't show anything, they must collect every piece of debris from the sea floor, reassemble the aircraft, and find what failed. If you had a simulator of the two-thirty, we could play and try to find out.'

'Well, I don't, and we're visiting Mauritius, so let's forget about it.'

'Then we must avoid watching the TV in bed.' Dexter grinned, 'I can think of better things to do.'

Day 40
Tuesday

'An advantage of overnight flights that arrive early is that we have the entire day ahead of us. What would you like to do?'

'First, get the limo to the hotel; I want a shower, then a swim in the sea and a change from uniform to casual.'

Dexter grinned. 'How casual? Did you bring your Tanga?'

'Naturally, but I'll make you wait to see me wearing it.

'After that, we can decide on lunch. I arranged with Shrivarah, Mum's boyfriend, to meet him at the Moka cemetery entrance at 15:00.'

Dexter didn't notice the hotel receptionist press a button below the desktop, but the manager was there to greet them less than a minute later. Dexter noted the name on his jacket.

Mr Rajeev smiled warily, 'Good morning, Captain, or rather Captain's. I'm the day manager. You didn't warn us that you were aircrew, so we didn't tell you we don't offer aircrew discounts. In Mauritius, only the hotels near the airport do so.'

'Mr Rajeev, we aren't on duty; we've come for a holiday, so please ignore the uniforms, we don't expect a discount.'

The smile became broader and more welcoming. 'Then welcome to the Sugar Beach; I'm sure you'll enjoy your stay.' He turned to the receptionist, 'Is 2101 available?'

'Yes, Sir.'

'Then, allocate it to them.' He turned back to Dexter. 'I can't offer you a discount, but I can upgrade your room. Please do not hesitate to ask your butler for anything needed.'

'Thank you very much, Mr Rajeev.'

'Wow, this is fantastic, our feet almost in the sea and a private swimming pool.'

'It's much more than I expected.'

As they stepped from the golf buggy and the hotel porter unloaded their bags, a smartly dressed man came down the steps to meet them. 'Good morning, sir, I'm Rajat, your butler. Welcome to the presidential suite. Anything you require, please ask.'

Jenifer replied, 'Good morning, Rajat; thank you for your welcome. I would appreciate a cup of tea. Dex, you too?'

Dexter had just given a tip to the porter, who drove off. 'Yes, please. Tea would be great.'

'I shall bring a tray to the veranda.'

•••

Although Jenifer had to attach her bikini top, she was faster than Dexter, and less than two minutes later, they were in the warm sea.

'This is heaven.'

'I agree. I'll race you to the buoy out there.'

He beat her there, then let her win the return heat.

'You cheated, you let me win.'

Dexter wrapped his arms around her. 'No, I enjoyed watching you from behind...this one.'

'The tea's on the veranda.'

•••

'Shall I pour, ma'am?'

'Please, Rajat. We'll laze around this morning and have lunch wherever you recommend. Then we must be at the Moka cemetery at three o'clock this afternoon. We must get a big bunch of flowers to place on a grave; a taxi could take us to get the flowers on the way there, and then it must wait there to bring us back. Can you arrange it?'

'Certainly, ma'am, I shall reserve a table for you at the Buddha Bar restaurant for twelve-thirty and have a taxi waiting at one forty-five. Traffic is slow on the island, and you'll need time for the flowers.'

'We noticed on the way from the airport. Thank you, Rajat.'

Jenifer had never met Shrivarah, but the moment she saw the man beside the cemetery entrance, she knew it must be him; he was as her mother had once described him. Tall and very spare, with a mop of long, unruly greying hair and a beard, wearing Indian clothing. It was the flowers in his hair that convinced her.

'Are you Shrivarah?'

'I am, and you're Beth's daughter; you look like she did when I met her.'

'I'm sorry I didn't manage to come for her funeral. I had an anxiety attack before boarding the flight.' She indicated Dexter, who held the bouquet, 'Captain Rawlins of the airline rescued me from being carried off to the hospital.

'What caused my mother's death?'

'It was a sudden and devastating stroke. Beth died at sea; we had gone to dive with the dolphins. She loved doing it because she loved the dolphins, but this time, she dived and didn't resurface. There had to be an autopsy. I should have noticed that she'd become less stable over the previous two years, often dreaming for prolonged periods. The doctor said there were signs of brain deterioration over many years.'

'Please, we can't bring her back. Can you show me her grave?'

'Come this way.'

•••

Jenifer was surprised to see the grave had a cross and a small statue of Parvati; she recognised it, for her mother had kept the Hindu goddess statue in the house when she was a child.

Dexter handed her the flowers and stepped back well out of the way; Shrivarah said a quiet prayer, then silently joined him, watching Jenifer. Dexter couldn't hear what she said, although he could see her lips moving, for she whispered as she placed the flowers in little bunches so they would cover the grave.

'Mum, you loved me and left me with Dad to spare me from pain. I wish we had met again, but I'll tell you something I will believe all my life. Your death brought me the man I'm learning to love, so I can't help thinking you died for me. Thanks, Mum. I'm also sure you aren't here in this grave, although you may visit occasionally. I believe you stayed with the dolphins you loved, and I know they love you as the ponies love me. I shall remember you with love, Mum, and when I speak to Dad the next time, I'll tell him, for he loved you too.'

With eyes full of tears, Jenifer turned away from the grave and stepped into Dexter's waiting arms. They stood for a long time until Jenifer took a deep breath, opened her bag and extracted a tissue to dry her eyes. Then, with Dexter's arm around her and Shrivarah on the other side, they walked to the gate.

'Shrivarah, thank you for looking after my mother all these years. I know she loved you.'

'Thank you, Jenifer. There are two things I decided not to tell you, but I think now your mother would like me to. The first is that we married before we came to live in Mauritius. The second is that after the autopsy, I asked the doctor if my stepdaughter might suffer from the same degeneration. He didn't want to give me an opinion, but as I left his office, he relented, saying, "I have seen the same degeneration in the brains of several cases of suicide. In every case, not due to an illness or genetic disorder, but from taking dangerous drugs when young."'

'Jenifer, you don't need to worry. Let me leave you with Lord Brahma's blessing, and if you return to Mauritius, please call me.'

They returned to the hotel. Dexter spoke to Rajat, and that evening, the hotel served a quiet dinner for two on the sand in front of their room. Dexter also ordered morning coffee at 08:00. Due to the time difference, they walked for three hours along the sandy beach and back, holding hands but lost in thought without speaking.

Jenifer was thinking. *Dex said he would take me to put flowers on my mother's grave, and he's done this. I'm sure he wants to stay with me. I want him to stay, but I don't know if that will last. I must persuade him to stay with me.*

Dexter's thoughts differed. *We must come back when we have no worries and nothing to do. This afternoon must have been hard on Bo. We must go before the sadness in her grows.*

Day 41
Wednesday

———

They heard Rajat when he brought coffee to the veranda at eight.
'Shall I fetch two cups?'

'No, let's put on the dressing gowns and sit on the veranda to look at the sea.'

Cup in hand, after a mouthful of coffee, Dexter asked, 'Tell me, what do you want to do today?'

'Go kite surfing, Dex.'

'Ok, let's ask Rajat how to do that; press the call button.'

Rajat appeared in two minutes. 'Rajat, we want to try kite surfing. How do we do that?'

'Do you have equipment, sir?'

'No, I thought a school might supply that.'

'Not the clothing, sir. Harnesses rub on bare skin, and the water can hurt when falling at speed, so partial wet suits are necessary. A taxi can take you to Le Morne, where the surfing schools are, and it can stop halfway at La Gaulette, where there are surfing shops. They will sell you the necessary gear.

'A warning, sir: never leave phones, watches or wallets on the beach. Please put them in the safe here or give them to the school for safekeeping. You could buy waterproof pouches and carry them.

'I suggest you leave by ten; it will take an hour at least to shop and reach the schools. An adequate supply of sunscreen is also necessary.'

'Ten is fine, Rajat; we'll swim then go for breakfast.'

Rajat left, and they changed into costumes. 'Bo, we'll put everything in the room safe except a credit card and cash; I'll buy a waterproof pouch for them.'

'How do I look?'

'Lovely from the front, turn around...'

'Can I take a photo?'

Jenifer turned back. 'Why?'

'I just saw a beautiful backside; a Tanga suits you. Now I know what you'll look like from behind when you're naked!'

'Into the sea, lecher, I'll drown you.'
I wore it! I did, and I didn't freak out!

They reached the broad bay south of the island at eleven and chose one of the two surfing schools housed in caravans extended by poles and canvas. The taxi driver said he would return after four hours. Half an hour later, dressed in wetsuits and wearing rubber surfing shoes, an instructor gave them their first lessons on the narrow beach. Dexter felt slightly foolish, for the instructor was almost young enough to be Jenifer's son. However, he was professional.

'Kite surfing is all about flying your kite, better called a wing. So, I'll teach you how to manage it for an hour. There is a second instructor who will join us in an hour. Then we can try getting up in shallow water and follow on from there.'

Dexter was surprised at how easy it was to fly the wing; he and Bo understood how it worked and had a pilot's natural sensitivity to its reactions. Bo thought it was like flying Slinky. At first, it was challenging to remember which line controlled what, but soon, they mastered the technique in the steady breeze blowing off the sea.

After a quick Mauritian lunch bought from a caravan vendor, a bowl of fried noodles mixed with shredded vegetables and chicken called *Mines Frites*, they moved on to the next phase.

When the taxi arrived, the driver could see them riding back and forth parallel to the beach, enjoying themselves. Bo, trying to zigzag at speed, fell frequently, laughing every time. Dexter was trying to U-turn without crashing and finally managed it twice. When they packed up, the instructor said, 'You're both excellent; pilots must find it easy to kite surf. You must send us more pilots. I hope to see you again.'

Jennifer announced in their room, 'I'll sunbathe until dusk.'

'I'll join you, but first, I must fetch my phone and check for a call about a return flight...

'I have a message. There are two seats tomorrow morning, and the next ones available are Monday morning.'

Jenifer was about to say book Monday when she had a thought. *Does Dex want to stay?*

'Do you want to stay?'

'Very much, but if we leave, we must plan a return; there's much to see here. Looking through the brochures, we could spend a month at least; I'd like to rent a place and a car.'

'How much leave did you take?'

'A week. The office expects me back on Monday.'

'Then block those seats, Dex, if they're still available.'

'Right, I'll call.'

'International Air Mauritius, good afternoon.'

'Good afternoon, Captain Rawlins here; I received an SMS saying two seats are available for us on tomorrow's flight.'

'Let me check, Captain.'

'I'm sorry, Captain, not tomorrow, but Friday. A couple with a problem asked to go a day earlier. Would that suit you?'

'It does; please block them for us. Thank you.'

'Done, Captain, a pleasure, goodbye.'

'Bo, we now leave Friday.'

'That gives us some breathing space, we'll ask Rajat what to do. If we can, I'd like to see the dolphins. We'll be stiff tomorrow after the kite surfing; can you reserve a massage at the spa? We must get out of the sun before five.'

'Turn over, the Tanga covers less of your bum than a bikini, and you'll have sore red patches soon; they're already pink.'

Is he letching over my backside or looking after me? Funny, it doesn't matter; I like both thoughts.

Lying on adjoining massage tables while the massage therapists worked hard to relax muscles, Dexter asked, 'Are you okay with Rajat's proposal? It will mean we're in a crowd of strangers on the boat and at the beach lunch. We won't be wearing bars. I can hire a private boat if you wish.'

'I must learn if I can support a crowd. I expect people will introduce themselves; it might help if you say I'm your wife, then they'll know I'm not alone.'

'I will, and I hope we can continue like that forever.'

'I'll learn how I feel.'

The massage therapists asked them to turn over, and then Dexter asked, 'Does visiting where your mother died upset you?'

'No, it will be like visiting her grave; if her spirit is still around, it will be with the Dolphins. I'll pray for her.'

DAY 42
THURSDAY

The day was uneventful. The boat took them to swim with the dolphins.

When Jenifer dived into the sea to swim with the Dolphins, Dexter was beside her, and only once, when she remained motionless underwater, did he worry, but then she shot up and left him behind. *She was praying for her mother.*

After the Dolphins left them, they motored to Le Benitier Island, where they swam, and then they and the other tourists enjoyed a wood-fired beach barbecue of prawns. Dexter introduced Bo several times as his wife Jenifer and sensed her relaxing as the day passed.

Jenifer found it strange being Mrs Rawlins, but after five or six introductions, she'd become so used to it that when a strange woman asked, 'Is that handsome man your husband?' She felt pleasure in replying, 'He is, ma'am.'

After returning to the hotel, a taxi took them to the top of the nearby mountain at Chamerel to admire the view, then to the tourist attraction where seven distinct colours of volcanic sand were on show, culminating in a visit to an artisanal rum distillery.

'Dex, that was a marvellous day. Can you ask Rajat to bring two tiny glasses of that delicious *Rhum Arrangé*? The vanilla and pineapple one. Just sipping it at sunset will be ecstatic. Then we can go to Le Patio for dinner; they have a buffet of Mauritian dishes.'

***

'Would you like to finish the day in style? There's a Sega dancing display on the beach, and we can try dancing. It's a traditional Mauritian dance.'

DAY 43
FRIDAY

Their flight to London landed at 17:00.

Jenifer checked her emails. She couldn't access her metabox because she didn't have the equipment, but she did have an email. It came from someone she didn't know; the address was charioteer@gmail.com.

> Hi Jenifer,
> I hope we can get together for a ride soon. Very soon.
> Bye.

Jenifer put two and two together. It had to be Henry Mancuni. He drove 'Chariots'. There would be something in her metabox, and she bet herself that the email address would no longer exist if she replied.

'I suspect Henry Mancuni has sent something to my metabox, so I'd like to return home as soon as possible.'

'Then we'll leave for Coventry once we collect our bags.'

Jenifer was thrilled. *We have something to do together; Dex won't leave me.*

Dexter turned into Jenifer's driveway two hours later and continued around the back. 'I'll take our bags in; you fire up your system and find out what's worrying Henry.'

Dexter brought everything in, took their bags to the bedroom, and made coffee. When he took a cup to Jenifer, he found her looking at rows of data scrolling across the giant screen.

'What are those numbers?'

'The FDR data from the crash in Asia. I also have the cockpit voice recording.'

'Can you play it?'

'Yes, but I'm scared to.'

'Play it in the lounge. I'll sit in one of the big chairs, and you can sit on my lap. If it frightens you, block your ears with your fingers, and I'll hug you.'

The recording started with the words from a radio call, 'Permission to start engines.'

For the next nine minutes, the routine sounds, radio calls, and voices of the pilots and copilot while the aircraft took off and began to climb under full power, retracted the wheels, and Dexter and Jenifer assumed, raised the flaps. Then all hell broke loose, with terrified voices, shouts of horror and the screams of passengers loud enough to hear as a background to the cockpit recording. It lasted less than fifty seconds, and then the recording cut abruptly to a silent hiss...

Dexter had an agonizing knot in his stomach, and his chest hurt; he realised he was holding Jenifer so tightly it hurt them both, so he released her. She began to shake, so he tightened his hold, but not as tightly. Her arms were around him, her head buried against his chest, her hair filled his nostrils and blocked his sight, but he bent his head down and kissed her gently on the forehead, once, twice, three times. Her shaking stopped.

To Dexter, it seemed ages, but it was less than five minutes before Jenifer gave a sigh and whispered. 'That was horrible. That wasn't a computer game. They were real people.'

'Yes, I had a painful stomach cramp. For a moment, I felt I might crap in my pants.'

'Kiss me again, Dex.'

He did, and then she sighed. 'I could stay like this all night, but I must ask Henry for help.'

'Then ask. I'll make supper for us, and then we can go to bed.'

The message Jenifer sent to the charioteer's metabox was a URL to a file with three lines of text.

> FDR decoder for type.
> Must rebuild/program sim for tests.
> Inputs calibration.

The reply, a fourth line added to the file, came in seconds.

Est 8h+.

Jenifer shut down and went to the kitchen, 'We have eight hours or more before we have the first lot of data.'

Dexter asked, 'Why did Henry send that to you?'

'I don't know; I'm sure that was data from the plane we read about last Monday. CNN announced they had found the black boxes.'

'I agree, but why send it to us?'

'Your guess is as good as mine. That CNN program said salvage operations had begun. You said the experts would collect everything, lay the parts out in a hangar and try to find what parts broke. They think something must have broken. Like the tail falling off.'

'But Henry must be worried about something. What could it be?'

'It's a new plane, Dex, and a new model. On old ones, the maintenance guys may have changed a part for the incorrect one. Henry might be worried that there's a flaw in the design, and another one will crash.'

'But why send it to you?'

'Dex, do you think the designers will accept that they've made a mistake? I don't. Remember the attitudes of Brian Deever and Jack Strang when we first met them? They were ready to deny any fault. I'll bet that no one has suggested that a test pilot fly their simulator until something breaks.'

'Could they do that, Bo?'

'They could, but I don't know if their simulator includes the necessary programs; I have used mine to design aircraft, and I expect theirs only flies the way it should so they can train pilots and check the cockpit layouts. Simulators all have stops to prevent a pilot from breaking it. They cost too much to allow a careless pilot to crash it.

'Henry might be on the sidelines and hopes we can crash the sim using the FDR data as a guide and then tell him what will break before the next accident – if there is one. Let's go to bed now, and I can get up early to start the download.'

DAY 44
SATURDAY

When Dexter woke, Jenifer was not beside him. He rose and went to the bathroom, but she wasn't there either, so he went downstairs and found her, still in pyjamas, in front of the big screen in the lounge.

'Good morning. When did you wake up?'

'About half an hour ago, I had to start the download running. It will take two or three hours, then the rest of the day, to decompress and verify.'

'And you haven't had a coffee?'

'No, you haven't put on slippers or socks; you'll catch a cold barefoot. Go and put some socks on, two pairs. I don't have any man-size slippers. Then you can make our coffee.'

Ten minutes later, Dexter came back with two mugs of coffee. 'What data are you getting?'

'The first is the FDR decode data. He sent numbers yesterday; my decoder can understand most of them. They're standard codes, but some are specific to the aircraft type. Once I load the type codes into my decoder, you can directly read altitude, speed, and other things with each time tick.

'For example, the decoder changes the number pair 18739-45781 into "Undercarriage switch up at 4578.1 seconds from the start of recording, or one hour sixteen minutes and 18.1 seconds."'

'And then?'

'You can match the voice recording ticks to the FDR, then you can hear the instruction "Gear up" and how long it takes for the copilot to select gear up. You might notice if anything happened without verbal instructions.'

'Does "you" mean "me"?'

'Yes, I'm also getting calibration data for the simulator inputs, so I must recalibrate all my sim's sliding controls, like throttles. Then, I must install the plugins for this aircraft so I have a simulator that works. I must program a test run as well.'

'How long will that take?'

'Probably until Tuesday before we can fly the sim. Today is download day, so most of today is waiting. Tomorrow and Monday installation and testing.'

'Right, I'll make breakfast. Do you fancy bacon and eggs?'

'Please.'

'Then afterwards, will we have time to talk?'

'All day, I must occasionally check that it's still running.'

…

'That was lovely; you make a mean fried egg. Far better than me. You don't burn the toast, either. I'll check on the download and help clear up.'

'Jenifer, it's all done; I'll make another coffee, then we can sit in the lounge to drink it.'

'What do you want to talk about?'

'Us, Bo. I said I would take you to validate your licence and put flowers on your mother's grave. The engine failure and the Phoenix enquiry diverted us, but we have now put the flowers on her grave. I want to know if I must gallop into the sunset.'

His words were a shock, like a cold shower had turned on. Jenifer asked herself, *why?* Then she thought, *at least I can tell him not to ride away.*

'When you said that, it gave me cold shivers. I don't want you to leave me; I'm no longer alone with you beside me.'

Then Jenifer thought, *that sounds weak and selfish; I must explain.*

'It's not just that, with you beside me, I learn more about myself daily. I've spent years avoiding relationships and have no references to judge how I feel about you, except that I don't want you to leave me; I hope to learn enough to say that I want you to stay forever or that my life will be with someone else, but right now, please stay with me and help me learn. I know you'll think I'm selfish, but I need you.'

'Please, I don't want to leave; my greatest wish is to be with you forever.'

'Then do what you want to do, Dex. I can't make you stay without saying something dishonest, and I can't do that, but I can say it hurts to think of you leaving, but I don't honestly know why.'

'I'm staying, subject closed.'

'I must check again on the downloads.'

'Will you be alright while I do some shopping? We'll be here at least until Wednesday.'

'Yes, buy some fresh salad, vegetables and fruit; I'll make salads for us.'

⁂

When he returned, Dexter carried several bags into the kitchen, and Jenifer came to help him store everything. 'You're good at this; you have everything we need. Why did you buy salt?'

'I checked; Bo, there's only a little left.'

Jenifer chuckled, 'You might have been married once, but you've forgotten; you should have looked in the tin labelled flour.'

Dexter grinned, 'I did, and there's only a little left!'

'Remind me later, you've earned a hug.

'Now I must go and check again. The download and decompression are almost complete, and I need to decrypt and verify.'

'I'll prepare jacket potatoes and cream. I have some haddock and peas as well for tonight.'

'You'll spoil me; that's far better than a reheated Pizza.'

'Come and eat. I bought white wine. Will you have a glass?'

'While we try to sort out this problem, no, but tonight, yes.'

Dexter poured and served the poached haddock, jacket potatoes and peas, and they sat to eat.

'Do you have everything you need?'

'I think so.'

'Do you have the pilot's manual and the load data for the flight, the one the pilot signs?'

'Thanks, you're not just a pretty face; I'll ask for it.'

'Would you like a little dessert?'

Jenifer smiled, 'What have you prepared? Are you trying to earn another hug?'

'That's for sure. I have a surprise. Don't look.'

Dexter went to the fridge and returned with two small plates. 'Now look.'

'Cassata! That's worth another hug.'

'I've asked for all that information and data. It's early morning there. We can expect it tomorrow morning. It's huggy time!'

They both showered and changed into clean pyjamas, then

climbed into bed feeling happy with a touch of excitement and anticipation.

Jenifer turned to him and said, 'The salt hug first, Dex; hold me again.'

Dexter wrapped his arms around her, and she said, 'Now kiss me.'

He kissed her on the forehead as he'd done when they watched the voice recording. Then Jenifer pushed herself up until their eyes were level and said, 'Now kiss me properly, Dex. I want to know what it feels like.'

It lasted a minute, then she said, 'Now it's the Cassata hug,' and rolled on top of him.

It lasted a lot longer, and Dex felt the stirring of an erection. 'If we go on, we may go too far.'

'You mean sex?'

'Yes.'

'What do you mean too far?'

'There are two kinds of sex. One is casual, with no commitment or love, only a brief encounter with physical pleasure. Men may refer rudely to it as "Bam, bam, thank you, mam." The other is when it means something, like a commitment. I'm sure that if I make love to you, it's more than sex. I'll be saying that I want us to stay together forever, and if you don't mean the same thing, it's more likely to force us apart, so we must be honest with ourselves and avoid making love until we're both sure.'

'Are you sure?'

'Yes, are you?'

She didn't answer for a minute, 'No, Dex, I'm not sure. It may be because I've never loved anyone like that or had the experience of sex.'

'Then kiss me again if you wish, and let's sleep; you'll know when you are sure.'

Day 45
Sunday

Jenifer woke, remembered last night, smiled and turned to look at Dexter beside her. She leaned forward and kissed him. As she drew back, without opening his eyes, he said, 'Now you've done it, my darling.'

Puzzled, she asked, 'Done what?'

'Tripped my D switch.'

She grinned. 'Destruct switch?'

'Darling switch. From now on, you're now "my darling"; I'm programmed that way. If a gorgeous woman in pyjamas kisses me in bed in the morning, it trips my switch, and there's no way I can turn it off.'

Jenifer leaned forward again and kissed him, this time longer. 'And that doesn't turn it off?'

'Nope, no hope. It might work after a hundred and one tries without anything more.'

Jenifer's grin had grown. 'I must start counting. Is that one or two?'

'One.'

'I'll wash; I have work to do, and you have coffee then breakfast to make.'

'Coffee coming up, my darling.'

Jenifer went to the bathroom, chuckling; *if he goes on like this, it'll be sex coming up, my darling.*

'Here's your coffee, how are you doing?'

'It would be better with a few "my darlings". Where did they go to?'

'That's an odd thing; once out of the bedroom, they become random, and without morning reinforcement, they eventually disappear, although they can be shocked back into line by all sorts of things.'

Jenifer grinned, 'What things?' *I'm sure this will be interesting.*

'Like walking around in lace underwear!'

'Oh, that kind of thing. I'll suffer the randomness, but I'll try to remember the morning reinforcement. If I'm desperate, I'll leave off my underwear.'

'Breakfast in an hour, my darling.'

'What brought on that "my darling"?'

'The thought of you with no underwear.'

Jenifer was still laughing as Dexter went to the kitchen – smiling.

⎯⎯◦⎯⎯

'Breakfast is ready, my darling.'

'Just ten minutes more, then the first install program will run.'

...

'I could become used to you making breakfast.'

'I like making breakfast because there's two of us. I might become fat from overeating. I'm lazy alone; it's just coffee and a pastry.'

'Then I'll insist on salads at lunch.'

'What are you installing?'

'The simulator core program. It'll take an hour, so after breakfast, I'll set you up with a terminal in your room and run the FDR decoder.'

'My room?'

'Yes, I've finally accepted that my dad has gone. It's your room now, does that worry you.'

'No, it makes me happy.'

'Another cup of coffee, then I'll return to work.'

'Here's your terminal; I've loaded the program to look at the decoded FDR data and the voice recording. Click the *run* button, and both will run together; if they are out of sync, click *stop* and adjust the voice recording cursor so it matches. I have copies so you can reload if you mess it up. Try and learn how to work it.'

'Roger.'

'Call me if you're stuck; I'm about to load the calibration data, then I'll go to the sim to set limits. You'll find me there.'

…

Dexter struggled at first; the program and what it did was strange, but at least he knew about the run button. He clicked it, listened to the voice recording and watched the data from the FDR that ran across the screen. After running it twice, he understood that the two were uncoordinated, so he picked on the pilot's order, 'Flaps', and saw the FDR signalled the flaps were up thirty-five seconds or so afterwards. After playing around for a while, he fetched a piece of paper and a pencil and wrote two lines:

> What is the time it takes for the flaps to move?
> Why is there no FDR record of when the co-pilot selected the flap switch to the up position?

Then he went to find Jenifer with the paper in his hand; she was in the barn with the simulator.

'Are you progressing?'

'Yes, I'm glad you're here. Can you help by operating the levers and the control column? I can't set the limits and move them at the same time. We can go much faster if you help.'

Dexter sat in the pilot's chair and asked, 'Which one first?'

'Left engine power, full power.'

Dexter slid the lever picture forward; Jenifer read a number from her screen, then another from a table on a separate screen, used the two in a calculation and entered the result in an input field on another.'

'Now back to idle...'

'Now full again...'

'Now full reverse thrust...'

'Back to idle...'

'Same again, the other engine...'

Suddenly, Dexter felt part of the team and understood what Jenifer was doing. An hour later, they had worked through the engine controls, pressurization, control column movements, Flaps, Trim, undercarriage, fuel indicators and several others.'

'We've done them all. I need to ask one of my contacts in the metaverse for an engine performance data set for these engines, but I'll start the actuator program installation now.'

'Then take a break, start the installation, ask for the data set, and come for lunch. I'll do the salad. Then you can answer two questions I have.'

⚜

'You're as good with a salad as with bacon and eggs.'

'My remaining cuisine skills are limited to heating stuff in the microwave, anything more than three ingredients, and I'm hopeless.'

'Well, we won't starve. What questions do you have?'

'These.' Dexter gave her the paper.

'I must show you how to share a note file with me. I don't know the flap movement time, but I can tell you when the sim is alive tomorrow. Why the FDR doesn't record the flap switch activation is a puzzle; it may be because they ran out of available recording time and decided that recording the flap position was the only thing required. If I give you the flap movement time, you can work backwards from the position record. I have the pilot's manual; I can show it on your screen or print it for you.'

'Showing it onscreen is enough; I'll mark it up with notes and save it.'

'I must return to setting the actuator limits. I don't want the wheels coming through the floor.'

'Okay.'

Dexter spent the afternoon reading the pilot's manual. He read the takeoff procedures with extreme care and highlighted the instructions on flap operations. Something was bothering him.

Jenifer returned from the barn. 'Dex, I'm running the first test programs. They'll run all night, and I'll have the results in the morning; I've also set up a shared notebook for us. Just click on the icon "Shared."'

'What will you do now?'

'A bit of research. Would you like a coffee?'

'Go and research; I have tea and cake ready.'

...

Dexter entered the lounge with a tray, 'Tea's up. I'll pour.'

Jenifer sat down, 'This is homely.'

'It's supposed to be a British tradition. What have you been researching?'

'My Darling.'

'I don't follow, Bo.' Then he saw her grin. *Oh-Oh, somethings up.*

The web says 'My Darling' is an affectionate nickname, so I looked up affectionate nicknames. It's a shocking revelation.'

'What is?'

'There are twice as many different ones for men than women. Men have no imagination!'

'Accepted, we're unemotional.'

'So, I looked at what I could use for you. The names are all classified and labelled as more or less affectionate. I eliminated the erotic ones, although I fancied "Pussy".'

'For a *Man*?'

'Yes, and there's a list based on food. The French are hot on those; one favourite is "*chou*", but I can't see myself calling you cabbage.'

Dexter grinned, 'So what takes your fancy?'

'I eliminated "carrot" and "parsnip"; "spud" has a low rating on the affection scale, and then I found "pumpkin", which is common, but "dumpling" has a higher rating. So that's my best choice – dumpling.'

Dexter laughed. 'You're delightful but taking a big risk.'

'Why?'

'Maybe dumplings will turn off my darling switch.'

Jenifer smiled, 'I know how to turn it on again, but if you put on too much weight, I'll call you dumpling. Then it's your fault.'

'Fair enough – my darling. Now it's time for a walk. Two hours to keep dumplings in the pot.'

⊸∘⊸

'Bo, will you hug me tonight?'

'You deserve one, Dex, for helping me, perhaps a kiss too.'

A kiss later, Jenifer said, 'I liked today. It wasn't just the work; it was with you doing the ordinary everyday things that made it so good.'

'Then we must keep at it, and we'll learn about each other. What are your plans for tomorrow?'

'I'll run evaluation programs and adjust things all day. The sim won't be good until I have the engine plugins; they might take until Friday. I must also ask Henry for an FDR set from his simulator, recorded on a standard test flight. Then, with the plug-in, I'll prove the sim gives the same results as his. Then we can start playing. We can do that on Saturday. I'll give you the flap times first; then, you can do more work on the FDR results.'

'I must return to work Tuesday and return here for the weekend.'

'I'll be busy. Kiss me, and let's sleep.'

Day 46
Monday

Dexter got his 'my darling' reinforcement, and then Jenifer disappeared to the barn wearing pyjamas and slippers. They spent the day working separately, meeting for what seemed to them to be overly brief encounters for breakfast, lunch and supper, with interspersed visits for coffee.

Dexter managed to synchronise his two recordings by lunchtime and afterwards sat puzzling over what he'd found. He typed them into the page of shared notes.

> Voice instructions for flap calls are not according to the pilot's manual.
>
> The time from the 'flaps fifteen' call corresponds to the numbers Bo supplied.
>
> Time from call 'Flaps' to fully up record does not.
>
> The pitch angle change after the 'flaps' call is sudden, nose down, and huge,

> Call 'Up-damn it, up' immediately after the pitch change with the whole rearward movement of the control column. Implies pilot addressed call 'Up-damn it, up' to the aircraft.
>
> Pitch nose up follows only seconds after control column movement but is sudden and excessive.
>
> Aircraft stalls-crash.

Jenifer came to see him at four, 'I read what you wrote. We must see if we can do the same in the sim when it's working.'

'How far are you?'

'I have a sim that works, but I don't think it's right. The engines need changing, but it also needs fine-tuning. I'm waiting for Henry to send me a recording from his sim. I'll work through the items tomorrow, but we won't have a sim until Sunday. I need some fresh air. Can we walk again?'

'Of course.'

After the walk to Baginton Aerodrome, back, and supper, Jenifer said, 'You must leave early tomorrow, so let's go to bed.'

'My darling, will you be alright after I'm gone?'

'If you promise to come back Friday, I will. It will also give me time without "my darlings" to think about us.'

'I'll be back. I'll call and tell you when.'

'Then kiss me, and we'll sleep.'

•••

'If you don't stop, you won't sleep.'

'It's not me, it's you.'

'Right, on the count of three, we'll both turn over. One-Two-Three...darn it. Good night, Dex.'

DAY 47
TUESDAY

Dexter rose at 05:15, showered and dressed, and found Jenifer had prepared him a cup of coffee. After a two-minute kiss and a 'Bye, my darling', by 5:45, he was driving to Gatwick. Dexter arrived at his hotel in time to change and return to work on the hotel bus. His breakfast was a chocolate croissant with Greg, where he studied and approved the pilot checks Greg had done before returning to the revisions he was making to the operations manual. Before the day ended, the rewrite of the crew change procedures was complete, and he sent it to Greg for proofreading and began a new chapter titled Fuel Transfer.

Jenifer made breakfast. With no pressure to begin work, she made French toast.

She connected to the metaverse, found a message from Henry, downloaded the FDR data, and then ran it through the decoder. It was what she expected, so she extracted all the control inputs and prepared to run the simulator automatically. An hour later, she pressed the test button and watched as the simulator did what Henry had done. Two traces, one above the other, tracked across her monitor. At first, the tracks matched, and then, as the difference in engine performance became significant, they diverged. Jenifer shut down and returned to the house. *I can't check for errors until I have that engine data.*

She sat in her kitchen, nursing a cup of coffee and thinking about Dexter and sex; it was an hour before she concluded. *I've never had an orgasm. The dildo never worked, nor did the metaverse sex. I might be frigid. If I have sex with Dex and it doesn't work, I'm sure he will know and leave me, although I love him.*

She thought after rolling the problem around her mind and looking for a solution. *It seems ridiculous. But I could ask the ponies!*

Half an hour later, she'd packed a bag, found the key to the farm cottage, cleaned the kitchen, locked up, and was ready to leave.

I can still make it before dark. It's only three hours and a bit.

At seven, she arrived at the cottage, let herself in, found Dexter's GPS and plugged it in to charge, put the food she'd brought in the fridge, ate two sandwiches, and went to bed. As sleep took over, she thought, *it's odd, but I feel more at home here than Coventry; Dex must have left a presence here, or there's a welcoming ghost.*

In London, Dexter was in bed in the hotel and felt lonely for the first time in fifteen years. His last thought was, *I must think about this. I'm no longer an airline pilot.'*

DAY 48
WEDNESDAY

W hen the sun was up, Jenifer woke and decided she deserved an egg for breakfast with toast and marmalade. She had to search the pantry for marmalade, found an unopened pot of thick-cut old English marmalade, mentally recorded that Dexter must like it, and then fried her egg.

As she ate, she felt a calm relaxation growing. *Hello ghost, I like you.*

After dressing for a day of walking, she made sandwiches, packed her rucksack, and then planned her walk. She looked at the map of the moor, selected two stone circles and two tors to visit, and set each as a waypoint in her GPS.

The Nine Stones Circle became waypoint number one when she remembered her name in the poem.

Then Jenifer set a waypoint called home on the GPS, decided on the Tor Inn at Belstone as a starting point, and saved it as a way-point in the GPS memory; she did one other thing.

She took four bunches of clover from a box beside the kitchen door and put them in her rucksack. Then she locked the house, put her boots and hiking stick in her car, and drove off following the GPS instructions.

The ten-kilometre walk would take three hours, giving her time to watch ponies if she found any. Feeling cheerful, she set off; the first stone circle was only a kilometre away. Jenifer thought the stones were small, but the ring was almost complete.

This stone looks like Jenifer's rock. I'll sit on it and look at the view.

⚘

Dexter was in his office, working on the manual. He struggled with the words to describe the 'Centre of Gravity' called C of G and 'Centre of Mass'. He wished Jenifer were with him to help. A knock on the door interrupted his thoughts.

'Come in.'

'Hello, Dex; I hope I'm not interrupting. I came to ask if we can have lunch together.'

'Greg, I need a break; my thoughts have gotten tangled.'

'What's the problem?'

'What's the difference between "C of G" and "Centre of Mass".'

'Nothing.'

'They can't be the same, Greg.'

'But they are. The C of G is the point where a single support will hold the aeroplane off the ground without it touching anywhere, so support for all the weight or mass is at that point.'

'Greg, imagine an aeroplane with a short nose and a big weight and a long tail with a small weight. Then, a stubby wing with a heavy weight and a long wing with a lighter weight on the other side. It balances at the same point. Where's the centre of mass?'

'Hell, Dex, you need an engineer to answer that; call Joe Cantrell in maintenance.'

'That's a clever idea, I will. I'll also join you for lunch. I have something else to discuss. Where?'

'How about the Sushi place? I'll meet you there at one.'

⚊⚊●⚊⚊

After twenty minutes of absorbing the panorama, Jenifer finally stood up. *It's so peaceful, and the view is magnificent. I could sit here for ages. But the ponies are waiting for me.*

She set off to walk the next kilometre to Higher Tor. She saw it at a distance and decided it was a far more exciting granite outcrop than those she had seen, and when she was closer, she decided to climb to the top. When she finally reached the top after climbing onto several huge boulders, she stood on the top. *I'm the queen of the world but a foolish queen. If I fell, there's no one to help and no phone. Next time, I must tell someone where I'm going.*

She looked at her GPS and turned until the route she had to take was before her. *It's three kilometres to White Moor Circle, and there's a valley I can follow; there might be ponies in the valley; I can stop halfway and have lunch.*

When Dexter asked Joe Cantrell, the reply was intriguing. 'They're the same if the only force acting on the aircraft is the static force of gravity; that's why we call it the centre of gravity. The Centre of Mass is not at the C of G under other conditions.

'Pilots don't bother much with the Centre of Mass because designers try to have the two as close as possible on the centreline, but there is a difference. Remember what happens when there's a sudden updraft? The nose pitches up or down. If it's up, the centre of mass is behind the C of G, and vice versa. We define C of M as the point where we can apply a dynamic force without rotation occurring.'

'Thanks, Joe. That makes it clearer.'

'It's more complicated than that because the centre of lift, which in level flight is at the C of G, has an effect. But that will do for a simple explanation.'

Dexter returned to composing his description for the manual.

Jenifer followed the valley and was about to stop for her lunch when she saw ponies on the opposite side, so she crossed over the small brook to reach them, pleased that the mud didn't go higher than her boots.

She found a rock near them that she thought had rolled down from the valley's top, sat on it and extracted her sandwiches and water. She ate slowly, pausing between sandwiches while examining the ponies individually. After fifteen minutes, she thought. *I'm alone, and they're curious; I'm sure they're getting closer.*

She finished her sandwiches, put the box in the rucksack, and took a bunch of clover in each hand. *Would one like some clover?*

She then sat motionless while the group of five drifted closer. After several minutes, she thought. *They're looking at me; they look now and then, and if I look at one for a long time, it looks at me as if it knows I'm looking.*

Wonderment began to grow as the ponies continued to close on her. *The brown mare is curious.*

Dexter went to lunch.

'Hi Dex, have you solved your problem?'

'Yes, they aren't the same thing but they can be in the same place. C of G is just a name for the Centre of Mass when the only force acting on the mass is the constant force of gravity.'

'Well, now I've learnt something new. I must think about it. What else do you want to talk about?'

'Let's go and fill our plates from the buffet, then I'll tell you.'

The brown mare drifted closer, and Jenifer watched her until she was only a metre away, looking at her curiously. Then she opened a hand with clover. After the mare had scrutinised it, and Jenifer thought she had recognised or smelled it, she slowly extended her arm.

The mare hesitated but didn't spook, then stepped forward and reached forward until she could take the clover from Jenifer's open palm. After chewing in obvious enjoyment, she didn't step back but took a small step forward and sniffed. *She can smell the other half!*

'Greg, you know I've lived either in my Dartmoor cottage or one of the hotels here for years. That's been a great life because when I came here from Dartmoor, it was a one- or two-night stay, and then I took off for Timbuctoo or somewhere for at least two or up to seven days.

'Now that my scheduled flying is over, if I stay on as training Captain, I'm likely to be here for four or five days every week, and already I feel the hotel is not where I want to be.'

'What does Jenifer say?'

'I haven't discussed it with her. Our relationship is platonic; she's young, and I don't know if she wants to take it further. She could be my daughter; she should be looking for a younger man.'

'What do you want, Dex?'

'Marriage if she would accept.'

'Then sort that out with her first before you buy a place near here.'

⟨✈⟩

Jenifer opened the other hand, and the mare took a step closer and delicately picked it from her hand. As the clover disappeared, Jenifer leaned forward to blow air against the mare's head in front of her ear. The mare didn't step back, so Jenifer raised her right hand and caressed the area she had blown with two fingers. When the clover was gone, the mare raised her head, and to Jenifer's delight, she felt the mare blow air into her face. *I think we're friends.*

She reached down for her rucksack with her left hand while stroking the mare with her right, and the mare didn't move until, smelling the rest of the clover, she bent her head down to nuzzle the bag. Jenifer removed another bunch while extending her stroking and then the last bunch. *The clover's gone; what will she do now?*

Then she noticed the other horses. *They're all close, and watching me, they know I'm a friend.* Still stroking, Jenifer slowly stood. Beside the mare, she could stroke more of her. *I need a curry comb. If I had one, I bet she'd love that.'*

When Jenifer saw her shadow, she realised how much time had gone. She slowly picked up her bag and strolled away. The ponies didn't move. After ten metres, she removed the GPS from her rucksack, shouldered the bag, looked at the GPS, pressed 'go to' then the waypoint for her car and set off along the indicated track. The feeling of euphoria that filled her brought the thought. *This valley is a magic place. I'll find the horses tomorrow.*

⚜

When Jenifer parked in the courtyard, she was thinking about where to buy a curry comb, and as she left the car, she saw the stables at the end of the barn. *I wonder if there's stuff for horses in there.* There was an old wooden box with assorted items, and one was a brush with short, stiff bristles.

After preparing everything for the following morning, including six bunches of clover, all she could find, she went to bed and slept well.

DAY 49
THURSDAY

Jenifer was up early, made her breakfast, cleaned up, and then set off. As she hadn't reached the white moor circle the previous day, she had planned a different route and drove through the village of Throwleigh to where the road stopped at the open moor. She visited the farmhouse beside the track to ask if she could leave her car, where she met the farmer's wife. When Jenifer gave her name, the wife replied, 'So you're Cornish! I'm Morwen; come in, come in, and have a cup of tea.'

For Jenifer, it was a new experience. Morwen was curious, and Jenifer became the subject of investigation. It wasn't more than three minutes before she had to admit she was staying at the Rawlins farm.

'And where's Dexter, then?'

'He was here last weekend but had to go to work yesterday; he'll be back tomorrow night. Do you know him?'

'When I was young, we were kids together, ran wild with the other kids, swimming naked in the river, and lots of larks. Dexter was a lovely young man. I would have taken him to the Tolmen Stone if he hadn't gone off to become a pilot. How did you meet him?'

'I'm also a pilot; we met at Gatwick.'

'That's good, doing the same work as your husband.'

'We aren't married yet.'

'Then take him to the Tolmen, first chance you have. He's been waiting for the right woman since Bethkin died. I heard he was doing some work on the farmhouse. What have you done?'

'Not me, only him; he knocked out the wall between the dining room and kitchen. The kitchen is much bigger now, and he has a small study. There are now only two bedrooms upstairs, but the bathroom is bigger.'

'I hope he kept Brean's pantry.'

'The old stone piece?'

'Yes, it was a croft before the Rawlins built the farmhouse. An old peasant farmer called Brean lived there. His family buried him in the next field, and folks say he visits.'

'I'm sure he does. Dexter kept the pantry, and I liked the friendly feeling there.'

'Why are you going onto the moor?'

'To take clover to some ponies I know and to see if they will like a brush down.'

'Like you, do they?'

'Yes, and I love them.'

'Dexter always loved the ponies. How much clover do you have?'

'Twelve small bunches.'

'Can you carry twelve more?'

Jenifer thought, 'I think so, but eight will be enough for two each.'

'Then I'll give you eight.'

'Thanks, the ponies love the clover. I'll leave my phone in the car, it doesn't work out on the moor, and leave the keys with you if you want to move the car; I should be back between four and five.'

'I'll be here; I'm not going out today.'

⊰❧⊱

Dexter arrived at his office in Gatwick when Jenifer walked onto the moor. He still had much more to write on fuel balance, but his first task was a mock crew change according to the new manual. Greg was in the simulator when he arrived and said, 'Dex, what you wrote won't work.'

'Why?'

'Too much paper.'

'Why, and then what do you suggest?'

'You want the departing crew member to fill in a sheet with the panel's status and the replacement crew to sign it. Can't we use a book of sheets already marked with an item to report on each line and several blank columns? If the fuel temperature light comes on, the crew member in the seat in front of it must put the time at the top of the next blank column, and against the fuel temperature item, write "ON" in the column; if it goes off, he uses another column.'

'And what happens at changeover?'

'The last page has a column for time and two signatures on each line, departing and arriving pilot. The arriving crew must check the status of the panel and report to the other any discrepancy between the display and what's in the book.'

'A different book for each aircraft?'

'Yes, no different to the different weight and balance for each aircraft we have now.'

'Make up a book for your sim and have a crew do a flight. Flip lights and then do a crew change.'

'Okay, I'll use your sheets as an example. Have you heard from Jenifer?'

'No, I must call her tonight. I'm seeing her tomorrow evening.'

Jenifer set out on the hour's walk to White Moor Circle. A few minutes later, Morwen's husband Breock came in from the fields for breakfast and asked, 'Who does the Mini outside belong to?'

'Jenifer, Dexter Rawlins's girlfriend, she's gone onto the moor to feed clover to the ponies.'

'She'll be lucky to find any.'

'They'll find her; she's Fey. Name of Boscawen. She says she met old Brean.'

'Oh, like you then?'

'Yes, and Dexter. They'll visit the Tolmen stone soon.'

The rucksack with the clover seemed heavier as she walked, and she was glad to reach the stones and sit on one. Jenifer thought yesterday's stone circle was much nicer. Nevertheless, the panorama was as good. After half an hour, she lifted her rucksack again and set off to find the ponies. She had less than a kilometre to go.

When she spotted the five ponies three hundred metres away, happiness flooded her. *They're waiting for me!* At fifty metres, she stopped beside a dry patch of grass with a convenient stone, then propped her bag against the rock and sat on the grass to watch the ponies. After a few minutes, she lay down on her back and relaxed, looking at the sky and a flock of birds she thought might be ducks.

Jenifer turned her head when she heard a snuffling sound. The brown mare, only a metre away, looked hopefully at her. Jenifer sat up, reached for her bag, and removed a clover bunch and the curry brush.

Half an hour later, the mare had eaten two clover bunches, and Jenifer was standing beside her, running the curry brush along the mare's sides; she had already combed her back and rump. The other ponies had closed and watched with interest. Jenifer felt she and the pony understood each other. She was about to offer clover to another pony when she felt an itch between her shoulder blades. She saw the ripple of the pony's skin, and without thinking about it, she ran the comb over the rippled area, and the itch on her back disappeared. *Is that what Dexter said? They can feel where the other has an itch.*

By 16:00, Jenifer had fed each of the five ponies, had eaten her lunch sitting in the sunshine surrounded by them, and had carefully brushed them all. They gleamed in the sunlight. *What a marvellous day!*

Jenifer took an hour and a half to return to her car, where Morwen welcomed her with open arms, more tea and scones with Cornish cream.

'You look like you had a happy day!'

'I did; let me fetch my phone. Dexter may call, and then I'll tell you.'

...

'I had a wonderful day; it was marvellous, the same five ponies. They ate two bunches each, and I gave them all a good brushing. By the end, I knew they were my friends, and we could feel each other. A lovely feeling.'

Morwen looked at her, surprised, 'Feel each other?'

'Yes, I'm sure that one of them, the brown mare I had brushed earlier, came and stood next to me, and I felt itching between my shoulder blades, and when I brushed her in the equivalent spot, it went away.'

'Then you're one of the rare people who have the gift. Dexter does, but not that strong.'

'And you, Morwen?'

'The ponies know me. When the weather's bad, I leave the barn door open, and a few always come here to shelter.'

Then Jenifer's phone rang.

'Hello Dex.' Jenifer pressed the speaker button.

'Hello, my darling, what a relief to hear your voice; what are you doing.'

'Why's it a relief?'

'For three days, I've had nightmares of you disappearing into your metaverse, meeting a handsome dragon, and not returning.'

'Well, I have made six new friends but no dragons; five are ponies. And the sixth is your ex-girlfriend from long ago.'

Morwen, with a broad grin, pushed a piece of paper into Jenifer's hand; she read it and smiled.

'She must have the wrong Dexter; I don't remember having a girlfriend in the Midlands.'

'Then she must be wrong unless you have a red spider-shaped birthmark on your upper thigh – on the front.'

The two women were now broadly grinning as they listened to

strangled sounds from the phone.

'*Where* are you?'

'I don't know, your girlfriend can tell you.'

'Hello, Dex, it's Morwen.'

'Morwen, it's been years. Are you now in Coventry?'

'No, on our farm by the moor.'

'And Jenifer's there?'

'Yes. Jenifer's a lovely young woman. She went onto the moor to talk to the ponies and left her car with us.'

'And I'll bet you've let all my secrets out of the bag.'

Morwen smiled, 'Only a few. You can speak to her again, but promise to come by and see us.'

'We will do, Morwen.'

'Hello Dex.'

'Why are you there, my darling?'

'I'm still waiting for data. I felt lonely, so I decided to come to your farm to think about us, but the ponies on the moor side-tracked me. And then I met Morwen.'

'You can tell me later about the ponies. I planned to go to Coventry tomorrow night; shall I come home?'

'That would be best. There's nothing to do in Coventry until the data comes.'

'Then I'll see you tomorrow at about seven. Bye, darling.'

'Bye, Dex.'

'Morwen, I must go; I need to visit the supermarket; I've nothing left in the house.'

'Just don't forget us now.'

Jenifer drove out to the supermarket, and minutes later, Breock arrived.

'She's gone then? Did she find the ponies?'

'Yes, as I said, she's Fey and has the gift.'

'So, you think she and Dexter will marry?'

'When two Fey people meet, it's like mixing two reactive liquids. There's either an explosion or a blending; I hope it's the latter.'

⁂

At check-out, Jenifer asked, 'Where can I buy some clover?'

'If you want tons, you'll have to talk to the farmers, but at the vegetable stall beside the Exeter Road to Okehampton, as you leave the village, the woman sells clover to visitors for feeding the ponies. There's a sign that says, "Feeding the ponies is illegal unless it's clover."'

Jenifer replied, 'Thanks, I'll see if I can get some.'

She did, then drove back to the cottage and filled the clover box.

When she went to bed with everything prepared for the next day, Jenifer tried to imagine what it would be like with Dexter lying next to her every night as her husband. She could not. No matter how she tried, he was still the same Dexter in the Dodo pyjamas.

I must get rid of those pyjamas.

DAY 50
FRIDAY

Dexter rose earlier on Friday morning. He intended to leave Gatwick by 15:00, so he washed, dressed, had breakfast, and then returned to his room. Dexter then packed his suitcase and sports bag, checked out of the hotel, took his bags to the car and drove to the employee parking. He had a meeting scheduled with Greg at nine.

'How did the crew changeover work, Greg?'

'We have it smoothed out. Here's the wording and the procedure that two separate crews have done, and they agree it's sensible and workable. Check it out and put it in the manual. What's next?'

'Did you see what happens in the sim when you transfer fuel?'

'Yes, nothing. The fuel indicators show that the fuel levels in the wings are different, and the unbalanced fuel indicator lights up, but it doesn't affect how the sim flies. The pilots must correct it as per the manual.'

'Then you must speak to the makers and determine what it will cost to change it. I'll send you Henry Mancuni's email address at CamAirCom. I don't know who made their sim, but he's doing the same thing. Once you have a baseline cost, ask Jenifer what she can do for you. Her sim does what you need to train pilots in asymmetric flight and landings.'

❦

Jenifer parked her car at a different spot at the moor's edge. She wasn't sure it was where Dexter had parked because there were two places, but they were close to each other. Jenifer set the GPS waypoint called KAR, sent a dropped pin to Dexter, shouldered her rucksack, and began walking. Her objective was a leisurely walk to Gallavan Brook, only a kilometre and a half, where, she hoped, she would find more ponies.

Forty minutes later, Jenifer arrived and continued along Gallavan Brook along the north bank, as there were no ponies. After a further hour, the brook turned west, and Jenifer had to decide, so she slipped off her rucksack with its load of clover, sat on a rock, and looked at her GPS.

If the ponies are still there, it's about an hour and a half, so I'll arrive at about twelve. Then I can feed them the clover. Straight back to the car is an hour-forty, allow two, so I'll have two hours with the ponies.

She stood, shrugged on the rucksack and headed along a well-defined track to White Moor Circle. It took longer than she had thought, and when she arrived at the circle, feeling tired, she sat on a rock and ate her lunch. As she finished her second sandwich, she heard steps and turned. The ponies she knew, in single file, were walking towards her with one of the stallions in the lead. *They've come to meet me!*

For an hour, Jenifer fed them the clover and scratched their backs with the curry comb, and then suddenly, the stallion neighed, and they began to walk away. *I wonder where they're going.*

When the brown mare stopped and looked back, Jenifer felt she was saying, 'You come too'. So, she shouldered her bag and did, soon catching up. They had gone a kilometre before Jenifer looked at her GPS and found she was north of the route to her car, so she stopped. The brown mare stopped, looked at her, and neighed; the other ponies stopped while the mare came to her and gently pushed her with her head. *There's no doubt what she wants, and the moor's edge is this way: I can always find someone to take me back to my car.*

Jenifer started walking, and the brown mare walked beside her. After a few minutes, Jenifer thought. *Now there's two in front, two behind, and I'm in the middle with the mare! Something must be wrong, and they're walking to a safe place.*

With an eerie suddenness, Jenifer lost sight of the horizon, and then it closed in until she was walking in a grey cloud beside the mare; she felt fear. *It's the mist Dexter talked about.* She put out a hand and rested it lightly on the mare's shoulder and felt less frightened. *The mare knows where to go and is taking me with her.* Within minutes, she felt cheerful, but the damp air condensed on her hair and clothes, and she began to feel the chill.

Two hours after leaving the White Moor Circle, the first shivers began as the constant exposure began to take effect. She walked with her body against the mare and arm over it, trying to get as much warmth as possible.

She hardly noticed when the ground became a hard road, and they crossed a courtyard and entered a barn. When the ponies stopped walking, she let her rucksack drop to the ground, staggered into the barn, collapsed in a heap of straw, and tried to burrow into it, shudders wracking her body.

Dexter had left Gatwick at three, and his drive down the motorways to Exeter went like clockwork, but when he turned onto the A30, he could see the low cloud in the direction of Dartmoor and thought mist was coming. Fifteen kilometres from Whiddon Down, he slowed. Less than a kilometre later, Dexter was creeping along at a walking pace. When he reached it, he took the Cheriton offramp, found a place to stop, and called Jenifer. Dexter got no answer. Seriously worried, he drove back onto the A30 until he reached Whiddon, took the off-ramp, and repeated the call unsuccessfully; then, he went the remaining kilometres to the house, praying that Jenifer's car would be in the yard. It wasn't. He switched his phone to the phone map to look at Jenifer's dropped pin, pressed the go-to-pin and started the car. Then his phone rang.

Whether Morwen heard the horses arrive or not, only she could say, but she knew when they came and felt something was abnormal, so she wrapped a shawl around her, stepped into her gumboots, and went to the barn with a powerful torch. Jenifer's rucksack was the first thing she saw on the ground in the doorway. She hurried, found Jenifer buried in the straw, pulled her up, put an arm around her and ordered, 'Come, Jenifer, walk!' Jenifer stopped shaking once in the warm kitchen, with a blanket around her and her feet in a bowl of hot water. Breock handed her a mug of hot tea to sip that she held in both hands.

Morwen said, 'Breock, fill our bath with hot water, then go to the barn, fetch her rucksack, and look for her phone; we must call Dexter.'

'Jenifer, finish your tea, then I'll help you up the stairs, and you can soak for half an hour.'

With Jenifer in the bath, Morwen came downstairs to heat soup on the hotplate. 'Breock, have you found her phone?'

'Yes, I've just switched it on, but what's the code?'

'I forgot that, give it to me.'

...

'Jenifer, look at the screen...

'Thanks.'

Dexter almost dropped the phone when it rang because he grabbed it too fast; when he finally had it upright, he pressed the answer button with trembling fingers.

'Bo, where are you.'

'I'm glad you didn't use darling, Dex; it might have got me into trouble.'

'Morwen, where is she?'

'In the bath here, she'll be fine. If you can drive here, Breock will go with you to fetch her car. She has its position on her GPS. You can leave it at your home and then come here. I'm inviting you to dinner. Jenifer will be in bed with hot soup but can talk to you.'

'Thanks, but where are you?'

'I'll drop you a pin...

'There, I've sent it.'

'Got it.'

'Don't drive fast, there's no hurry, she's not going anywhere.'

•••

'Jenifer, are you ready to get out?'

'Yes, the water's cooling.'

'I'll help you dry, then you get into the spare bed; I'll bring you some hot soup.'

...

'Thanks, I'm feeling much better now.'

'You can tell me what happened when I bring the soup.'

...

'Breock, fetch Jenifer's car keys, and when Dexter arrives, go with him to fetch her car. You should take it to Dexter's farmhouse so she doesn't need to drive it tomorrow morning.'

With the soup bowl on a tray with a knob of farmhouse bread, Morwen returned to Jenifer. 'Here you are, spoon this into you. I'll fetch you a bed jacket so you can sit up when Dexter comes. Now tell me what happened.'

'I walked out via Gallaway Brook to White Moor Circle and ate lunch. Then the ponies came to me. I gave them my clover, and after a while, they lined up and walked away east. I didn't know where they were going, and they wanted me to go with them, so I did for a while.

'Then, when I realised we weren't walking towards my car, I stopped and tried to go further south. Then they stopped me. The brown mare came and walked beside me; two went in front and two behind. I sensed something was wrong, and they were heading for a safe place, so I went along. Then the mist came, and it became cold and wet. I walked and leaned against the brown mare with my arm over her back. When we arrived here, I didn't know it was your barn, and just collapsed in the straw and tried to get warm.'

Morwen said, 'Having good friends you can rely on is one of the joys of living. They saved me once, many years ago, and I leave my barn open for them. They don't always come every time the mist comes down; they have other places.

'I'll fetch that bed jacket. Dex will be here any time now, and I must make dinner. I'll send him up when he comes. Tell him if you want him to stay the night with you.'

'Thanks, Morwen.'

Now warm, inside and out, but exhausted, Jenifer fell into a deep sleep within a minute. She didn't hear Dexter come into the room, look at her, and leave quietly after leaving a clean tracksuit, socks, jersey and underwear on a chair.

⁂

In the kitchen, Morwen said, 'Sit here, Dex. Is she sleeping?'

'Yes, best to let her sleep until morning.'

'You must be tired too; help yourself to lamb stew and potatoes. There's more bread in the bin. I told her you could sleep with her if she wanted you to, but we have a truckle bed down here if you wish to stay without disturbing her, or you can come for breakfast at eight tomorrow and fetch Jenifer.'

'I think it best to let her sleep; I'll go home and come for breakfast. What happened?'

'Let her tell you. You may already know: She's one of us, so be gentle.'

'I thought she might be.'

'There may be clover at your house; bring it all in the morning.'

DAY 51
SATURDAY

Dexter arrived before breakfast. The mist had gone during the night, and the day promised bright sunshine in a cloudless sky. He brought the bag of clover.

When he arrived, Jenifer was with Morwen and Breock in the kitchen; she almost ran into his arms. Morwen approvingly watched as Deter kissed Jenifer thoroughly.

'Are you fine now? Yesterday, I was frantic.'

'I was safe; although cold, wet and tired, the ponies looked after me. Morwen said you would bring the clover; let's go and feed the ponies before they leave.'

When they entered the barn, the ponies all came to her, and the brown mare nuzzled and blew as Jenifer caressed and scratched. The others gathered around her, and the stallion placed his head on her shoulder from behind her, so she stroked the hair above his nose. Then another pony spotted the bag held by Dexter, and he was surprised they included him in a welcome; he felt it.

'Give me two bunches of clover.' He did, and she fed the mare and the stallion while he fed the other three. Five minutes later, the clover had gone, and Jenifer said, 'There, we can go to breakfast, and they can return to the moor.'

⁕

While eating a typical farmhouse breakfast with homemade sausages, Jenifer told her story to an amazed Dexter and a smiling Breock. When she reached the end, Dexter looked at Morwen. She smiled and slowly nodded at him, then lifted her hands and formed a circle with her thumbs and forefingers touching. Dexter knew the sign for the Tolmen Stone.

While Dexter unloaded the Aston, Jenifer bustled about cleaning boots and muddy clothes at Dexter's farm. An hour later, after Jenifer had hung their clothes on a line in the sunshine to dry, Dexter said, 'Let's go to lunch at the Gidleigh Park Hotel. I'll call and book. It's a beautiful day to walk in their gardens. The restaurant is fabulous, and its wine cellar is enormous.'

'I must change if it's a snazzy place.'

'Not snazzy, it's like the Oxenham, old fashioned, it looks medieval.'

'Then I can't go in a tracksuit. It was thoughtful of you to bring this one last night. Thanks.'

'What about the sim and Henry's problem?'

'I tried to forget it, Dex, and I haven't had any messages; the engine plug-in should arrive today. We can return to Coventry tomorrow night or Monday.'

As they got into the car, Jenifer said, 'Dex, we need a bottle of milk and butter. Can you stop at Dunn's dairy?'

'On the way back, it will heat up in the car. I booked a table for 13:00, so we could walk in the park and gardens and then go into the bar for a drink before eating. We can look at the menu and wine list in the bar.'

They walked in the gardens and park for an hour, holding hands and in secluded spots, stealing an enthusiastic kiss; both felt euphoric. Dexter couldn't help thinking, *tonight; I'll ask her to go to the Tolmen Stone tomorrow.*

In the typical country pub bar with a collection of old photographs, flags and other memorabilia decorating the walls, they sat together on a well-stuffed leather couch at a low table facing the bar itself. Dexter saw the small TV on the wall behind the bar, surrounded by bottles of exotic spirits. With the volume turned down, it showed a rugby match.

Dexter ordered and fetched two Campari's with soda; then they became engrossed in the Menu and wine list.

When the grandfather clock in the corner chimed, Jenifer said, 'We must go to the restaurant.'

They both stood and then Dexter said, 'The TV has switched to the one o'clock news; let's hear the headlines.'

They stood, frozen in horror, when they heard the news flash. 'An airliner crashed in Africa after takeoff only two hours ago. A spokesperson at the airport has stated that no survivors are likely. Operations to identify the dead are underway. We will report further when the news is available.'

'If that's a second one, we must drive to my house this afternoon. Let's have lunch but no alcohol; you might need to drive.'

'We won't appreciate the meal. Stay here; I'll find the restaurant manager, explain the situation, then we'll go home and have a scrambled egg or something while we follow the news.'

The euphoria had vanished, dread building in its place.

• • •

An hour later, after scrambled eggs and coffee twice, they were in the farmhouse lounge watching CNN when the news came.

'Our reporter at the crash scene has said there are no survivors from the two hundred and thirty-one persons on board. The aircraft, a CamAirCom two-thirty, their newest airliner model, crashed, airport officials say, only minutes after takeoff, within seconds after it disappeared from the airport's radar.

'Our aviation consultant says similarities with another accident in South-East Asia two weeks ago will raise questions regarding the plane's safety.

'Aviation experts will be on-site shortly to remove the black boxes that should reveal the cause of this mysterious disaster. Further reports will follow.'

'It's the same plane, although a different country and airline. We must go to my home.'

'Do we both drive? Or leave your car here?'

'We don't need my car. Let's go in yours.'

'I'll fetch my stuff, you clear the pantry and fridge into bags, and then I'll load the car and put your car in the barn while you pack your bag.'

Cruising comfortably in silence along the highways, Jenifer slept for half the three-hour trip, and then Dexter parked behind Jenifer's house.

'You look for your data; leave me to do everything. I'll heat a pizza. And call you when it's ready.'

'Thanks.'

It took only a few minutes for Jenifer to warm up her equipment and access her metabox. Then, she noted the list of URLs and began the downloads. She estimated four hours.

She took two short breaks, the first for a slice of pizza, a coffee, a toilet visit, and then a kiss.

'How's it going, Bo?'

'The engine stuff is all there, Dex. The last file from a guy arrived this morning. I'll know when it's ready to install. If it goes well, we'll have a two-thirty sim tomorrow night.'

The second break was for decaf, toilet, and kiss. Dexter was surprised by her passion.

'It's going well, Bo?'

'All downloaded; it's now the decompression, decryption, and verification. Go to bed; I'll come about midnight. I'm not tired because I slept in the car.'

When Jenifer went to bed, Dexter was sleeping soundly. She slipped silently between the sheets and then snuggled close. *I'd like a husband, especially this one.*

DAY 52
SUNDAY

When Dexter woke, Jenifer wasn't there, but he could see by the pillow that she had been. He put a robe over his pyjamas, put on his slippers, and padded downstairs. Jenifer, wearing pyjamas, was in front of her giant screen. Numbers were scrolling up from the bottom.

Without turning, she said, 'Good morning. Can you make coffee?'

'I will. Have you finished the download?'

'Yes, it's all here; now I'm installing it into the sim software. After breakfast, I'll calibrate and check the engine plug-in, and then it's the rest of the calibrations. You must help me again, Dex. Then by tonight, we should have a sim that does what Henry's one does, and we can try to crash it.'

Dexter didn't count the number of flights that he did in the simulator that day. The only break they had was for lunch. Some flights were Bo's automatic flight program; others, Jenifer or Dexter, flew manually, taking turns as captain. A scrutiny of the differences between the FDR data from Henry's sim and Jenifer's followed each flight. Then, careful adjustments became smaller as the day passed until Jenifer said, 'One more time, Dex, I'll fly, and you co-pilot. It should be spot on.

'I should write an auto-calibrate program, but that would take time, and I don't know how often we'll be doing this.'

...

'That's it; tomorrow, we can try to follow the recording of the first crash. Let's go to bed.'

...

'Kiss me, like before.'

... 'Have you done any thinking?'

'Yes, a little. I'm a bit more confident, and I have learnt something.'

'What.'

'That we must visit the Tolmen Stone before I tell you.'

'Then, I'll take you back when this is over. Good night, Bo.'

And if I say no, I can drive my car home.

DAY 53
MONDAY

———

At breakfast, Jenifer asked, 'Are you ready for today?'

'What's special about today?'

'We must run the FDR recording and voice recording that you synchronised and try to fly the sim accordingly. Those shouts and screams terrified me when I listened to them in your arms; what it will be like when I'm flying the plane, I don't know.'

'Can you shut down the sim and the recordings immediately after the FDR diverts from the sim status? Then, if the sim doesn't do the same thing, we don't need to hear it.'

'I can, Dex.'

'Then do that. Can you put a small screen with a large stopwatch to show the time in seconds so we'll have a reference for the control movements we must do?'

'That too. I'll put your FDR screen and the stopwatch beside each other. But what will this tell us.'

'Exactly when things went wrong. It's just the first step.'

…

'Ready?'

'Yes. Simtest one zero one, request engine start.'

The takeoff Jenifer did followed the FDR recording: The aircraft left the runway, climbed away, the captain throttled back to maintain the speed until the climb reached the right height, the wheels came up, the aircraft accelerated, and after a pause, when the altitude reached another safe level, the call 'flaps fifteen' raised the flaps, and the plane accelerated again. The captain raised the nose to increase the climb and pushed the power lever further forward. At the max speed for the partial flaps, with full power, it was climbing fast, and as it reached another altitude limit, the captain called 'Flaps', and a second later, the sim shut down.

'Dex, what happened?'

'I don't know, a flap might have stuck or broken. But it happened immediately after the call "Flaps".'

'Reset everything for engine start, and let me fly it.'

…

Thirty minutes later, with Dexter in the left seat, Bo called, 'Simtest one zero two, for engine start.' Dexter noted she had said *for* engine start. International Air procedures stated *request* engine start.

The test gave an identical result.

'Dex, where do we go from here?'

'Let me think, Bo.' His earlier thoughts about the commands came to the fore, and he thought, *what happens if you select flaps down at high speed and full power? I cannot imagine that. A pilot would never do it.*

'Bo, reset again, take the left seat and repeat the process.'

…

'Simtest one zero three, request engine start.'

It went as smoothly as the other two runs until the flaps call. Then the nose pitched down violently, and Jenifer instinctively hauled the control column back. Then the call 'Up-damn it-up' came from the speaker, and the nose rose so quickly that although Jenifer tried to push the column hard forward, the plane continued to the vertical, and then the sim shut down.

Shaken to the core by the unexpected and the screams heard in the cockpit, Jenifer began shaking, and Dexter reached over and pulled her to him. She clutched him tightly.

A few minutes later, the shaking stopped, and she asked, 'What did you do?'

'Selected flaps down, and then up at the shout "Up-damn it-up".'

'Why did the sim shut down.'

'After the aircraft stalled, it was uncontrolled, and the FDR data diverged from the sim; maybe it fell a different way.'

'Then we've found the problem. Do we tell Henry?'

'No, Bo. We must get the recordings of the latest crash. It may be different. And then we must plan a presentation.'

DAY 54
TUESDAY

———

The call came at 07:00. Jenifer was about to make a fruit salad.

'Good morning, Dexter Rawlins.'

'Captain Rawlins, this is William Faulker; we met after the CamAir Three-Ten incident.'

'I remember, sir. What can I do for you?'

'I'm sure you're aware of the recent Two-Thirty crashes. I'm calling to ask for your assistance in determining the cause.'

'Captain Boscawen and I are available, sir. We would be glad to help. Can you send us the FDR and CVR of the latest crash? I suggest a shared directory on the cloud.'

'You should have it within an hour, Captain. I'll call to check if you have it. Goodbye.'

'It's eleven at night in Phoenix. The investigation is a top priority, and the VP from the CamAir Three-Ten is in charge.'

'Four hundred and fifty dead people and two three-hundred-million-dollar aeroplanes is an expensive business.'

It took fifteen minutes for an emailed URL to arrive in Jenifer's inbox.

'I've received it. I'll put it through the decoder, and then you can synchronise the two.'

At 08:00, the phone rang again. William Faulkner was in a midnight meeting with several staff members.

'Captain Rawlins, I'm told you have the recordings.'

'We do, sir, and have decoded the FDR and listened to the voice recording. My first reaction, sir, is that to find a problem, it is often far easier to make comparisons. Can we ask for the same recordings for another take-off and two landings with the same crew and aircraft, with the load sheets?'

The reply was positive and frighteningly firm. 'If the recordings exist, you'll get them immediately.'

He called back only minutes later. 'Captain Rawlins, every flight's data and voice record has been in our library since the first crash. Which ones do you want?'

'The last six takeoffs and landings by the same crew in the same type with load data.'

'The recordings are on their way.'

'Thank you. We would appreciate it if you could dedicate Henry Mancuni and a simulator to us; we're modifying our simulator and programming it to the identical pre-take-off conditions. We want to cross-check test FDRs with him.'

'I'll arrange that immediately and give you his phone number. Thank you for your rapid action. Goodbye.'

•••

The VP then turned to his meeting and asked. 'Why do they want those old FDRs?'

Captain Strang replied, 'I guess they're trying to identify if pilot error is the cause. Having several may reveal inconsistencies.'

'Then we have the right guys on our team. Would you know what they're doing with the simulator?'

'Another guess, sir. Simulators shut down when a pilot exceeds acceptable pre-set conditions. I would guess they're removing all such limits and will fly their sim into the ground to see what breaks. It takes guts to *crash an aeroplane purposely and survive the trauma,* and it might damage a sim.'

Faulkner said nothing.

'So, what do we do?'

'I'll talk to Henry about limits and conditions, and we'll run tests and confirm the sync of our two sims. You finish the sync of the crash FDR and then the three other takeoffs and landings.'

'Then tomorrow we crash our sim again.'

Jenifer came into Dexter's room. 'Are you finished?'

'Yes, I've synched all seven of them, and both the captain and the co-pilot ignored the pilot's manual instructions in every case.'

'So how will we prove the infringement caused the crash.'

'Only one thing, Bo, the time from the "Flaps" instruction to the time the FDR recorded it was up. The FDR decode list includes a code for a flap motor overload trip, and that code doesn't show up, so the motor was running.'

'Then let's go to bed.'

...

'Bo, we make a good team, don't we?'

'I've been thinking the same thing. You asked me to think about sex, but it's not just that. Staying together means doing things together, and I've been thinking about working together in Aviation consultancy.'

'I have also, but I have another idea.'

'Explain, please.'

'After you demonstrated a single engine landing with offset fuel, and I've tried to rewrite that bit of the manual, I've realised that no airline simulator, anywhere, can teach a pilot what you did. I don't know what's required, but I reckon selling simulators that can, or kits to modify them, is another business.'

'That's smart, Dex, but we aren't business people.'

'Then we find a way to own a chunk of a simulator company that we don't need to run but can influence and to which we provide consulting services.'

'That's even smarter, but you'd be far smarter if you gave your partner a little attention....'

Day 55
Wednesday

'I'm ready.'

'Let me put in my earplugs. I don't want to hear the screaming again.'

'Do they work?'

'Yes, they're also noise cancelling.'

'Simtest one zero four, request engine start.'

...

'That was spot on, and it happened the same way.'

'So, are we finished?'

'We must do one more; I want to see what will happen when we fly Henry's sim; it won't have the shutdown switch when the FDR diverts from the sim.'

'Give me half an hour, and I'll remove it, then we'll have tea, discuss our presentation, have lunch and return to do it.'

'You can shut your eyes when the pilot calls "flaps".'

'No, I must see it at least once.'

'Right, Simtest one zero five, request engine start.'

After the flap calls, the aircraft reared up to the vertical. Dexter could see nothing but blue sky, but then he noticed. *The vapour trail from the engines is going the wrong way; we're sliding backwards!* Suddenly, the nose snapped down, and a small cloud streaked across the view, followed by the ground that slid up until it filled the screen. Dexter involuntarily brought his arm across his face as the top of a tall tree raced towards him. Then the screen went black.

Shaken to the core, Dexter dropped his arm and looked at Bo. She seemed frozen in her seat. He stood, picked her up, stepped from the back of the sim, and held her in his arms. When he felt her hands grip his waist and she pressed her head against his chest, he knew she would be fine.

Jenifer whispered, 'Hold me, that was horrible. Now I know what a skydiver must experience when his parachute fails to open.'

Half an hour later, Dexter had two seats on the next day's flight to Phoenix and called William Faulkner. It was early morning in Phoenix.

'Good morning, Sir.'

'Good morning, Captain, although should I say good evening? Do you have something to report?'

'We do, sir. Captain Boscawen and I will be aboard the International Air flight that arrives tomorrow evening. We request the simulator to be ready at 05:30 your time, and a meeting room with a large display screen with sound to run videos must be available two hours later. The attendees are up to you, but we request that the FAA be present at the meeting.'

'Why?'

'Sir, anything you tell the FAA will be subject to suspicion; if the FAA sees what we'll show you, direct from the horse's mouth, as it were, you're more likely to have immediate support.'

'The helicopter pilot will meet you, Captain. And everything will be ready.'

'Goodbye, sir.'

Day 56
Thursday

'We must leave by midday at the latest, Dex.'

'Are you packed? I am. I think we can make it by eleven.'

'That gives us four hours to mix the two demo videos correctly.'

'An hour each, although it might be much quicker as they're only fifteen minutes long.'

The arrival routine was identical to the last time they had flown into Phoenix, although the helicopter pilot wasn't the same man. By 22:00 Arizona time, they were in bed.

'Good night, my darling. Does JenDex Aviation consultants sound good to you?'

'It will do if the Dex part kisses the Jen part.'

'I can think of many parts to kiss.'

'Keep those until after we've succeeded in our first job. Do you want to visit Nance when we finish here?'

'If it's okay with you.'

'It's for you. I think we should, and I want to meet Nance and your granddaughter.'

'Then we'll arrange it after the meeting.'

DAY 57
FRIDAY

The limo collected them from the hotel at 05:00 and took them to a building on the airfield.

Standing outside, the welcoming committee was two men. When Dexter and Jenifer descended from the limo, one of them stepped forward. 'Good morning, Captain Rawlins, Captain Boscawen. It's a pleasure to see you again.'

Jenifer exclaimed, 'Captain Strang, are you part of a different team now?'

'The urgency of this enquiry has meant doubling up on test flights, so the boss seconded me. As I've met you before, I have the job of welcoming you.'

'That's very considerate.'

Jack Strang stepped to one side and indicated the man with him, 'Please, you met William Faulkner, the VP of the CamAir Three-Ten program when you were last here. He, too, is a secondee.'

Dexter and Jenifer shook hands as the VP said, 'A sincere welcome to you both; I'm praying you'll pull the rabbit from the hat as you did the last time. We have covered every avenue we can think of with no success so far. If there's anything you need, please ask.'

Jenifer asked, 'I asked for a simulator because I couldn't bring mine. Is there one here?'

'It is waiting for you in this building. Where did you get one?'

'We built it, it takes time and money, but without it, finding a problem is near impossible.'

'Will you do another demonstration?'

'That's what we planned; we'll crash your simulator in front of whoever you nominate to witness our crash.'

'Why?'

Dexter replied, 'So your FDR and VR analysts can certify that we've done precisely the same as the real crash, and the FAA will not question our results.'

'And then?'

Dexter replied, 'If the FDR records correspond, and you have organised the meeting as I requested with the FAA present and with the display equipment Captain Boscawen specified, we'll show you how we crashed it.'

'Then please go in with Captain Strang. I'll have your witnesses and the analysts here within half an hour.'

'Sir, several people will need a strong coffee or a tranquilliser after the demo.'

'That sounds ominous.'

'It is.'

'Then I'll make sure both are in the room next door.'

Henry Mancuni was in the simulator. When Jenifer saw him, she exclaimed, 'Henry, what a pleasure to meet you again.'

'Likewise, Captain. Since your request came, we've worked without pause to ensure the sim has the same configuration as the crashed aircraft, including the AD status and no shutdown limits.'

Jack Strang said, 'Henry suggested to the VP that he should ask you to come.'

'Thanks, Henry.'

'Just my job, but Captain Strang backed me up.'

Surprised, Jenifer turned to Captain Strang, 'Then thank you too.'

'Since you taught me how to land a CamAir Three-Ten on one engine, I believe you can do anything. Supporting Henry's suggestion was an easy decision.'

'Then, if all goes to plan, Dexter or I will ask you an embarrassing question at the meeting. Have the pilot's manual ready.'

'I will do. Thanks for the heads-up. Now, what configuration did you ask for?'

'Identical to the crash at engine start, fuel load and distribution, passengers, cargo mass and distribution, temperature, altitude and air pressure, and anything else you can think of.'

Henry added, 'There's one difference: out of respect for the two hundred and thirty-one passengers and crew who perished, the flight call sign will be Heaven two-three-one. The airport is identical to the real one, but the name is Angel Field.'

Dexter said, 'If everyone is here, shall we start?'

Strang checked, 'Yes, all present; getting nine into the sim won't be easy, but I'll try to position them where they can see the monitors. I hope you don't mind, Dexter, but we have a video camera focused on the panel from the control room behind us.'

'Not at all. It will provide further evidence.'

Jenifer took the left seat, Dexter the right, and Jack Strang sat on a jump seat behind them. Dexter warned, 'Strap in tight, please.' After strapping in, they put on headsets, and Jenifer called. 'Angel Field, Heaven two-three-one, good morning.'

'Two three one, go ahead.'

'Heaven two three one, request engine start.'

The words spoken and the following sequence were copies of their last practice, their timing exact to fractions of a second with the help of the large stopwatch Dexter stuck on the unnecessary navigation display. Then everything went haywire: the nose dropped violently, the sim shuddered and shook, Dexter, Jennifer and Strang were thrown violently from side to side, their headsets flew off, the nose soared up with more shaking and screeching, the aircraft stalled, the sim went into a frenzy of abrupt and random movement, and forty seconds later, the ground hit the screen, and the sim went dark.

Behind them, after a deathly pause, Strang said quietly. 'Holy fucking *shit*.'

Suddenly, a hubbub of voices rose from the profound silence behind them. Strang unstrapped, turned, strode forward, and shouted, 'Everyone out; only the data recorder team can return. Let the flight crew out.'

Once outside, Strang said, 'I need a coffee badly; it should be in the next room.'

Sitting in a corner with Dexter, Jenifer and Henry, Strang said, 'I've had some hairy landings and some terrifying crashes, both real and simulated, but that's the first time I understand the expression, "The ground came up and hit me in the face." May I call you Jenifer? And you, Dex?'

'Yes, please do.'

'Jenifer, that was a perfectly timed and executed display; how often have you practised it?'

'Not practised, but we did it three times before we found the answer, then two practices, and today.'

'How you can stand that experience more than once, I cannot comprehend; if Henry had included the passengers' screams, I would be a mental case.'

'Ask Henry to show you, Jack. He knows.'

Henry smiled, 'Gaming, Jack, the horrors imagined by twisted minds can be far worse.'

'Then, Henry can give me a lesson when this is over. We scheduled the meeting for eleven; I'll check if the analysts will be ready.'

'Bo, I'll call Nance.'

•••

'Hello, Nance.'

'Dad, this is a lovely surprise; where are you?'

'Phoenix. If we finish here today, can we visit you?'

'Of course, Dad, who's the "we".'

'My partner, Jenifer Boscawen. She's a captain like me.'

'Call me when you know your arrival time; I'll fetch you from San Jose airport.'

'Thanks, Nance, we'll see you tomorrow.'

There were more people at the meeting than the last time; Dexter estimated about twice the number around the U-shaped arrangement with the giant screen on the wall opposite them. Henry introduced them to the technician, who would run their video sequences, and people filed into the room to find their places and name tags. The VP brought a man with a mane of pure white hair and a buffalo bill moustache to meet Dexter and Jenifer and introduced him as the FAA representative, Colonel Bill Grady; then, they went to their seats. Dexter and Jenifer sat on two chairs beside a desk in the middle of the U where everyone could see them. The VP had a gavel and tapped it on the desk.

'Good morning. I see everyone is here. We have two consultants visiting CamAirCom today. They're from England, and Captain Rawlins and Captain Boscawen are specialists in Aviation operations and aircraft. CamAirCom engaged them to investigate the most recent crash independently, and they asked for this meeting to report. You'll have heard by now that they crashed a simulator this morning, and I can confirm that our analysts state the recordings are identical to the actual crash. As most of you here did not witness the simulator test, Captain Strang has asked we view it, and then our consultants will tell us how they did it.'

Dexter and Jennifer had not seen the video, which began with a view through the cockpit door, as they, followed by Strang, took their seats. The final scenes, if anything, exaggerated the simulator's movements and the horror of the dive into obliteration.

When, after a pause, Dexter stood, there were many white faces. Two people left the room and returned.

'Ladies and Gentlemen, I have trained pilots for many years and don't believe a few words or a piece of paper will work well, so my style is to show my trainees, and I hope to show you. As an introduction, we'll show the data recorded when the aeroplane landed the day before the incident. The crew, God bless them, was the same.' Dexter nodded to the technician. 'You'll hear the cockpit voice recording. On the screen, you'll see an icon of the plane landing with altitude and airspeed changing.'

The landing was perfect, except the flap calls were 'flaps fifteen', then 'flaps.'

Jenifer stood, 'That was a perfect landing, and I can confirm that the heights, speeds, flap operations, and undercarriage deployment occurred as designated in the pilot's manual. However, there is one small, almost unnoticeable error in the procedures followed.'

'Now we'll show you a similarly constructed video of the crash.'

When it ended, more white faces were around the table; the terrified voices of the captain and co-pilot and the screaming background horrified most of them.

After thirty seconds of complete silence, Jenifer stood and said, before the VP could say anything. 'We were at first completely flummoxed trying to identify the cause of the crash. However, I was with Captain Rawlins three months ago in International Air's CamAir Three-Ten simulator at Gatwick. He suspended a qualified airline Captain who had flown several thousand hours and sent him for medical and psychiatric examination. The recording of that pilot's landing, apart from the aircraft type, was the same as the first one shown today. Captain Strang can, I hope, tell you why the pilot received a suspension. Captain?'

'It seems a drastic punishment, but the pilot manual states that the Pilot in Charge must call for flaps with the words "Flaps Down Fifteen", "Flaps down Thirty", and "Flaps down full." The calls made in the first video were "Flaps Fifteen" and "Flaps". If anyone wants to hear it again, I'm sure we can do so.'

Dexter took over, 'Captain Strang, did you notice the calls for flaps in the second video?'

'Yes, there were only two, "Flaps Fifteen" and "Flaps." Neither are according to the manual.'

'Thank you. Did you hear another shout? "Up, up".'

Strang replied, 'According to the data record, the captain was hauling back hard on the stick at that moment. We assumed he was shouting at the aircraft, and before the recording terminated, the flap indicator showed the flaps up.'

'Thank you, Captain Strang, Mr Mancuni, you were with me this morning in the simulator. I had a large stopwatch to synchronise our flight with the actual crash. Before we began, what action did I take?'

Mancuni replied, 'You cycled the flaps down each step, then up again. A classic pre-take-off checklist item for sticking flaps.'

Dexter took a tiny notebook from his pocket. 'I can report to everyone here the exact time it takes for the flaps to travel between each designated setting. The data recorder will register a code if the flap motor trips under overload and no such code appears in the record.

'I can also confirm that the time between the instruction "Flaps" given by the captain – until the time recorded by the FDR that the flaps reached full up – is the time it takes if flaps *DOWN* is selected, followed by a flaps *UP* selection at the time of the "Up-Up" call.

'The data shows the first officer selected the flaps down inadvertently; I suggest due to work overload and the habit of selecting flaps down in response to the call "Flaps" on the landing approach.

'He did this well above the maximum allowable speed, and the aircraft, at full power, immediately and violently pitched down as it did this morning in the simulator, then accelerated, making the situation worse. The pilot put as much back pressure as he could on the control column and shouted "Up-Up" as he realised the flap error, and when the flaps came up, the nose rose rapidly, uncontrollably, and the aircraft stalled.

'At that altitude, no recovery was possible.

'Before terminating, I would like to make two further comments.

'First, the FDR does not record the movement of the flap switch, only the flap position.

'Second, a preliminary examination of the earlier crash of a two-thirty appears to have happened for the same reasons.

'Thank you.'

Dexter sat beside Jenifer and drank over half the glass of water on the table. She whispered. 'You've staggered them, Dex.'

The silence dragged on.

Then, the FAA rep leaned toward the VP and said something. Then the VP asked.

'Captain Rawlins, Captain Boscawen, thank you for a masterful analysis; what are your recommendations?'

'Sir, I know this is not an official enquiry, but Captain Boscawen and I have compiled the following items for implementation, especially the first that we believe is urgent and should not await an official investigation.

'One. An immediate circular with FAA approval to all the type operators to emphasise the gravity of not following the procedures in the manual. The crashes were pilot errors, and that is the quickest way to reduce the risk of it happening again.

'Two. CamAirCom designs an interlock preventing flap movements outside the approved operating parameters of speed, altitude and power, and with FAA approval, issues a mandatory AD for earliest installation.

'Three. CamAirCom should upgrade the data recording system to record flap switch operation and increase the sampling rate during flap movement to determine flap position.'

There was another silence while the VP conferred with the FAA.

'I would like to thank Captain Rawlins and Captain Boscawen for solving a complex problem. We'll break, and three committees will convene to discuss and implement the recommendations. The FAA asks that we issue the circular before 17:00 today. Captain Strang will lead that committee.'

⚊⚊⋙✇⋘⚊⚊

The VP came and thanked them; then Strang promised to meet them at their hotel once the circular went out.

The VP reported to the president.

'William, that's a huge relief. As it was a pilot error and the manual instructions are clear, we aren't at risk, and the FAA won't suspend the aircraft. Without those two experts, what would it have cost us?'

'I believe Bill Grady came today because the FAA was ready to suspend all aircraft tomorrow. In that case, several months, cancelled orders, insurance and warranty claims. Anywhere between twenty to sixty billion. We would have offsets shifting the workforce, and one of our guys might have found the problem, so, say, thirty billion. The standard fee to JenDex would be one per cent, so three hundred million.

'May I add that they built a simulator in England and crashed it several times to prove the cause. I don't know how they did it so quickly, and a simulator is not cheap. They didn't ask for payment in advance; their only concern was saving lives. If you want to see the video, you'll experience the trauma they did while doing so.'

'That's the cost of one aeroplane. We would have lost orders for hundreds. Get that interlock done in a hurry. The insurers will raise their premiums, and the purchase cost will increase. One per cent extra premium would add three million to the annual operating cost. Pay our consultants but negotiate a payment schedule over five years. Murphy's law says we'll need them again.'

Jack Strang was as good as his word. He met them in the reception hall and brought a copy of the FAA circular that warned of the danger of deviating from the flight manual.'

'Dex, this is for you; you can frame it. But I have something else to say.'

'Go ahead, Jack.'

'Jenifer said you suspended an experienced Captain when he didn't make the correct calls during a check ride, and I said it seemed excessive. I was wrong; when it's a matter of safety, that is the right action. I'll lobby the FAA to change their cockpit management training guidelines to emphasise this.'

'Thanks, Jack. I'll send you my modifications to the International Air operating manual. One is about crew changeover in flight; Jenifer pointed out a flaw in the old procedure. If you're lobbying to change an FAA doc, you might include it.'

'Thanks. When are you leaving?'

'We're visiting San Jose to meet my daughter. We'll return to the UK from there. Can you suggest a flight?'

'Where in the San Jose area?'

'Her husband works at the Ames Research Centre. They must live nearby, but she said she could pick us up at the San Jose airport.'

'Ames is at Moffet Field, and we have regular flights there. Let's go into the bar and have a drink, and I'll make a couple of phone calls.'

⎯⎯✺⎯⎯

In the bar, Dexter fetched the drinks while Jack Strang spoke into his phone, then said,

'Dex, a limo to take you to the plane at 07:30, then our corporate jet to Moffet field, arriving at 09:50. Will that suit you?'

'Perfect, Jack. Thanks.'

Strang spoke again into his phone. 'That's fixed, Dex. It'll be a Citation.'

'Then I'll call my daughter and tell her.'

⎯⎯✺⎯⎯

Jenifer asked when she climbed into bed, 'Dex, what are your family like?'

'I don't know. I was in East Asia when I received an emailed invitation to their wedding with only a few days' notice; I couldn't attend. I received photos some weeks later. Nance looked a little fat, so I figured it was a rapid wedding.'

'So, what is she like?'

'Dark hair, mid-length, she looks more like Bethkin than me, about your height but a bit heavier. I haven't seen her for fifteen years, and she's now thirty-three. She was a difficult child; often, I thought she was somewhere else. She became enthusiastic about animals and had every kind of pet you can think of. When she was young, she always had something like a rabbit or guinea pig in her arms. I wasn't surprised when she said she wanted to become a vet. I *was* surprised when she married a scientist.'

'What's he like?'

'His name is Frank Beerman. Short fair hair, a brush or crew cut, and in the wedding photo, spectacles with thick frames. He might have contacts or had an op by now. Quite a bit taller than her but not heavily built.'

'And your granddaughter?'

'She must be getting on for ten now; she was six in the last family photo I received. I would say a copy of her mother, although she may not be the dreamy kid her mother was.'

'Would she like a rabbit?'

'Where do we buy one?'

'It's still early. Let's ask the concierge if they can get one in a box for tomorrow morning.'

Dexter called and, without ringing off, turned away from the phone to ask Jenifer, 'What colour?'

'Just say for a ten-year-old girl.'

•••

'You'll feel like a grandfather for the first time. I hope it won't change your behaviour.'

'If you feel that happening, kick me.'

'I'll buy you boxers with naked nymphs all around it in lewd po-sitions.'

'Is it your night to kiss me?'

'Yes, and it's given me an idea.'

'Another?'

'I'll have those boxers especially printed with a photo of me.'

'Can I be the photographer?'

'Shut up, I can't kiss moving lips.'

DAY 58
SATURDAY

—

They had breakfast at six, collected their cases, and then a white baby bunny with black eyepatches in a box and carrier bag. At 07:30, the limo driver collected their suitcases.

Two hours and fifteen minutes later, they landed at Moffet Field.

The Citation drew to a stop before the Executive Terminal. Two minutes later, the engines had stopped, the door had opened, and Dexter went down the steps carrying the shopping bag, followed by Jennifer. Then they walked together to the building and through the automatic doors.

He instantly recognised the three people standing a few metres ahead: Frank, with his hands on Linnette's shoulders as she stood before him, and Nance beside him.

Nance ran forward with a broad smile spreading from ear to ear, 'Dad, how marvellous,' and wrapped her arms around him. Dexter felt fifteen years younger as memories flooded him. She looked at him and said, 'You feel the same, Dad.' He kissed her as he had done years ago on the forehead. 'So do you, Nance.'

'You have someone to meet, Dad.' She turned and gestured at Linnette, and Frank pushed Linnette forward. 'Lettie, this is your grandfather.'

Then Nance turned to Jenifer. 'And you must be Jenifer. You're lovely and so young to be a captain.' Then she looked into Jenifer's eyes, and the two women looked at each other in silence. Fortunately, Dexter and Frank were looking at Linnette, for the two women stood silently, their gazes locked. They sensed the tension and insecurity in the other, and then it drained away, replaced by curiosity and finally by comprehension. Nance spoke first.

'So, you and Dexter?'

Jenifer smiled, 'Adore ponies.'

Nance smiled too, 'So do I – and Linnette.'

Dexter had stood looking at his granddaughter for half a minute, the little girl looking at him curiously. He was at a loss until he remembered the rabbit in the shopping bag, so he dropped to a half squat, one knee on the floor so his face was at the same height. 'Lettie, you look just like your mother when she was ten.'

Lettie was serious when she replied. 'That's what mom says.'

'Well, that's true, and your mom loved animals; I remember I had to be careful in the house because she had so many, I could easily step on one. Are you like that?'

'Yes, but mom won't let them out of my room when I play with them, and I must keep them in cages outside.'

'Well, that's a good thing if it stops big feet squashing them. Have you got a rabbit?'

Still serious, Lettie answered, 'No, I had one, and he escaped; Mom says she won't buy one until I'm more re-spon-si-ble.'

'Well, I feel sure you're old enough to have a rabbit.'

Linnette seemed to lose her seriousness; she smiled, and Dexter thought it was a happy smile. 'Will you buy me one?'

'Should I ask your mother?'

Linnette was despairing, 'She'll say no.'

'Lettie, the name of the pilot who came with me is Jenifer, but I call her "Bo", and yesterday we saw a little rabbit in a pet shop window, and the name on the cage was "Bo". So, we bought the rabbit.'

Linnette, clearly excited, asked, 'Did you bring it?'

Dexter moved the carrier bag from behind him, 'We can look in here.'

Thirty kilos of an excited child who threw herself at him almost knocked him over; then she hugged him with her arms around his neck. 'Can we look now?'

'Yes, but we mustn't let her out. She might run across the airport.'

Dexter opened the bag, took out the box with a grille on one side, and Lettie breathed. 'She's beautiful, thank you, grandad.'

Frank had watched and heard the interaction, and when Dexter stood, he reached his hand forward. 'That's what she's wanted for months. I'm glad to meet you at last, Dexter. Nance has talked about you for years, and I can see they weren't tall stories.'

And I thought I was persona non grata. I wish I'd known.

He shook Frank's hand firmly, 'Frank, the feeling's mutual. Let me introduce Jenifer.'

Dexter turned and found himself facing two women standing close to each other, smiling happily. Experienced in body language, Dexter immediately knew that they were firm friends. *They have a bond.*

'Bo, come and meet Frank and Lettie.'

Jenifer shook hands with Frank; he reminded her a little of her father, then dropped to speak to Lettie.

'Hello, Lettie.'

'Hello, is your name Bo?'

'Some people have two names, Lettie. My outside name is Jennifer, but Dexter calls me Bo because he loves me and knows that inside, I'm Bo.'

'Do you like rabbits?'

'All animals, Lettie. I especially like ponies and talking to them.'

'How do you talk to them?'

'Like you do, Lettie, with your hands and fingers.'

Linnette looked at her, her eyes bright. 'And they understand you?'

'Like they understand you and your mother. One day, your parents can bring you to see where we live, and you can meet our wild pony friends.'

'I'd like that.'

'Then I'll invite them.'

Nance had listened. She whispered to Dexter, 'You must tell me where you met her, Dad, and never let her go. She's a rare find.'

'I know.'

'Now let's go to our house, where Lettie can let little Bo out of the cage.'

Jenifer played with Lettie and her menagerie while Frank, Dexter and Nance were in the kitchen. While preparing lunch, Nance sipped a glass of wine; Frank and Dexter had beers. The three-way conversation interested all of them.

'Dad, why do you have five bars on your shirt?'

Dexter had to explain and then admitted that he could no longer fly scheduled airline flights as captain due to his age.

'So, what will you do?'

'I could stay on as training Captain for another five years, but I'm hoping Jennifer and I can do something different together.'

Frank, familiar with the comings and goings at Moffet Field, asked, 'That was a CamAirCom jet that brought you Dex; what were you doing with them?'

'Bo and I are consultants to CamAirCom; we've done a couple of jobs for them.'

'Is Jennifer an airline captain?'

'She's fully qualified, Frank, with over two thousand hours, but she doesn't fly full time. She builds simulators and flies them to improve aircraft.'

'Then they must be very different simulators.'

'They are; if you're interested, ask her about them.'

Nance asked, 'How did you meet her, Dad?'

'That's a long story; I think she should tell you because I'm still learning about her.'

'Frank, I have no idea what you do except what the word research conjures up. Is it hush-hush, or can you tell me?'

'Some of what I do is a secret, but not my role. I'm a reliability engineer, and Ames does space research. I'll ask a question that you know the answer to. Would it arrive if one of your airliners had to fly continuously for a year to reach the destination?'

Dexter replied, 'No, and now I know what you do. Is it self-repairing or microduplication?'

'Both, although the first is still a futuristic dream.'

'If you two space explorers would spare a moment for an over-worked Terran woman, would you please help put our lunch on the terrace table?'

⊱•⊰

Jenifer and Linnette arrived on the terrace. 'We put the animals in their cages, mom. Bo showed me how to tell them they would be safe.'

'That's worth learning, Lettie. Thanks Bo.'

'A pleasure. Lettie tells me you have a big practice with many animals.'

'Sometimes a pet needs to stay a day or two for treatment, and as it's Saturday, I must go this afternoon to feed them. Would you like to join me?'

'With pleasure, is it in the country?'

'I wish it were, but having it near the clients works best. If visiting the vet is easy, they do and don't let the animals suffer.

'Help yourself to the salads and Bratwurst.'

'Nance, your animal hospital is super modern, all this lighting and ventilation.'

'You might like the smells of a farm, Dad. I do, but the neighbours object, especially those who don't love animals. Frank did it all for me; it's temporary accommodation, I can adjust the cage sizes, the lighting that mimics day and night, all the waste goes in a composter, and the fan system filters and UV sterilises the air.'

Jenifer asked, 'Do you only have house pets to treat?'

'Mostly, but you'd be surprised at the pets some people have. But there are at least ten zoos or animal petting farms in the San Jose area, and I'm on call for them; I go to one once or twice a week when an animal is sick. Then don't forget the animal shelters; if they call, I don't charge.'

'Are strays a problem?'

'The same as in Europe and the UK, it's cyclical, many more during the holiday season. Bo, can you do the small animals and birds at this end? Ignore the reptiles. Linnette knows the routine and the feed in the bins; the codes are on the cages. Dad and I'll feed the dogs and the Tapir. Then we'll go home and prepare a barbecue for this evening.'

Dexter had a feeling he hadn't had for years when they assembled on the Terrace later. *We're a family; not just Nance, Lettie and me, but also Frank and Bo.*

Linnette had a little kitten on her lap, and Frank had handed each adult a glass of California wine when Nance asked.

'Bo, Dad said I must ask you how you met him.'

'I went to Gatwick to fly to Mauritius for my mother's funeral. In the departure terminal, with all the strange people, I froze with an anxiety attack, and Dex rescued me. I'm a pilot, and when I recovered, I saw his bars and thought, "He's a friend", and we have stayed together since.'

Frank asked, 'Dexter said you build simulators to make better aeroplanes; that's unusual. Why?'

'Because I was a gamer when I was twenty. I then caught the flying bug when flying a computer game, so I went to get a license. Still, I knew I couldn't be a pilot for a living because I might have an attack and freeze, so I flew my simulator, modified the software to resemble a real aeroplane, and then experimented to make it fly better.'

'Jenifer, I'm still a little in the dark. To do what you describe requires an enormous amount of data and sophisticated structural analysis programming. Can you do that?'

'No, I started with control systems. I had to learn programming and found the languages were difficult to use, so I invented my own. Before I started the structural stuff, I had gathered many friends who helped. I tell them what I need, and they send me a plugin.'

Frank wondered if Jenifer was telling the truth, so he asked, 'What language did you invent?'

'I called it Linky.'

My God, the creator of Linky is sitting on my terrace!

All his doubts fell away. 'Jenifer, can I take you to work on Monday? I'll show you around and introduce you to people who will be thrilled to meet you; they all use Linky.'

'If Dex can come too, I'd love to.'

Day 59
Sunday

At breakfast, Frank said, 'On Sundays, Nance often has a fellow animal lover come to feed the menagerie because they aren't at work. That gives us the chance to get away. East of here, the mountains are a wonderful place to go. We don't hike many trails because Lettie must grow more before she can do the longer and more rugged ones. However, there are many picnic spots in or beside woods, with lovely views; we take lunch, barbecue some ribs, and sometimes meet our wilder cousins.'

'Are there bears?'

'The bears are often a nuisance in the bigger campgrounds and picnic places with dozens of people, but the more remote single places don't interest them. If one visits us, then we jump into the car. I do have pepper spray.'

'We've never visited the mountains here; that will be great.'

<hr />

'Nance, that was delicious, and Frank's ribs are five-star.'

'Thanks, Bo, we've had lots of practice. Frank proposed at a picnic in Derbyshire, so for us, these picnics are a memory.'

Dexter whispered, 'Lettie, we have a little friend visiting.'

'Where, Grandad?'

Dexter pointed. 'Under that bush.'

'Oh, I see him, it's a rabbit.'

Dexter took a lettuce leaf from the bowl on the table. 'Shall we invite him to our picnic?'

'How?'

Dexter tore off a piece of leaf. Take this, then crawl slowly towards him; I'll come too.'

Dexter whispered, 'That's close enough; lay the lettuce down in front, then come back.'

'Now we've invited him. Just wait and see if he accepts. Concentrate on how much you love rabbits and him.'

The rabbit was reluctant but habituated to the presence of people he didn't run, and after three minutes, felt the lettuce was worth the risk, so it lolloped out from under the bush and began to nibble.

'Here, Lettie, take the lettuce, crawl again, tear off a piece, put it close to him, then wait. If he eats it, hold out another piece, and he might take it from your fingers. Keep thinking how much you love him.'

When the rabbit had eaten the rest of the lettuce from Lettie's fingers, it turned and lolloped back to the bush.

'Grandad, how did you know it would come?'

'I didn't, Lettie, but if you tell an animal you love it, often, they like you and won't be scared.'

Jenifer, Frank, and Nance had watched them, silently sitting as if frozen; Nance had a smile on her face, Frank an expression of amazement, and Jenifer one of wonder.

Only love could calm a wild rabbit. Although Lettie had never met him before we came here, she loves Dex, not because he's her grandad, but because he loves her. Nance loves him too, even though they became separated years ago, not because he's her dad, but because Dex loves her. Dex loves me too, and now I can compare; I know it's not as his daughter but as his wife, and I don't love him as my dad. I felt it in Mauritius. I love him as my husband. We must return to Dartmoor.

Day 60
Monday

———

When they woke in the morning, Jenifer asked, 'Dex, are we leaving on the flight tonight?'

'I think we should, if there are seats, we don't want to overstay our welcome, although it has been completely different to what I expected.'

'Then, when we arrive in London, can we go straight to your farm?'

'Of course, I'm on holiday until the end of the week.'

'Do we wear bars today?'

'If you want to, but I won't.'

'Then I won't either.'

———

Frank went to work early, taking Lettie to school, then returned to collect Dexter and Jennifer after Nance had left for work. He drove them back to Moffet field, to a building that Jenifer remarked. 'Isn't a glass building a mistake in this climate? Although it's tinted.'

'The glass reflects heat; it's surprisingly effective. But the trees on the south side help with summer shade. There's a central quadrangle, and that has more trees.'

Dexter asked, 'Who are we meeting, Frank?'

'I'm not sure, Dex; I sent out a message inviting anyone who wants to meet the creator of Linky to come between 10:00 and noon. We'll be in the big conference room, with drinks, so the guys will dribble in when they have a moment. They're an easy-going crowd. Either I'll introduce you, or they'll introduce each other. We all use first names.'

Dexter thought. *Bo's not wearing bars. I must watch for signs of anxiety if the crowd is too big.*

Frank's first introduction surprised Dexter. 'Dex. I'd like you to meet the Stanford Professor of Reliability Sciences, Wu Chen. Half our reliability staff followed his courses, and we have the privilege of collaborating with him. As he was visiting today, I invited him to meet Bo.'

Dexter shook hands, 'Professor, meeting you and this group is a rare privilege.'

'No, Captain, the privilege is mine. Meeting the person who created Linky is not something I would miss.'

Frank took the professor to meet Bo, and Dexter felt immediately at home amongst a group of people at the forefront of aviation research.

He had expected rocket scientists but learnt within minutes that the problems they researched might be more severe, but they were the same as those aviation engineers had studied for a century.

He kept glancing at Jenifer and, after ten minutes, realised she was enjoying herself immensely, so concentrated on the subject that had risen spontaneously when one of the scientists had said, 'Dexter, we can make the hardware more reliable, but I believe the weakest link will always be the human being.'

'So, you're an advocate of automation?'

'Essentially yes.'

'Do you mind an amateur remark?'

'Not at all, please go ahead.'

'I agree that you can human-proof a machine like an aeroplane by using automation, but no matter how good your AI program is, in the development chain are some humans, so the automaton itself can be unreliable.'

In the silence that followed, Dexter glanced again at Bo; she was in the centre of a group of seven or eight scientists arguing about something, including Frank and the professor. She looked up at him, and he saw her eyes sparkling and happy. *She's loving it!*

A woman, introduced to him as Karen, said, 'I've heard that before. My answer was that I don't support automation to eliminate risk and failure but to reduce it. If I say we test an automaton under every possible circumstance, you can justifiably say, "Not those circumstances a human cannot imagine. We aren't perfect."'

Then she added, 'I don't want to be rude, but I want to know what's going on over there.'

Dexter and the others looked at the group with Bo and saw her walk to the whiteboard on the wall and pick up a marker.

The discussion amongst the scientists around Bo stemmed from a question she had asked. 'Why are you either "Repair" or "Micro Duplication" researchers?'

Frustrated by her difficulty explaining her viewpoint after saying there should be no division, she said, 'I don't know what you can do physically, but in software, this should be possible,' stepped to the board, and began writing program code in Linky.

As the groups merged, Karen whispered to another scientist, 'What's she doing?'

The reply was *sotto voce*, 'She's merging "Repair" and "Micro Duplication" using Linky.'

Silence fell until Jenifer finished the sixth line, stood back, and spoke. 'There, I think that says what I mean.'

In the silence, Dexter thought. *Bo must be over the anxiety. There's no sign of it.*

Then one of the men said, '*My God!*' He took his phone from a pocket and photographed the board, followed by the others taking photos.

Frank stepped forward and asked, 'Bo, can you sign the board, *please!*' She did.

Then Frank said, 'Guys, I know you would like to spend the next week with Jenifer, but I must drag her away because she and Dexter have a flight to catch. However, I'm sure it's not the last time we'll see her here.'

After applause from everyone, the professor accompanied them to the door.

'Captain Boscawen, today has been a great privilege for me. I look forward to our next meeting.'

'Thank you, Professor, you're very kind to say so, goodbye.'

'Not kind, Captain. Honest. Goodbye.'

Dexter asked in the car during the drive back to Frank's home. 'Why the signature on the board, Frank.'

'Dex, if that program code proves to be true, then that board, framed and glass-covered, will hang in the entrance hall.'

'Why?'

'That code mimics how a human body repairs itself to last a hundred years.'

Frank drove them to San Jose International, and the International Air flight left at 16:25

DAY 61
TUESDAY

The Jet stream gave them a boost; they arrived fifty minutes early, and at 11:05, they drove onto the M25 on the way to Dartmoor.

After a break at Amesbury for a snack, they arrived at 15:00.

'Dex, are you too tired to walk?'

'No, where do you want to go?'

'Change, take our sticks and water, drive to the Fernworthy car park, and then walk to Manga Brook. If the ponies are there, I want to ask them something.'

<hr>

'We can go now. The ponies have told me everything I need to know, but I must ask you something.'

'What?'

'Do you remember when we were on the plane flying to Tampa? I asked you about your plans for the future when you passed your sixtieth birthday.'

'Yes, I do.'

'Well, you're about to pass it, have you decided?'

'I have, at least in the short term.'

•••

I wish he had said long-term. 'So, you'll stay on as the training captain for International Air?'

Dexter smiled at her, a smile that somehow gave her hope. 'No, I said I wanted to do something different, so I'll do something different until I'm discarded.'

'Out with it. What?'

Dexter said, 'Give me your hands.' She felt her heart leap then race as he took them and looked tenderly at her, then said, 'What I do is up to you. The last two months have been so much fun that whether you marry me or not, I'll stick to you like a leech until you throw me out, and then I'll fly as an instructor at Exeter airport.'

Jenifer smiled at him, trying to slow her heartbeat; Dexter thought she was struggling with a reply, then she said, 'Come, we have something to do,' and walked away.

He had to walk behind her when the path narrowed, and when he managed to walk beside her, talking was impossible; he was sure she was going as fast as she could. Twenty minutes after they crossed the clapper bridge, Dexter was sure he knew where she was going, and fifteen minutes later, he was confident when the Tolmen stone came into view. As they reached it, she climbed down to the rocks in the lazy trickle of water and spoke. 'I want to climb up through the hole. You must help me, go on top.'

He climbed on top and looked down through the hole at Jenifer. *This is a test. I hope I pass.*

'Give me your hand.'

As their hands clasped, Jenifer looked up into his eyes, and he stared silently into hers for ten or fifteen seconds; then Dexter asked, 'What does this mean to you?'

'Pull me into your arms, and I promise to marry you. It's forever; it's your last chance to escape. The ceremony is a formality.'

He pulled her up through the hole in one smooth lift, and she fell into his arms. The kiss lasted until Dexter said, 'We have company.

'It's Dolly and her stallion, with two others; they must have followed us. Let's go and tell them…'

'They know.'

'Yes, I can sense it too. Let's go home.'

Dexter was already between the sheets when a grinning Jenifer came from the bathroom wearing the pyjamas with the hand imprints, and he burst into happy laughter. 'Darling, do you believe I need instructions?'

Jennifer chuckled, 'Well, you're a training expert, Dex, but only flying training; maybe you need help with another kind of flying.'

'Come here and judge for yourself.'

Smiling, Jenifer slid into bed beside him, and for what seemed ages to her, he looked into her eyes – and then asked. You're sure, Bo?'

'Forever, Dex. Now. Blow and caress me like the stallion you are.'

He began as he had done once before, breathing warm breath on her eyelids and then caressing them with his tongue and lips, and continued. Their pyjamas landed on the floor minutes later, with the ripping sound of Velcro tearing apart, and the caresses continued. The clock stopped ticking for them both, and then Jenifer felt him in her mind and knew he sensed her. Small fires began under her ears and then joined with others that spread from her nipples and continued to grow. She felt his caresses everywhere as their skins, the sensitivity raised to almost unbearable limits, brushed together, and when she felt him enter and caress her from inside, she could feel what he felt, and he knew her feelings. When she squeezed, she felt *his* pleasure, and when he moved, he felt *hers*, and together, the fires grew until finally, silently, she thought, *NOW, DEX, COME!* He heard, and their minds joined as their bodies locked together in muscle-straining ecstasy.

An hour later, Jenifer woke. 'Dex, what are you doing.'

'I feel your toes are lonely, Bo.'

'Then why are you kissing my nipples?'

'Because of the TV Ad.'

Jenifer smiled. *I love this man.* 'Which one?'

'The one that says, "Life's a journey; enjoy the ride." I'll enjoy the journey to your toes – and then the ride.'

'Then enjoy the voyage, but please pause there longer.'

•••

'Dex, why have you stopped travelling?'

'I found an interesting place, darling, especially the little Tor here...'

'Dex, I seem to have an interesting visitor.'

'Then say hello...'

'I'll turn over; my back needs scratching.'

She could feel where she itched, and Dexter scratched in precisely the right place. Jenifer felt his feelings, and several gentle scratches later, she drew her knees underneath her waist and felt him enter as the fires grew again. They guided each other's desires until they collapsed in a tight embrace with Jenifer's final thought after an ecstatic shaking and shuddering. *He will be my stallion forever.*

Day 62
Wednesday

When they woke the following day, they were both reluctant to leave the bed, and tender kisses and caresses kept them there for an hour until Jenifer said. 'Now that we've decided to marry, we have decisions to make.'

'Yes, my darling, where do you want to start.'

'What seems like ages ago, but after I met you, Susan said I must buy some condoms.'

'Why?'

'She said if I went to a tropical island with you, anything could happen, so I should buy some.'

'How many did you buy?'

'Twelve.'

Dexter laughed, 'So I have a sex-mad wife. Why are you telling me this.'

'Because I forgot about them last night, and you did too.'

'Bo, we love each other. Would you like a child?'

'Yes, it would make us a family.'

'Me too, so let's just go on and see if it happens. If it does, we must decide how many we want. What's next?'

He could sense when she grinned that the unexpected was coming. 'Which of us will get up first to make the coffee in the morning?'

Dexter chuckled, 'Bo, we'd better get this right, or our marriage will fail before we get out of bed. How about taking turns? But we make it one-year stints. For one year, you make coffee, and for the next, I will.'

'That's fair, but whose year is this one?'

'We could toss a coin?'

'Then, fetch a coin, and I'll toss it.'

A minute later, a naked Dexter had found a ten-penny coin. 'Here, heads, and it's my year.' Jennifer, also naked, stood beside the bed, took the ten-penny piece, spun it into the air, and said, 'Abracadabra!' before it fell on the floor.

She took two steps forward and bent over to look.

It was too much for Dexter, and she felt him gather her into his arms from behind.

'Dex, that's cheating.'

As he lifted her and fell back on the bed, he said, 'You said "Abracadabra", the genie has come to fulfil your wish.'

'Then turn onto your back.'

...

'It was heads; you make the coffee.'

'It was worth it.'

⎯⎯◦◦⎯⎯

'I'll call my architect.'

'What for?'

'We need re-organizing; you must take back your barn. Build another in a corner of your fields for the farmer if necessary. Make it big enough to take those farm implements away.'

'Why?'

'I need the barn for my sim and workspace, and the architect knows what I want. Then the woodshed must move, and the toilet can include the woodshed to be a bathroom, and the implement store becomes a bedroom.'

'Again, why?'

'So, when Nance visits, they can have the upstairs, and we can move there. Then, one day, Linnette can use it.'

'What about the mud?'

'Don't be difficult; we'll have a paved terrace.'

'You seem very sure, Bo.'

'I am. Linnette will come because the ponies will ask her to when she meets them on their first visit to us.'

'That's great.'

'Then, when you return to Gatwick, resign, and JenDex will sell simulator updates and solve aviation problems. The headquarters will be our barn. From now on, if we need to go somewhere, we charter a jet out of Exeter.'

'Can I tell Philip he can call on us if he has a crew problem? I'll ask him to let us do our line checks with Greg. You must fly as captain.'

'It will be fun, Dex, especially if we go to unusual places, but not too often. Tell him.'

'Bo, there's something else we must do. Can we go to Exeter tomorrow to the courthouse and get a marriage licence?'

'Are you in a hurry, Dex? I promised, what's the rush?'

'We'll get a licence, Bo, then once we have a marriage date, we can notify the registrar. It can take up to six weeks before the ceremony. You mentioned condoms; I want to be sure we're married if a baby comes.'

I am in a hurry. Doris said Jenifer has all the time in the world, and I don't.

'Okay, Dex. Tomorrow.' *Is he worried I might run away with another guy?*

Day 85
Friday

'**D**earest, I've received an email from Stanford University.'

'From the professor?'

'No, it's an invitation from public relations to attend the degree awards ceremony in three weeks. It says Jenifer Boscawen and partner. I've no idea why.'

'Then you must call Frank and ask.'

'I'll wait until this afternoon when they're up.'

...

'Hello, Jenifer, Frank is in the shower.'

'I can call again, Nance.'

'He won't be long; you must be excited. We hope you can stay a few days with us.'

'Nance, why should I be excited?'

'Don't you know yet?'

'Know what?'

'That Stanford is awarding you a Doctorate in Information Technology.'

Jenifer sat down with a bump, and Dexter took her phone from limp fingers. 'Hello Nance, I think she's passed out, or close to it. I heard. That's fantastic. We have an invitation, but it doesn't say why.'

'That's typical; you'll get an official award notification soon. Frank's out of the shower; let me give him the phone.'

'Hello Dex.'

'Hi Frank, can you explain to Bo why she's awarded a doctorate? She's beginning to recover from the shock.'

'Hello, Frank.'

'Hi, Bo. When the IT professor heard you had visited Ames, he decided Stanford should award you a doctorate for creating Linky and got a unanimous vote. You'll get a fancy certificate, cap and gown at the award ceremony, which is as much for Stanford's prestige as yours.'

'Thanks, Frank, this is overwhelming. Let me talk to Dex about coming.'

'Fine, Bo. Call me or Nance when you decide.'

•••

'I'm not sure I could stand on a stage with a huge crowd watching me.'

'They won't be a normal crowd, Bo. They'll be scientists and engineers like the guys at Ames, and you enjoyed that.'

'But this will be a much bigger crowd, and I won't have bars.'

'Something better. Bars are suitable for airports. At the ceremony, you'll be wearing an academic gown like all the others, a doctor's gown, that's like having four bars.'

'I'll think about it. If we go, when would you like to travel?'

'We could fly on Tuesday and return on Saturday. That's more than enough for a visit to our family.'

He said our family. 'Ask Nance if they would prefer us to go on Wednesday and leave on Monday afternoon; then we can go into the mountains with them.'

'That's a great idea, but don't forget that it's Friday, tonight we're going for another evening at the jazz club. They have a visiting band.'

'Do they have a name?'

'They call themselves *Basin Street*; the lead player is Jerry Somers, an ex-US serviceman who stayed in the UK.'

I'll take her trumpet with me; if she plays, it will give her confidence in front of a crowd.

'This is the jazz I learnt to play; it's lovely.'

'If I ask the bandleader if you can play a bit with them, will you do so?'

'I don't have my trumpet, Dex; I can't play another without practice.'

'I have yours in the car. I brought it because I want to hear you play.'

'For you, fetch it and ask. I can try.'

Dexter didn't have to ask; Jerry Somers saw him carry in the trumpet case, and as the band returned to the little stage after a break, he came by their table. 'Hi, Bro, do you play the horn?'

'Not me, my wife, Jenifer. Could you let her play a tune and say what you think?'

'Sure, Bro. Jenifer, what would you play?'

'A kiss to build a dream on. Satchmo'.

'That's a great one. Bring your horn, and we'll try.'

Dexter watched as Jerry introduced Jenifer to the band members, the base, trombone and percussion players, picked up his saxophone, and said something to Jenifer. She nodded.

She brought the trumpet to her lips and tapped her foot, one, two, three. The first crisp, clear note soared, defying space and time, and Dexter saw Jerry close his eyes. The band was frozen.

She played the first six notes alone before Dexter saw Jerry open his eyes. He didn't hear his words, 'Oh man, play guys, play with the lady!' But he saw the band galvanised into action. He looked at the audience, silent and unmoving, some with eyes closed, then listened to the music and felt the song's words.

When the song finished, the audience leapt to their feet; the applause was deafening, with shouts of more. Dexter saw Jerry say something to Jenifer, then she turned to the audience, raised the trumpet, and silence fell. After *Hello Dolly*, they played three more Satchmo hits, then Jerry stepped to the front and announced, 'That's it, folks, we need a break.' The audience didn't agree. After three or four shouts of *The Saints*, they began to chant the title. Jerry said something to Jenifer; she seemed to disagree, and then he said something else, and she turned to the audience. Silence fell instantly.

Dexter had heard the song played a dozen times, but never with such wild abandon and joy. As it ended, the audience exploded.

Jerry brought Jenifer to the table, and Dexter could tell how happy she was – her eyes were shining.

Jerry said, 'Jenifer, tell me when you want to play, and I'll be here anytime. You're the best I've ever heard.' Then he turned to Dexter, 'You take care of that horn, Bro, made in New Orleans by a master, and take care of its mistress.'

'Thanks, Jerry.'

'Bo, why didn't you want to play *The Saints*?'

'It's a song for a rambunctious band, Dex; I was always alone, so it didn't sound right. Jerry told me to play and that it would be great with the band, and I learnt he was right. It was marvellous fun.'

When they went to bed that night, Jenifer kissed Dexter passionately. 'Darling, I'll attend the awards ceremony; it must be like tonight.'

It worked.

DAY 103
TUESDAY

'Dex, I've called Doris; I need a makeover for an award ceremony. Can we go to Gatwick tonight?'

'Of course, I'll check with Grant at Exeter; it will be easier to fly to Gatwick.'

'Remind me to take my trumpet; we might find a jazz club in San Jose.'

They flew into Gatwick that evening and checked into the Holiday Inn. Dexter said as they got into bed, 'I must savour the next three nights.'

'Why.'

'After that, I'll have to sleep with a doctor.'

'Then hug me and enjoy.'

DAY 104
WEDNESDAY

Jenifer visited Doris and met Dexter at check-in for lunch and the San Jose flight. Nance, Frank and Lettie were at the airport to meet them.

DAY 105
THURSDAY

———

'Dex, I can't sleep any more. Do you think we can go for a walk?'

'I'm sure we can; let's slip out quietly and return for breakfast. I'm going with Nance to the clinic.'

'That's great; I'm going with Frank to thank the guys at Ames.'

DAY 106
FRIDAY

———

You look lovely; the Stanford gown suits you.'

'It would suit most women; it's mostly black, and I'm glad you're in uniform. If I need it, I can look at you for reassurance.'

'You won't need it, but I'll stay in view. Let's go.'

They sat with Nance and Frank in the front row with the other award recipients, and Frank explained the procedure, 'The minor degrees go first, then the more impressive ones. According to this list, you're at the end, so we have an hour or more to wait.'

They waited and clapped and waited some more, and then Frank said, 'Two more, Jenifer. You must go with Dex to the wings.'

When Jenifer's turn came, before the Professor of Information Technology stepped up to the podium, Dexter had to step aside when two men carried the whiteboard from Ames onto the stage. 'What that for, Dex?'

'I guess he'll talk about it.'

'Mister President, members of the faculties of Stanford, Ladies and Gentlemen.

'It is not unusual for Stanford to make awards to people who have not studied at Stanford; however, these awards are to people who have made massive contributions to our world of knowledge, commonly through fieldwork in medicine or archaeology. Information Technology is a young subject, and I have not encountered such a case in my speciality before today.

'However, it gives me enormous pleasure to say that I shall award the degree of Doctor of Information Technology to a young woman who created a computer language because she found the existing ones challenging to use in writing control programs. Six lines of code are on the board, as you can see. Control systems today are the core of all complex machinery, and her language, known as Linky, is now in worldwide use because it makes an engineer's work much easier and far better.

'I present, Jenifer Boscawen.'

The audience was clapping when Dexter said, 'Go, Bo.'

Jenifer did. The professor shook her hand, hung the collar around her neck, gave her the scroll, and asked, 'Would you say a few words, like why you created Linky?'

'Can I say what I want?'

'Of course.'

She began with the opening line she'd heard, 'Mr President...' then continued, 'I'll take this opportunity to say a few words to the students at Stanford. When I decided to design an aeroplane and then build a simulator to fly it, I was alone, and it didn't take long for me to realise I couldn't do it without assistance. So, I asked every person I could, and the world of engineers and scientists helped.

With them assisting, the problems dissolved, and the aeroplane I called Slinky became visible on the screen. Then, I designed and wrote the program code for my simulator. That meant learning several programming languages, but when I tried to link my simulator to the aeroplane, the languages were difficult to use and tedious, and my results were unreliable. I asked many IT experts, "Why must I write hundreds of lines of code to make the tailplane move?" And got the answer, "There's nothing else; that's how it's done." They couldn't explain why, so I thought, "If there's no reason behind it, I'll do it myself," so I invented the language that linked my aeroplane to my simulator. That's why I called it Linky.

'So, my message to the students is. Don't believe something is impossible; if you can't find why it's impossible, do it.

'I thank Stanford, the President, Professor Banerjee and the academics for awarding me this honour.'

As the thunderous applause died, the IT professor said, 'Jenifer, please wait by the whiteboard.' Then, he turned to the microphone. 'Professor Wu Chen of reliability sciences will say a few words,' and stepped back to allow the professor the microphone.

'Mister President, members of the faculties of Stanford, Ladies and Gentlemen. Two months ago, I was at the NASA Ames Research Centre, where I met Doctor Boscawen with a group of reliability research engineers. The discussion centred around a division between two groups; one advocated self-repair and the other microduplication. Doctor Boscawen was visibly annoyed, but I learnt she was annoyed with herself when she said, "I may not be able to explain what I mean, but in Linky, this is what I want to say."

'She stepped to the board and wrote the code you see on the board which now hangs on the wall at Ames. Code that links the two fields of research into one.

'It may not be as simple as Einstein's equation, $E = mc^2$, but the *unifying* impact on our world may be more significant. The Stanford board unanimously decided to award Doctor Boscawen the Doctor of Philosophy degree.

'Mr President.'

Jenifer came forward; the President gave her the degree and the collar, shook her hand, and said, 'I never shook Einstein's hand; I'm honoured to shake yours.'

Instead of leaving the stage, Jenifer stepped to the microphone. The applause died after a minute, and then she said, 'That proves that when you're frustrated, you can get some great ideas.' The laughter and applause were deafening, then when it died again, she said, 'While standing by the board, I found this marker,' She waved it in the air, 'It may be the same one that I used at Ames, and the professor has presented me with a challenge. I'll present another.' She turned and quickly wrote on the whiteboard in large letters:

$$L^3 = J + D.$$

'I announce an annual award of twenty thousand dollars for scientific excellence decided by Stanford. However, the first award will be to the student who proves, using Linky, that this last equation is equivalent to the above code. I guarantee it is. I think Einstein would approve of the equation.'

The silence was stunning until she waved and walked off the stage. Then, the audience exploded. They stood, clapped, and whistled.

'Bo, you're fantastic.'

'It was just like the jazz club, Dex. I know I'll never be frightened of people again.'

Professor Wu Chen joined them as Frank and Nance arrived. 'Jenifer, thank you for that award. It will be known as the Jenifer

Boscawen Award, and thank you for that equation; there will be a lot of bright minds working on it. Are you all coming to the cocktail party this evening?'

'Is there music?'

'There's always a group, I don't know who they are.'

'Then we'll come.'

<hr>

'Dex, bring my trumpet. You can leave it with the coats.'

The party started soberly, with a group of students and staff around each new graduate, but Dexter soon decided the alcohol consumption would change it; he and Jenifer stuck to fruit juice and soda.

Dexter did his best to shield Jenifer from the endless handshakes and congratulations. He was grateful when Professor Wu Chen joined them and adroitly diverted the students who hoped for an enlightened answer to a question.

The band filed onto the small stage; two young men played the drums and double bass, and two much older with saxophone and trombone. The music they played was post-Second World War.

Dexter asked, 'Bo, do you want to play with them?'

'I don't think I can, Dex; it's not intimate like a jazz club where I know everyone would appreciate it; there are too many strangers here.'

'Okay, Bo, although I would have liked to hear you play.'

'Maybe one song, Dex, after everyone has fuelled up and before boredom sets in.'

•••

As the queue of wellwishers tailed off, Jennifer turned to Dex. 'Darling, can you fetch my trumpet.'

Dexter returned with it. He saw Jenifer take a deep breath, and then she said, 'Dex, this is for you, for us. I must try.' She went to speak to the bandleader.

'Where's she going, Dexter?'

'To ask if she can play with the band, professor.'

• • •

'Hi, do you guys play Satch?'

'Sure do, ma'am, we love it.'

'*The Saints*? It would wake up this crowd.'

'Can do, ma'am, but we don't have Satch with us, so it doesn't sound the same.'

She lifted the horn into view. 'Is it okay if I play the horn? Just one jam.'

'Sure, ma'am. That'll be a great jam.'

• • •

Jenifer joined the band and said, 'Okay, guys, follow me on three, and let it rip.' Then, she tapped her foot, one, two, three, and blew the first four notes.

Several people had stopped talking when they saw the unusual sight of a woman wearing a doctor's gown holding a trumpet step onto the stage.

The audience stopped talking as she hit the fourth high note, and then the band, fired up by Jennifer's trumpet, played their hearts out.

The stunned listeners were silent when the song ended before thunderous applause broke out. The professor said to Dexter, 'My god, *what a woman!*'

Dexter replied, 'I couldn't say it any better, Professor.'

DAY 107
SATURDAY

Before they rose, Dexter asked, 'Darling, yesterday before you played *The Saints*, you said "This is for you, for us. I must try." I love you, and you can play Satch for me any time; why did you have to try yesterday.'

'Dex, when you pulled me through the Tolmen stone, I had decided we love each other, but there was something else. Finally, I believed we could be a couple, an equal partnership. Remember our coffee in the morning agreement? That was part of it: equal shares. I don't want to spend our life thinking that I'm leaning on you but standing beside you. If you had played the trumpet, I knew you could have stood on the stage and played. I had to prove to myself and you that I can too.'

'Bo, I like it when you need me, but I won't hesitate to tell you when I need you. We must both do that.'

'Dex, that's a promise. Kiss me.'

The professor was right, what a woman!'

For the next three days, Jenifer and Dexter relaxed; Frank had a rented cabin in the mountains beside a lake. Dexter fished with Lettie on Saturday, and Jenifer sat with her while Lettie tried to catch some tiddlers on Sunday. However, when they compared notes, they agreed that Lettie was extraordinarily bright and enthusiastic about animals. Dexter listened as Nance talked about life with his ex-wife Bethkin, and they decided that when Nance came to England, they would ask Bethkin to join them for a visit.

On Monday, they boarded their flight to Gatwick at 18:00. Their jet would collect them on arrival the next day, and they would be home that evening.

Day 124
Tuesday

'Kiss me, Dex, then I must get up.'

'What's the hurry?'

'Not a hurry, Dex, just a problem.'

'You've buried yourself in the barn for the past week; what are you up to?'

'Now that the move from Coventry is over and the barn contractors have left, I've installed my sim, library and workspace. Come and see it later. I have lots of data on the E Three Ninety to download, and I want to convert my sim.'

'We said that we would plan an official marriage after the move. Have you thought about it?'

'Not much, Dex, it seems unimportant. I feel married, and that's that, but I know you want a marriage certificate.'

'It's like having a pilot's licence that's not valid, Bo, it's a waste! I can't help thinking like a pilot.'

'Then we'll do it. You can do the terrace now that heavy machinery is unnecessary, and after you finish the extra room and bathroom outside, we can ask Nance and Frank when they can come here for a wedding. I guess it must be during a school holiday. Morwen, Doris and Susan will come with their husbands. You must reserve the Oxenham for the people you invite from International

Air. Can we organise it in six weeks?'

'That's possible. Where? Here or at the Oxenham?'

'The reception at the Oxenham, Dex, but I want to say "yes" in the nine stones circle, then the ponies can come.'

'Ok, Bo, I'll get Morwen to help. We'll go to Exeter today and notify the registrar.'

'And I'll get the sim running.'

'I approve because we may have a use for it.'

'Are you being mysterious, Dex?'

'No, I've been looking for a simulator manufacturer we can buy. There's one that seems attractive in Switzerland.'

'What name?'

'SwisSim.'

'I know of them, Dex, but they only make baby sims for training aircraft.'

'I thought we could start small; you have a Cessna 150. However, they won a contract to build an E Three-Ninety sim and appear to have problems because they haven't delivered, and their share price is dropping.'

'Who are they building it for?'

'The manufacturer.'

'That's surprising, they must have easy access to data. Can you find out more?'

'I'm trying, Bo. I'll tell you when I know something.'

Day 126
Thursday

———

'My darling switch needs reinforcement, Bo.'
'Sorry, my darling, I didn't think.'

'Why not?'

'Because I've had the downloads running all night, they should be complete about now.'

'Not until after some reinforcement…'

Day 128
Saturday

——————

'Bo, that's enough.'

'I thought there could never be enough reinforcement.'

'There can't, but I meant that burying yourself in the barn for five days and half nights is enough. You need two days to walk with me on the moors. The plumbers, tilers, electricians and painters don't work on weekends. We can visit the ponies.'

'I'll come, Dex; the sim is running but not calibrated. I can do that Monday.'

'If you need help, shout.'

'Have you uncovered anything else about SwisSim?'

'I know who owns it; the two founders share forty-five per cent, they're the engineers, a man with an address that is a Zurich bank owns eight per cent, and multiple shareholders hold the rest in small quantities. The Zurich exchange lists the stock, and it's still going down.

'The bank lists the same man as their president, and the aircraft manufacturer lists him as the chairman of their board.'

'Does that explain why SwisSim, a baby simulator manufacturer, got the contract for a big one?'

'Perhaps, Bo, but it would certainly mean their tender received serious consideration.'

'Have you bought any shares?'

'I would tell my partner first, but I have the company's net asset value, so I could tell a broker that if the price drops to NAV plus ten per cent, we'll buy any available shares.'

'Do that, Dex; let's have breakfast and go for a walk.'

'I like running this company.'

'Why?'

'Board meetings in bed, with naked participants, brings harmony.'

'Then we should make it standard practice. Come on, you proposed walking, you make breakfast, and I'll shower.'

DAY 130
MONDAY

Jenifer came to bed late, although she tried not to wake Dexter; tiptoeing to the bathroom and to the bed, he was awake. When she slid between the sheets, he put his arm around her, and she snuggled, then sighed.

'What's the problem?'

'Kiss me ..., breathe on me, make me forget my sim problems.'

...

'I needed that orgasm. I'll tell you in the morning.'

DAY 131
TUESDAY

'Bo, you must tell me your problem this morning.'

'If you stop eating my ear and we can have breakfast, you can come to my sim.'

A large photo of a silver aeroplane with 'E390' in the lower left corner was on the wall to one side of the sim.

'So that's the beast?'

'The port side, I don't have other photos. One of the metaverse guys sent it.

'Dex, I got data for the E Three Ninety from five people. Some were duplicates, so I eliminated them and ensured I only deleted identical data.'

'Who were the sources?'

'I don't know, but an aeroplane takes time to build, so some data must be older than the rest; performance data will be more recent. But it does all fit together, and the sim flies.'

'So, where's the problem?'

'The plane is an advance on all previous airliners. The design specifies above forty thousand feet and in a critical control envelope. It must fly on autopilot once at cruise altitude.'

'Why?'

'You know that the C of G is critical to fuel consumption; the further aft it is, the lower the fuel used, but the sensitivity of the aeroplane to control movements builds until a human can't react in time, but designers set limits. When you fly the sim, the fuel consumption is as specified for climb and descent, but once at altitude in level flight, the fuel used is higher than the given fuel. If I move the C of G back, the control sensitivity increases and the fuel consumption decreases. I must minimise the autopilot reaction time for the plane to fly stable. I think it's dangerous, and if the autopilot fails, a pilot must dive to a lower altitude if he can do so before losing control.

'There has to be something wrong with the data because I don't think the designers would have exceeded the accepted limits.'

'What about their test aircraft, Bo? Would they have found this?'

'I don't know; flight tests that use max AUW and max aft C of G occur later in a testing schedule. They can specify a reduced max aft C of G to avoid the problem, but the sim is supposed to match the actual specs.'

'You check the data, and I'll try to learn more about the E Three Ninety.'

'Thanks.'

⟫◦⟪

After checking on the plumber's progress, Dexter went to his office and connected to the internet. He entered E390 in the browser search field and then began reading the entries. Thirty minutes later, frustration had built; the first eighteen entries were in two groups; one of each group must have been the first, and the others were repeats of the same information stolen from the first one. Dexter grumbled audibly. 'These guys are destroying the web as a useful tool; to get advert money, they steal other people's content.'

Wikipedia was dependable but limited, and Dexter decided the other websites had expanded the wiki information with hearsay. As he clicked on the following search response, he remembered joining the plane spotters after his Tiger moth ride and the group of passionate youngsters who amazed him with how much they knew about the aircraft they studied.

He hadn't logged on to the Plane Spotters website for years and found that although it was free, he had to register and then learnt he could order photographs of aircraft for a fee.

Within seconds, he had over a hundred pictures of the E390 to look at.

Dexter had patience learnt through many hours waiting to arrive at a distant destination, and three hours later, he'd whittled down the pictures to five; all were high resolution, taken with a powerful telephoto lens on a clear day, showing two different aircraft, one labelled 02 was unpainted, the other 001 had an airline livery. They showed the left and right sides. The fifth photo showed a fatigue testing rig with a silver aircraft inside the structure.

Dexter paid, downloaded the photos, and clicked on the aircraft history menu item.

There was an article with more information than Wikipedia and the name and email of the member who posted it.

Dexter fetched a cup of coffee, thought for a few minutes, and then composed an email.

> Dear Gunter,
> The E390 interests me, and you appear to be the expert. I have bought
> five pictures; can you tell me where is 01? And what is the current
> status of 02 and 001? Is there a 002?
> Regards, a fellow spotter, Dexter.

Then he went to tell Bo what he'd done and ask what she wanted for lunch.

⬥

The reply came minutes after Dexter finished washing up.

Dear Dexter,

It is a pleasure to hear from a fan of the E390.

01 was incomplete; used to check the routing of cables and pipes and then as a dummy for jigging. The factory then scrapped 01.

02 did fly to establish actual parameters compared to theoretical ones. Fitted inside are thousands of stress, load and pressure sensors. Then, the factory built the fatigue testing rig in the photo around it. It will cycle for sixty thousand cycles, double the estimated life.

001 is the first E390 they will deliver to an airline – at a reduced cost – because it is currently test-flying for certification.

002 came out of the factory a month ago. It will do certification flying and crew training before delivery of 001 and 002.

The first production aircraft for which parts are on order will be 0003. They hope to deliver more than 1,000 aircraft, hence the extra zero.

I hope that answers your questions; if you have others, please ask.

Gunter.

Dexter did something unusual. He sent the photos to a printer, asked for three prints of each at the highest definition, and asked for immediate delivery. Then, he forwarded the mail to Bo and went to the barn.

'Hi, have you uncovered anything?'

'No, all the numbers are correct.'

'Open my email, read Gunter's words, and show the pictures on your big screen.'

'What he says seems normal.'

'Yes, but I'm a suspicious person. He says they used 02 to establish parameters, and it is now in the fatigue rig, and 001 is flying. Two different aircraft, Bo. They should be identical, but if they aren't, and you have parameters from 02 and performance from 001, then that might explain why you have a problem.'

'How do we find out if they're different?'

'We can look at the pictures for a starter.'

•••

'I can't see any differences except the paint scheme.'

'Bo, you're the computer expert. These images are from different angles and are of assorted sizes. Is there software that can change the pictures so they're all taken from the same viewpoint relative to the plane, left and right sides?'

'I'm sure there is, but even better, a guy who helped me with the transformations for the sim; those use a 3D object and make it flat; we need to convert to 3D objects first. I'll ask him for help, then we can go for supper. He's in the USA; we might have an answer to-morrow morning.'

'Would you like to go out, Bo?'

'Not yet, we can celebrate when we solve this problem. Can you grill two soles?'

'Tonight's menu, with shrimp, lemon butter sauce, chips and roasted carrots.'

'I'll get you a chef's hat next time we invite Morwen for dinner. Let me ask for help, then I'll join you.'

While Dexter rattled pans, Bo downloaded the pictures to a metaverse depository, then added the drawings she had of the E390, copied the URLs, logged on to the metaverse using the code of her helper, and placed the URLs in his metabox with a message.

> I need identical side views from the same viewpoint so I can overlay aircraft. Please help, thanks, Bo.

Then she shut down for the night.

DAY 132
WEDNESDAY

———

Dexter woke to find no Jenifer in bed. Three minutes later, in slippers and dressing gown, he found her in the barn, also wearing slippers and a dressing gown. 'Have you got pyjamas under that gown?'

'No, but I'm not cold. There is a reply, I'm downloading.'

'Then come, get dressed and drink a coffee.'

'Thirty seconds, I'll enter my code and come to the kitchen.'

———

'Here's your coffee; why do downloads take so long?'

'They're huge, Dex; I download one file, decompress and decrypt it, only a part is usable, and the next five files' instructions arrive in sequence. Only the last is valid. It's a security system.'

'Do we have time for breakfast?'

'I'm sure we have.'

'Then go and put on something warmer.'

———

'Dex, there's a note.'

'What does it say?'

Jenifer read it: '02 and 02 in the rig, left sides, appear identical. 02 and 001 right sides appear similar. 02 and 001 left sides – check the rear fuselage door where paint might disguise a difference – drawings show the door of 02.'

'Let's compare the pictures; magnify that area.'

...

'Dex, I'm sure the rear door on 001 is wider than 02.'

'I agree. It isn't easy because the line might not be the door but the edge of the paint. I'll ask Gunter if he can help.'

> Dear Gunter,
> Thank you for the magnificent photos. I have one question. The left-side rear door on 001 appears wider than on 02. Is there a way you can confirm this, and if so, how much wider?'
> Thank you, Dexter.

'Now we must wait. Meanwhile, what does it mean if it's wider?'

'Dex, I think you must ask the FAA.'

'Why?'

'I think doing fatigue tests on an aeroplane different from the one being certified is enough to delay certification.'

'I would agree, but let's try to find out more. What does a wider door mean?'

'I couldn't ask for help without a drawing of what they did, Dex, and that might be impossible to get. If we talk to the FAA, they may insist on receiving a drawing.'

'The FAA is the government, Bo. They might refuse a certification but won't say why. That would put them in the hot seat.'

'Then I'll talk to Silver.'

'Who's he?'

'An avatar who supplied some of the data.'

⁘

It was about the same time that I first met him. He should be watching the sunrise. Two minutes later, using the code Jenifer had used the first time, she entered the metaverse space, a green valley between snowcapped mountains. She had to walk quite far before she saw Silver sitting on a rock looking down the valley, wearing the same closefitting one-piece silver costume. She spoke.

'Good day, the view is lovely.'

He turned leisurely and looked at her. 'Sunrises are. Have you been successful in your endeavours?'

'Partially, I have a problem.'

'And that is?'

'The drawings I have of the rear fuselage are those of serial number zero-two, yet it appears they're outdated for zero-zero-one has a wider rear door.'

'Ah, I'm surprised you noticed. Does it make any difference to a simulator?'

'It should not, but it does. I believe the C of G has changed.'

'I didn't consider that; it is possible. I shall try to get you updated drawings of the rear fuselage. I'll also give you a warning. Beware of the Chief Executive; keep everything you obtain from the metaverse in the metaverse. Goodbye.'

'Goodbye, Silver, and thank you.'

Jenifer logged out and went to find Dexter; he was with the electrician in the new bedroom.

'Hi, Bo, this is Colin; he will do the electrics. He disagrees with the switches and fittings we chose.'

'Why?'

'Please, ma'am, the light switches are fine if you want the old-fashioned look, for the lighting is low power, but the sockets are different. The law says they must be safety sockets, and I can't find sockets with the look you want; I can't put in used ones. You could change both.'

'Then go ahead with the lights and the other stuff, pull the wires for the sockets and give us a few days to choose something different.'

'Thanks, ma'am.'

'Dex, Silver will try and send us the drawings; what do we do if he does? He also warned me about the CEO; he thinks he's dangerous.'

'That's worth knowing. The broker called. He says we may soon be owners of a chunk of SwisSim and wanted confirmation of my order. I told him yes, but not to push the share price, only to accept offers to sell.

'What would you normally do with the drawings?'

'Not much; I received torsional and longitudinal stiffness data with the original drawings. We can add the new rear to the old forward section drawings, but someone must calculate the stiffness. I've just realised they widened the door towards the front to allow standard containers through it, but that's the wrong way for stiffness.'

'Don't you have a friend who can calculate that?'

Jenifer shrugged, 'Once we have drawings, I can ask.'

'Are we going out for dinner tonight?'

She perked up, 'Yes, it'll take my mind off the sim problem.'

'Then we'll go to the Gidleigh Park Hotel if I can reserve a table.'

'Admit it, Bo, you couldn't stop thinking of the E Three-Ninety. You were elsewhere for most of the dinner.'

'Kiss me, and let's sleep. I was thinking of something quite different and will tell you in the morning.'

Day 133
Thursday

'Bo, you nearly earned a divorce last night, leaving me alone with my thoughts over a plate of food.'

'I had a crazy thought; why does the aircraft industry put an entire aeroplane in a huge steel structure and then bend and twist it for thirty years.'

'Because no one's found a better way.'

'But it could be calculated.'

'Are you sure?'

'Yes, I'm certain that's not the problem; I think it's a power limitation.'

'Explain, please.'

'Imagine the power we expend in a fatigue test rig over thirty years, then think of doing that in one hour with a computer. Even at much higher efficiencies, it would use a huge amount of power; no computers are that powerful.'

'Frank would love that suggestion. He and his buddies fear a rocket falling to bits en route to Mars, and they can't imagine fatigue testing rigs for rockets.'

'Then I'll arrange a conference call with Frank once I get those drawings.'

Day 134
Friday

—

'Bo, I have pictures from Gunter.'

'Then send them to me, and we'll look at them on the barn screen.'

He's a superb photographer. This closeup of the o2 door in the rig is in the dawn sunlight.'

'It's not a closeup, it's a telephoto picture, the lens must be at least 1000mm.'

'The 001 door was taken in the afternoon, probably when it returned from a test flight.'

'Oh wow, look at this one, it has a graticule overlay. Does Gunter say anything?'

'Just one line, Bo.'

The door on 001 is 425mm wider than o2 towards the wing.

'That's conclusive. You make breakfast; I'll connect to the metaverse and check for drawings.'

Between bites of toast and marmalade, Jenifer said, 'I'm downloading the drawings. Can you call Nance and set up a conference call with Frank?'

'If I call at 14:00, they'll be waking up. I'll call then.'

•••

'Frank says he will call us at 17:30.'

'I've looked at the drawings, and they seem complete, so I've put them in a shared directory and sent the URL to Frank. I scrubbed all references to E Three-Ninety and the manufacturer.'

'He should call any minute now.'

The screen changed, and a moment later, Frank's face appeared.

'Hello, Frank.'

'Hello Bo, Hello Dex. This call is a surprise. Especially when I saw your mail.'

'How are Nance and Lettie, Frank?'

'At the surgery and school, Dex, well and looking forward to coming over for your marriage.'

Jenifer replied, 'It's getting closer, but we have a problem to solve, which is why we called.'

'Go ahead.'

'The drawings I sent are of an aircraft fuselage; I need a torsional and longitudinal stiffness. That should be easy for you, but I don't know why the builders must put it in a massive steel structure and torture it for thirty years to discover where it will break due to fatigue. Why can't we calculate it?'

'The simple answer is that we don't have a computer powerful enough. The math and the formulas exist, and we calculate small structures; a supercomputer is inadequate for an aircraft.'

'How big a computer is required?'

'No one has tried to work that out, Bo. It's like diving into the Marianas trench; we know it's impossible, so don't try to calculate how long it will take to reach the sea bottom.'

'Then I can tell you how to do that easily.'

Holy Shit!

'Bo, can I call you in two hours? I want to get the guys connected to this call.'

'Sure, Frank.'

Dexter and Jenifer were in the barn when Frank called back. The screen lit up, and rows of faces smiled at them. Dexter counted eleven. Bo recognised them all and welcomed them with a broad grin. 'Hello everybody, this is marvellous, and Professor, you're an unexpected but welcome addition!'

'Frank told me of the call, and I couldn't resist connecting. How are you, Jenifer?'

'Well, Professor, and so is Dex.'

'What have you told Frank that has him all excited?'

'I asked why we can't calculate the fatigue life of a complex structure, like an aircraft, instead of subjecting it to physical stresses for thirty years.'

'I expect he said we don't have a big enough computer.'

'That's right, so I asked how big.'

The professor answered. 'We know how to get the answer. We must do a stress analysis on a static structure, then run cycles of alternate stresses and measure the time. That's a lot of computer power, and the result is that it takes longer than doing it physically. So, we don't bother.'

'I understand that professor, but if you can estimate the power consumed by a test rig, say at CamAir or Boeing, and the power consumed by a computer to do one test cycle of the stress calculations, the ratio will give an approximation of how big a computer is required.'

'Jenifer, that's a unique and brilliant suggestion, but it doesn't solve the problem; where would you get that computer?'

'Professor, there are thirty-six supercomputers in the world. If you can tell me how many I need to link together, in the interests of science, I can try to persuade them to connect for the duration of the analysis.'

In the silence that followed, Dexter looked at the expressions on the faces in front of him. Most he thought were awe.

Frank was the first to speak. 'Jenifer, I have everything we need. Leave it with us. Guys, we need to have a conference. Professor, will you join us at Ames, or shall we come to Stanford?'

'I'll come to you.'

'Thanks, Jenifer; I'll send the stiffness figures and tell you what happens. Goodbye.'

After a chorus of goodbyes, the screen blanked.

'That went well; I could see you staggered them.'

'We'll get the stiffness figures in three or four days, Dex, the rest, I don't know. While we wait, let's visit the ponies. There must be a different group on the far side of the moor; I'd like to find them.'

'How will we do that? We could spend a month wandering and never find them.'

'You said they sometimes group into bigger herds. We'll find Dolly, and I'll tell her we want to find other ponies, then she and the others will show us.'

It sounds unbelievable, but I feel that will *work. Bo is a continuous surprise, and now I'm in awe.*

DAY 138
TUESDAY

———

'Dex, the stiffness figures came from Frank. I'll load them into my sim and do a flight.'

'I'll come with you.'

•••

'I'll level off now, set the autopilot to cruise, and let the speed settle.'

•••

'Bo, that's the speed you expected; you've solved the sim problem.'

'But we still have two others. The control sensitivity is too high, and the fuselage is bending. They can shift the C of G limits, but we still have the fatigue problem, and they may have made it worse. The plane may crash early in its life.'

'Then we must tell the FAA.'

'That's your job, Dex.'

•••

Dexter called William Faulkner at 16:00.

'Good morning, Captain Rawlins; I hope this call is not something serious.'

'I hope not, sir. I want to talk to a senior official of the FAA and thought of Colonel Grady, but I have no number to call him and expect an email to the FAA might take days to reach him.'

'In that, you're quite right. Are you and Captain Boscawen well? Or should I call her doctor?'

'Both well, sir, and she prefers captain.'

'I'm glad to hear that. I'll ask Colonel Grady to call you as a favour.'

'Thank you, sir; I hope we'll meet again. Goodbye.'

The call came minutes later.

'Good morning, Captain Rawlins. William Faulkner called and said you want to speak to me. Let me add it's a pleasure to speak to you again and to hear you're still active in aviation. JenDex, I hear, produces excellent simulators.'

'It's a pleasure to speak to you, sir. I'm calling because we would like to share information regarding passenger safety.'

'It surprises me that you have such information, but not that you wish to share it. Go ahead.'

'We have built a simulator of the E390, sir, for the potential market is large, and in the process, we identified anomalies in the data we used. We have solved them, but our investigations discovered that serial number zero two in the manufacturer's fatigue test rig is different from serial number zero-zero-one they use for certification.'

'That's a serious allegation. Do you have proof?'

'Yes sir, photographs, and I'm sure you can send an FAA rep to verify their accuracy. I can send them to you if you give me an email address.'

Grady thought for a few moments and decided there was something more.

'Captain, do you have something else?'

'Off the record, Colonel. Zero-zero-one has a reduced fuselage stiffness, both torsion and longitudinal. The maximum C of G is also so far back that the aircraft is beyond acceptable stability limits when cruising. Unfortunately, we cannot certify this because we have no contract with the company and have no official data. However, our simulator performance matches their data.'

'Captain, I assume someone else calculated the stiffness? Can you tell me?'

'NASA Ames and Stanford, sir.'

'Send the photos; my email is Grady at faa dot gov, and a heartfelt thank you. You may have saved the lives of a thousand people. I'm grateful I won't need to view a horrific video like the last time.'

⊂〇⊃

Dexter sent all the photos, including Gunter's notes and a short line of text.

While sending, an incoming email popped up, and he read it and then turned to Jenifer.

'JenDex now owns forty-seven per cent of SwisSim.'

'That's great, what will we do with it.'

'Invite the directors to lunch at the Oxenham, but not until our company is the registered owner.'

Day 141
Friday

———

Frank called.

'Hello, Bo, I have some news for you.'

'Good or bad?'

'Depends on your viewpoint. We finished programming the structure, and the weakest point using the loads you gave me is the top left corner of the rear door. If there's a fatigue failure, I would guess a crack would propagate from there, and the tail would fall off.'

'Thanks. Have you tried a fatigue cycle?'

'No, you want to link computers together, so the IT guys at Stanford have said they want the structure divided into separate units with similar calculation needs and will run them in parallel, talking to each other. We must do that; they will run a fatigue cycle on Monday.

'CamAir came through with an estimate of the energy consumption of their fatigue program. Those guys are good; they were struggling until one of the guys there produced a solution. They asked accounting for the total cost over a rig's lifetime in today's money, then converted that to kilowatts using the electricity price.'

'Was the guy's name Henry Mancuni?'

'Yes, how did you know?'

'I know him, and that's typical of his thinking; he's a simulator man. Dex is here if you or Nance wants to talk to him.'

'We're both at work. I'll tell Nance to call later.'

'Tuesday, you should have your answer. Bye.'

DAY 144
MONDAY

One thing happened on Monday. Dexter received a copy of an email to the manufacturer of the E390.

> We regret to inform you that the FAA has suspended certification of the E390 due to irregularities and inaccuracies in the submitted documentation.

Dexter showed it to Jenifer, 'Look at this email; it will put the cat amongst the pigeons.'

DAY 145
TUESDAY

Two things happened on Tuesday.

Frank called and told Jenifer that thirty-one supercomputers were needed to do one year's fatigue cycles in four minutes.

'Thanks, that's great news; why the odd number?'

'Thirty will do the calculations; the one is the master coordinator that talks to all of them, sets up and manages the cross-links.'

'Is the Ames computer powerful enough to fill that role? Then the Stanford super can be one of the thirty.'

'I'll check.'

'I'll try to round up some help.'

'How will you do that, Bo?'

'I don't work alone. I talk to whoever might help, and I have a worldwide community of helping friends like you guys at Ames. We're all keen on solving problems.'

Jenifer posted on the metaverse bulletin board.

> I need to arrange for 31 supercomputers to link for a massive calculation to solve a problem for a doctorate at Stanford University. If you can help, I will tell you why.

Then, she began an explanatory document.

⚜

The second thing that day was a call to Dexter.

'Good afternoon, Martin Leiton, personal assistant to Adolf Schnieder, Chief Executive of *Schweizer Flugzeughersteller*. Can I speak to Captain Rawlins, please?'

'Rawlins speaking, how can I assist, Mr Leiton?'

'Herr Schnieder has asked me to arrange a meeting with you.'

'What is the subject?'

'We have received a notification from the FAA suspending our application for E Three Ninety certification. They refuse to explain or justify it, and we understand you might assist with an explanation.'

'Mr Leiton. I cannot assist you. Neither the FAA nor your company employ us, nor are we informed as to why the FAA do things, and I'm sure the FAA would never suggest you contact me. Goodbye.'

'That must have made you popular.'

'When huge sums of money are at risk, we must be careful what we say. *Schweizer Flugzeughersteller* can hire a hundred lawyers, and we don't want to waste our time in expensive squabbles. It's better to say nothing. I won't talk to the CEO under any circumstances. I'll only talk to the chairman, initially only in private.'

'Where will you do that?'

'On the moor.'

DAY 147
THURSDAY

Frank called again. 'Bo, count Ames in as the controller.'

'Great, I have fifteen so far. I'll explain how it will work. You'll get a list of IP addresses and passwords. You won't recognise any of them; they're dark web and will be valid only for the length of the test, which must run until the failure probability of any point in the next cycle exceeds twenty per cent.

'The master computer, Ames, must connect to all those addresses, send a Linky program to them all, with the address list, and then the program for their segment. The Linky code will establish all the cross-links, report they have finished setup, and then notify Ames when the computer is idling. Ames can trigger the operation when all the computers are idling with a message to each computer. It contains a current time plus a fraction more than the comms link time. They will run at that start time. The results will be in a set of files that I can recover and send to you.

'Have you copied that?'

'Yes, I've recorded it.'

'Then I'll let you know shortly before the list is complete. I assume you guys will be ready to go any time, day or night.'

'Absolutely. Most of us are already living in the lab!'

DAY 151
MONDAY

On Monday, the chairman of *Schweizer Flugzeughersteller* called personally.

'Good morning, I'm Axel Meier. Can I speak to Captain Rawlins?'

'Speaking, and I'll be pleased to meet you and take you to lunch if you fly into Exeter airport at 11:00 UK time, alone.'

Dexter thought the voice sounded surprised, but the reply was unambiguous. 'Tomorrow morning. Thank you.'

Dexter booked for lunch and asked for a discreet table.

Jenifer connected to the metaverse every hour and, at 16:00, called Frank.

'Frank, be ready, I'm guessing, but we may have a window between 23:00 and 01:00 our time, that's 15:00-17:00 in San Jose.'

'I'll tell the guys.'

'Dex, don't wait for me to go to bed; I'll likely be late as we may run the fatigue program tonight.'

'I'll be with you in the barn, Bo.'

'The list is complete, Dex. I'll download it from the metaverse and send it to Frank. Can you call him? Tell him it's coming, and he'll get the results in seven hours. Then let's go to bed.'

DAY 152
TUESDAY

Dexter woke and found Jenifer had left, he found her in the barn, studying numbers on the giant screen. 'Good morning, darling, what's up?'

'A perfect run; the program simulated ten thousand eight hundred and seventy-two cycles, then shut down. The projected failure point is the top left of the door, but we must examine others.'

'What does that mean, Bo.'

'Roughly speaking, Dex, the aircraft might break up in flight after two point six years and will after seven point four. Most importantly, we can calculate and forecast a fatigue failure at a cost far less than the existing methods. I hope the professor has understood that.'

'I imagine he has, but you can ask Frank.'

Dexter was standing in the XLR Executive Jet Centre terminal when Axel Meier exited arrivals, carrying a small briefcase. Axel smiled broadly and extended a hand as soon as he saw Dexter.

'Captain Rawlins, this is a pleasure!' Dexter liked him; the smile, deep blue eyes and once yellow hair, now faded and surrendering to white, suited the comfortable face. Slightly overweight, Dexter thought he didn't resemble the double-chinned bank manager mould.

'Likewise, but please call me Dexter.'

'And I'm Axel. Where are we going?'

'A forty-minute ride to an old Coaching Inn.'

Dexter described Dartmoor and the countryside, said he was born near the Oxenham Inn and that he and Jenifer had their offices in a barn behind the house.

When they arrived, Dexter took a document folder from the car. Once seated and their meal ordered, Dexter said, 'Axel, you have two questions to ask me. I'll answer both. You want to know why we bought the shares of SwisSim.

'We build simulators, and I have a watch on all simulator companies; when the share price tanked, I thought the opportunity too good to miss.'

'Will you take over as chairman?'

'No, I hope you'll stay. I said we build simulators; we don't manage companies.'

'I expect you'll be at least a board member?'

'No, Jenifer has someone else in mind. We'll let you know.'

'Thank you. And the other staff?'

They discussed SwisSim until the food was on the table.

While eating, they discussed Cornwall and Devon and the origins of Cornish cream. Then Dexter said,

'Your other question is why the FAA notified you they had suspended the E Three Ninety certification process.'

'Did Martin Leiton tell you that?'

'Yes, and I'll tell you that we have built an E Three Ninety sim, but in doing so, had a problem with data discrepancies. We have no official data and don't know where it comes from, but when we ask the aviation community, it dribbles in. We investigated. We have close ties with the

FAA, manufacturers, and airlines and a reputation for safety conscious-ness that we vigorously protect. We had no choice but to give the FAA information in the public domain, nothing more.'

'Why did you build a sim, and what information?'

'If you sell a thousand aeroplanes, at least a hundred sims are necessary.'

Then Dexter handed Axel the document folder and said, 'These photographs, I downloaded them from plane-spotters.com.'

It took Axel four minutes to examine the photos, then he said. 'It seems conclusive that the plane in the test rig differs from the one in airline livery. Why would the FAA react as they did?'

'The fatigue test is part of certification; it guarantees that the plane will not fail in flight due to fatigue before the rig test shows a failure. The FAA will never certify an aircraft unless an identical one is in a fatigue test rig.'

'So, we have a major problem and a budgetary crisis coming? What can we do?'

'Axel, we don't build aeroplanes, and we don't run companies, so I can't tell you. You have employees to do that. But something has gone wrong; your team is dysfunctional. I learnt long ago that a flight crew that doesn't work well together is dangerous, and the first step is fixing that.'

'You know much more about aviation than I do. If I chair a meet-ing with the senior engineers, would you and Captain Boscawen come and listen to their suggestions? It's in the interests of JenDex and SwisSim that the E Three-Ninety flies.'

'Can we fly into Emmen? I know it's a military base.'

'If it's to visit us, there's no problem with clearances.'

'If there's no obligation to stay if we don't like it, then we'll come. Now we'll visit my wife. Then I'll show you the moor and take you back to Exeter.'

Day 155
Friday

The meeting took place in a large room with a long table on each side and a small desk that seated three at one end. Axel Meir was in the middle of the small desk, with Jenifer and Dexter on either side and nine people behind each long table. The CEO was at the closest end of one row, and the Chief Financial Officer on the other. Dexter concluded Axel had arranged the seating so the CEO was not at their table.

The chairman opened the meeting. 'My guests, either side of me, are Captain Jenifer Boscawen and Captain Dexter Rawlins from JenDex. They're aviation consultants. I have invited them to hear your suggestions for solving the current problem. If anyone here hasn't seen the photographs I circulated, please say so. As each person speaks, please introduce yourselves and what you do. A microphone is in front of you and is recording.' No one spoke, so Alex said, 'Right, the meeting's open for suggestions.'

The CEO launched into an attack. 'Adolf Schnieder, CEO. Before suggesting changes, I want to know why we can't get the certification process back online.'

Axel asked, 'Dexter, can you answer that?'

Dexter was annoyed; Jenifer could sense it. 'Because you have broken one of the established rules for proving reliability, the photographs show that. However, the FAA has consulted Stanford University and considers your aircraft unsafe.'

'How do you know that?'

'The United States is not secretive about safety, nor are the universities.'

'Why's it unsafe?'

'Because it will break up in flight before it's five years old.'

'Bullshit, they don't have a test rig; if they say that, we'll sue them.'

Jenifer replied, 'I hope you won't; you'll destroy the lives of too many people in your company. Stanford doesn't need a test rig; they calculated it.'

'Now I know that's bullshit, there isn't a computer in the world big enough to do that calculation.'

Dexter stood, 'Mister Chairman, we didn't expect insults or to hear we are liars. Goodbye.' Then, he turned and walked out with Jenifer beside him. No one noticed the young man at the opposite end of a table quietly exit a side door.

The chairman spoke. 'The meeting will adjourn; it will resume in ten minutes. Mr Schnieder will remain.'

When the people had left, Axel said, 'Herr Schnieder, not only was that a disgusting display of bad manners, but to do so when the company is in trouble that occurred with you at the helm is unbelievable. By the powers vested in me as the Chairman of the Board, I'm suspending you with immediate effect, pending a full board decision. Please leave the premises immediately.'

⌖

When Jenifer and Dexter left the room, a young man who looked vaguely familiar confronted them. 'Please, I'm Hans Muller, head of stress analysis. Can I ask Doctor Boscawen a question?'

'How do you know I'm a doctor?'

'I looked you up. Twice a doctor, like there are two of you.'

Jenifer laughed, and Dexter smiled. 'Then ask.'

'I know you calculated the fatigue life, but the boss was half right; how did you do it without a computer big enough?'

'Only a bit, Hans; we cycled until one node reached twenty per cent of the allowable energy. It's experimental and needs proving, but it's a step forward. We used extreme parallel computing.'

'A massive step forward, doctor. You could fix that node and run again. Was it the wider door?'

'Yes. But you can't fix that on 001.'

'I know, we'd have to put it in a test rig. Thank you, doctor.'

'Then consider two things; the first is never hesitate to ask others for help; secret science never solves problems. You must have learnt the other, but we often forget. "Step back and take a different path when no solution is possible." Goodbye.'

Dexter turned to continue and found Axel standing behind them. 'Dexter, I didn't want to butt in, it was interesting. I have dismissed the CEO. Now I have another problem: finding someone to take his place. Would you like a temporary job?'

'No, I'm the wrong guy. Building aeroplanes is a high-tech business; you need young people at the helm. That young man, Hans Muller, is an example. Talk to him, you'll learn what I mean.'

Jenifer added, 'A hi-tech company is unlike a bank. It doesn't need a CEO. You need an accountant and administrator to manage the non-technical stuff and a COO to build your planes.'

'I knew this would be a useful meeting; thank you for coming, and have a good trip back. Can I get someone to take you for lunch? I have a lot to do today.'

'Thanks, we'll get something ourselves. We can have lunch together when we have a SwisSim board meeting. Bye.'

⌇⌁⌇

'I'm sure Alex arranged that meeting. He now has a tape recording to prove firing the CEO is justifiable.'

'I agree. If Axel appoints Hans, they'll scrap the wide door version and certify a narrow door with a wide door as a later addition with an STC, but it will be Hans's idea, not ours, and will cement his position.'

'Now, Bo, no more diversions, let's get married.'

DAY 184
SATURDAY

At Jenifer's request, Dexter wore his uniform with five bars. Greg, also in uniform, was his groom. Jenifer's dress was a simple white gown with no train, but she had flowers in her hair and carried a posy of clover. The nine-stone circle may have witnessed many marriages, but never one where the bridesmaids, Susan and Lettie, were followed by the ponies, Dolly and her stallion, who stood patiently through the ceremony. A dozen other ponies ringed the circle and the crowd of the bridal couple's friends.

Henry Mancuni with his wife and children, Tim, Bethkin with her husband, Nance and Frank, Doris and her husband, Morwen and Breock, Philip Macintyre and his wife, Rhys Jones and his wife, and David were there.

Dexter had arranged a surprise at the reception in the gardens of the Oxenham, Jerry Somers, and Basin Street were there on a small stage in the park. The band had an extra member, recruited for the day by Jerry, 'Dexter, if we're gonna play Satch, this is Spokes; he sings Satch superbly.'

•••

'Dex, did you bring my trumpet.'

'Of course, my love.'

'Then later, I have a song to play for you.'

Jenifer remembered to ask Bethkin about the poem. 'Bethkin, is there a story behind the poem about the nine-stone circle?'

'Yes, Jenifer, it was given to me by a childhood friend. She left our village when her family moved to London. I was surprised when Dexter said your name had one "n", like the poem.'

'I'm not surprised; my mother's name was Petronell; I think she named me from the poem.'

'Was your mother a very dreamy woman? She might have been my friend.'

'Very dreamy and impractical. Mother died of a stroke six months ago.'

'I'm sorry to hear that; I would have liked to meet her again.'

⁕

'Dex, where's my trumpet?'

'I'll fetch it.'

Jenifer went to Jerry and said, 'Jerry, can I play *La Vie en Rose* with you?'

'Jenifer, anything you want to play is what we want to play.'

'Ok, then I'll announce it.'

Dexter handed her horn to her. 'Sit in that chair in front of me, Dex,' she said, turning to the microphone.

'Hi everyone, I know there are long, boring wedding speeches, and Greg is probably ready to entertain us with amusing stories about Dexter. Brides don't have to make speeches, and I'm not very good at them, but instead of saying how wonderful Dex is and how happy I am to be married to him, I'll play a song, especially for him. Dex, this is my message to you.'

She turned to the band, raised the trumpet, tapped her foot

three times, and the first note soared.

Everyone, including the band, stood like stone statues as the final notes screamed to the sky.

In the silence, she lowered the trumpet, smiled and said, 'After listening to the speeches, we'll dance.'

The applause was deafening. Late in the evening, the party swelled when the hotel staff and other guests joined in.

Moments before Dexter slept that night, he thought: *I guess I've answered the question, 'What do I do now?'*

Many Days Later

Dexter died at 92, and Bo, still an active sixty-two, continues the business and lives with another woman captain she's training at her house on Dartmoor.

They had a daughter, and Jenifer insisted they name her Arisa from the poem.

Henry Mancuni still lives in Phoenix, but he left CamAirCom to become the COO of JenDex Simulators.

Whenever they visited Nance and Frank, Jenifer would spend a day or two in the big glass building. The sign outside reads:

Dr Jenifer Boscawen institute for fatigue research.

The whiteboard still hangs in the foyer.

Linnette became a vet with a practice in Okehampton; she has a partner she met on the moor.

Jenifer went to London with Dexter and spent two days with Jerry Somers in a recording studio. The disc became a hit amongst jazz fans; the title is *Jerry Somers, and Jenifer Boscawen – Satchmo returns*. Their photos are on the cover, so in every jazz club they visited, Jenifer played a tune or two by invitation.

There are five barns around the moor, built by JenDex. They're called Bo's barns; one end of the barn is empty except for a bed of hay. The doors are marvels of technology; when temperature, humidity, wind and video from high masts unite to forecast mist or rain on the moor, the doors swing open, havens for the Dartmoor ponies.

Arisa is a vet and works with Lettie. They walk with Bo on the moors and have a unique veterinary practice. Once each week, Arisa opens one of Bo's Barns for business, and she is the only vet that treats Dartmoor ponies that come for treatment voluntarily without a handler.

Jenifer has no interest in men, but once a month, she retires to her room, switches on her computer system, undresses, puts on a virtual reality helmet, clips on movement sensors and lies on the bed. The scene she sees is a hotel room. Dexter enters the hotel room, the same one where they spent their first night together; unchanged, he joins her in bed. They make love; she doesn't need a dildo; the gentle caresses are enough to bring ecstasy.

She did tell him what the formula $L^3 = J + D$ meant *to her*: *Love cubed equals Jenifer plus Dexter.*